P9-CFY-696

THE
DICKENS MIRROR

BOOK 2 OF THE DARK PASSAGES

WITHDRAWN

ALSO BY ILSA J. BICK

The Dark Passages
White Space

The Ashes Trilogy
Ashes
Shadows
Monsters

THE

DICKENS MIRROR

BOOK 2 OF THE DARK PASSAGES

ILSA J. BICK

Fitchburg Public Library
5530 Lacy Road
Fitchburg, WI 53711

EGMONT
Publishing
NEW YORK

EGMONT

We bring stories to life

First published by Egmont Publishing, 2015
443 Park Avenue South, Suite 806
New York, NY 10016

Copyright © Ilsa J. Bick, 2015
All rights reserved

1 3 5 7 9 8 6 4 2

www.egmontusa.com
www.ilsajbick.com

Library of Congress Cataloging-in-Publication Data
Bick, Ilsa J.
The Dickens mirror / Ilsa J. Bick.
pages cm. -- (Dark Passages ; book two)
Summary: In the second book of the Dark Passages series, Emma wakes
up trapped in the body of a grown Victorian woman trapped in an insane
asylum, and must find a way a way back to Reality or else her friends and
family will die with her.
ISBN 978-1-60684-421-2 (hardback)
[1. Reality--Fiction. 2. Horror stories. 3. Science fiction.] I. Title.

PZ7.B47234Di 2015
[Fic]--dc23

2014034621

Printed in the United States of America

All rights reserved. No part of this publication may be reproduced, stored in
a retrieval system, or transmitted, in any form or by any means, electronic,
mechanical, photocopying, or otherwise, without the prior permission of
the publisher and copyright owner.

For Carolyn:

Honestly, kid . . . count your lucky stars. You're still standing.

I am not who I am.

—*William Shakespeare*

NOW

1

EMMA'S JUST TURNED twelve. She will not pass through White Space, fight a thing from the Dark Passages, lose her friends—lose Eric—and nearly die for five years yet. But every life turns on a dime, and sometimes several: pivot points after which everything changes.

This is hers.

This is what happens a week after down cellar.

2

"SAAALLL!" SCREECHING, EMMA blunders up their cottage's front steps and yanks the ancient screen door. Caroming on a *squawww* of old hinges, the door slams stone with a resounding *fwap* that rattles windows and makes the glass buzz. Beyond the house, down in Devil's Cauldron, the surge pounds sandstone in a relentless *ba-boom-ba-boom-ba-boom* that echoes the crash of her heart. Bulling through, she straight-arms the front door, tattooing a handprint in drippy blood. The other hand's clapped to her chin. Having taken the two miles home at a dead-out, panicky run, she's winded, terrified. Her bike's a tangled heap down the road, front wheel bent out of true, the rear pancake-flat because she just never *saw* the stupid pothole and the gravel was really slippery, and she *was* wearing her helmet, only it popped off, and she *tried* to do a Lara Croft, but she is *so* sucky at gym . . . and no no no no, who *knows* how long she was knocked out, and *why* do they have to live *so* far from town, with *no* neighbors, no one she can go to for help, because she's *cut*, she's *bleeding bad*, and her face, her face, her *face*! *"SAAALLL!"*

No one answers except Jack, the big orange tabby, who appears at the top of the stairs with a teeny-tiny *mew?* As if to ask, *Whoa, Emma, why all the fuss?* The only other sound above her frantic huffing and the *plip-plip-plip* of her blood dribbling onto the floor is a thin, scratchy line of melody dead ahead: the radio tuned to golden oldie big band crap.

"J-Jasper? *Jasper?*" Gulping sobs, she streaks into the kitchen, trailing blood, hoping against hope. When Jasper paints—more like slaps monsters onto canvas, if you ask her—he mostly listens to Dickens novels on tape. (Why? Beats heck outta her. Her guardian is truly loony in so many ways.) If there's no Dickens, though, Jasper just might be sober and actually useful for a change. Music like Ol' Frank—Jasper's on a first-name basis with the entire Rat Pack—he saves for when he's out on the boat or perched in a camp chair to sketch, *getting down with his bad self*, as Sal, Jasper's lizard-eyed live-in housekeeper, says. (Emma has *no* clue what that means; honestly, it's not bad enough that Jasper's pretty permanently shnockered and the village nutjob? Why *does* he have to be so weird?)

A single glance around the kitchen, with its white vintage gas range, a rack of cast-iron pots on one wall, the potbellied woodstove, and century-old yellow pine floor worn to a high gloss, is enough. No one home. She's on her own.

"*Nooo.*" Her moan is bubbly and wet. Fresh tears stream down her cheeks. Her mouth tastes of salt and wet iron. Where *is* everybody? "I need *help*. It's not *fair*."

No one seems to care but Ol' Frank, who's very concerned about what's gotten under his skin. That makes two of them; she's a mess. Her shins are speckled with bloody, glued-on grit; her skinned knees are on fire; and she's pretty sure her left elbow needs stitches. No need for a mirror either. If her face is as torn up as she thinks, she's not sure she could stand looking anyway. She still remembers the sound her teeth made as the point of her chin banged rock: a snappy, crisp *tock* that also chipped a tooth. Her tongue aches from where she bit down. All the blood she's swallowed has left her queasy, but that's probably fear, too.

For a split second, she debates about 911. Sure, this isn't a heart attack, but *still*. Except that's stupid. She's not going to *die* or anything. (Oh *nooo*, her face'll fall off, that's all.) Madeline Island's not *huge*, but Jasper's cottage is almost twenty miles away from La Pointe, the island's only town. Everyone sane lives there, so, of course, Jasper doesn't. An ambulance will cost money, and she doesn't need to give him one more reason to *kill* her, which he'll *do*. All the surgeries to make her face normal, and *now* look. She's *ruined* it, she's messed up, and you watch, buster: he'll throw her back, just like an undersized salmon. She'll wind up in foster care so fast, make your head spin.

"Stop it, you baby, *stop it*." Her voice is blubbery and little-kid small. At her feet, Jack leans against her ankles, kind of propping her up as her chin *plip-plip-plips*. A lot of blood hits the floor, though some drips onto Jack, who paws and shakes his head—like, *wuh?*—but doesn't budge otherwise. (She loves this cat, but boy, she wishes he were a dog right now; dogs'll eat anything, even blood.) "Stop crying and do this, Emma. You can do this." Right? Sure, she can; Jasper's always getting dinged up, and Sal's cleaned him up in this kitchen plenty of times. "It's not that hard."

First thing, she's got to get out all this crap. You can't leave dirt and grime and old blood in there; she'll get an infection, and then you watch: her face will get all pussy and bloated. It'll sag like molten candle wax and then slide right off in big, ooky, rotten green slabs. Huge chunks of her skull and all her teeth will fall out and *tik-tik-tik* all over the floor like an overturned mason jar of buttons and . . .

Stop it, Emma, stop it. Scuttling to the sink, she rips off a double handful of paper towel for her chin. With her free hand, she paws open the cupboard beneath the sink and wrestles out a first aid kit Sal always keeps there. But when she pushes up, a sweep of woozy vertigo whirls through her head. Her lips ice; deep in her belly, her stomach does a loop-de-loop. There's a distant clatter of plastic on wood as the first aid kit slips from her fingers and the kitchen kind of *smeeears*.

Uhhh. She rests her forehead on the counter. A fine, gritty patina of ancient bread crumbs pebbles the thin skin over her titanium skull plate. *Don't throw up.* Gulping back a sour surge that tastes suspiciously like hours-old gamushed peanut butter and strawberry jam, she swallows her tummy back where it belongs. When her dizziness passes, she knuckles away the petrified bread and straightens cautiously, worried that if she passes out she might lie there, limp as Jasper after a bender, until someone finally remembers, *Saaay, isn't there this kid we're supposed to be taking care of and, you know,* responsible *for?* and decides to show up.

Careful not to move too fast, she scrapes up the kit, drops it on a countertop, and pops the lid. Pay dirt: the kit's packed with gauze rolls, surgical tape, scissors, alcohol swabs, squeeze packets of antibiotic ointment. Ducking back underneath the sink, she unearths a bottle of Hibiclens and a basin Sal uses to mix antibiotic soap with water. Still keeping one hand pressed to the paper towels wadded on her chin, she uses the other to squirt a gooey pink stream of Hibiclens into the basin. Twisting the spigot, she stands, shifting from foot to foot as she waits for the water to warm up (listening as the old water heater down cellar *chugachugachugs* to life; silly thing takes *forever*). She watches the water change from a murky brown to clear as it sluices gore and grit from her free hand.

You're going to be fine. But she has her doubts. There's this steady throb that's started up above the bridge of her nose as her brain pulses *ba-boom, ba-boom,* like IT on its dais (*sooo* creepy). Real whopper of a headache coming on.

"Hey, boy," she says to Jack, who's jumped onto the counter to supervise, "it's going to be okay, isn't it?" But Jack only grooms himself and offers no opinion. So she answers for him: "'Course it will. You betcha."

But she's not sure, mostly because she's never been exactly *right* or normal. She may look okay *now,* but *she* knows what's under her skin. Fifteen months ago, the craniofacial surgeon in charge of her reconstruction had shown her blank-eyed masks, one of which would become her face. *They're all possibilities,* the surgeon explained, swapping out one face for another. On the monitor, each new mask settled like clingy Glad Wrap over a computer rendering of her deformed skull. *See?* The doctor grinned, really revved, like he was playing *Grand Theft Auto* with his brand-new, shiny Xbox. *I can give you any number of looks that fit your underlying bone structure.*

She doesn't recall who finally chose. The surgeon, most likely. All she cared about was getting rid of the monster in the mirror.

Yet even now, months later, she still doesn't know this new girl. Her eyes are the only constant: a deep and unearthly cobalt blue so pure they ought to be glass. The right holds a queer golden flaw that the doctors say is a birthmark but that glitters like a faraway star. But the rest of her face is . . . strange, the mask of a normal girl she has no right being. Every morning, she expects her reconstructed skin to slough like the dead husk of a lizard or snake.

The doc said she'll eventually grow into her looks: *Just like that duckling.* (She noticed he omitted *ugly.* That word wasn't in his dictionary, apparently. No, no, she had *cranial deformities* and *severe anomalies.* She was *in need of repair.* Bone saws, chisels, skull plates, skin grafts. Hours and hours and multiple surgeries during which the doctors broke and ripped and sawed and drilled and stretched and grafted and stitched—and then the bandages, a haze of pain, the salves and treatments. The craniofacial guy says it's a good thing she scars so well. Running her fingers through her hair and the train track of all those skillful scars is like reading the chronology of her reconstruction in braille.)

Now, when she and that stranger in the mirror lock eyes, she thinks, *People look at you, and they see someone . . . someone who's . . .* Her brain stumbles over *pretty.* She'll never be that. If she even *thinks* the word, it'll be like stepping on a crack or telling a birthday wish. *They see someone who looks normal, but you're only the mask. I'm still in here, and I'm weird and ugly and nobody's kid, and nothing can change that.*

At school, the other kids pegged her right off the bat, first day. Walking the gauntlet of the lunchroom was like listening to the Doppler effect of an aural wave of Badger fans at a UW football game:

. . . here she comes she's so weird so strange **so totally lame I heard her face was really gross like she had these horns** *what a geek* such a spaz my dad says Jasper's a drunk . . .

They're like wolves that way, cutting the weakest deer from the herd and running it to death. Under the skin, she's the same *Emma Lindsay, Loser.* Thank God, school's out for the summer. Maybe it'll be better next year when she goes to Bayfield on the mainland. Madeline Island's so small, everyone knows from a fart what you had for supper.

If she had her way? Go live on an island, *waaay* far away. Maybe hang out in a sea cave, get herself a wolf, and eat fish and abalone, like that girl from *Island of the Blue Dolphins.* Or do like Sam and run away to live in a tree on a mountain and tame a falcon or hawk, maybe even an eagle. Or, you know, just set up house on Devils Island, where hardly anyone goes except a couple charters so the tourists can *ooh* and *aah* at the sea caves. When Superior really gets going, the caves' roars and booms carry clear to Jasper's . . . which is, you know, impossible. The island's more than twenty miles northwest of the cottage. But she hears them. The Ojibwe say all that racket's because of this big old honking evil spirit, Matchi-Manitou, who guards the entrance to the underworld, and only the bravest warriors go down there and blah, blah. She doesn't *believe* it, but sometimes she daydreams about packing up and heading out there in her kayak, slipping that Scorpio into the deepest, darkest cave she can find, and checking it out. Maybe there's a whole under-ground world down there, bunches of tunnels and all these creatures, and here, she's the only kid brave enough to face up to all that. Is that totally Lara Croft or what?

Before the surgeries, the craniofacial doc made her see a shrink. Standard procedure, he said, to help with the adjustment before and after. The shrink was okay. Nice lady. They drew pictures. Played a lot of Uno. The shrink asked leading questions that, you know, a moron could figure out, mainly stuff about what life might be like after the surgeries, what Emma expected, did she think she'd become this fairy princess or something. One afternoon, Emma got onto islands and running away and Devils and Matchi-Manitou. Don't ask her how; just happened.

At that, the shrink got this *look*—and then said the one thing that's stuck with Emma all this time: *Monsters in the basement are easy, Emma. That's where they're supposed to live. It's the day the monsters stare from the mirror that you should worry.*

3

THE WATER'S WARM enough now to steam. On the radio, Frank is still going on about reality and what's so deep in his heart that it's really a part of him. *Strange.* Frowning, she cranes over her shoulder at the kitchen table. How long is that song, anyway? As with Dickens novels, she's pretty familiar with Ol' Frank. The song's . . . four minutes, max? Even with the big, vampy trumpet doo-dah in the middle? Yeah, and she could swear she heard *that* right around the time she turned on the water. Hand still clamped to her chin, she turns to peer at the wall clock. As she does, her elbow catches the Hibiclens bottle. She makes an awkward grab but misses. The bottle's plastic, but of *course* the squirt top pops, releasing a spume of goopy pink soap.

"*No.*" She stamps her foot. Can't she get just *one* stupid break? The backs of her eyes sting, and she can feel her lower lip beginning to quiver again. She needs to fix her chin, but that big pink puddle of Hibiclens *glares* from the floor: *You bozo-brain.* Already, she can just imagine the soap soaking into and plumping up tired, desiccated pine to leave a great big stain. Same with her blood, which she's tracked *all* the way down the hall. God, she's in so much trouble already, and now *this.* "Fine, all right, *okay.*" Ripping off more paper towels one-handed, she squats and begins mopping up. In about two seconds, she realizes that she'll probably have to use the entire stupid roll and thinks, *I can't do anything right.*

As she starts to push up again, the kitchen begins its topsy-turvy, pre-passing-out spin. *Ugh.* This time, her head goes empty; her stomach bottoms out. Then, just like that, she's starting to fall, she's falling, the floor's opening to swallow her up as furry black spiders scurry over her vision . . .

And everything goes dark.

4

OHHHH. HER BRAIN leaks back into her skull a drip at a time. She comes to, splayed like roadkill, from some dark jumble of a nightmare. For a disorienting second, there are no walls; there's no floor. Instead, there is a matte-white glare, a little like the paint Jasper slops over his canvases when he's done. Like Meg Murry nearly tessered to a two-dimensional planet, she feels steamroller flat: a flimsy paper doll of a girl, with all the substance and depth of a molecule of ink on parchment.

Wow. She has the strangest idea that she's smeared sideways into ghostly afterimages running away into forever, as if she's wandered into a bathroom with mirrors front, back, up, and down, and no matter where she looks, there goes Emma and Emma and Emma and Emma and on and on and on, and every Emma is different, can be anything anywhere anytime. A split second later, all the Emmas collapse like a deck of cards in a complicated shuffling trick where the guy's got perfect control and all the cards *shooo* together in a blur until there are only two Emmas, twin selves: one sprawled . . . well, wherever she is, and the other *swooshed* back to that gravel road for a redo. If she opens her eyes, reality might just kick-start again in the *hoosh* of the wind, the nip of sharp stones against her back, and the mocking *a-hah-hah-hah, look at the stoopid huuumannn* laughter of faraway gulls spinning lazy circles against a bright blue sky. (Flying: now yer talking. Come back as a bird. Don't see birds doing headers off bikes.) For an instant, she wonders if *this* time is when she finally wakes up for real.

Then, her chest struggles for a breath, and she lets go of a groan: *"Uhhh." That's* not flat; that sound's round as a balloon. And like that, her world goes 3-D: floor under her back, walls stacked on a foundation to support a ceiling, the open cupboard beneath the kitchen sink. Like she's stuck in a game of *SimCity* that's hit a glitch and only now decides to cough out details. Her hands, sticky with gore, are limp as dead starfish. Her stomach pulses against her teeth. She feels sluggish, though her head's oddly *full*, like her brain's been *verrry*, very busy. With what?

With cold, she thinks—and *that* makes no sense. It's June. She's sweaty and hot and grimy and so scuzzy bugs will snuggle in the jungle of her hair for a nice long visit. But *cold* is what jumps to the center of her skull: that, and *snow*. Some kind of valley, too, and there were other kids stuck down there, and they were trying to find a way out. A couple of them *died*. And there was a . . . a . . .

"House," she whispers. Her tongue's thick and gluey, and there's a strange taste, too, almost like . . . gasoline? Yeah, and she can almost smell it, sticky-sweet, steaming from her clothes, but that's crazy.

The house had been strange, too. Was it . . . *alive?* She thinks so, and House had a lot of rooms. *Library—that was the most important room of all.* Only she didn't go *inside* so much as step *through* it—through some kind of weird mirror? *Yeah, like Alice in Wonderland.* She'd gone somewhere else: into a summer's day, on a street she didn't recognize. She'd been different, too, not the same age as now but older, a teenager. *There was a bookstore called . . . Come on, come on . . .* She can feel the nightmare beginning to evaporate. *What's the name?* Her teeth grab her lower lip as if to snag the words . . .

Between the Lines. "Yeah," she breathes, "yeah, that's right, and there was a boy, too." *Someone I really liked, and he was talking about a . . . a necklace?* Her fingers drift to her chest, and she swears she feels smooth, cool glass where she *knows* there's nothing. "Galaxy pendant," she says, and wonders what the heck she means. Something special about the necklace. About *her.* And then . . .

Oh. Despite her muzzy head, a clot of fear sears her chest. *Blood.* Her eyes jerk down to her arms. *I got cut, real bad, worse than now, only on my arms instead of my chin, and my blood . . .* Her blood had *moved,* like a snake, and when her blood touched a book—a really important book, but what was its name; what had it been about?—when her blood *licked* this book . . .

"M-monster." An invisible hand seems to close around her throat. *Sick, I'm going to be sick, I can't breathe, I don't want to remember anymore . . .* "A m-monster came out of the book and it wanted *me.* It said it w-wanted to *p-p-play . . .*"

Stop. Pooling with frightened tears, her eyes squeeze shut. She doesn't want to remember any more. *It's just a dream. Just a b-bad dream. Let it go.*

At that, inside her skull, something unclenches, her brain relaxing as the knot of that nightmare unravels into disparate strands as insubstantial as fog. In moments, the dream—those visions of a valley and snow and monsters and that boy—is gone.

5

GROGGY, SHE LABORS to a stand. In the sink, a geyser of steam chuffs from hot water still gushing from the spigot. Her shorts, sodden where she splooshed into Hibiclens, stick to her butt. And to heck with the floor.

She twists on cold water. Steam dews her face, and she can feel her eyes pooling again. The sink wavers and glimmers as if someone's dropped a stone into a still pond. *Crap.* She blinks against a salt sting of tears. *Why does everything have to be so . . .*

That thought trickles away. Because that's when she realizes that the *waver* has spread from the center of her vision to encompass the sink, the countertop. The walls. Jack's body looks like a furry orange sack filled with worms. She can feel the same squirming inside and under her skin as wave after wave ripples from head to toe, her skin actually *rolling* as if she's suddenly no more substantial than water. If she could put a *sound* to this, it would be a whining wiggle, like music drawn from a whippy handsaw: *wuh-WHINGWHINGWHINGWHINGWHING.*

"What?" In the time it takes for the word to leave her mouth, however, the sensation's fled. The kitchen solidifies again, and so does she.

But then Jack growls.

Now, she loves Jack to pieces, but cats are definitely weird animals. Dogs are easy; most are big, goofy galumphs, and you can tell what they're thinking. Cats are plain strange. Times when Jack's staring up at trees or between shadows, and then his mouth twitches open in no-sound meows as his tail *swish-swishes*—you could swear he's tuning into some alien cat-channel, or seeing things slipping in and out of dimensional gateways, like in *Star Trek* or something.

But she's never seen him like this: ears flat and tight against his skull, a Mohawk of hackles on his spine, tail like a bristle bottle brush. Growling, the cat is staring out the kitchen window above the sink.

"Jack?" Puzzled, she follows his gaze. "Is there a . . ." Maybe she was going to say *bird* or *another cat*. Really, she doesn't know. Her mind blanks. If she were a cartoon, there'd be that empty thought bubble and not even a question mark.

Then, her brain kicks in, and she thinks, *What? Huh?*

6

THE KITCHEN LOOKS northeast, and it's late in the day, after three, so the sun's moved behind the house now. The view is one she knows well and loves: the curve of Presque Isle Bay on Stockton Island on the left, a stretch of open water, and then Michigan Island, its two lighthouses on the far right. When the lake really gets going like it is now, the waves are so furious she can see explosions of white spray blasting from the tip of Stockton's rocky tombolo. This time of day, the sun dyes the lake a deep blue and splashes the islands with brilliant swathes of golden light.

That is not what she sees now.

In the glass, her face is sketchy, as if outlined in faint pencil, though her eyes are black as stones. Her birthmark is a white-hot cinder with no color at all. There's nothing normal about this reflection.

That is because what lies beyond the glass is flat and matte-white, like taut canvas on a frame that Jasper has yet to prime. A piece of her mind understands this has to be fog—wait, hadn't she just been dreaming about that?—but it is the strangest she's ever seen. It doesn't flow or seem like mist at all, and is so dense that if she didn't know better, she'd swear the house was floating in midair.

Whoa, wait a second. Her throat works in a nervous, liquid swallow. Except for Jack's growl, the steady *splash* of water against porcelain, and Frank still going on about his skin, his skin—*same song; it hasn't changed at all*—it is eerily silent. There is fog . . . but no foghorn. After another few seconds, she realizes that the sound of the lake is gone, too. No thump of waves against sandstone. No throbbing, relentless *ba-boom, ba-boom* keeping time with her headache. There's nothing.

"What?" Her voice is a reedy squeak. With a hand that trembles, she twists the spigot. The water quits. The house goes still. She holds her breath and listens. Except for Frank and the still-growling Jack, the silence is white. Empty. Craning over a shoulder, she looks back toward the front door. A glare the color of a fish belly shines through its pebbled sidelights.

"What is this?" She feels so small. The silence is crushing. Turning back to the kitchen window, she whispers, "What's going . . ."

And now, at the window, there is a woman.

7

BEYOND THE FACT that she shouldn't be there at all, Emma thinks the woman is both familiar and completely alien, a steampunky nightmare-vision straight out of Dickens. Her chestnut hair is done in an old-fashioned coil, and she wears a frilly, poofy-sleeved blouse with a high lace collar.

But what grabs her are the woman's eyes. They're purple as old blood clots. *Glasses?* Yeah, but *really* funky, with four lenses, two to a side. They make the woman look pretty *got a screw loose, a can shy of a six-pack* insane. For a very long second, the woman and Emma stare at one another while, on the kitchen table and a million miles away, Frank is urging Emma to wake up to reality.

No, Frank. The thought is dreamy, surreal. *No, you're wrong. This can't be . . .*

But that's when her brain drops out again.

Because that's the moment the woman reaches through glass and hooks a hand over the sill.

8

WITH A WILD screech, Emma blunders back from the sink as Jack rockets off the counter in an orange blur. Stumbling, she tries to turn and run after the cat, but she's doing too many things at once and has forgotten that slick, treacherous puddle of Hibiclens. Her right foot comes down and then shoots out from under. Crashing to the floor in a spectacular pratfall, she lands on her rear. An electric shock shoots up her spine, and she screams again, this time in pain and terror.

Above her, at the sink, the woman heaves herself over the sill:

first that hand and then the other. A long leg, draped in a jet-black skirt, stretches for the sink. For a disorienting second, Emma can't decide if the fog's spitting her out or the woman's a hungry spider who's tired of waiting for Emma to bumble into her web already.

Run, run! Rolling to her hands and knees, Emma plants a toe and heaves to her feet. Behind, she hears the rustle of fabric, the *clops* of boots on porcelain and then Formica. In that instant, she has three choices: front door, kitchen side door to her far left, or the door to her immediate right that will take her down cellar. All have their problems. Get herself trapped down cellar with a crazy woman and she's dead meat, because there are only so many places to hide. But outside there is the fog, and this woman came in or through it (or *is* it; there's no way to know). Front door or side, even if she gets away, bumbling around in the fog's a crummy idea. With her luck, she'll run into a tree and add a broken nose to her already torn-up face, *and* this crazy lady will still be on her tail. Worse, boogie out the side door and get herself turned around? There's no gravel out there, no way to tell if she's heading to the road. Dense woods hug this cottage front and back. Make the wrong turn, and she could find herself pinballing around trees only to finally step off the bluff above Devil's Cauldron. From there, it's a real long way down. Hit the rocks, she'll burst like an Emma blood-balloon. She'll be fish food. They probably won't find her right away either. Current'll sweep her north and east to drift until what's left beaches somewhere in Michigan. Or Canada. Or nowhere, ever.

"Emma." Unlike the high, scritch-scratchy spider's chitter Emma expects, the woman's voice is smooth as buttery caramel. Her accent, though, is straight out of Dickens. "Wait, dear."

She almost does. Because take away the glasses; hell, forget the fact that this woman just came out of fog and climbed through what had been solid glass . . . and she sounds so reasonable. Kind of how Emma's always thought a mom should sound, or like Mrs. Whatsit. And Emma's still just a kid. When an adult says jump, you ask how high; you don't tell an adult where to go and what she can do with herself. So Emma hesitates. "What?" She starts to turn. "Who are . . ."

The woman's hand flashes in a grab. Gasping, Emma jerks away as the woman's fingers whisk through her long hair. Turning, Emma hurtles through the basement door. Snatching the knob, she slams the door and jams the thumb lock. The key's long gone; when someone accidentally hits the lock now, Jasper or Sal jimmies it open with a long wire pick they keep above the header. She's hoping the woman won't think of that.

"Emma?" Still reasonable, so *now, honey, we can talk about this.* The knob rattles. Frank's still wondering what's under his skin, and if Emma never hears that song again, it will be too soon. "Emma, please open the door."

Oh, you've got to be kidding me. Huddled on the third step, Emma's eyes are level with the gap between the door and floor. The woman's shadow oils right to left and back again, like the photonegative of a ghost. The tips of her boots—very old-fashioned, with button closures—show beneath folds of black wool. For an insane moment, Emma worries that the woman will drop to her knees and then she'll be eye to eye with those crazy purple glasses.

The hard *bap* of a boot kicking wood makes her heart claw up her throat. "Emma!" Not so *there-there* now. "Trust me, this is for your benefit."

Oh yeah, like she really believes that. *But what do I do now?*

Emma clatters halfway down rough, open-backed steps. She doesn't need a light. This is a layout she knows by heart. Boiler on the right, next to the stairs; washer and dryer along the wall beyond that; shelves of canned food and jars Sal's put up that stretch three-quarters of the way down the left wall to end at the threshold for that back room. This, Emma explored just last week when she went looking for a book. The room's chockablock with boxes, canvases, an old Victorian rolltop desk—and something she's told herself never to think about again but can't forget: that inky square that might be a tunnel or trap or wormhole hidden behind the wall. In the week since, she's been tossing it around, whether she should tell Jasper or not. Mostly, she thinks not, because this is *obviously* something Jasper didn't want her to find. Sometimes, when her mind drifts back to the moment she reached inside, she's wondered if she hasn't found a whole other dimension, like on *Star Trek*. She really doesn't want to go into that room now if she can help it.

Sal . . . Jasper . . . someone, please come home! Darting under the handrail, she jumps to poured concrete. The air smells of laundry detergent and scorched cotton. Behind and above, she hears those boots thunk back and forth. *Probably looking for a key.* Gosh, she hopes the crazy lady doesn't think about feeling above the jamb. Or maybe hunting for something to break down the door. *Uh-oh.* Her heart freezes at the thought. All that crazy lady has to do is look out the kitchen side door, and she'll see Jasper's ax next to the woodpile. If the woman finds that, the cellar door'll be matchsticks in no time flat. It'll be just like the scene in that ancient fossil of a movie Jasper watched a couple days ago, about a crazy writer and his family trapped in some haunted hotel. (On the other hand, that chopping scene *was* the best part: *Heeere's Johnny!*)

As if the woman's read her mind, Emma hears her clop away. There's the crash of a door. Then, nothing . . . and more silence . . . and then the boots are back. This time around, they're heavier, like the lady's put on a couple pounds or is carrying . . .

No, come on. Emma's stomach plummets to her toes. *That's so not fair.*

The woman's back at the door. "Don't do anything stupid, Emma." Then, *BLAM!* The door lets out a huge bawl, and Emma discovers the sound of an ax biting wood really *isn't* a chop but a detonation.

"Don't run, Emma," the woman says. "Trust me, you'll only make this worse."

Running will make this worse? What could be worse than an *ax*? *What am I going to do, what am I going to do?* Her thoughts spin like gerbils racing on a wheel of pure panic. Another *BLAM!* Now, the wood actually cracks. She hears the clatter as pieces rain to the steps. A third *BLAM!* She's got to do something, try to hide—but where?

Suddenly, out of the corner of her eye, Emma sees a streak of orange shoot from behind the washer and dart into the second room. *Follow the cat.* Jack has the right idea. Lots of boxes in the second room, books, the desk. Maybe she can block off the entrance. Springing from her crouch, Emma races past the washer and dryer. As she passes the shelves, she thinks, *Why not?* With a great sweep of her arms, she sends jars and cans crashing to the floor. The air fills with a scent of vinegar that is strong enough to make her throat try to close and her eyes water. If her aim was any good, she might lob a couple jars, but while Lara Croft would peg that crazy lady, no sweat, Emma's truly hopeless at softball. Mainly, she's only trying to make as much of a mess as she can.

Above and behind, the tenor of the ax hacking wood changes as the door caves.

Go! Emma dashes into the back room just as boots clatter down wood steps. There's enough grainy yellow light seeping from the kitchen door the lady just killed for Emma to make out a dim jumble of boxes and books and Jasper's old rolltop, but not much else. Of course, the gloom cuts both ways; she'll be just as hard to see, especially if she holds herself real, real still. On the other hand, now she's out of running room. So maybe this was a really terrible idea after all. Where to hide? Terrified, she tosses a wild look. Duck behind boxes? The old secretary?

There's a slight crunch and pop as the woman's boots grind broken glass. *Wonder how come she hasn't turned on the light?* Maybe she can't find it, but that's dumb. The switch is right . . . Then Emma thinks, *What are you doing, you nut? Don't jinx—*

There's a distinctive *snap*. Flat yellow light flows into the gloom.

Stupid, Emma, you're so stupid. Emma's insides go all loose, like she might fall down in the next second. She's *always* jinxing herself. *You think too much.*

Another *snap*. The light goes out. "This is fascinating." The woman *snicks* the light on a second time, and then a third. "Worthy of study."

Worthy of study? What, she's never seen a light before? Still, the woman's done her a favor. To the left, Jasper's hulking old secretary looms, and she can see a larger, long wedge of shadow where the desk isn't completely snugged to the wall. The opening's just wide enough for a thin and wiry twelve-year-old kid. So she's got a choice. She could hide behind the Victorian, quiet quiet quiet as a mouse—maybe even do a Lara or something and jam herself into the crack, tuck and plant her feet like a rock climber so that crazy lady won't be able to see her feet. If Emma's *really* lucky (hah!), the crazy lady will look around and kind of scratch her head—*Huh, where's Waldo?*—and go back upstairs. Or Emma could do the same move and shove the desk really hard until it falls over. The desk isn't wide enough to completely block the way, but it would certainly slow this woman down.

Emma doesn't have that kind of time, though, and knows it. There's only one way out of here. *Should've bolted out the front door, taken my chances outside.* At least there would be room to run. But the fog was so thick, she'd get lost. She *even* might have—and this is a weird thought—run to another place and time.

Yet there is also Jack, who could have chosen anywhere else to go in the house but has taken himself down cellar and led her to this back room. The cat's long shadow dances up the wall as he bounds atop the boxes she wedged against white-painted cinderblock only a week before, as if he's pointing: *This way, Emma, move your butt!*

Oh boy. Should she? Because she knows what the cat wants her to do. Those tiny panic-gerbils in her brain shrill, *Are you crazy? Are you nuts?*

No, mainly she's desperate. Plowing across the room, she horses aside boxes. *Please be what I think you are.* Which is what, exactly? A tunnel? A door to another dimension or time? *I don't care, I don't care, just* be *there.* She is gasping again, and her heart is beating so hard that the harsh grind and hollow baps of the woman kicking aside glass and tin cans seem far away. A few seconds later, she feels a gush of very cold air around her ankles and she falls to her knees before painted cinderblock—

And the cinderblock is a white blank. Biting her lower lip, she corrals a small cry. That's not right. Last week, there was a pull-ring. *I couldn't have imagined it.* Could she? *But I opened this; I know I did . . .*

Oh! She sucks in a breath as that brass pull, just so right for her hand, sprouts like a mushroom, as if it's been waiting for her to get on with it already; to really, truly want this.

As if this is the pivot, the *now*, around which her life turns: the end in which she'll find her beginning.

9

EXCEPT FOR THE fact that she has no birthday candle now, everything's the same: that frigid wash of air, that flawlessly perfect black square, the icy burn when she touches it. Beneath her fingers, the dark square gives like thick cellophane, and sounds dribble out: a static-y *psst–spiss–spiss–psst* like Rice Krispies, or a big, whispering crowd. Then, a tiny *click* and her hand plunges into the dark. The last time, that's when something hooked her wrist. When she'd finally tugged free, her fingers were sickly white with cold and her blue birthday candle was frozen. Now, nothing snatches at her. Maybe going the whole hog is what the darkness has wanted all along.

Then Emma thinks, *What are you doing?* She wasn't really thinking of crawling inside, was she? There are *things* in there that might be just as bad as what's followed her down cellar. *Stay here, though—I'll get killed. But go in there and maybe, just maybe . . .*

By her side, the cat is shifting from side to side, like a stallion at a starting gate. "Jack?" Her whisper's as quivery as half-set Jell-O. Her lips have drawn back in a terrified rictus, and big tears roll down her cheeks. The tang of iron's on her tongue. "Jack, do you know where . . . ?"

A knife blade of shadow slashes up the far wall. "Emma."

Emma screams and whirls around. By her side, Jack springs about a foot straight up, the way cats do. Yet when he lands, he stays. He's not leaving her. She doesn't know if she likes that or not. What if this kook kills her cat, too?

"Emma." The woman steps to the threshold of this second room. "There's nowhere left to run. Let's not make a fuss."

"Not make a f-fuss?" Emma's chest is boiling over with fear. "Wh-who *are* y-you? What do you *w–want*?"

"Why, you, child. Although . . ." The woman's head suddenly cocks as she stares through those weird purple glasses. "What *is* that?" Her smooth, buttery caramel tone has gone brittle. "Is that another device? Or a back door? Have you accessed it? Where does it go?"

Access? Back door? "I . . . I don't . . ." It hits her then: *She can't tell I've opened it. Even with those funky glasses, she doesn't know.* From the woman's question, Emma thinks this nut will be on her in a second if she gets even the slightest whiff that it's open. *But she asked where it went.* That must mean the woman's seen this or something like it before and knows that it's an escape route, a tunnel, a door, and not just some black hole filled with stuff that'll have her for lunch. *If she doesn't know it's open . . . does that mean she can't follow?* The door opened for *her*; the pull-ring sprouted at Emma's touch. *So what if it closes up right after I go through?*

What is she saying? What is she thinking? She's not going in there. But Jack wants her to; Jack knows. *And the crazy lady can't get it open?*

"Emma." The woman moves into the room. "Come away, *now*."

Go on go on, do it, you big fraidy-cat, go! "O-okay." She sets her toes, tenses her thighs. "Okay, I . . . I'm c-coming, I give up; just p-please don't h-hurt me, d-don't . . ."

Then she shouts to the cat, *"Go, Jack!"*

And launches herself into the square.

10

LARA CROFT'S GOT nothing on a cat. Hurtling ahead, Jack's gone in an instant, lost to the dark. She is a split second behind. The transition's abrupt; the cold grabs her throat, and there is a rushing around her ears, as if a huge flock of blackbirds has suddenly startled. That static wash of whispers swells.

Maybe, if she hadn't hesitated so long, she'd have made it, too.

A pair of strong hands clamps her ankles. She bucks, trying to kick her way free. *No, NO!* Jack is probably safe *somewhere*, but she's been too scared, too slow, so stupid. No one will ever know. Sal and Jasper will find an empty house and a wrecked basement reeking of vinegar and smooshed pickles. But they also might see the square or, at the very least, that the boxes have been moved. Jasper might put it together. Will he come after her? *Can* he?

Help me, she thinks, furiously, to the dark and whatever lives here. *You were here before; you grabbed me before, so help me now!* Squirming deeper, she realizes that while there is *nothing* under her chest now—no floor, no concrete—she's not falling either. She also can't be quite certain, but are those lights? Stars? Open doorways?

Behind, the woman is hauling her back. Emma's shirt rucks over her tummy. In seconds, she'll be right back where she started, at this nightmare turn her life has taken.

Please. She grabs for the dark. *If you're here, please, I want this! Find me!*

And then comes the strangest thought of all: *Put me where I belong.*

That idea . . . is hers, and it is not. It feels far ahead and in the future and as distant as one of those bright lights, and yet the thought is immediate, present, *now*. Along with this, there is a sudden *blooming* in her head and a lurch, a tug like the set of a fishhook. Deep in her center, she knows: this is her chance.

Tearing a foot from the woman's grasp, she pistons her leg back with all her might. Her foot connects with a solid bang she feels in her knee. The woman lets out a screech of pain. Her grip on Emma slackens—and that's enough.

Emma launches herself into this black tide, and now she's moving, fast, fast, faster, the sensation the same as in the moment she angles her kayak in a swift stream churning through rocks, slipping into exactly the right shoot at exactly the right time. Emma hurtles through the cold and dark, the current sweeping her to . . .

PART ONE

AWAKENINGS

SNAPPING BOLT UPRIGHT, he jolts awake with a scream perched on his tongue.

Jesus. Swallowing the shout, he grimaces at . . . *gasoline?* His mouth tastes like he's been sucking on an exhaust pipe. Or that could be left over from his nightmare: something about a car or maybe a truck that jumped a guardrail and landed in a splinter of trees and . . . and snow? *Yeah, that's right.* What else, what else? A girl. Yeah, there was a girl he . . . he *liked?* Yes. A girl he *trusted.* To whom he felt a connection. He wanted to protect her. She was sad and . . . and *haunted,* like him. What was her name? Come *on* . . . But no face wavers up from memory. Shit, *shit.* It's all starting to drift away, like soap bubbles on a strong breeze. Yet what remains in his chest is a clot of deep, icy dread—and pain.

Because I got hurt. This thing *appeared all of a sudden, out of the dark.* Shivering, he hunches his shoulders and folds in on himself. *Cold.* In the dream, there was snow, a real blizzard. Then, from the dark, this big *something* came and . . . *pain. Blood. And I got hurt, I got really, really hurt.* An explosion next? He thinks so.

And then I died. The words are the mental moan of a kid ready to puke his guts out. God, this makes no sense. He took psych. You can be scared to death in a dream. You can think you're running like crazy but really in slo-mo, even though the slavering thing chasing you is a whisper away, a hair's breadth. In a nightmare, you might even see the knife or ax or claw. But you shouldn't die. At the moment the ax whizzes down or the monster opens its mouth, you ought to wake up.

Only I didn't. I died in my dream. I felt it happen. I-I f-felt . . .

He has to stop this. He's fine. He's awake now and in bed, in his own room, not out on the ice watching his life drain away in a hot, steaming red pool to mingle with gasoline. *Gasoline, what the hell . . . Come on.* He puts a hand to his chest. *Just calm—*

His thoughts stumble. *What?* Hair rising on his scalp, he mashes his hand to his ribs, right below his left collarbone. *What, WHAT?* No, that's not possible! He's sitting up. He's in *bed*. He's not *dead*.

So then where the hell is his heart?

2

IT'S AS IF he just has to think the word. Because, all at once, a knot swells behind his ribs. His chest heaves as if what's inside is just now shaking awake. A second later, he feels a knocking in his throat as his heart vaults to life.

Okay. His lips throb with the wild gallop of his pulse. *You're fine. Relax.* He . . . he was just freaked out. Anyone would be after a dream like that. He shivers again, the tiny hairs prickling on his neck. Best not to think about it. *Maybe sit up, read . . .*

Wait a second. Leaning forward, he sweeps blindly with outstretched hands. Where are his covers? He's *freezing*, and it's so *dark*—blacker than pitch—but he has no blankets. There are no sheets puddled around his waist. He shuffles his ankles but feels no spaghetti twist of a top sheet or rumpled wool. *What?* Stretching, he gropes but feels only the icy knobs of his bare toes. *Hunh.* Probably kicked off the blanket, or maybe it's balled up with his top sheet. And why the hell is it so dark? Twisting to his left, he drops a hand for his night table. *Has it ever been this dark*—

It is then that he realizes: his hand is still falling. Because there is no night table.

What? He goes rigid as a post. That can't be right. But there's no mistake: his hand is lower than his left thigh, and *that's* when he figures out that there's no mattress either. His palm's simply hanging there. *But there's got to be a mattress. I'm sitting on it. What's going on?*

The scream that followed him out of the nightmare and which he hasn't let go of is a knuckle in his throat. There is something beneath his legs; he *feels* it . . . but is it really his bed? Cautiously, he shuffles his legs, listening hard for a squeal of box springs, feeling for the mattress's many small dimples and quilted hillocks. The blackness beneath him is perfectly smooth, like . . . *ice, I remember ice and gasoline* . . . and there is no sound, no whisper of skin over a sheet or even a mattress pad.

He is balanced, in midair, on . . . nothing.

3

THIS IS NUTS. There *has* to be something here. A person can't be in *nothing*, much less *on* it. *But maybe that's why it's so dark. Nothing would be that way. Limbo would be like this.*

And he's just died. Okay, yeah, in a dream . . . but maybe at the end of your life, that's what dying's like.

No, my heart's beating. But it wasn't there five seconds ago; he had to think it into existence, didn't he? *No, I'm breathing. I'm thinking. I feel.* As if seconding this, his heart gives his ribs a good hard kick. *See? Relax.* All he has to do is turn on a light. But . . . wait a second . . .

Is there a lamp in this room?

He has no idea. None. Zip. Zilch. But that's crazy. *What does my room look like?* He knows that he shared it with Matt, before his brother went off to the Marines, but—

Oh God. He can feel himself trying to cringe away from this train of thought, but he can't unthink it now. Like *lamp* and *sheets* and *heart* and *room*, the name *Matt* holds no real meaning. *Matt = brother*, but that's all. No image splashes across the movie screen of his mind: no face, no true memories. *Matt* is just a word, and that's nuts. *Why can't I remember?* He *knows* he has a dying mother, and a pastor-dad always on him about getting right with God, implying that because he *isn't*; because he's one sick, ungrateful, unrepentant son of a bitch, and God punishes the wicked . . . say no more. Look no further. QED: your mom's rotting from the inside out, and it's your *fault*.

Yet he can't find his parents' faces in the file cabinet of his memory either. In fact, he can't find . . . *oh*. He feels his heart curl on itself. *No. No, that's not right; that's just* . . . But he's had the thought now, and it won't be denied.

He can't find the face of a mom or dad or brother—any more than he can his own.

4

THIS CAN'T BE right.

Of course I've got a face. I'm breathing; I hear *my breath. I'm . . . I'm . . .*

Oh. Oh shit. What *I? Who* am *I?* He can't stop shaking. *What's my name?*

Nothing happens in his head. Because he. Doesn't. *Know.*

Stop, stop. *Calm down. Stop trying so hard, it'll come to you.* Better to get in a rhythm, like a song: *I am okay. I am fine. I have a brother. His name is Matt. He's in the Marines. . . .* As he chants this to himself, he feels his mind tiptoeing to the edge of a big black hole where his memories must swim like koi in an inky pool. All he has to do is net the right memory as it glides by. *And Matt is gone, so this place . . .* And it's a room, it *is*; he just hasn't found it quite yet. . . . *It's my room now, and this room is in a house, and that's in . . . iiinnn . . .* A blank moment as the bottom of his mind drops out, and then the name comes: *Merit.*

That's right. He is so relieved he wants to weep. *I live in Merit, Wisconsin, and my address is . . .* His mind blunders again as if it's stubbed a toe. *My address is . . .* He doesn't know. Because he hasn't one?

No, I am real. But then what's his name? Where does he live? What does he look like? What . . .

All of a sudden, his hands move. He hasn't thought it, didn't plan this, but it doesn't seem to matter. His hands float toward the space where his face should be . . . no, where his face is, *is.* He thinks his hands are right in front of his eyes, but he can't be sure. His eyes, though . . . *Please. Please, God, they have to be here. I feel them.* I'm *not nothing.*

He's still in the dream. That's got to be it. There's a name for this, too, but it flits away with a silvery snap of its tail before he can capture it. His hands come closer and closer, the fingers wiggling like antennae. *God, they could be tentacles for all I know, just like that thing in the dream . . . No!* He slams down on that. *Think only of your face . . . your face . . .* His fingertips skim . . . something. Something smooth, smooth as

(ice)

glass, as

(ice)

perfectly unblemished marble.

No lips. He has no mouth. There is a shelf that must be his chin, but nothing else, and no whisper of air on his fingers either. He has no nose. No cheekbones. His palms graze where the hollows of his eyes, his sockets, ought to be, but when he blinks, and he *thinks* he's blinking, there is no flutter of eyelashes against either palm.

His face is a blank.

5

NO. **THE SCREAM** he has worked to hold back so long balloons in a mouth and on a tongue that are not there. *No no no! Please, God, help me help me, letmeoutletme—*

All at once, there is some seismic shift within himself, an almost indescribable sensation of something worming to life. From the space where his mouth is not, lips suddenly pillow. The ridge of his nose thrusts into being. His eyes bud like tiny mushrooms: first as nubbins and then as flowering caps. The dead space in his mouth clenches as the moist snail of his tongue curls from the deep cavity that is the shell of his throat, and now he is screaming on a tidal wave of terror blacker even than the nightmare; he is shrieking, the word exploding from his throat: *"NOOO NOOO NOOO—"*

TONY

Boy in a Box

1

TONY SUCKS IN a breath.

Everything has changed. Now he stands, towel around his waist and toothbrush in hand, before a bathroom mirror fogged with condensation because he's just stepped out of a hot shower. Michael Jackson's tinny falsetto splutters about how he might be trying to scream from a piece-of-crap Sony transistor, while from beyond the bathroom door comes the ceaseless, monotonous one-note song that is his mother: *kak-kak-kak.*

I'm back. There has been no transition, no snap to wakefulness, no *ka-BANG* and bolt of bright yellow light, shattering the darkness, because his father—hair standing in corkscrews, and sleep crumbs like snow in the purple hollows under his eyes—has come bursting in to see why his son's screaming his lungs out. He is just suddenly awake, like he's been dreaming standing up and with his eyes open.

And I've been here before. Déjà vu of the worst kind blasts through his body. On his electric toothbrush—which would be totally boss, if it wasn't for the fact that this is a little kid's Snoopy set (red-roofed doghouse and everything) that his pastor-dad unearthed at Goodwill—a bloated green worm of mint Crest oozes on bristles so worn they splay like the tired legs of dead tarantulas. *I'm getting ready for school.* His eyes flick to the mirror, where his face is an oval blur behind scummy moisture. *In ten minutes, I'll go downstairs and flush the oatmeal glop Dad's left, because he just doesn't get that I hate that stuff. I'll brush my teeth again, because Mom will want a kiss. I'll drive my piece-of-shit Camry to school. I'm where I belong, and everything is as it's always been.*

This should make him feel better, but only for a second. Sure, of course, he's doing a lot of the same *things*. But not *everything* is exactly the same now as it was, say, yesterday or last week, is it? No, that would be crazy. His eyes fall to a *Twisted Tales* that he really likes. The comic book's open to his favorite story, about these soldiers and their lieutenant, a guy named Hacker, who suspects that he and his men have been hunkering in their foxholes forever. Then his gaze slides right to the paperback of *Our Mutual Friend* he's supposed to be reading instead of his comic. (God, what a snooze, and Dickens was popular? The whole river rat thing—fishing bodies out of the Thames—is okay, but there are so many characters, and trying to keep track of that John Harmon guy and all his disguises and alter egos and who the dude's supposed to be *now* only gives Tony a headache. And he's got to cough up a ten-page paper comparing and contrasting Dickens's use of doubles in this monster with either *Great Expectations* or that story . . . *The Haunted Man and the Ghost's Bargain*? Gag him with a spoon. At least *Haunted Man* is short, the last Christmas book Dickens published, and anyone with half a brain can see that Evil Genius is really Redlaw. Thank God, they're going on to Sherlock Holmes next. *Hound of the Baskervilles*—now *that's* a story. That black dog gives him the shivers. He wonders if he can talk the teacher into trying Lovecraft after that. Talk about spooky.)

But how long have I been reading this stupid book? He can't remember. He starts to reach a hand to the Dickens he's placed facedown to mark his place . . . then hesitates. *Think.* Where, exactly, *is* he in the book? He knows the name John Harmon and the thing about river rats—what else can he recall about the story? *Jesus, why can't I remember?* He tries to dredge up some more facts, scenes, *names* of other characters—and can't. It is almost as if this is all the information he's *allowed* to know.

Oh, that is crazy. It's because the book is so boring he'd rather set his hair on fire, that's all. But come on, he *must* know what he's read so far, right? After all, he knows about John Harmon and doubles, and isn't there a girl? *Important girl . . . what's her name?* Prying the information from his brain is like worrying a piece of meat from between his teeth that's wedged in so tight he needs a toothpick to dig it out . . .

"*Lizzie.*" The name comes in an explosive hiss. He should feel a blast of relief—but all he gets is a jolt in his chest. Like the name *Lizzie* is totally bad news. But that *is* the girl's name in *Our Mutual Friend*: Lizzie, short for Elizabeth, and she . . . *sheeeee . . . Christ.* The fine hairs spike along his neck. That's all he knows about the chick. The name, and that's it. *This is like my nightmare, when I couldn't remember where I lived, when I didn't have a face . . .*

"Screw it. Not important." The words ride a dry croak. "Who the hell cares? All I have to do is look and then I'll know what page I'm on." But he's afraid to check. He has the funniest feeling: flip that book over . . . and everything will be a blur. Or blank. That the book is just a prop, like in a movie.

"This is nuts," he says as, on the radio, Jackson's wailing to some girl that she better hope this is her imagination. *Got that right*. The song grates. He doesn't particularly love Michael Jackson, but anything's better than listening to his mother *kak-kak-kakking*.

Only . . . *is* she out there?

Of course; you just heard her. Don't be dumb. Just that nightmare or daymare or whatever the hell he'd just had—of him as a blank-faced mannequin floating in midair—still eating at him.

On the other hand . . . is there anything beyond this bathroom? Trying to place details is like trying to remember scenes from that Dickens novel. All he has to do is open the door and check; pick up the book, scan a page, and he'll know. But that all feels too weird.

On the radio, Jackson has decided the girl hasn't got a snowball's chance in hell against something with forty eyes—and man, is that close to his nightmare or what? Spooked, he switches off the radio, Michael *urping* out before he can tell him that they—the monsters, the demons, these creepy zombies—will possess him, too.

"You have to calm down, Tony." He's tired; his mom's dying; his preacher-dad's wearing out his knees praying to thin air. If Tony's not careful, he'll wind up like Jack Nicholson in that movie a few years ago, which he'd never have seen if Matt hadn't worked the theater's ticket office. (Honestly, if he had to put up with Shelley Duvall, he'd go after her with an ax, too.) The little kid was okay. Come to think of it, wasn't that kid's imaginary friend named Tony? Was that in the movie or the book? Both? He can't remember, and no, he is *not* imaginary.

"Why are you even *thinking* about all this, you moron?" His eyes tick back to the fogged bathroom mirror where his reflection is nothing but a shimmering blob. Because of the nightmare he knows he's had but can't really remember anymore?

There is a sodden little *splot*. His gaze falls to the sink, where a light green glob of toothpaste shimmers wetly, like exotic bird shit, on porcelain. *Come on. You'll be late for school.* Turning on the tap, he uses a forefinger to edge the slick glop from the porcelain and down the drain. He shudders at the feel. Like a squirmy slug, like snot. Cranking on the hot water full blast, he rinses his finger and lets out a little *ugh* at the sudden burn. *God, stop it already*. He studies the angry red scald. Be lucky if that doesn't blister. *It's just toothpaste, you dope.*

Squishing out another rope of green goop, he lifts the brush to his mouth, then hesitates. Behind its watery film, his reflection patiently waits. He feels its eyes trying to bore through that mist—but for a split second, he has the eeriest feeling: *I don't know what you look like.* Which means he's not sure what *he* looks like either, just like that moment in his dream when he reached for his face and . . .

"Stop it." Yet . . . has he *ever* seen his face in this mirror? With his free hand, he skims the hollow under his left eye. In the mirror, the blob shifts, and its arm mimics his move, of course, of *course*, because that is just a reflection. But what color *are* his eyes? He waits for the answer to slot into his brain. Nothing comes. *Okay, what about the color of my hair?* No answer surfaces from the well of his brain; nothing drifts from the dark to settle on his tongue. Total blank.

That's crazy. I can't be nothing. But he's never looked at himself in the mirror now, has he? *Has* he? He can't remember. *Shit.* He feels the spit drying up on his tongue. This is just too close to that damn nightmare.

Well then, settle it. Go on. Check, you coward. Go on.

"Okay" —and then, casually, "No big deal." Which is *such* a lie, because it is, it *is*. Heart thumping, he uses the side of his left hand to squeegee water from silvered glass, and he *seeees* . . . him. He. Whatever. That is, he recognizes the kid with the cap of wet brown curls and light blue eyes in the mirror as the boy he's always imagined he is.

"Well, who else would it be?" Lifting his hand, he turns it this way and that. His hand, all right. Isn't it? How can you really tell something like that? Just because you keep waking up in the same body? How do you *know* that whatever you wake up *in* is yours?

"What's going on?" He raises his eyes to his reflection. "Do *you* know?"

For just a sec, he has the funniest feeling that the kid in the mirror will answer, like *that* kid stands on the other side of a pane of rain-spattered glass: different bathroom, another Wisconsin, whole other planet. A twin, all tangled up in his life the way Mr. Steele, his physics teacher, says might happen if you believe Schrödinger. (Although Einstein didn't. But the concept's cool, actually: that a cat can exist in between, both alive and dead at the same moment. When you look in the box—*collapse the wave function* is how Steele put it—Schrödinger's cat is either alive or dead because you looked. You forced that cat to be either/or. The cat can't be both.)

So he's stupidly relieved when his reflection perfectly syncs, saying the same thing right back at him at the same time. Still, he can't rid himself of this nagging sense that something has changed. Like . . . what has *he* forced by clearing fog from that bathroom mirror *for the very first time*? In a funny way, isn't this bathroom a kind of box? Who knows what's really beyond the door?

"You're a nut. You're going to drive yourself crazy with shit like this." Thumbing his stupid Snoopy electric to life, he begins scrubbing his teeth, hard and thoroughly. Yet he's also got this strangest swoop of déjà vu all over again, the sneaking suspicion that this whole routine is something he's gone through maybe more times than he can count: Michael on the radio, *Twisted Tales* by the sink, Crest on his toothbrush, and so much green foam on his mouth, he looks like a rabid dog that's escaped from the set of *The Wizard of Oz*.

Stop. But he can't. He spits, sucks water from the faucet, rinses, spits again. Fights the urge to see what the boy in the mirror is doing. Instead, he watches murky spit-water circle down the drain.

What's new is the nightmare. Now he does turn a look at his reflection. *And you. This is the first time I've ever wiped away the fog to find you.*

It hits him then: *the first time.*

But the first time . . . *when?*

2

BEIRUT HAPPENED IN October. So did Grenada. He knows that it's the week before Christmas, *buuut* . . .

Shit. His heart flutters against the cage of his ribs. He reaches for his comic, the movements as slo-mo as a dream. Being generally sucky at art, he doesn't know squat about perspective, but he thinks the view in the first color panel is foreshortened, the scene set as if you're looking up from the bottom of a foxhole to a soldier with a weapon balanced on his lap and the bright coin of a moon hanging in a purple, starless sky. His gaze skims the panel's last line, when Hacker thinks that maybe he and his men have been in this desert . . .

"Forever," he says, and wonders just who he's talking about here. Look at it a certain way, and isn't Hacker, stuck on six flimsy pages sandwiched between glossy covers, a guy in a box, too? Hacker's only *alive* when Tony's there to read him, right? *Yeah, but what really happens inside the comic book when I'm not looking?* Does Hacker go off and do something else? Maybe characters from other stories decide, *Hey, let's go visit those guys on page 20; that's waaay more interesting than here.* Or when Tony decides to start Hacker's story on page 13 instead of 10 . . . doesn't *that* become Hacker's present, his *now*, as opposed to *then*?

And what if *he*—Tony, a real live boy—what if *he's* the same way? What if *he's* like Hacker, and the only reason he's standing at his sink, brushing his teeth, getting ready for school, listening to his mother die . . . is because he's *not* a real boy but only a character in a book that someone just happens to be reading?

"What?" he says to his reflection. "What are you doing? Stop thinking this way." But he can't stop this, and isn't entirely sure he wants to. His brain is feverish, a steaming, belching runaway train, his thoughts whirring over the tracks *clickityclack-clickity-clack*. Because . . . here's the thing, the flip side, the whole *other* part of it all.

What happens to *him* when there's no one there, outside, looking at him and putting him together letter by letter, word by word?

Jesus. If this moment, this day, is only a couple three, four pages in a book . . . what about when the book is closed? When there's no one out there to read him? Or when they've skipped his chapter, started in a different place? What if he—his character—never shows up again? Does that mean he doesn't exist?

If there is no one to read him . . . *is* there any him—a *Tony*—
at all?

"Stop it, *stop* it!" Of course he's real; he knows about Michael
Jackson and Einstein and Jack Nicholson! But wait wait wait—
he's starting to hyperventilate, his breaths coming short and
sharp—don't writers put pieces of real life into books all the time
to make the *characters* seem more like people?

Damn. That's right. *Pop-cultural references* is what his English
teacher said: *Writers do this to ground characters in their particular time
periods or add a layer of verisimilitude to the narrative.* The references
didn't have to be books either, or movies, but slang, food, songs,
even people who'd actually existed. Like a writer could slot in
Einstein or Charles Dickens or Arthur Conan Doyle, use one
of *them* as a character to make the book seem closer to reality.
God, and if you *did* that, even if you changed them all around or
did one of those alternative-universe things, made them into the
people they *might* have become . . . would they *know* they were
characters?

"Shit." His forehead's slick with perspiration. *"Shit."* What if
he only knows about Michael Jackson or Crest toothpaste or *The
Wizard of Oz* because some writer—some crazy lady, hunched
over a typewriter and stuck in a room somewhere—is playing
God, sprinkling cutesy pop-cultural references to make some
point, and she's thinking, *Oh, that Tony, he's such an interesting
character; let's torture him some more.*

There's a sudden crack, like the snap of a branch, and a jump
of pain. Winking against the sting of salt, he stares at his hand,
then at the mirror and the red splotch on that kid's cheek. *Slapped
myself.* He just *hit* himself! Had he meant to do that? Or did the
crazy lady at the typewriter just put that in for kicks?

Stop this, stop this! Laughter gurgles in his chest, but he's afraid to start, worried he won't stop until he's clawing out his eyes and eating them like gumdrops. *Get a grip.* He grits his teeth and welcomes the ache in his jaw. He tastes copper. *That's real.* He tongues the small rip in his cheek. *I feel that. It hurts. I can taste my blood, and no one wrote that. I did that to myself.*

Unlesss . . . Unless someone wrote that he ought to do it. Unless the crazy lady at the typewriter's talking to her cat: *Oh, this is good, this is great, bwahahaha, go on, slap yourself. Take* that, *Tony.*

Which might happen if he truly *isn't* real.

"This is crazy," he says, and spits, the foamy red gob splatting like a squished mosquito. "Your mom is dying and you're freaked, and that's all. Hacker's the one who's only ink on crappy paper that you picked up from a drugstore."

But when did he buy this? He picks up the comic, listens to the rustle of paper. *That's real. It's got pages.* Flipping back to the table of contents—cheap, pulpy paper fanning past so that whatever's printed there is a blur—he looks for the date. It's there, solid and in black letters. *Okay, okay, this is good.* He says it out loud, feeling the words full and heavy and *real* in his mouth: "April. April, 1983."

Okay. Doesn't matter if he can't remember the exact date he tugged the comic from its rack. (Who pays attention to crap like that? No one.) But he'd done that in April, and now, it's the week before Christmas. Which means December. *That's right. Christmas happens in December, on . . .* He has to close his eyes and *think think think. Don't freak don't freak don't freak . . .*

"The twenty-fifth!" he blurts. "Twenty-five. Thirty days have September, April, June, and November . . . Jesus." In the mirror, sweat pearls his reflection's upper lip. "What's the date, Tony?" he asks that other kid. "Come on, it's not a trick question. What is *today*, right *now*?"

The other kid doesn't reply. His own head is blank, except for that same phrase:

it's the week before Christmas.

A slow shudder slithers the rungs of his spine. *Easy, take it easy. Think.* His gaze settles on the silvered plastic of his Sony transistor. *The radio.* He *snicks* it to life, thinking, *Yeah, there's a DJ. He'll tell me the weather and the time and the . . .*

And it's still Michael Jackson.

3

***NO.* HIS THROAT** catches and knots. *It's still . . . it's . . . the song's the sa—*

You try to screeeeam. Michael holds the note an impressive four beats. Again. And then he goes on about terror . . . but, Jesus, Ol' Michael doesn't know the half of it.

This is also when *he'd . . .* tuned in? *Faded* in? Awakened in this bathroom, doing the same thing in the same exact way and sequence in a day he's already been through over and over again and only *thinks* he's living for the first time? Because someone cracked the book of his life and this is the page where they started? Or they've started from the very beginning, page one, chapter one—where and when *he's* not—and now reached the point in the book where he—the character named *Tony*— finally shows up?

Get out of here. Go to school. Just . . . Slotting his toothbrush into Snoopy's red roof, he turns like a little robot boy and reaches for the knob with stiff, robot-boy fingers.

And then he pauses.

4

SAY HE'S THE cat or a character or a boy or whatever the hell he is. The second he pushes from this bathroom—cracks this particular box or book—a reality will assert itself. His life will be what he forces.

Or . . . he's the reflection, and what passes for his life will happen to the boy behind the mirror as he emerges into whatever world lies beyond the looking glass.

It really comes down to which of them is the boy in a box.

"Or you might just be kind of insane," he says, and twists the knob. The tongue slips back with a *click*. The hinges let out a very soft and mousy *squeee*. A balloon of cooler air pillows into the room, chilling his face. Condensed steam rains, falling in a gentle patter onto his head and shoulders. The mirror instantly fogs again, leaving only a narrow strip of silvered glass low down near the faucet. The staring boy disappears.

Teetering on the brink between this box and what lies beyond, he waits. For a split second, there's nothing. No *kak-kak-kak* at all. And he thinks, *God, what if it's really true? What if this is a different Merit where my mom isn't—*

"Honey?" His mother's voice is as faint as a cloud dissolving under a hot sun. "Is that you, sweetheart?"

For a second, he feels an absurd sweep of disappointment. *Shit.* It's the same. His mom's dying. God's an asshole. Nothing has changed. So much for reality.

"Coming, Mom," he calls. "Just a sec."

5

IF THIS WERE a book, this would be the moment he wakes for real and the clockwork of his life resumes ticking. At that second, in fact, the name of the phenomenon he's been searching for comes to him: *false awakening*. Or *double dream*. And of the two types he's learned in abnormal psych, he's having a Type 2: things are eerie, uncanny, terribly out of whack.

But his eyes don't snap open for the third time. He doesn't awake in bed with his covers bunched around his ankles, sheet creases stenciled in the drool on his cheek, and his hair in cork-screws. Yet what he does is kind of what you might expect, given the situation. Given that mirror he's cleared for the very first time that he can recall.

Even so, he hesitates. Thinks about the ramifications and the reality he might be forcing if he does this. Because what if . . .

If I see something weird, I'll just close my eyes. It'll be like the book where that black guy, the cook, tells the kid to shut his eyes and whatever he sees in that spooky hotel'll go away.

So, he snatches a look back at the mirror.

6

BIG MISTAKE.

Because you know what they say about curiosity, and the cat.

TONY

His Side of the Glass

1

THE ENTIRE BATHROOM, from the walls to the ceiling to the floor, wavers. The room ripples and shimmies as if he's standing atop a pond, still as a mirror, into which someone's just dropped a stone. *God.* Poised on the threshold, he feels the wobble in his chest. His eyes drop to his hands, where wave after wave chases over his skin and deep in his bones, through his mind. The air crinkles with odd glimmers that, if he didn't know better, actually might rip and pull apart to allow something on the other side

(other side of what? what's going on?)

to crawl through,

(crack the lid, take a peek)

and suddenly, he's not sure he's even real anymore.

By the time he registers all this, everything has firmed up again. It's taken only the blink of an eye. He is solid and so is the room . . .

In which he now sees something he shouldn't.

2

THE SHOWER STALL'S tucked in a far corner to his right, with the toilet squatting beside it, closer to the door. His sink is kitty-corner to the left. This means that the mirror offers a partial view of the shower stall, and a nice full frontal of the commode. This new scrim of fog hasn't lifted quite yet, although that narrow ribbon of silver is wider now, slowly peeling back like an eyelid reluctant to admit, *Yeah, crap, another damn day.* A third of the mirror is clear. He can see the entire toilet and that he hasn't put down the lid, but screw it: this is his bathroom, and he's got decent aim. Half the shower stall is visible; if he were standing inside, you would see up to his knees. Of course, he sees the reflection of the chromed faucet and even the strangled, half-used tube of Crest he's forgotten to cap . . .

Oh.

His lungs squeeze down. Every molecule of air drains away. His heart stills into that dead space between beats, and that high whine, the peculiar sound that only silence possesses, is loud as a pneumatic drill. He closes his eyes, thinks he ought to count to ten, but loses track somewhere around four. Honestly, he doubts making it all the way would do him a whit of good, because anything—a hand or bit of hip, an arm—would've been bad.

And the woman with the purple eyes is so much worse.

3

NO. THE WORD is tiny, nothing more than a squeaky, mousy mental *eep.* His lungs shrivel. He's not sure he's even breathing. He's very nearly back to the moment this all began: when he woke after a nightmare of fire and terror and cold and death to find that he had no name, no face. If he *could* turn to look, he's not sure his house would even be there. Because there is only *now*: this moment, the mirror, that woman, that *woman* . . .

With something close to awe, he watches as her hands spider up the glass. From his vantage point, he sees the pads actually blanch and flatten. For a wild second, he thinks, *She can't get out. She's trapped. She's . . .*

The woman's fingers press—and then *curl* to hook the mirror's edge.

"Guh . . . uh . . ." This choking little cry is as close to a scream as he can manage. A tidal wave of dread struggles up his chest, but nothing else comes out. In the bathroom—this box he's opened— the woman's fingers crawl over the lip of that mirror, and now there is a boot: old-fashioned, with buttons and a blocky heel. A leg, clad in black stockings and draped in folds of a jet-black skirt, kinks, and then this woman is clambering out of the mirror. She swarms over the counter, knocking Snoopy, who clatters to the bathroom floor hard enough to crack off that black plastic nose. *Twisted Tales* spins off in a flutter of cheap paper, and now there she is, balanced on the edge of his sink, leering like a hungry, long-limbed tarantula that's decided this juicy little fly will make for quite the snack.

No! Paralyzed, he can't scream, doesn't move, can only watch as the woman scurries off the counter, drops to the floor, and scuttles for him, nails *tick-tick-ticking* on tile. *Go, go, run!* But he can't, and now she's crawling up his bare legs and her lips, blue as death, peel from her teeth and her clawed hands reach for his face and then his eyes his eyes his *eyes* . . .

TONY

The Other Tony

"NUH!"HE JOLTED awake, eyes snapping open. For a fraction of an instant, the space around him seemed to tremble, and he thought he was right back where that awful dream had begun: floating in midair, surrounded by nothing. Then in the desert of his chest, his heart convulsed with a great shiver. But what surged through his veins was icy and black as a remorseless tide, and he thought, *God, it's the rot; it's the squirmers; I'm infected; they're eating me alive!*

"Tony?" A hand, wet and dripping, spidered over his face. "Tony, what . . . ?"

With a strangled sob, he lashed out, sweeping a wild fist. He felt the moment of impact and heard a gasp, the sound of something—someone—falling. The darkness before his eyes dissolved to a ruddy, pulsing glow, and in the dim and unnatural light, he saw a shape—*girl . . . no, the woman!*—in a tangle of worn cotton ticking. *Kill her, stop her!* Swarming over rags and burlap and rough brick, he pinned her, facedown. She let out a pained gasp and then a small cry as he knotted a fist in her hair.

No more nightmares. Baring his teeth, cocking a fist, he flipped her onto her back. *No more black visits, no more infection; kill her before she kills me, kill her before—*

"T-Tony." Her hands closed over his balled knuckles. "Tony, d-don't. Wake up. It's me, it's . . ."

"Rima?" Stupefied, he stared. Loosed from its braid, her hair was a tangled cloud around her head, and her eyes, so dark, were huge in her thin, pinched face. Through the gloom—*because it's night; we're above the retort; everyone's asleep*—he saw the darker blush of a new bruise on her cheek. A second later, he felt the warm seep over his lips and down his chin and realized he was bleeding from his nose again, too.

"Oh God." Shame swept his chest. Moaning, he sagged from her body, suddenly weaker than a kitten, his eyes springing hot. He cupped a hand to his streaming nose. The taste, brackish and dank, coated his throat. "I'm sorry, I'm sorry, I *never* . . ."

"Shhh, shhh, Tony, it's fine. I startled you. Of course you'd lash out. It's my fault. Here, let's stop that bleeding." Pinching the bridge of his nose with one hand, she pressed a rough cloth to his streaming nostrils. "Relax, Tony, the nightmare's over."

"Leave it." His voice was nasal and stuffed. He brushed her hand aside. "I can do this." He was getting worse. So were the dreams, each nightmare building on the other, growing more detailed and ever more horrifying. His eyes drifted right to a dull orange gleam of reflected light: a squared-off and wicked-sharp ten-inch steel blade set in a worn bone mount, dangling from its peg. He'd hung it that way on purpose, so there would always be that split second where he would *have* to sit up and reach for the blade—and thank God. If he hadn't, he might have buried his chopper in her skull.

"Rima, I'm sorry." *I'm a monster. Might have killed her.* Gulping around a stone of fear, he said, "I d-didn't know . . ."

"Shhh, Tony, you'll wake the others. It's all right. Let's just . . . hold on." She ducked around a ramshackle barrier he'd constructed of the broken slates of a rotted crate. With no privacy other than what he could make, he'd used these as a screen between him and the hundred other children crammed, cheek by jowl, like pilchards in a tin. Rima slept alongside in her own nest of threadbare burlap. He heard a slight rasp of metal, followed by a muted gurgle. In another moment, she was back, a small, sloshing cast-iron Dutch pot scavenged from a dustheap hooked over one hand.

"Here." Kneeling, she wrung out a cloth and began cleaning blood from his face and neck. "Let's put you to rights."

He forced even, methodical breaths, one after the other, through his mouth as she worked. The air was a mélange, heavy with the odor of soot, hot brick, musty burlap, clothes that hadn't seen a proper wash in months—and another, more peculiar, almost sweet aroma that anyone, if he didn't know better, might mistake for a roast pig on a spit, dripping molten fat. But he did know better.

"Try to relax." Laying a gentle hand over the fist bunched at his chest, she swabbed at his bloodstained palm. Wringing out her cloth, she touched the back of the hand that still held pressure on his nose. "Let's have this one now."

He let her. "What happened?" he asked, still in a whisper. Although this room above the retort was warm enough for them all to shed coats and mittens for sleeping, he was shivering. His skin was clammy with fear-sweat. His heart boomed in his chest, muting the chuff of a persistent roar from the furnace below. The gasworks had several retorts—gargantuan iron vessels in which coal or other fuels were carbonized to release gas—although only two furnaces still operated this side of the Thames because there were no more shipments of coal. No trains either, for that matter, and what this part of the city had left had to last until . . . well, no one was exactly sure. So they were forced to use a very *different* species of fuel now. "Did I shout?"

"No. I heard you moaning. When I checked, you were burning up, so I got a wet cloth for your forehead and . . ."

"Wait." He snagged her wrist. "You *touched* me? You didn't try to . . ."

"Quiet. Not so loud." She half-turned as, from beyond Tony's nook and the murky depths of the room, someone shifted in a rustle of burlap and straw. This place, with its demon's light and heat, was where he and the other rats—children with nowhere to go, who were desperate enough to do a job no one else would— lived when they weren't out collecting bodies to strip bare and then feed to the furnace as fuel. After another moment, there was a small mewling noise, like a contented kitten, and then a mutter as whoever that was settled back into sleep. Looking back, Rima gave the wrist he still held a pointed look. "No, I *didn't*. You made me promise, remember? I only felt for a fever. Now, if I might have my hand back?"

He wasn't sure he believed her, but he did as she asked. *Did she try?* Pressing a palm to his chest, he tried to reach beyond the thump of his heart. Normally, he could tell when she drew out sickness. Hard to describe, but the sensation was like a *clearing* in his soul, as if this black blight in his center was only soot that could be scrubbed clean with the right hand and good soap. For a little while at least, when Rima drew from him, he was stronger, stable, and more himself.

Now, though, he simply couldn't tell if she had, most likely because he was still so unsettled, his mind mired in the thick mud of that dream. That other boy—*himself*—had appeared in other nightmares, but only fleetingly. *This* time, though . . .

Bathroom. Was that a kind of indoor privy? The sink and spigot, he recognized; when the toffs cleared out of London months before, him and the others had ransacked their houses. Being rich, the high-class types had taken their nice threads and jewels. (Stupid. You couldn't eat diamonds, and how many clothes did one body need?) Furniture and paintings made for very good fuel, though. But he remembered the first couple houses he went through, round Regent's Park and further north in the very posh Crouch End. There, the houses had indoor plumbing, which meant sinks and spigots and separate water closets. Nothing worked, of course; without a reliable source of fuel, the pumping stations couldn't function. Light was much more important than being able to flush a toilet. There were plenty of public privies. Or you just dropped your drawers wherever. No one was paying much attention to the niceties these days.

So if *he'd* seen a sink and spigot in his nightmare, then this other Tony must be rich, a real toff. Indoor plumbing, toilet in the same room, and a shower, too. What else? *Crest.* What was that? Surely not the crest of a wave; he hadn't heard water running. *And a comic book?* Hadn't looked like any volume he'd ever seen. What wavered before his mind's eye was closer to a pamphlet but smaller, with odd writing that didn't look like proper printing. The drawings were wrong, too: in color and very crude, nothing as fine as anything by Doré or Cruikshank. In the drawing, the lieutenant? Or sergeant? He couldn't remember, but what the figure wore looked like a kind of bowler. The soldier had a rifle, too, though it wasn't a Henry; he was pretty certain of that. *And foxhole? What's that?* Why would soldiers be out on a foxhunt?

There was something else, too, that was very strange. An animal . . . come on, what was it? *Right.* He felt that muzzy sense dissipate, and now the image firmed. *That queer red-roofed house with a gigantic dog and . . . what's an electric toothbrush?* He knew what a toothbrush was, but his had a bone handle and the bristles were a threadbare splay of macerated hog's hair. But electric? Like lightning?

"What?" Rima said. "Electric toothbrush? What's that?"

Startled—he hadn't realized he'd spoken aloud—he said, "Something I saw in the nightmare. In that other T-Tony's bathroom." God, that felt so strange in his mouth. She listened as he stammered out the rest, the entire sequence from beginning to end, and then she said, "So you got a good look this time."

"At him? Yes. I think it's because something happened to really scare him."

"Like what?"

"Not sure. I want to say"—he could feel the word poised on the tip of his tongue—"that he had a nightmare, too. As if we both had one at the same time. He just felt *different* this time."

"Not like someone you'd read about," she said. They'd talked about this before, when the dreams had begun. Back then, the other Tony had seemed like a boy in a fairy tale or serial: something flat as paper, with no more substance than a thin character in a bad novel. Yet with each dream, this other Tony had drawn closer, in the same way that the fog, so relentless, crept ever nearer. "He was fleshed out. A person."

"Yeah, and I think *he* noticed it, too, because he *did* something. Changed things up somehow." *Mirror*—the word popped into his brain on a thrill—*that's it.* "He's always been hazy; can't quite ever make him out. But this time, he wiped away mist or fog or something like that from a mirror, and then, all of a sudden, I could see out of his eyes. I wasn't able to do that before and . . ."

"What?" she said when he broke off. "Tony?"

"What in God's name are we talking about?" *I'm sick; I'm going mad, that's it.* He pressed the heel of a hand to his forehead. "Rima, there *is* no other Tony. This *has* to be the rot. I'm infected. It's burrowed into my brain."

"No. Tony, the last time you let me *draw,* I could tell. Rot feels different."

"How many rotters you actually drawn from? Two? Three? No more than a half dozen before you realized you couldn't help. Checking for squirmers doesn't count." So far, they'd been lucky enough to avoid a rotter with a bellyful. *Oh, but the day is coming. Eventually, our luck's going to run out.* "Maybe, in me, the rot's up to something new."

Perhaps the rot had taken root in his brain, and this was how it would be: he going slowly insane as squirmers wriggled and munched and hollowed him at his core. Even worse, what if he didn't snap out of it next time? He might kill her without meaning to. *I should leave, take myself away while there's still time.*

He felt movement, heard the Dutch pot slosh, and then she was stretching out alongside, careful not to touch. Eyes still shuttered, arm over his face, he said, "You shouldn't."

"Be quiet. Don't tell me what I ought and ought not do. Aren't things bad enough?"

"Yes." There was something strangely comforting about speaking into the dark before his eyes. "But they'll get worse, and you know it. Forget the rot and the fog. Horses are all gone.

There are no more dogs, no cats. No one's seen a bird since the Peculiar made it to the Tower." The raid on the zoo, with its turtles and snakes, gazelles and hippos, an elephant, had been well before the toffs and Parliament and their good King Eddie decided to abscond in the middle of the night. None such as *him* had so much as a mouthful; the price for a quarter pound of civet had been three pounds, sixpence, which was more scratch than he'd seen in his entire life. Only those families with money, and there were plenty in those days, actually supped on zebra in raisin sauce, or a duck-and-hippo cassoulet, which he'd gathered was some fancy name for bean stew. Although he'd heard that the toffs complained about elephant. Said it was tough and too greasy, so much bowwow mutton. While a few animals had been spared—the lions, a few tigers, several monkeys, and a great black bear—that was only because some scientists thought monkeys were too close to people, and killing lions was too difficult. And where were those poor creatures now? Starved to death, still in their cages, behind a dense milky shroud? Or had they somehow *become* fog?

No one knew. Once the fog lowered, not a soul came out again, and no one was stupid enough to wander in.

"All that's left is what vermin we can catch and what hordes we find. But how many more of those, you think?" Deep in his heart, he also thought they weren't very far from consuming the dead. (In another, even more inaccessible part he didn't let himself stare at for long, he thought some people were already there. Meat was meat.) But then it was a choice between heat and food, wasn't it? Freeze to death with full bellies, or starve away to skin and bones on a warm brick floor. He moved a shoulder in a shrug. "Can't be limitless. Soon there won't be food to be had for love or money. It'll be whoever's left, and the Peculiar boxing us in on all sides."

"Well, until then, we do the best we can," Rima said. "That day may be a long while off. It's *been* like this for as long as any of us can remember. Who's to say this won't go on forever?"

What she said was true. Everyone's memory held the same black absence at the core. No one could recall a time before the coming of this weird, suffocating fog—the Peculiar—that was denser than any London Particular before it. (Pea-soup thick, a nauseating mixture of coal soot and smoke and fog, the Particulars had been bad enough, like to choke a fellow or turn spit brown and stain garments piss-yellow. But *this* fog was *peculiar*, like nothing anyone had ever seen, and the name stuck because it was so apt.) The doctors thought the Peculiar was responsible for all the holes in their memories, too. *Noxious fumes and debilitating miasmas* was what they said, fancy words that said nothing at all but carried weight and felt important.

There were days, in fact, when Tony was convinced that he'd only just now come alive; that this was the first day of his life. He had a *history*, of sorts. Well . . . as much of one as any foundling left in swaddling clothes on Coram's doorstep. He knew things. Staffers from the orphanage, for example. That Coram's cutlery had lambs stamped into the metal, and they got roast instead of boiled beef on Sundays. He remembered a book he and Rima loved, all about the Isle of Mull off Scotland; they would take turns, spinning a future in words of high cliffs and a blue sea and a cottage with a good stone croft for sheep and always snow for Christmas; of the monster in its deep, dark cathedral cave on Staffa and how they might listen to it roar at night. He could recall the summer one boy, Chad, had gotten it into his head to take a dip in the Thames round the old Battersea Bridge, only to be pulled under by the current.

He recalled all that—the book, the talk of a future, that boy—or thought he did. But damme if there weren't days when his past felt flat and as insubstantial as air: no real *feeling* or true memories. That was what the Peculiar was doing to them all.

Yet, so far as he knew, he was the only person with nightmares. (These days, the least little bit of news rippled through Lambeth like lightning, so he'd have heard if anyone else had them.) Was that the fog's doing? He wasn't sure, but he felt a deep foreboding. *Something's about to happen, and whatever it is, I think it's nearly here.*

Then what? He should leave. Protect Rima. *Yes, but go where?* As far south or east or west as he could, until he reached the fog's edge? *Or go to Westminster or Tower, any of the bridges, and walk into the Peculiar, let it take me?* Just the thought froze his blood. Who knew what waited inside all that?

"Rima, this is getting out of control. This other Tony . . . it feels like he's *bleeding* into me." And yet even that wasn't quite right. *Not bleeding:* stealing *from me, emptying me out.* The image of some parasite, latched on his mind, sent another stab of cold terror through his heart. "How long before he takes over and I *don't* wake up as me anymore? Or what if he hollows me out, and I don't ever wake again? What if I"—his throat tried to fist—"if I really h-hurt you? K-kill . . ."

"Stop." A light flutter of her fingers over his lips. "Don't blame yourself for what you can't help. You were having a nightmare, Tony, and that is all."

"But your dreams aren't like mine." When she didn't respond right away, he drew his arm from his eyes. Shadows swarmed over her features, though her eyes were somehow even deeper and more limitless than before. "Rima? *Are* they?"

"No." She didn't say it cautiously. "But that doesn't mean I don't have bad ones. Sometimes, I think it's the fog trying to . . . to talk to us, perhaps. Or maybe it's only reaching a finger into our minds, trying to decide if . . ."

"What?" When she said nothing, he skimmed a tentative thumb over her chin. A brief touch, nothing more, and still a clean, clear arrow of desire—more potent even than his fear—struck his heart through. *Stop.* Swallowing, the taste of dying blood still strong on his tongue, he took his hand back. *Surrender to that and you'll kill her for sure.* "What do you mean about the Peculiar talking to you?"

She sighed. "I don't know what I mean. I'm just . . ." Her hand slid onto his chest, and he gasped as he felt her—oh so fleeting—reach beyond the shell of his skin. "Please, Tony, let me help you. Just a little. I promise," she whispered, though he could barely hear her over the groan that her touch pulled from his throat, "I won't draw too much. Only enough to strengthen you. Please let me do this for you, please."

For a second, he wanted to surrender. So good, *so good* . . . better than a moist cloth or cool drink of water. He couldn't describe what she truly did, but when she laid on hands and drew out sickness, it felt the way he imagined the sun would over high cliffs edging the sea: a burst of warmth that bathed his face and chest and body and left him as languid and drowsy as a lizard. For a time—shorter and shorter these days—nothing hurt, and he wasn't afraid and allowed himself to see a future when there would be enough food and no fog and sweet relief and their cottage with its stone croft and . . . *Rima, Rima,* he heard himself moan again . . . *Rima, there's only Rima, please take it, draw it out, draw as much as you can bear and . . .*

"*S-s-stop.*" The word came out ragged and rough. Clasping her wrists, he pulled her fingers from his chest. "I c-can't let you, Rima. I *won't*. You can't possibly take it all away, and it only makes you weaker and . . . *no.*" He tightened his grip when her mouth opened in protest. "Don't. Don't tell me that you'll take just a bit and stop yourself before it's too late. You want to help me now?" It took all of his self-control not to crush her to him. Instead, he turned and showed her his back. "Go away. Get some sleep, Rima. It'll be morning soon, and always more work." *More bodies for us rats to gather.* "And promise me, Rima, you have to give me your word: don't touch me while I sleep. Don't try to draw this sickness or whatever it is from me."

"It is my choice. This is mine to give."

"And mine to refuse. Rima . . ." He could hear his voice try to break, and he swallowed. "Rima, it will kill you. *I* will."

"You don't know that."

"I don't want to find out, because if that happens . . . I might as well slit my throat right now. I won't be responsible for that. You can't ask me to."

For a long moment, she was silent. She also didn't move. He waited, eyes staring, his ears tingling as the others slept and, beneath, the furnace chuffed and thrummed like a gigantic hidden heart.

Finally, there came a stir of fabric and then the slash of her breath across his jaw. "Damn you, Tony." And he thought she really was crying this time. "Damn you to hell."

"That's not a promise."

"No," she said, "it's not." But she went back to her side.

RIMA

That Other Rima

1

DAMN HIM. RIGID with anger, Rima lay with her hands balled. Above the background cough of the furnace below, the air prickled with the sighs, soft moans, and musical murmurs of the others. She strained to parse out Tony above the rest. Normally, after a nightmare, sleep was a fugitive, which meant that between hours of toiling through snow by day and wrestling with the demons in his mind every night, Tony was hardly resting at all. Every morning—well, such as it was in daylight that was leaden and short-lived, the sky as likely to gray and blacken several times over—Tony's eyes were sunken even deeper in his skull. He was dwindling to nothing but tough, knotty muscle and sinew, what with the dreams eating him alive.

Well, not tonight. Because she *had* lied . . . well, *omitted.* Before he'd thrust her hands away, she'd made a very small *suggestion* that sleep could come for him, and soon. Whether that would work, she hadn't a clue. This was the first time she'd tried. *But damn him, I* will *help, whether he likes it or not.* Spreading her hands, she studied the lick and dance of shadows cast by the dim and ruddy light along her slim fingers. *What use are you if I can't? Two lolly daddles, that's what, if you can't draw away his suffering and lend him strength.*

Sighing, she folded her hands to her chest. She'd also lied about something else. Tony's nightmare? She'd had it, too. She'd seen another Tony, in agony and covered with blood, so much blood, and then there had been a bright, distant leap of fire and then a monstrous . . .

2

BANG.

Rima's eyes fly open. An explosion? The image of that bright burst sheeting her vision—*fire, explosion, Tony, TONY!*—is still so vivid. God, has the other retort gone up? Floundering to her knees in a puddle of frayed burlap, she holds her breath and listens, nerves still jangling. But there's nothing. No shouts or screams, only the background chuff of the furnace and the soft *shush* of many people, deeply asleep. On the side opposite, she hears Tony drag in a long, muttering breath. A word or two in there: *mom* and . . . something about a cat? She loses it after a moment as Tony settles. Beneath her, the bricks are warm and still. *No shudder.* Not that an explosion's required for a wall to buckle or a roof to cave these days, but for right now, the floor is still solid.

She draws in a deep, steadying breath. The air smells of soot and roasted flesh, but she holds it a moment before letting go. *Just another dream.* But she's lying to herself, and knows it. This has not been *just* another nightmare of some weird doppelgänger. She concentrates, trying to dredge up more detail besides that explosion. Before, all she got was a bizarre mélange: visions of a broken-down tenement, strange metal carts that rumbled along smooth roads with no cobbles, some sort of gigantic dustbin, much cleaner than any dustheaps she knew, but which the girl in *her* dreams thought of as *Goodwill ghost-bins.* (What could *that* mean? Ghosts that weren't harmful but all Christmas cheer? It was a puzzle.) There was a woman, too—*Mother,* the word was a whisper over her brain; *Anita*—with bad teeth, sores on her mouth, and scabs beetling her arms. The girl was afraid of Anita, and it worked the other way around, too. Something about a . . . a knife? *Yes, and it cut. I felt it.* With a fingertip, she traced a thin phantom grin over the tender skin below her jaw. *Right here. The other Rima's mother thought that Rima was evil and tried to kill her.*

The snow is a new detail, too. Of course, there is snow everywhere these days, and cold. But she doesn't think that's it. *There was also a valley.* Which is odd because she's never seen one in her life. The only valleys she knows are those she's read about in that book she and Tony loved, all about Staffa and the monster in the cave and the Isle of Mull and mountains and soaring eagles and black cliffs edging the sea. (She would dearly love to see an eagle. She would love to *be* an eagle and fly away from this awful place. Skim an indigo sea and then climb and climb and test the limits of the sky.)

In this dream, the snow was relentless, coming down in buckets. She'd been freezing, too, dressed in very odd clothes. "Parka." The word is so strange on her tongue. "Duct . . . *tape*?" Or was that *duck*? And . . . "Jeans." She runs a hand over a thigh and feels coarse wool, the slide of thin linen drawers beneath boys' trousers. She thinks *jeans* are trousers. *How odd.* In her dream, that other Tony had also worn similar clothes: *Parka. Jeans. Although the muffler*—she caresses the loose coil of wool around her neck with a thumb—*was exactly the same. Green, wasn't it?* That other

Tony had given her, the other Rima, the muffler—*scarf,* he called it—twining it around her neck. This was exactly what *her* Tony had done, snatching up a green woolen snake from a pile of cast-offs. (Weeks ago? Months? She can't recall.) *This will keep you warm,* her Tony had said. *All you need now is a pair of proper mittens.*

One hand caressing her muffler, she concentrates on teasing images from the general swirl in her mind. *Snow. A valley. Other people . . .* "Bode," she whispers, and feels the shock thrill through her. *He'd* been in that nightmare valley, too, though so different: hair shorter, different and very odd clothes . . . dark green. A lot of pockets.

All right, that's not so surprising. You've known Bode all your life, ever since Coram's. No mystery there. She and Tony and Bode had been foundlings together: orphans growing up in the same sprawling hospital. Did that explain the others in the dream? All roughly her age . . . although wasn't one a *little* girl? A flash of blonde pigtails and very blue eyes. *Dark blue, like mine, though with a fleck of bright color.* Copper? Gold?

There was a boy who stood out, too, though his face was indistinct. *His eyes were queer. Stormy.* Did that mean gray? She's not sure. It's a word that occurred to the *other* Rima, and now it's stuck in her brain like gristle caught between her teeth. Something else about that boy. *When I think about him, I feel a tug. In the dream, he's important to that other Rima. She cares for him.* Something happened to him, too, as well as to the other Rima. She just doesn't know what, but she thinks . . .

Oh. She claps a hand to her mouth to catch a moan. "That Rima *dies.* She dies in the dark." Or is close to dying. *Is dying right this very second? No, no.* Gulping back a sob, she smears a fine line of sudden sweat from her upper lip. *Don't be absurd. That would mean the dream's still going on; it's happening right now in some other reality.* "But I'm awake." Her hands clench, the ragged nails biting into her palms, but this is good, because *that* pain is real; it's no dream. "I'm awake and this is not happening; I am *not* that Rima, and this *never* happ—"

Tony suddenly moans, a long and frightened lowing, and she hears him begin to thrash. *God.* She lurches around the slats to kneel by his side. His breathing's ragged. *Fever?* She lays a hand on his forehead, meaning to check . . .

A white blaze breaks over her mind, the full force of his dream smashing like the blow of a hammer. Her head snaps back, and she actually gasps. For the briefest moment—in the background of what she sees—she is *positive* there is that *same* bright burst of fire that sheeted through her own dream, except it is very close, right in front of her eyes: a searing gush that incinerates flesh from bones in seconds.

There are other images, too many to grab hold of, and Tony, still asleep and in the grip of this nightmare, is trying to scream now because something monstrous *is* coming for him, scuttling not out of the ice but from a . . . a *mirror*, and then there's a face— lean and wolfish, with purple eyes—leering in his mind.

At that instant, right before he wakes and strikes her in his panic, what she thinks is, *My God. I know you.*

3

NOW, SLEEPLESS, SHE was as certain of *that*—that she did indeed know this woman—as she'd been less than a half hour ago. *But where from? Where have I seen that woman before?*

Sighing, Rima sat up. Maybe a turn in the cold night air

would clear her head, blow away the cobwebs of that nightmare. Noiselessly, she rose, slipping into a thick woolen shirt. The shirt had a rip, and her socks needed darning, and she would dearly love a pair of mittens. After lacing on her cloddish hobnails and checking on Tony one more time, she wrapped herself in her green muffler and bulky coat and cautiously picked her way around sleeping children as she headed for the far catwalk. In the past, when there were still trains and regular deliveries, men would maneuver iron cars along high rails between the different retort-houses and offload coal through shoots. Nowadays, with no trains coming, the catwalks were the staging point for bodies destined for the flames. Already sweating—it was either wear the clothes or carry them, and she needed both hands free—she climbed down an iron ladder to a large brick room. Long-idled, huge bridles, gigantic iron scoops once used to dump a charge of coals into the furnace, depended from the ceiling. Down here and so much closer to the furnace, the air was sweltering and the orange-yellow light bright enough to scorch tears. Blinking, she averted her eyes and hurried to a side door.

That first step, from jungle heat to mind-numbing cold and the constant snow, was always a jolt that stole her breath. Driven in near-horizontal sheets, snow stung her eyes, and she could feel the sweat on her neck already chilling. Spilling from the retort-house's windows, squares of orange light throbbed on the snow. The outside brick wall was toasty, warm enough to melt the snow back a good foot, although days when bodies were in short supply could also mean daggers of ice frilling the retort's eaves.

She began trudging against icy gusts through Battersea's grounds, tossing a look back every few feet to make certain she didn't lose sight of the retort. Her heavy boots stumped through calf-high drifts. After a minute, she was panting and fresh sweat lathered her neck. Already getting tired, too. Her heart thumped in her temples.

Have to do something about Tony. Pulling up, she stood, hugging herself and breathing hard. But other than trying to draw the sickness out, which he wouldn't allow, what could she do? *Maybe Bode will have an idea.* Tomorrow, when she and Tony went to the asylum for bodies, she'd get Bode alone to talk. She wondered if he'd had the nightmare, too. *Wager he has.* But then what did that . . .

And that was when the wind suddenly died and the snow stopped.

What? Startled, Rima threw a look at the sky. No stray flakes. No icy wind. Nothing. But the *air* was trembling. It glimmered like water over black ice and then . . .

Oh God. Her throat tried to squeeze shut. *No, you don't belong here, not yet. Why should I see you in my dream, and* now?

Of course, there was no answer, though she really did think that *it* was a thing, with a purpose. After all, it had just chased her and that boy with the stormy eyes through a nightmare, and then followed her here, into her waking life, ready or not.

Where there had been snow and gloom . . . now, there was only the fog.

RIMA

Imagine Her Surprise

NO. STAY BACK. She felt herself cringing. *I'm not ready. Go back into my nightmare where you belong. I don't want to die.*

The Peculiar only hovered. This close—only feet away—she could see that it was solid, with straight, crisp edges, and motionless as a pristine curtain or blank piece of paper. She noticed, too, that this area had brightened, the air glowing with a milky glare. The Peculiar had an odor, too, one she recognized because she got a noseful every day from every corpse: old blood and rotting purge.

Odd sound trickling from the fog, though. Something *fizzy*, like bicarbonate. Despite her fear, she felt herself leaning forward, trying to parse it. Were those *voices*?

With no warning, the Peculiar dimpled, drawing in on itself as if a giant mouth were on the other side and had decided to inhale. Before she had time to react, something *shot* out.

Throwing up her arms, she floundered back a step and nearly came down on her rear, but then she got a good look and her mouth fell open.

"My *God*," she said, dropping to her haunches. Purring, the large orange cat nuzzled her hands and began to weave back and forth across her knees. "Where did you come from?" She hadn't seen a cat in *ages*. Other than London's endless supply of rats (the eating kind, not Rima and Tony and their ilk) and assorted vermin (cockroaches, principally), there were no animals. Everything else had been eaten. *But now here's a cat, come from the fog.* She ruffled the animal's ears, felt its rumble deepen. Could she keep it? Hide it somehow? Considering the cat's sudden appearance, it felt wrong to eat the animal. On the other hand, the cat would need food, and they weren't catching enough rats to keep themselves going as it was.

Or have you *sent this cat as a sign?* She eyed the Peculiar. Maybe the cat's from north London, the other side of the Thames? *Are you trying to show me there's something worth trying for?*

Beneath her hands, the cat suddenly spat and arched. Flinching, Rima quickly clambered to her feet, worried the animal would bite, but it was prancing, its gaze riveted to the fog. *Another animal? A person?* Really, she was hoping for an animal, preferably one she wouldn't feel bad about eating. Though she'd skin this cat, if she had to.

2

Imagine her surprise.

PART TWO

UNDER MY SKIN

ELIZABETH

London Falling

no not that way cut like this

God, couldn't that nasty little voice *shut* it? "Under my skin, under my skin . . ." The words, those insane lyrics, skated on a breathy undertone, the tune tangling in her mind like a ball of yarn mauled by a lunatic kitten. Her mouth was foul as a sewer from that gutter swill Kramer called morning tea. Her head throbbed, the pounding worse than before. The voices were much louder, too, like squirmers teeming in her brain:

so never digging around a Goodwill ghost-bin

         black echoes kill you nine ways to Sunday

you ever stop to think that maybe God's just a kid

     that's not your father

         a whisper, like blood, leaves a stain

         can't you see how sick she is

   and we're the dolls

Ever since that morning's session, she'd felt this anvil of doom on her skull that matched the pressure in her chest. The voices were worse, even her mother's popping up from memory, something overheard from a long-ago argument,

    that's not your father

which she never had understood. Why her mother

    can't you see how sick she is

should torment her—so odd.

Kramer's mesmeric passes weren't helping at all, though of course he blamed *her*: *If you'd only take your medicine, Elizabeth.* Kramer was a slithery spider with a ruined face and serpent's hiss, who wanted nothing more than to scuttle through her brain and its dark, secret clefts, picking, probing, *pickpickpick* . . .

Well, not just yet. Squatting cross-legged on her filthy mattress, she grit her teeth and tried coring through a dull pink grin of scar tissue on her left forearm. *Get out of this accursed asylum and find the Mirror, determine which symbols will build me the* Now *I need, and leave this wretched London behind.* Yet no matter how hard she dug, there was no sparkle of pain, no

Blood of My Blood

blood. They kept her nails trimmed so short, she'd have better luck peeling a lemon with a thimble. She'd once considered using her teeth to gnaw through skin and down into muscle and through the stubborn fibrous tubes of arteries and veins, but she wasn't insane; she didn't want to *die*, no matter what Kramer said about those other slashes on her arms. (Those awful black stitches were the handiwork of the surgeon, Connell, the quack who'd mended her like a tatty piece of burlap.) Kramer insisted she must've made those cuts, and it was only luck that Constable Doyle happened by to save her from bleeding to death.

Luck? Oh *yes,* she was just *sooo* lucky to have landed in Bedlam with all these lunatics. And *happened by*? Happened by *where*? She couldn't recall. All she could remember was that she'd been running, running, running from

the whisper-man

a monster? Or had it been—the image of a man, black hair, glasses, glimmered through her mind—had it been her *father*? Wishing to *use* her for something? Or perhaps—now this was a lunatic thought—put something vital *in* her, *hide* it away for safekeeping?

not doing it right

Will you plug your damn cakehole? Panting, a brackish taste on her tongue, she paused, finger cocked, nail over her skin. Her heart thudded against her ribs, and she heard the slight *tick-tick-tick* of glass against tin from the necklace Kramer let her keep. Now *why* Kramer didn't take that away—a very pretty glass bauble strung with two squares of tin on a strange beaded chain—was a mystery, just as she was unsure how she'd come by it. The tin had a good edge. She could easily cut . . . and yet she never did. The necklace was *special*

no, not special yet

and had a strange name that boiled onto her tongue without her understanding what it meant or how the words came to be: *Sign of Sure.* What was that? The knowledge was there, but elusive. She had a sense it was like the Mirror: some kind of device, but one that needed . . . well, energy? Or perhaps the right wearer to make it work? Whatever the case, the glass was unique, and so was the tin. Not right to use them. Which probably proved just how mad she was.

So—she gnawed a loose bit of skin from dry lips—maybe pry

up a scab instead? New skin under there, pink and tender. Cut that, squeeze out some nice fat drops.

PLIP-PLIP-PLIP

No. She winced against this one, a different and clearer voice that rose above the swamp in her mind to bob at the surface. *Please be quiet. Not you too.*

SO DEEP IN MY HEART

Fresh cold sweat sprouted on her upper lip. Of all the many voices, this very strong *Other*, with its thoughts of UNDER MY SKIN and STARBUCKS and MATCHI-MANITOU, IN HIS DEEP DARK CAVE and PLIP-PLIP-PLIP, frightened her most. Sometimes she actually felt it rustle and then shift, the way a dog turned on a bit of rug. One day, perhaps soon, she would look in a mirror and the *Other* would peer back through the glassy portholes of her eyes and give her a tiny wave with one jointed leg: WHY, HELLO, I DON'T BELIEVE WE'VE BEEN PROPERLY INTRODUCED.

Come on. Attacking the scab with a will, she gave a little cry of triumph as a long, rust-colored strip peeled away. *Yes.* "Got you now," she muttered.

"Miss." A voice, not in her head but close to her ear, and about as real as things got these days. "Miss Elizabeth, you must stop."

"Yes, *thank* you," she said, then wanted to kick herself for replying at all. She didn't mind talking to some attendants; she liked one boy, Bode, best. Which did *not* please that old crow, Nurse Graves, who'd probably whispered in Kramer's ear, because, all of a sudden, here Elizabeth had herself a companion. *To better anchor you in the here and now* was what Kramer had said. *Ha! Companion, my eye.* This girl was a spy.

"It's my body to harm." She slipped her eyes up and to the

right to find the girl's impenetrable blue gaze. If it were possible for Babbage to build a difference *person*, a mechanized automaton that clicked and ticked through theorems and problem sets, that was *this* girl. She had all the heat and passion of a toad. "I didn't ask for your opinion, and I don't require your permission."

"But you know that I will have to stop you one way or the other," the girl said in that maddeningly reasonable tone of hers. (God, she was so rigid and proper, she must have a broomstick jammed up her bum.)

"Are you *threatening* me?" A dart of surprise. This was new. She gave the girl, clad in her assistant's navy wool skirt, white blouse, and over-apron, a longer look. Elizabeth supposed the girl was pretty, though she was bigger boned and taller, with an angular face and luxuriant coils of copper hair that never seemed out of place. Physically, they weren't at all alike except for their eyes, which were the same deep cobalt. If the girl had possessed a golden flaw in her right iris, their eyes would've been an exact match. In one of her father's twisted fantasies, they might've been distant relations. "What, has meek little Meme found a speck of courage?"

"It is not courage." Meme stood next to a rickety table upon which she'd squared a tray of toiletries and two basins: one of cold rinse water and the other hot enough to steam. "I do not enjoy being a watchdog any more than you like having me here."

"You're right; I don't enjoy you. And see?" She showed a dazzling smile. "We agree on something. Who says I'm not making progress? Now why not leave and make your report of my miraculous breakthrough to your precious doctor?"

"You know I cannot, not the way you are now. Please"— crossing to stand over Elizabeth's miserable cot, the girl reached a tentative hand—"you would feel so much better if you at least let me give you a good wash . . ."

All at once and out of nowhere, the air split with a harsh, shrill sound like nails dragging over a slate school board, sending shivers racing down Elizabeth's spine and a gasp leaping for her tongue. An instant later, something *pinged* and then *tick-tick-ticked* off brick.

"Oh!" Meme sounded breathless—surprising for a girl who showed so little emotion—and Elizabeth thought, *Good, she heard that, too.* Her shoulders sagged with relief. That was the problem with this place. Sometimes she didn't know which sounds were real and which were in her head.

But now she looked across her room. One of the few privates on this ward, hers was a long and deep brick throat bounded at one end by a high narrow sliver of a window fenced with iron bars. (If she wanted to see out, she had to jump and hang like a monkey at the zoo. Apt, considering.) Everything else—her rickety metal cot, a standing wardrobe with her very few changes of clothing, the stand upon which Meme had laid her tray—was either bolted to the floor or, as was the case with a high shelf, the wall. She now saw that the shelf's right half dangled, held to the wall only by a single bolt, like a diseased tooth on a fleshy thread of rotted gum.

The other bolt snapped. Where had it gone? Her eyes swept the floor. Such breaks and cracks and spontaneous ruptures were common nowadays. As the fog advanced, this bizarre Peculiar no one understood, London was rotting away. Buildings slumped. Roads cracked. Wallpaper suddenly blistered and peeled, sloughing from the walls like flaps of dead skin. That very morning, the top rail of Kramer's guest chair had split. London and this *Now* were falling down, falling down, falling down. *But the bolt, that bolt* . . . Her pulse gave a hard thump as her eyes fixed on a jagged metal nubbin. *Excellent.* That would be sharp enough to—

"No, Miss. Do not even think of it." Meme clapped the sole of a boot on that bolt, then scooped up the broken bit of iron to drop into a pocket of her over-apron. "Now, please, let me help you wash. Your hair is positively crawling."

"No!" Elizabeth batted the other girl's hand away. God, she'd been so stupid, hadn't moved fast enough, and now her chance was gone, and it was all this girl's fault! "Don't tell me what I need! Keep your filthy . . ." Her throat suddenly clutched, and she felt the old familiar tearing in her ribs as the coughing jag seized her.

"Miss, here. Let me . . ."

"N-no!" Choking, she backed away, doubled over, hand cupped to her mouth. Another spasm of coughing, and then a warm, slick splash on her palm. *No, no.* "K-keep . . . keep *away!*"

"Miss, you are working yourself to a frenzy. Calm yourself."

Calm? Oh, that was *brilliant.* "I'm in a *bloody* . . ." Dragging in a gargled breath, she swallowed back a mouthful of wet rust. *Getting worse.* She grunted against a blade of pain knifing her right ribs. *Die in here if I don't get out soon.*

"Miss Elizabeth?" Meme reached for her arm. "Would you like . . ."

"I said don't *touch* me!" Elizabeth whipped her open palm in a slap. There was a sharp *crack*, followed by Meme's pained gasp. "I don't need your help! I don't want it!" She spat a ruby-red gob that splatted onto Meme's over-apron, then slowly slid, painting a slug's trail of gore. "T-take your basins, your *tr-tray* . . ." She was racked with another coughing fit. "G-get out," she managed. "Get *out!*"

Although, in her mind, she thought—in her own voice—*My God, I am becoming a monster.* She wasn't like this; she never *had* been, although what could she *really* remember of herself? She didn't know. Some days it felt as if all she'd *ever* known was this wretched place, this horrible, squalid little room; that *this* was the only moment, the span of her life. The voices were so bad, too, and she was alone, sick, more frightened than she'd ever been in her life. (*Life*: such a simple word, but what was that, exactly? What life had she led?) It was easier to be cruel. It helped her feel as if she wasn't losing this battle.

"I am only trying to help." A smear of blood showed on Meme's left jaw and, beneath it, the purple splotch of a new bruise. "Do you not want to get better?"

"You hanging about only makes me sicker!" *Stay angry; stay strong.* She worked another bloody gobbet she let fly to a far corner, where it quivered like claret aspic. "G-get *out!*"

"No." Pulling herself straighter, Meme turned to take up a cloth that she then swirled in a basin, releasing a scent of warm vinegar. "I cannot, Miss Elizabeth. I have my masters. I am their creature, and Mrs. Graves says I am to help you wash, put on some clean clothes, and make yourself presentable before Inspector Battle arrives for his interview. I do believe he's bringing Constable Doyle as well."

"Battle?" Scowling, she smeared blood from her mouth with a sleeve. A pity this blood wouldn't do for what she wanted. It was polluted, full of sickness. *What is wrong with me? Consumption? Cancer?* Her gums bled at a touch, and she was so weak. "What does Battle want now? I've told the inspector that I don't remember where I was, who was doing what, or where my father is."

"Nevertheless," Meme said, picking up a boar bristle brush, "the inspector wants to see you. So come now. Let us go to work on those snarls—"

"No. For the last time, *get out!*" Cursing, Elizabeth upended the tray in a clash of brass. Meme let out a small shriek as water sloshed her blouse and face. By some miracle, none of the bottles shattered, which really was a shame. But a pot of bicarbonate of soda burst into jagged, toothy ceramic shards and white dust. A comb skittered and spun its way to lodge in the crack where the far brick wall met the floor. An obvious weapon, and one she'd never get past Meme. Then, to the far left, Elizabeth spied something wedged behind a leg of a wardrobe that made her heart leap: a bone-handled toothbrush, its head completely broken off. That shattered finger of bone pointed, as if it had singled her out of a crowd: *Yes, that one there; that's the girl for me.*

Her mouth dried up. *Yes!* But she had to keep Meme from seeing it first.

"Didn't I just tell you?" Jumping her gaze away, she moved swiftly to her right, interposing her body between the comb and Meme, who was busy chasing after bottles. *Misdirect, misdirect.* "Didn't I say I want you gone?"

"Yes." Dropping shards of ceramic into her over-apron, Meme dropped to her knees and reached beneath the cot for the brush. "I heard you."

"Then what are you waiting for?" Such a tempting target. Aim a good strong kick into those buttocks . . . what she wouldn't give for a nice sturdy pair of hobnails. Do too much damage, though, and Kramer would drug her senseless, then spirit her away to a dank little padded cell in the bowels of this place. (Actually, Weber would probably like that. The pig was always looking for an excuse to bundle her into a strong dress. A good, long grope—that's what he wanted.) "Go."

Pushing to her feet, Meme swept her gaze round the room. "And I will, just as soon as . . ." Her cobalt eyes narrowed as she spied the comb. "Please move aside."

"Why?" *Give her a good show. Keep her eyes on the comb.* "I like it here."

"Oh yes. Quite the palace."

A flush of heat. "Don't make fun of me."

"Then do not say ridiculous things just because you have a tongue. Either kick out the comb or go sit on your bed where I can see you."

"Fine." Struggling to keep the glee from her face, she gave the comb a savage swat with the side of her foot. "Take it."

"Why are you so hateful?" The comb joined that broken bolt and those ceramic shards in Meme's over-apron. "Can you not take friendship when it is offered?"

"Friendship?" For some absurd reason, tears pricked. "I don't need a friend, and even if I did, that would not be you. You are Kramer's creature."

"Oh, and you are so much better off: a mad girl with no family, no friends, left to rot in this place." Turning away, Meme shook her head with something close to bewilderment. "And to think that he treasures you."

ELIZABETH

Little Alice

1

TREASURES ME? **AS** soon as the door closed, Elizabeth dove for that bone handle. *Who? Kramer? That snake? And she calls* me *a fool.*

She had to be quick. That idiot would be back with reinforcements—Graves and Weber, for certain—and soon. Dropping to her knees, Elizabeth swept a hand. As her fingers closed over the bone handle, however, she felt the nip of something else jagged. *"Ohhh."* She drew out first the toothbrush handle—and then a shard of ceramic from that shattered pot of bicarbonate. *They're both perfect.* So which to use? Should she even try right now? Wouldn't it be better to pick loose stiches from her mattress and hide these? *Meme will be back.* The girl had said Battle was expected. *I won't have time to cut every symbol.* She didn't even know in which order she should. The smart move would be to do nothing. Yes, but what if she got it right this time? Would she even *need* the Mirror?

won't work, not the right place, not the right one

"Right place? Right one? I don't even understand what that means," she muttered. Ceramic first, she decided. She would save the bone spike for . . . well, for something. Slipping the handle under her right thigh, she pressed the sharp bit of pottery to a scar midway up her right forearm. There was a small hiccup of pain as the point dimpled scar tissue. An instant later, a miniscule bead of bubble slowly welled. All right, this was good; this was what she wanted. *Left to right.* Twisting the point back and forth, she cored and dug. The bead widened into a slim dash and then the minute curve of a red smirk. She gave it a critical look. Not much of a cut. Pause too long and this would quickly clot. But there was blood, and that was all that mattered. She only wished she understood precisely why.

Then on to the next. She licked pearls of pain-sweat from her upper lip. *That symbol of a pitchfork with horns . . .* what was its name, anyway? The *luxl* she knew; that was the symbol with three interlocking spirals. But this one she couldn't quite remem—

no, not right, not for you

"I GOT YOU UNDER MY SKIN." Her throat was full of razors. "DEEP IN THE HEART OF ME." God, she hated this song. Why couldn't she sing something nice, like "The Fine Old English Gentleman"? Or "The Ratcatcher's Daughter"? Now, there was a jolly tune. "But the ratcatcher's daughter had a dream, that she shouldn't be alive next Monday." Thinking, a little abstractly, *Dream? Such an odd word.* She punched out the next line: "So he cut his throat with a piece of glass, and stabbed his donkey arter . . . in spite of a warning voice that comes in the night and repeats, how it yells in my ear . . ."

It was no use. The song was *really a part of me,* and she was fated to rot in this hellish place, fall apart a piece at a time: a finger here, a leg there, a nose. Lose an eye like Graves. (Her only consolation: like as not, no one would eat them. Her eyes, that is.

She didn't think. Actually, she didn't know. It wasn't as if any of them were dining well. Now the *rat* they'd used in that thin soup instead of a quivering wobbler . . .)

"Oh, for the love of God." A new voice, hard as a boot grinding sand onto stone. "What do you think you're doing?"

2

BLAST. SHE WENT absolutely still. *You fool. You knew they would come, but you had to try, didn't you? And now look.* But she couldn't. Instead, she kept her eyes riveted to her forearm. All she'd managed was a pathetic red dribble and a bit of broken crockery now smeary and slick as a . . .

PLIP-PLIP-PLIP

No, snail, SNAIL. She heard the ferocious *chuck* as her jaw clenched and her teeth clashed. *I don't care what you say. I was thinking* snail*, not plip-plip!*

"How did you . . . Oh, I see." Kramer clucked like a spinsterish aunt over a gravy spot on a lace collar. "Drop it, Elizabeth." When she didn't move, he added, "At once."

Fine. Without looking up, she pitched the smeary bit of crockery aside. *There. Choke on it.* The spike of bone toothbrush was hot as a brand under her right thigh. Just so long as she didn't move, wouldn't get up, that was hers.

"Thank you." A skeletal hand swam into view and clamped its fingers around her wrist. Through the curtain of her hair, she watched her hand flop as Kramer turned the arm over and back to assess the damage. "Thank heavens, she's only managed a few scratches. A plaster ought to do."

"I suppose no need to disturb the surgeon." Graves sounded

a tad put out, as if she'd have welcomed something with a trifle more gory flair. "We're only fortunate she didn't decide to swallow that bolt. I shudder to think of the internal damage."

"Oi, sir." Weber always sounded as if he had a mouthful of gravel, although Elizabeth suspected he was a little disappointed, too. Perhaps he'd have welcomed the chance for Connell to gut her like a rabbit. "*I* think you might consider removing everythin' but the mattress. No telling when her cot'll give way, or that stand. Next time we walks in, she mighta opened her jug'lar."

"Thank you, Mr. Weber, but I don't believe we've quite come to that." Kramer relinquished her wrist. "On your feet, Elizabeth. Inspector Battle and Constable Doyle will be here any minute to query you again, and we don't want to keep them waiting any longer than necessary. Unfortunate, but since you refuse to bathe properly, you'll just have to come as you are."

No, leave me alone. She most certainly wouldn't budge an inch. If she did, then the toothbrush would be lost to her, too. *Go away. I'm busy. Can't you see I'm busy?*

"Elizabeth?" Kramer said. Another pause, and then Graves picked up on the refrain: "Elizabeth, you will do Doctor the courtesy of looking when he addresses you."

Not bloody likely in my lifetime. In point of fact, she was afraid to. The last time she'd looked at *Graves*, that crow's face had *changed*: skin and eyes turning runny to drip in thick, murky gobbets like

the monster-doll's head

GLASS SLUMPING FROM A BLOWPIPE

in a Kugelrohr oven turned too high on accident

IN A FURNACE'S GLORY HOLE

no, a Kugel—

"No, shut *up*! Candle wax! *I* was thinking candle wax!" She clapped a hand over her traitorous mouth. *Idiot*. But *God*, it was like trying to follow a cork ball in a game of lawn tennis, the voices volleying back and forth from ear to ear.

"Excuse me?" Kramer paused. "Am I speaking to Elizabeth, or someone else?"

"Mmm." Thinking, *Yes. No. Maybe. Really, it's anyone's guess.* Using her index finger, she scratched at the *luxl*'s leftmost spiral, beginning at the center, wincing as her nail lifted a corner of scab and bumped over black thread stitches.

that's not right

Oh, please, shut up. She just had to dig deeper, that was all. Claw the meaning from those symbols, wring them of

thought-magic

energy. Find the right symbols in the right sequence, and that would get her out of here, whisk her away to her proper place, the correct *Now*—and away from

Dad eyes Daddy eyes oh Daddy

WHISPER-MAN

this place before it was too late.

"Look at me, Elizabeth." When she still wouldn't, Kramer added, "This instant."

"Sir?" A different voice, but one she also recognized. Through her lashes, she saw a pair of legs in trousers come to stand next to Kramer. "It's not my place, but . . ."

"Bode." Now Elizabeth did look and saw Meme, her face pale. "Do not get involved," Meme said, her voice tight.

"Yes, do listen to her." Kramer turned Bode a frosty glare. "And you are quite correct. It is *not* your place."

"Nevertheless, sir, I get on with her. She can be quite

reasonable if you know how to handle her," Bode said. "Isn't that right, Miss Elizabeth?"

"Bode." This time, Meme touched his arm. "Please, let Doctor handle this."

"But I can help." Bode was a plain boy with pocked skin, a blunt jaw, and a crooked nose, probably broken one too many times. Scraped back from his face and secured with a scrap of leather, his shoulder-length hair was muddy brown. The thin, pale whip of a scar trailed down one side of his neck. Yet his eyes were very fine, and they never wavered from Elizabeth. "Right, Miss? Won't you let me help?"

"Yes." She knew him. Of course she did. The color of those eyes was so close to what the sky once was like that a pang speared her heart. And then she thought, *My God, I remember what color the sky was? When? Where had I been?* She couldn't place it, if it really was a proper memory. She pulled herself a little straighter. *Now's not the time to worry about the sky, you idiot. Focus on now.* "Hello, Bode."

"Hello, yourself." Of all things, he threw her a wink that was so *normal* and friendly, she wanted to cry. "You'll get on now, won't you? Tell Doctor what he wants to know?"

"Well, I . . ." She let that go. As much as she liked Bode, she didn't know about *that*. In his long white doctor's coat, Kramer loomed like something born of the ice and snow. She owed him nothing.

Bode opened his mouth again, but Kramer cut him off. "*Thank* you. That will do. Now back away. Remember your place. Do not interfere again." Without waiting for the boy to move, Kramer gave him a rude shove, then turned her a glare. "I see from the stains you've had another bout of hemoptysis. Are you ill?"

Ill? Oh, that was good; that was brilliant. *I'm in a* madhouse, *you arse. I'm coughing up* blood. *What do you think?* She held her tongue.

"Well then, you leave me no choice." Kramer snapped his fingers. "Meme!"

"No!" she said as the girl swept forward with Kramer's medical bag. She knew what he would do: drug her senseless. When she woke, she'd be down below, cocooned in a strong dress. *Yes, yes, that much I do remember.* But God, there were moments when she could swear that every single thought, each memory, was scripted, written for her—perhaps even by her own father, who'd stuffed her full of these many voices and pieces—only so much ink on paper, with no substance. In a book, a character could *remember* . . . but recall what? Life beyond the book? Absurd. "What do you want to talk about? I'll be good, I'll be . . ."

"Wait," Bode said as Meme brushed past. "Let me . . ."

"What did I just say?" The underside of Kramer's jaw was scarlet. "Be *silent*."

"Bode." Meme's voice was toneless. "She is not worth it. Please, back away."

"Don't tell me what to do." Exhaling in exasperation, Bode held his hands out to the other girl. "Meme, can't you see? Scaring her like this, it's not right."

"She is a patient, Bode." Frowning, Meme threw the catches on Kramer's bag. "We all do our duties."

"What's wrong with you?" Bode gave Meme a wondering look. "Yes, you're his assistant; we *all* deal with nutters every day, but even you got to see that kindness . . ."

"Sometimes the kindest thing to do seems cruel but is necessary. What Meme *sees* is her *place*," Kramer hissed. "As should you."

"My place?" Bode rounded on him. "Then what about yours? You're a *doctor*. You're supposed to heal, not bully."

Before Kramer could answer, Elizabeth heard a new and deeper voice rumble, "Is this how you people at Bethlem get on?"

"Oh, bloody shite," Kramer muttered, and turned a look over his shoulder. Following his gaze, she saw what the doctor had been too distracted to notice. Blocky as a monolith, Inspector Battle loomed in her doorway. Just beyond Battle's left shoulder was Constable Doyle, looking decidedly pale and sweaty. Judging from the pewter smears under his eyes and the way he fidgeted, Doyle was as ill as she felt.

"Treatment by committee?" Planting his huge fists on his hips, Battle leaned in and squinted as if inspecting a suspicious leg of mutton. "Well, you're certainly living up to your nickname; this is positive bedlam. These are your creatures, Doctor. Control them."

"*Thank* you, Inspector. How good of you to remind me." Kramer's tone was brittle as hoar ice, and she could see the effort he put into grabbing back some nastier retort. "Now, if you will all let me get on with my *job*."

Bode tried again. "But sir . . ."

"Bode." Meme snatched at him. "Stop. Do not task him."

"Yes, you would do well to listen to her. You *overreach*, young man!" Graves snapped at the same moment that Weber grated, "Watch your mouth around Doctor, ya damned hobbledehoy."

Bode ignored them all. "Please, sir. I mean no disrespect, but I'm sure I can get her to cooperate. You saw before, yeah?"

"Nonsense." Kramer had his bag open now to reveal an array of gleaming instruments—scalpels, a saw, clamps—as well as glass tubes, steel syringes, and small brown phials filled with colored liquids. "The time for talk and persuasion is past. What she *needs* is for you to step aside and let me get on with what needs doing."

"Wait," Bode began—and that was when Kramer uncoiled, fast as a snake, and cut a vicious backhanded slap to Bode's jaw. The boy's head whipped to one side, and as he staggered, Kramer bore down, shouting, "*I* am the physician here, *not* you!"

"No!" Elizabeth shouted. It was one thing for Bode to reassure her; it was another for him to take a beating. This was her fight, not his. Why didn't someone stop Kramer? That idiot Meme only stood there, eyes wide, hands to her mouth. From his place by the door, Battle was a stone. "Stop! He's only trying to help me!"

"This is *my* patient!" Kramer thundered at Bode. "*My* asylum, *my* charge, and I say what is right and what is not, do you hear?" The right half of Kramer's face went the color of a ripe plum while the half-mask of tin hiding the left remained eerily like porcelain with its coat of faded flesh-colored paint. "I offer *you*, a foundling, a boy with nobody and nothing . . . I give you protection, safety, *food*." He cuffed the boy again, a brisk, smart snap. This time, a spurt of blood jumped from Bode's mouth. "*This* is how you show your gratitude?"

"*No.*" Eyes watering, Bode backhanded blood from his lips. "I'm only saying . . . there's no call for you to—"

"Don't!" Elizabeth's fingers tightened about her spike of bone. *Come here, you; try that with me.* "It's my fault. Here, I'm talking! Isn't that what you want?"

This seemed to catch Kramer off his stride. "Yes. What am I thinking, wasting my time with this . . . this *whelp*?" Turning, Kramer crooked a finger. "Weber!"

No! Cringing, her courage fleeing, Elizabeth pressed herself against cold brick. At the door, Battle still stood, impassive, his gray eyes fixing her with a look of detached interest. Doyle only fidgeted. Meme—her very *good* friend—was useless.

"N-no tonics, no more t-teas." That pressure in her chest was growing, unfurling in a hot, dark, menacing rose. Above her eyes, the *Other* was trying to claw its way out of her skull. "I promise, I'll—" Her scalp gave a shout as Weber wrenched her hair with one huge paw.

"Open your mouth, Elizabeth." Selecting a phial, Kramer withdrew a minute stopper. "Don't make me force you." When she still didn't budge, Kramer sighed, then flicked a finger. "Weber? If you please?"

"Right," Weber said, and pinched her nose shut with his free hand.

"Wait! You don't need to *do* that!" Bode said.

No! A bolt of panic ripped through her. Her right hand closed around the bone spike as she dug the nails of her left into Weber's wrist. Her chest was already churning; she could feel her throat working, trying to get her to open her mouth and breathe, *breathe*!

"Don't hurt her!" Bode tried shoving Weber to one side, but it was like trying to move a monument. "Let me, sir. I can get her to take it."

"We're managing, thank you," Kramer said. "Open your mouth, Elizabeth."

"*Nuh.*" Parting her lips just enough to suck a breath through the gate of her teeth, she fought to twist away from the mouth of that small brown bottle of poison. "*NNN—*" She kicked and tried to bite as Kramer grabbed her face in one hand, but then he was straddling her, using his greater weight to crush her into her mattress. She heard the *tick* of glass against her teeth, and then she was coughing and choking against a thick, unctuous yellow liquid first seeping and then gushing into her convulsing throat. Rearing, she spat out what she could but knew: too late.

"Stop fighting." A dribble of tonic and her spit trickled over Kramer's tin cheek in a viscous yellow tear. Kramer studied her a moment, then nodded at Weber. "Open her mouth."

"Nnnuhhh." But she could feel the drug working its black magic in her veins, and when the slow slide of it next moved over her tongue, she swallowed automatically.

From the door, Battle spoke up. "Is this really necessary, Doctor? The girl's in a frenzy."

Kramer's face darkened. "Balls. Don't tell me my bloody business," he muttered, too low for anyone but her to hear. Pitching his voice a little louder: "She needs calming, Inspector. Agitation only fuels the *dédoublement de la personnalité*, the splits in her mind."

"Yes." Battle's tone was dry. "My French is adequate, thank you."

Kramer turned a look over his shoulder and said . . . something. She wasn't sure what. All at once, everything outside her own head was beginning to rush away. It was the drug, she knew, dissolving the last of her resistance. She heard herself let go of a long sigh, and as she did, there came an even stranger sensation of something loosening, as if her mind was a fist and just now decided to relax.

No. A muted clutch of fear in her throat. *Don't. You can't. I won't let . . .*

But it really was too late. She felt the sudden squirm as the *Other* wriggled and began to work its way free, one long jointed leg rising from the dark to hook a claw on a lip of pink tissue. Then another leg, a new claw. And another and then another . . .

"Yes." Kramer's weight was on her chest, which was going icy and still even as the *Other* quickened. Everything and everyone else was gone: Weber, Meme, Graves. Battle and that constable, Doyle. Bode. "It's just us now," he said. "There is no one to stop you. She's been dealt with, so come. Come back."

"Whaah?" The word pulled at her tongue like warmed taffy. She couldn't see properly. Her eyes weren't working, wouldn't focus. She'd a sense he wasn't talking to her at all. Then who? *Oh God.* He was talking *beyond* her to the *Other. No, no . . .* Her head moved in a sluggish negative. "L-leave m-m-meee . . ."

"No, shhh, shhh, don't fight. It's too late for that anyway." Kramer's tone was intimate, pitched only for her. His breath feathered over her face and neck. "Let it come back, Elizabeth. Let her return to this *Now.*"

It? Her? She felt her eyes struggling to latch onto his, set deep in their sockets of flesh and tin. And he'd called this a *Now.* "H-how do you . . . kn-know a-about . . ." As Kramer slid his hands under her shoulders and gathered her up, her blurred vision caught on a glint of brass in his breast pocket. She squinted, forcing her gaze to sharpen. Brass, yes, and a wink of . . . *Purple. Purple glass.*

Oh God.

Kramer had a pair of panops.

3

SHE HAD NO time to wonder how, or why. That would come later. For now, what mattered was this: Kramer knew about *Nows.* With the panops, he must've seen past her mask, and he *knew* what lived in her, understood that she was a vessel, filled with many voices, many pieces, the creations that were her father's doing. All those tonics and teas were to sap her resistance, and now all that she was teetered on the brink of oblivion as he called to a very particular voice and presence, the *Other*, to fill her up, take over.

"Wh-what have you done?" Her awkward fingers tried working their way into his pocket for the panops. "Where . . . where d-did you g-get . . . where is m-my mother, my m-muh . . ." She dragged in more air. "Wh-*why*?"

"Stop fighting." The slink of his whisper was all the more awful because he was so close, he might have been a lover. "Let her take you. She will save us, Elizabeth."

Save them? *No. I can't lose myself.* But she was sinking fast, the mattress seeming to evaporate beneath her.

"Come." Kramer's voice hummed in her ear as he called *past* her to something—someone—else. "Now. If you can hear me . . . now, Emma. *Now.*"

"*N-nooo,*" she moaned. "No, you . . . you m-mustn't summon it by *name.*"

"But I must. I will *have* her." Kramer held her so close she could smell him: the salt tang of his skin, the mustiness of wool, the dank reek of wet, exposed muscle from the half of his face that rot had claimed. "Come, Emma, come to me. Come *nowwww.*"

All of a sudden, her vision purpled; the air wavered, as when the walls tried to buckle, or Mrs. Graves's face decided to slump. In the center of her forehead, hot pain, bright as a comet, blazed a path through the heart of her mind. She thought she must have cried out, because Bode's alarmed shout came to her, but muffled by distance, as if she were a star, dwindling to nothing more than a flicker, drowned out by this *Other*, the strongest of the many voices, all the pieces of her,

PUT ME WHERE I BELONG.

A voice that resolved into that of a girl, some girl now storming through her body. This was a voice belonging to a girl who would risk everything: DROP ME INTO THE NOW WHERE I'LL FIND THEM AGAIN: ERIC AND CASEY AND RIMA AND BODE AND—

Bode? It *knew* him? No, that couldn't be right. Unless Bode wasn't who he seemed either. A black fist grabbed her heart. *No, not him, too. He can't possibly be a piece. Please, God, help me, leave me something, someone* . . . And then she was swooning into the abyss, just as little Alice fell forever; even as something else was rushing up, erupting to fill the void she—Elizabeth—left behind.

In the next second, she felt the switch as it happened—as the *Other* swamped her mind, shoving everything she was to one side, and opened her mouth and . . .

4

. . . SNARLED, *"NO!"*

This voice was huge and so fierce even Kramer started and was, for one precious moment, off-balance.

Seizing the bone spike, the *Other* exploded with a new, manic energy, and on a bellow: *"NOOO!"*

5

IT WAS A miracle Kramer didn't lose an eye or wind up with that rough dagger impaled in his throat. The *Other* drove hard and fast enough for either, but he was already falling back, and the bone's jagged tip instead jammed into that tin mask. But by then the *Other* was on her feet, diving for that open medical bag and all those shiny knives. Neither fully Elizabeth anymore and not yet completely Emma, the *Other* made it past Bode, who tried a grab, and as far as halfway down the hall, where she was cut off.

After that, things went very badly. Breaking Weber's nose with a bell jar was quite satisfying, even though Elizabeth was receding to a bright point by then, like a spider scuttling to the safe center of its web, thinking to the *Other*, this Emma, *This is no way out. They'll trap you the way you've trapped me.*

Yet the *Other*—Emma—tried. The mad chase through the corridors, with the others thudding after, and Emma, the *Other*, chanting to herself: *I am Emma Lindsay, I am Emma ... I remember Eric, how he felt, his voice, his eyes . . .* Praying to the rattling glass bauble and strips of tin around her neck: *Get me out, get me out, take me anywhere but here; just get me out!*

There is no Sign of Sure. This Emma was a fool. *It's only glass. You're a mad girl in a ruined world.* What was left of Elizabeth, now so deep down inside her own skull, looked through the backs of her own eyes and saw a mirror, growing huge in her sight, and this fool, this Emma, rushing for it. In the instant before that catastrophic smash, what remained of Elizabeth registered Emma's surprise, the girl's shock at what she saw, and felt just the slightest sense of vindication: *Yes, that's me, you see. Look in the mirror, Little Alice, looooook.*

After that—through the aftermath of Bode and Doyle wrestling her into a strong dress, and then Kramer, again, holding her close, crooning into her ear, filling her with drugs, claiming her—well . . . the only mercy was that Elizabeth wasn't really all there anymore.

That is . . . most of her.

DOYLE

Poppet

1

CHRIST. EVEN BEFORE the whole debacle—that mad chase through corridors before manhandling that screeching girl, gory and slick with blood let from barbs of the mirror she'd shattered—Arthur Conan Doyle thought the whole business, this *murder* investigation Battle was so keen on, was a bloody mess. Now, still winded, Doyle stood with the inspector at some distance from Kramer, who sat cross-legged in a pool of smeary, red, jagged glass, cradling and crooning to Elizabeth as if she were a child.

God, get me out of here. Doyle skimmed sweat from his lower lip with his tongue. Three days gone without, his guts in a twist, and a positive *deluge* of shite ready to spew out his bunghole—if Battle didn't let him off this bloody ward with its bloody nutters; if Doyle didn't find a pipe or a syringe or a pint of gin or a good half glass of laudanum soon—Doyle thought he might just pop out the inspector's eyeballs with his thumbs.

Now, now, poppet. It was that insidious, guttural snarl steaming from the muddle of Doyle's mind. **Calm yourself. That temper will be the death of you.**

The voice was nothing new. That it was *right* wasn't new either. He thought that if it had a face, it must be that of the black dog with the maddened red eyes tattooed on his right biceps. Whenever he felt the urge for another drink, one more dose, a third pipe, a second needle, his right arm squirmed like a bag of worms, and then the black dog was husky and full in his ear: **Ahhh . . . there, my beauty, there, that's it; take that pipe, down that drink, use the needle and aaahhhh, that's good, so gooood.**

Why he'd gotten the tattoo of this hulking, muscular, fire-breathing black hound with its hellishly infernal eyes and slavering fangs was a mystery, though it was probably because he'd been drunk as a lord when he let the first mate have at him with his needles. *God,* he missed all that. Best kip of his life was his berth aboard the *Hope* after a long spell on the ice: reeking of seal blood, biceps and thighs aching, exhaustion creeping ever so deliciously from the tips of his toes to the roots of his scalp. Never slept better than when he'd bashed the brains of fivescore baby seals with his spiked club.

Although . . . here was something he didn't understand. If he tried to dredge that first mate's face from memory? Nothing came. Same for the ship, its captain, the other men. *Hope* was correct, but there was nothing meaty under the word except those few sensations—the twinge in his muscles, the stink of dying seals. The tattoo of a ravening black dog on his arm was real enough. But the rest was mist.

Probably the drugs muddying his memories. Or that damned Peculiar. God, he needed a drink. A needle. Or a pipe. *Something.* His eyes felt full of pins. *Anything.*

Or what? The black dog bunched under his uniform coat.

You'll make paste of Battle? Have a care, poppet. Your lolly daddles have always been a problem, ever since you were a wee bairn running the slums of Edinburgh. The black dog was nothing if not a little mocking. And *oooh*, who can forget that *nasty* business with your pap?

Plug your cakehole, can't you? He may be a cock-up, but he wasn't stupid enough to talk out loud to something that wasn't there, thank you *very* much. Anyway, his father

Arrrtieee . . . Arrrtieee

was ancient history. He never thought of the man. Never.

Why, of course not. The black dog slavered. **I suppose that's why you carry his *sgian-dubh* everywhere, isn't it? That's why that black blade's at your hip this very moment— because you never, *ever* think of him.**

No, he didn't. Ever. Regardless of the knife, which he really oughtn't have whilst in uniform, but he didn't trust the weapon not to find legs and walk out of his rooms in the policemen's dormitory. Anyway, the pipes, the needles, the drink all did their jobs, thank you very much. Of course, exhaust his supply as he'd done and the old nightly jimjams would return: when he jolted from sleep convinced that some great green and moist moldering monster—dripping with rotted flesh and absolutely *crawling* with maggots—hunched over his bed. Then he might be in for a touch of trouble.

A *touch* of trouble? The black dog seemed to croon. Battle'd be keen to know, don't you think? Say . . . about your little problem? That left arm? I'm sure he'd find your black blade's provenance of great interest. Black blade, black dog . . . poetical, don't you think?

No. He didn't. Absurd. *The Peculiar's going to eat us alive until*

London's nuthin' but skin 'n' bones, and ya think anyone's going to care about a Billy born drunk? History was winding down. Besides, who would Battle ask, anyway? Edinburgh had gone silent . . . oh, ever so long ago. Not exactly sure when. Didn't matter, didn't.

He exhaled, slowly, through his teeth. He needed to get out of here, this *asylum*. Place worked on his nerves. The close, chill air stank with a lunatic fug of sour flesh, rancid piss, and sweaty desperation. Worst of all was that *gabble*, so like that miserable top flat on Sciennes Hill Place, where they'd crammed into squalid rooms in an even filthier tenement: mother, father, a brother, and, good Christ on a cross, more sisters than he could count yammering day

NOT EATING THIS SLOP, NOT FIT FOR A MAN

and night.

In a way, *this* place was like that. It was the many voices rising like steam through floor-set iron grates; all those fists and feet and heads thumping walls and doors; and the mad wailing, *Letmeoutletmeoutpleaseletmeoutletmeout.*

That sound was, he thought, how it would be at the end, when the sky blacked completely, cold settled on a buried city, and the fog, that Peculiar, finally lowered itself like a specimen jar to trap them all like so many doomed flies.

2

"ARE YOU ALL right, Doyle?" A voice, gruff and peremptory, by his right elbow.

"Fine, sir," he said, turning Battle a tight smile whilst strangling a groan. His guts clenched, the long innards twisting and knotting as if a giant had plunged in his fist to rummage around

Doyle's belly after a dropped penny. "Right as rain."

"You don't look fine." Something the inspector saw or heard didn't tally, because his eyes narrowed to an analytical look that was cold silver. "Are you quite . . . Good God, your arm." Battle used his chin to point. "Do you know you're bloodied, Constable? Did she bite you?"

"What?" Startled, he spied a wet purple pucker halfway up the right forearm of his grimy uniform coat. For a bizarre second, he actually thought the black dog might be chewing its way free. How could he not know he'd been hurt? Thank God, the *left* arm wasn't cut. Roll up that cuff and sleeve and, besides the souvenirs from his dear pap, there was a scattershot of some truly fascinating scabs and nicks and pricks. Even an exhausted sclerotic and inflamed vein or two. (A wonder he'd not yet died of blood poisoning, actually.) He wasn't eager to be examined, in any event.

"Must've cut myself on the mirror glass, that's all." Doyle clamped his hand over the squelchy rent. *Blast.* While rumpled and a touch threadbare, this was the only uniform coat he owned. He thought about digging out his kerchief to staunch the flow, then discarded the idea, not from pride or the concern that he wouldn't look very manly—*and sod Battle, the old gob*—but the kerchief hadn't seen a wash in nearly a month, same as his uniform. The pathetic brown shard of soap he'd been issued had to last ten more days, and here he was, down to practically nothing more than a bare fingernail. That his smirking sergeant had the balls to call it *soap* and *go on, boys, let's see you scrub yourself pink and pretty . . .* oh, that was *hilaaarious.* Soap felt like pulverized gravel held together with crumbly candle wax. Scrape your arse to bloody ribbons.

"Thank you for your concern, sir. But it's just a scratch." He pulled himself a little straighter, aware of the rancid tang of hair oil rising in a cloud from his scalp to mingle with the ward's general reek. *Come on, Doyle. Hold yourself together a few more minutes.* "I'll manage, sir."

"Don't look it. Is there something troubling you, Constable? You're fidgeting. Or"—Battle's eyes, so light blue they seemed like chips of mica, sharpened—"have you something to tell me? How that girl came by your Christian name?"

"My name." Doyle's mind was a complete blank. And besides, it was an excellent question, wasn't it? Because that girl, Elizabeth—after she'd battled her way out of her room and right before she turned to run pell-mell into that mirror—had known him . . . as *Arthur.* But how? Fresh, clammy sweat oozed into his constable coat's high collar. He'd never told her his Christian name. So how could she *know* a thing like that?

He turned a look down the hall at that ghoulish doctor and the girl. Elizabeth's pale features were smeary from that nasty gash on her forehead, over which Kramer had slapped a crude bandage that was going the color of claret from the ooze. Still, she was a beauty. A girl like that, he was positive he'd recall meeting before the night she appeared, covered in blood and on a scream.

Bad luck that, too. He was no place he'd any business being at the time, him off his beat like that, hustling to purchase a bottle of morphia; then—*poof!*—there she was, as if a curtain had suddenly drawn aside to let her through from someplace off stage. Then, of course, he'd had to lead Battle back to the scene. But the most ridiculous part of it all? He couldn't bloody remember precisely where he'd been. At all. Not the street, the lane, the alley, the buildings, or if there were carts (there were always carts) or Judys (there were always Judys and dollymops happy to oblige) or a pub on the corner (plenty of them, too, though whether you trusted what was in that pint glass, considering the trains had stopped running long ago and no grain to be had or even potatoes . . . well, your funeral). He'd wandered for hours, hoping to recognize *something* that would lead them to an entrance and then to catacombs or tunnels or caves or *whatever* in which the girl claimed she'd been held, where she'd come on her father doing something over bodies that she couldn't quite remember.

Came up empty. He'd have more luck finding his own bunghole with two hands and a candle. Worried him. How could you forget a thing like that? Maybe his brain was going spongy from all that morphia.

Whatever the case . . . nothing. No trapdoors, no hidden passages, no catacombs, no caves, though there were bodies, apparently. Only later had Battle taken himself back and found . . . well, whatever he'd found; the gob was playing it close to the vest. Other than Battle, no one else had seen the bodies, not even the police surgeon.

And why was that?

3

"SHE MIGHT HAVE overheard my name from one of the other constables," he now said to Battle, the lie rolling smoothly from his tongue.

"Indeed." Battle's tone suggested he thought that a bit of a stretch. "You're all in the habit of calling each other by your Christian names."

"At times." In truth, he was "Doyle" or "Constable" or *crusher, nose, slop, blue devil, pig,* depending upon which slammer or fadger or breaker he happened to snag on any given day. These days, and with his needs? One thing positively rum about signing on as a constable: you got to know who all the crooks were. Grease Doyle's palm with some chink, a little of the old smoke, or, better yet, a phial of seven-percent, and most sneaks never saw the inside of a jail. "At any rate, I suppose you'll want to leave the doctor to it?"

"Don't be ridiculous, Constable." The quicksilver dart of another careful look. "Are you sure you're not in pain from that arm? You look a little peaky."

PEAKY? For a split second, the words were poised to leap from his tongue: *You old gob, I need a bloody* needle, *and don't nobody CARE about murder when we're all done for!*

"What? Sorry? Pain? No, just . . . ," he fumbled. Just what, *what*? "I might need a moment, Inspector."

"Out of the question. Control yourself," Battle said, and Doyle thought, *Oh yeah? Dump a nice steaming load on that toff pair of leather clamshells you got on your feet, I bet you change your tune.* "Mrs. Graves has gone to fetch the surgeon or an assistant . . ." Battle made a dismissive gesture. "He'll see to your arm."

"Really, Inspector," Doyle said, trying to squash the plea in his voice, "it's only a scratch. Nothing to bother about."

"Nonsense. The surgeon will attend you and that's final." Planting his fists on his hips, Battle worked his lower jaw in a hard jut. Everything about the man, from his steel-colored bowler to his checked flannel trousers and houndstooth coat, was a study in gray and as obdurate as granite. "In the meantime, I want to know exactly what went wrong, because I will have what's locked in her mind, Constable." Battle strode off without a backward glance. "Now, come along and be smart about it."

4

AT THEIR APPROACH, Kramer half-turned, the flesh-and-blood side of his face showing in profile. Doyle read the man's annoyance in the splash of high color staining that right cheek and the tiny downward curl of his mouth. No love lost between these two: you could light a fire from the sparks.

"*Yesss*, Battle?" Distorted by the mask and what it hid—no jaw and probably not much of a tongue—Kramer's words came in that slithery and strangely guttural lisp and hiss. At the same time, he slipped something into the breast pocket of his long physician's coat, once grayish-white but now splotchy with the girl's blood. Spectacles, Doyle thought, with lenses that were . . . purple? Odd. Kramer had something else he was just now sliding into another pocket: a glass bauble and bits of tin on a chain.

"What is it you want now?" Kramer said. "I should think you'd leave me to more important matters, and my patient."

"She's unconscious, Doctor." Arms akimbo, Battle loomed like a gray vulture. "It don't look to me that she'll be the worst for your answering to what's happened here."

"I think that depends on how you look at it," Kramer replied, coolly. "She needs to wake, so she and I can talk about it."

That necklace, Doyle thought, *it don't tally.* Patients weren't allowed anything with a sharp edge or point. The chain would have been confiscated. Too easy to choke herself with, or swallow.

But he lets her keep it . . . and only now *takes it away? Why?*

"She needs to wake," Battle echoed. "After all the tonic you've poured down her gullet. And when shall that be? The next century?"

"Don't lecture me." No ordinary man would hiss those words, but Kramer was anything but ordinary and perhaps not much of a man, Doyle thought, depending on what else might be gnawing at his innards. Just because Kramer had managed to have the rot hacked from his face didn't mean it wasn't also crawling around the juicier bits inside. Kramer's hand fell to a small bottle by his knee. "This is my asylum. Badgering the girl will not force memories she doesn't want found."

Battle said something else, but Doyle didn't hear. His gaze nailed itself to that bottle. *Oh.* A knife of want sliced his chest. A groan slid up his throat. *Oh shite, oh good Christ.* The sudden buzz in his head was very loud, and so was Black Dog: **Oooh, you want that, don't you? Well, go on, poppet, nick it. Make a scene. Show them what you *really* are.**

No, he couldn't; he *wouldn't.* He pressed an arm to his grumbling belly. *Control yourself, Doyle.* But, *God*, he had to get off this ward, and soon.

"So what, then?" Battle asked as Kramer expertly uncorked the phial with a flick of a thumbnail. "Do you at least understand precisely what happened back there?"

"Of course." Kramer's grip tightened around the girl curled like a baby against his chest: *She's mine, you; now bugger off.* He pressed the bottle to the girl's mouth. At the touch of ruby-colored liquid (oh, Doyle could *smell* it, the too-sweet aroma of laudanum cut with passionflower and fortified wine), she tried turning her face aside, but her movements were lethargic and slow. Doyle thought she'd more than enough drug.

Quit wasting that on her. Give it to me, *you old fool, give it to—*

But look, Black Dog interrupted. **Isn't that odd, poppet? Why would this doctor keep feeding that girl more when she don't need it?** Black Dog paused, and Doyle could imagine it tapping a paw to its chin in thought. **If I didn't know better, I'd wager the prissy cove's trying to keep her under.**

Why, yes, excellent point. Black Dog was always so observant. Why *would* the doctor want the girl so *completely* petrified?

"Well?" Battle said. "What, exactly, transpired, Doctor? Would you care to enlighten us all?"

"Not here. My office." Kramer gestured with the bottle to some point beyond Doyle. "I need to have her moved to a treatment room for the surgeon."

"And given a bath," Battle said. "A thorough wash. I *insist*."

"Leaving aside that she's been incorrigible and we *have* tried . . . don't be so melodramatic," Kramer said dryly. "You've not rescued her from the gutter, Battle. Anyway, what does it matter? Do you . . ." Cocking his head, Kramer gave Battle a crooked grin. "Do you *truly* care? She's mad, Battle. Once she's no longer useful, you'll move along to the next crisis and the next. But it's how you cope, isn't it? Deluding yourself that justice matters at all these days."

"I won't even dignify that with a response. But look in the mirror, Doctor, and ask yourself the same questions." Battle's tone was as flinty as his eyes. "Now, sir, will you bathe her? Or shall I send round my sergeant's wife to do the job?"

"No need. I'll make sure Graves and Meme see to it." Kramer looked up as the younger attendant—*Bode,* Doyle remembered— and Weber (nose probably out of joint, judging from that broad bib of tacky crimson) came forward with a stretcher. They were trailed by that pretty young girl with the dark blue eyes and coppery hair. "Take her to the treatment room. Has Graves gone to fetch Connell?"

"Yes, sir." Bode gave Kramer only a fleeting glance before bouncing his eyes away. His jaw was beginning to swell, and that lower lip looked liverish as a blood sausage. "He's on the men's incurables, tending to a few biters."

Elizabeth was so limp, when they lifted her to the stretcher, her head swooned back. Her hair dragged through blood to paint the worn and dingy carpet a faint scarlet. When she moaned again, Bode put a hand to support the back of her head and murmured something into her ear.

I think he quite fancies her. Black Dog sounded impressed. **Awful chance he took, don't you agree? Trying to shield her the way he did?**

"All right then." Kramer gestured toward the floor and the array of bandages and pins still strewn about. "See to my equipment, Meme, and then have another attendant clean the blood, will you? Oh, and Weber, tell Graves to prepare the girl a bath."

Pausing, a small brown phial in hand, Meme looked up. "I could do that, sir."

"No." With a deft movement, Kramer plucked the bottle from her fingers. "You'll escort the inspector to my office."

That bottle. Kramer's voice dwindled to a buzz as Doyle watched the doctor disappear that bottle into the pocket of a blood-spattered brocade vest. *How to nick it, how to get at that?* Doyle's jaw was so tight it was a wonder his teeth didn't explode to pebbly bits. If he could only find a way to get his hands on it, or something similar. The surgeon, perhaps? No, no, that wouldn't do. If he complained about his arm, then the man would likely wish to examine both. That he couldn't afford.

". . . take a look at that, Doyle?"

"What?" Startled, he looked up to see both Battle and Kramer giving him an expectant stare. Christ, had they been talking to him? "Ah, sorry, I . . ." He swallowed and decided to just come out with it. "I'm sorry, sir. Wandered off there. You said?"

"He didn't." Kramer's gaze strafed him from head to toe and back again. That right eye narrowed. From its socket of tin, the left glinted. "*I* said that you were looking rather unwell. A little gray, actually. Your arm pains you?"

"Oh." His gaze dodged to his left hand, still clamped to that cut. His fingers glistened as if he'd dunked his hand in red paint. "I just need a plaster, is all."

"You let me be the judge of that." Kramer looked at Battle. "If you've no objection and don't think I'll poison the boy, I've an examination table in my office. As soon as I've finished with Elizabeth, I can tend to him there. I spent some months as a mortuary assistant during my studies, and Meme is very skilled. It will also save you a bit of time waiting on Connell."

"I wouldn't want to be trouble." Doyle didn't like the way Kramer's eyes touched him here and there.

"No, you need to be examined." Turning to Kramer, Battle said, "The constable accepts."

"Really, sir." Kramer would make him remove his jacket and shirt. Might as well take his Webley and blow his brains out right now. Or cut his own throat with his *sgian-dubh*. "I don't *need* . . ."

"Oh, do be quiet, Constable, and come along now." Kramer fluttered his fingers in a *get a move on* gesture. "I'm certain we'll find *something* that you do."

BODE

That Damnable Nightmare

1

THE SURGEON, CONNELL, was *not* pleased when Bode and Weber delivered Elizabeth, doped to the eyeballs, to be stitched up. Gave them an earful about the sooty light of a solitary oil lamp and didn't they understand that wounds of this nature required prompt treatment and a lot of other blather Bode only half-heard.

Weber was a worry, too. When the older attendant wasn't bleating about how he might be dying, his skull had broken open, his head ached, and oh, his *nose*, the looks the arse threw at the girl as they laid her on the surgeon's examination table in the adjoining consulting room made Bode's stomach churn. Bode thought the surgeon agreed to tend to Weber first just to shut the man up and get him out the door, but then Weber got all *that poor girl* and *I can wait.*

That decided Bode then and there. Didn't take a scholar to see that Weber would hang around and *volunteer my services, seeing as how you're shorthanded.* Bode just didn't trust Weber's hands not to wander.

So Bode spoke up about how Kramer wanted Elizabeth

bathed. The surgeon went into a snit: *That will put me even further behind.* And, *Who can be expected to work in these conditions?* And, *It's not as if she's the only patient.* Etcetera. After giving them both strict orders to remain in the outer room and away from Elizabeth, Connell finally stomped out to complain. Which was fine. Just so long as Graves got herself in here double-quick.

Once the surgeon was gone, Weber gave a nasty grin that, with the cove's beat-up mug and a nose the size of a turnip, would've looked at home on a gargoyle. "Oh, I know what you're about. You're hoping Connell does *me* while Graves puts *her*"—a hook of his thumb over one shoulder toward the inner consulting room where Elizabeth lay—"to rights. Then I'll have no need to hang round."

Just so long as I keep you out here and away from her. "It's not up to me. I was only relaying *Doctor's* orders."

"Hmm." Weber screwed up one blackened eye. "You know, I *do* believe I'm feeling even worse now. In fact, I don't think I ought to be around patients the rest of my shift. A pity. Means *you* got double duty. Best get cracking."

Crossing his arms, Bode leaned against a wall. "I'll wait."

"*Oooh.*" Weber's lumpy nose twitched. "Worried about your little Guinevere?"

The tips of his ears flamed. "It wouldn't do for only one of us to stay. Graves'd have my head."

"*Graves.*" Weber said it almost like a curse. He crossed to a high, wheeled wooden stand upon which the surgeon had laid out his box of instruments and a bowl of diluted carbolic acid that gave off a sour fume. There was also a double rank of various phials. Weber plucked up a bottle, tilting its label to the light. "You're lucky the asylum's shorthanded. Any other time, Graves'd press to have you put out. Though maybe Doctor likes to exercise that fist of his." Replacing the bottle, he picked up another. "I can still get you sacked, you don't mind."

Bode said nothing.

"First intelligent thing outta your mouth all day." Returning the second phial to its place, Weber squinted at the label of another and grunted his approval. Pulling the cork with his teeth, he tipped a swallow, rolled the liquid around his mouth a moment, then sighed. "That's more like it. *Much* better."

"That's for patients." He should've kept his mouth shut, but he couldn't help it.

"Yeah? Well, aren't you the pot calling the kettle?"

"Whatsat mean?"

"What I said." Weber plucked up another bottle and waggled it. "Ah . . . there we go." Uncorking the second phial, Weber carefully dispensed more tonic into the first bottle. "Not as if you've not blagged your share of what ought to go to the nutters." After a pause, Weber threw him a quick smirk. "Wish you could see the expression on your dial. I know it was you nicked Graves's old skeleton key."

Shite. His guts turned leaden. Secreted in an inner pocket stitched to his waistband, that iron key was suddenly as cold as an old bone. "That laudanum's gone to your head."

"Oh, I think not. We live on the same floor. I know every squeak of every board. 'Sides, you're not the only one with keys. So imagine my surprise when *I* come downstairs and find the kitchen door unlocked. After that, it was a matter of taking myself into a nice dark corner and waiting to see who slithered out. But here's what I can't figure." Punching both corks back in with the flat of one hand, Weber replaced the somewhat depleted second bottle. "Where you're hiding all that food. Can't be putting it all down your own gullet. So you're hoarding it, or maybe giving it over as barter."

No, he'd been gathering it for Tony and Rima. "If you were going to turn me in, you'd've done it by now. So what you want?"

"You keep your mouth shut about my helping myself here, and I'll let Connell take care of your Guinevere. Mum's the word, and we're all square."

"She's not mine."

"No? Coulda fooled me, what with you so quick to step in, defend your lady love? Although, tell the truth, I always thought you was sweet on Meme."

More like the other way around. Bode liked Meme all right; she was very pretty. But there was also something about her that bothered him: an emptiness that was hard to put into words. That she was also Kramer's assistant made him doubly wary. "None of that's your business."

"So you wouldn't mind? If I had a go at Meme? Because *there's* some sweet velvet I wouldn't mind tipping."

"Watch your mouth. She's not a Judy."

"Boy, all girls is the same under their knickers." Slipping the first bottle into a trouser pocket, Weber turned his attention to Connell's open bag. Rummaging around, he said, "Oh now, this *is* lovely," and came up with a gurgling silver hip flask. Untwisting the cap, he wafted the open insert beneath his nose and snuffled. "My beak's off, what with all this swelling, but I *do* believe . . ." Upending the bottle, he took a quick snort. *"Ohhhh!"* Shaking his head, Weber exhaled and gave a dog's shiver. "'At's strong enough to peel *paint*."

Yeah, hope it strips your gullet. He watched Weber disappear the capped flask into an inner pocket and then turn to inspect an array of instruments laid out on a velvet cloth from an open, two-tiered case. Weber lifted out the removable tray to reveal a second rank of surgeon's scissors, forceps, a large bone saw with an ebony handle, scalpels, and a coiled metal chain with two ebony handles. "Oh, lovely." Tweezing up an ivory-handled scalpel, Weber tested the point. "Now, where was I? Oh yes, tipping velvet and our dear Elizabeth."

"I don't follow."

"Oh, come on. That girl's petrified. Kramer poured so much laudanum, it's a wonder her eyes ain't met above her nose. Big strapping boy like you, don't tell me you haven't thought of her, pretty girl like that. Haven't you never wondered what Kramer *does* during those mesmeric sessions, closeted away, in *priiivate*?"

Bode's chest simmered. *He's baiting you.* Never mind getting sacked for stealing; throw a punch and Weber would crack his skull like a walnut, or jam that scalpel in his eye and call it self-defense. *Hurry up, Connell.* He clasped his bunched fists behind his back. *Move your ruddy baby backside.*

"What's a matter? *Oooh*, now." A dried half-moon of scant blood formed a rust ring under Weber's nose. He looked like a mournful bull. "Is it that you've never popped a cherry? Or maybe you're just a bit of a meater."

"I'm not scared. Just waiting on the right girl, is all." *Bode, shut your sauce box.*

"Really? From all your ruckus, I'd've thought she's the one. What made you take on Kramer like that?"

Damfino. He knew Elizabeth, sure. (How long? He couldn't recall.) They talked; she was nice when she wasn't raving.

(Actually, she was a sight better than most even when she was.) He wasn't exactly *sweet* on her.

In truth . . . he thought the urge to protect her came from the dream: that damnable nightmare.

2

SNAPPING AWAKE THAT morning, eyes bugging, sweat pouring. Never had anything like that happen in his life. So much was a muddle, but God, he could still feel it, see it, taste it: the fierce determination in his blood, a bloom of orange light, a wicked blast. Faces of the friends he knew, Tony and Rima, jumbled with others, including a little girl who he actually thought might have been a much younger Elizabeth and . . . Meme? Yes, but weirder still, whenever he'd seen Meme's face in the dream, his mind kept whispering, *Emma*. Made no sense.

But what scared him most: he had *died*. In the nightmare. He'd felt it happen in that blast of heat he barely registered before his body simply . . . went away.

There was even more: explosions and blood and broken bodies. A war waged in steamy heat and a dense jungle. An older man, someone he trusted. (And so very much like the inspector that when Battle appeared on the ward, Bode nearly cried out, *Christ, Sarge, I thought you were dead!* He'd caught himself just in time. What was *that* all about?) There were also tunnels in this other nightmare world, where something black waited.

But he was awake now, and helping Elizabeth was something he *must* do. It sounded mad, considering he'd known her . . . how long? A week? Two? Ten? He wasn't sure—blame the Peculiar— but deep in his bones he was certain he was *supposed* to get her out of this place. That saving *her* was the reason he was here in this accursed asylum.

Which was enough to make a stuffed bird laugh, it was that ridiculous.

3

"DOING HER DON'T have to be nuffin' fancy." Weber's lips parted in a wide grin that was more gap than tooth. "If you need instruction, I can always do with a dog's rig. You could watch. Take notes."

He was *this* close. Weber was bigger and heavier, but he was a touch taller. He *could* pull it off. Let Weber have it with a quick snap of his elbow behind the ear, in the throat, the jaw. It didn't matter. Anything to put the cove down.

So, thank God, the surgeon picked that moment to return with the starched and disapproving Graves and Kramer in tow. Thank God for Graves, who turned that one gimlet eye and suggested he had work to do. Thank God for Kramer, who only stared daggers. Thank God. If he never again saw that gob Weber, that would be too soon.

DOYLE

Strange Ink

IF BATTLE'S POCKET watch was to be believed, Kramer had kept them safely off the ward and out of the way for more than two hours. (The doctor was all apologies: Elizabeth to look after, a new admission to assess, yet another patient who required his immediate attention, and blah, blah.) Now, having cleaned away dried blood with a carbolic acid wash, Kramer ran a thumb over Black Dog's slavering maw. "What strange ink," the doctor said. "The color of the eyes is astounding. So *red*. These eyes are coals. Exquisite workmanship. Did you specifically request a Ghost Dog?"

"Ghost Dog?" Doyle had no idea what that was, and he was distracted. The acid had made his raw flesh sing with new pain. "Not that I recall. What is it?"

"Devil Dog," Battle answered. "Bearer of Death. Or Hellhound, a guardian of the Underworld, depending. Cerberus was of the same ilk, and there's, of course, the Barghest of Yorkshire." He ticked it all off with the boredom of a teacher who's taught the same lesson more times than he can count. "It's a very common image and superstition."

"Oh." Doyle shifted uncomfortably on Kramer's examination table, which occupied a corner of the doctor's boxy office. When Kramer had finally deigned to appear and asked him to shuck his uniform coat, he'd done it by halves, shrugging out of the right arm, worried about his decidedly nonregulation *sgian-dubh* in its black leather sheath. His shirt was the next hurdle, but Doyle had gotten by with simply rolling up his sleeve to expose both a fleshy four-inch rip and Black Dog, who had so captured Kramer's interest. He was sweating again, although a chill draft feathered through a gap in the office door, which sagged on its hinges. A rank of floor-to-ceiling bookshelves lining three walls had gone off-true and made Doyle a little ill if he looked too long.

"I just wanted something"—he floundered for the word he wanted—"unusual."

"Well, this qualifies." Running a magnifying glass over the tattoo, Kramer angled Doyle's arm closer to the sputtering flame of an oil lamp. "You know, he even initialed it and inked in a date? Here, along the tail." Kramer squinted. "*F.* I think that's an *S* or perhaps a *J.* Hard to tell. And an *M,* I believe, or *N,* followed by a 7 and 4."

The initials didn't ring a bell, but he recognized the year. "Yes, six years ago. Joined the whaler when I was fourteen."

"Really?" Battle said. "How many years?"

"On board?" Something in Battle's tone Doyle couldn't decipher. "Six."

"And then you came south, to London?" the inspector asked.

"Yes, sir, I . . ." He stopped at a light knock. A moment later, the door opened, and the girl, Meme, came in with a small tea cart.

"By my desk, Meme, if you please." Clapping a linen over

Doyle's still-oozing wound, the doctor said, "Keep pressure on this, Constable, if you will. Inspector?"

All right, so he obviously wasn't invited to take tea. Pressing the linen cloth to his cut, he watched Kramer shuck his soiled vest and hang it on a coat tree. And the bottle . . . *Ah*. Doyle's eyes zeroed in on a bulge in the right front pocket. How to get it?

"So." Clearly impatient to get on with it, Battle perched on a red leather wingback. "You were going to explain."

"Do let's not spoil our tea, Inspector. We've so few pleasures these days," Kramer said as Meme poured from a squat pot into cups arrayed on a silver tray. An aroma of black tea laced with bergamot bloomed. Beneath a napkin, a miracle: a lemon, impossibly yellow in the gloom. Doyle hadn't seen something that beautiful in . . . well, ever so long.

"Oh." Meme's eyebrows drew together in a frown. "I am sorry. I forgot a knife. Let me fetch . . ."

"Nonsense." Kramer looked over at Doyle. "Constable, might I trouble you for that knife of yours?"

"Sir?" *Shite*. He managed to look confused. "I'm afraid I've no fruit or penknife on me."

"Oh, come now, Doyle." Kramer twitched a forefinger. "That nasty business on your left hip. I saw the hilt when you unbuttoned your uniform coat."

Blast. This was just *so* his luck. Conscious of the questioning look Battle tossed him, he let go of his bleeding arm, reached beneath the folds of his coat, and pulled the knife free of its tooled leather sheath. Turning the steel blade, he pinched the business end between two fingers and extended the knife so Kramer could grasp its stag-horn hilt.

"Ah." Kramer arched his one functional eyebrow. "Scottish,

isn't it? A *sgian-dubh*? Isn't a black knife meant to be worn in a boot or long stocking?"

"Yes, sir," he said through clenched teeth. "But that's only good if you're wearing a kilt. Not much use to me if I've got to fumble."

"And the hip is better?" Battle said.

Doyle couldn't tell from the inspector's tone what he thought. Knives were against regulations. So was his Webley, for that matter. "Not the way the uniform's designed, no sir." He chewed over how best to say this, then just came out with it. "I modified the coat. Picked the stitching of the pocket."

"Ah. Transformed it into a slit then." Battle cocked his head. "So you could reach your blade without having to unbutton your coat."

"That's right, sir." He'd done the same with the right, too, the better to get at his truncheon in its long trouser pocket. In his opinion, whoever'd designed this uniform ought to be hung. Too many buttons, and except for his bull's-eye—his policeman's brass lantern which sported one huge lens that focused light to a tight beam and which could be strapped to a belt—he was forced to cart his cuffs, rattle, keys, and snips in pockets. By the time he might pull his truncheon or rattle, any self-respecting criminal would be long gone.

"Very resourceful, Constable." Kramer showed a sliver of a smile that revealed the man's blue grub of a tongue. "Black dog, black knife . . . your young man's full of surprises, Battle. Scalloped filework here is first-rate. Wicked sharp. Something your father bequeathed, Doyle?"

Yeah, you could say that. "Yes, sir."

"Well, quite the useful tool." Handing the knife to Meme,

Kramer tweezed chunks of sugar with silver tongs. "One or two?" he asked Battle.

"None for me. You've kept us waiting for hours. One might even suspect this was deliberate . . . yes, yes." Battle held up a hand. "You've your duty. I've mine as well, and it does not include taking tea." With a pointed glance to the girl, who was readying a cup for Doyle: "That extends to my constable."

Speak for yourself. The scent of that fruit had made the spit pool under his tongue. Hell with the tea or a biscuit; he'd settle for a juicy slice or two. "No, sir," he said, with a tight rictus more at home on a corpse. "Of course not."

"Sorry," the girl murmured as she returned his knife. Her skin smelled of lemons, and so did his black blade. Her eyes brushed his face. "I did not mean to cause you any trouble."

"You didn't." Her concern touched him. "Thank you for . . ."

"Meme," Kramer called. "That will do. Come stand by me."

"Yes, Doctor." The girl backed away, but not without shooting Doyle a look of apology.

"We're going to talk about this in front of your servant?" Battle said as Meme came to stand behind Kramer's left shoulder.

"As I've made clear, she is my apprentice," Kramer said.

"Highly irregular." Battle favored Meme with a long look. "And a little indecent, if you ask me. She's a girl."

And you're an arse. Doyle dodged his eyes away, embarrassed for her and furious with Battle. *If you weren't in charge, if this was any other place and time . . .*

Yes, Black Dog simpered. **You keep telling yourself what the gallant you could be.**

"Why, you know"—Kramer twisted round to give Meme a look of exaggerated astonishment—"Battle, I believe you're correct. She *is* a girl. How astonishing. No wonder you're an inspector." Kramer dropped a lump of sugar into his tea with a small *plik*. "Now, shall we get on with this, or do you wish to chide me further on my choice of assistants or how I run my asylum?"

"Very well." Battle's expression went stony. "Perhaps you would care to explain what happened to your patient."

Kramer took an experimental sip of his tea. "It was an abreaction."

"An abreaction." If Battle knew he was being baited, it didn't show in his face or tone. "And that is? Pretend I am a student and you, the master mesmerist."

"Think of an abreaction as a catharsis," Kramer said, the tail of the word rattling in a snaky *ssss*. As he settled into his wingback, the chair let out an ominous creak, and Doyle saw that one of the arms had split from its rails. "It's the mind's way of releasing unwanted emotions."

"But why attack you when you're trying so very hard to be helpful? Unless she sees you as the enemy. You did, after all, fail her parents."

A faint purple blotch stained the underside of Kramer's jaw. "An intractable patient is not a failure, Inspector. It is a tragedy. The mother's melancholia was unremitting, and she persisted in the delusional belief that her daughter had died. The father was driven to despair by his wife's condition, and the lot of them descended into this"—Kramer made a vague gesture—"contagious insanity. Psychotics can be quite charismatic. You saw the effect Elizabeth had on that young attendant, Bode? He may mean well, but he's suggestible."

"Really," Battle very nearly drawled. "And here I thought the boy might like the girl and want to help. How does that apply to Elizabeth McDermott now? She *is* ill, after all."

"Because she's no different from, say, Meme here." Kramer tossed an airy wave in the girl's direction. "Meme is an orphan, no family, no friends. No one cares for her, so to whom should Meme turn for guidance? Why, to me, of course."

God, Doyle marveled, *you are a bastard.* He'd seen her flinch and the color climbing her cheeks. She kept her eyes down, but her fingers knotted. He could swear something glimmered at the corner of an eye. *She's not a damn dog.*

"What's your point, Kramer?" Battle asked.

"Only this." Kramer put a finger to his lips. There was the tiniest *tick* as his nail struck tin. "If you grew up on a remote island with only your parents for company and no other influences—no friends or teachers or companions, nothing to read but what your father allows and half that his own wild writings—is it so hard to imagine that you would fall victim to the same unshakable beliefs?" Warming to his subject, Kramer laced his fingers together as if forming a web. "*That* is the McDermott family: a father, mother, daughter knit together by a singular, elaborate, and bizarre delusional system. Travel between *Nows*; the idea that every moment in time exists as a separate *Now* forever, that there are multiple versions of us all in an infinite array of possibilities. That *only* a select few could access relics from an unknown and far more advanced civilization, quite possibly beyond Earth. And the notion that there's an energy source from which one may craft characters and fictions that might come to life? Yet McDermott could be *so* persuasive. His writings, even the fragments"—Kramer's face grew intense, and he sat forward as if to better make his point—"quite compelling. You could *feel* how you might easily slip inside and become lost in those stories. Of course, he was mad."

"Stories. You mean, the novel McDermott was working on when he escaped?"

"Indeed." Kramer busied himself with tearing a lemon slice into quarters. "The title was absurd. An imaginary novelist with imaginary works in possession of a magical mirror and assorted other fantastical devices—glass pendants, all-seeing spectacles?" Snorting, Kramer slid juicy bits into that fissure of a mouth. "Ridiculous."

Spectacles. Doyle felt a tiny start of recognition. His eyes jumped to Kramer's breast pocket. *Those purple glasses.* And hadn't the doctor confiscated Elizabeth's glass bauble, that pendant on its queer chain? *If it's all so absurd, then why?*

"And yet McDermott was *absolutely* convinced that this novelist actually existed. He always said the name as if we should all know it. But I ask you, Inspector, really," Kramer said, around lemon, "who the bloody hell was Charles Dickens?"

EMMA
Monster of My Mind

EMMA CAME TO consciousness with a glassy smash, as if brought to life on a surge of electricity like Frankenstein's monster.

And that's what you are. You're a monster of my mind. Why can't you die DIE—

What? That wasn't her thought, not even her voice. She wanted to ask, out loud, *Who are you?* But she was afraid to talk to it, worried that would mean the voice was real, and it couldn't be, it just *couldn't*.

Yes, but I remember the valley, pushing into the Dark Passages, and then landing in . . . Her throat worked. Beneath her still tightly shut lids, her eyes burned hot. *Landing in an asylum.* God, maybe she *was* insane. Was that what everything had been about? Her madness? Eric and everything else only a hallucination? The valley had never happened and neither had her life: Jasper, Madeline Island, Sal, Holten Prep . . . all of it?

No. It's all been so real. So . . . a dream, maybe? Like *A Nightmare on Elm Street* or something?

Nightmare. The voice was back, and now it paused, as if rolling an unfamiliar word around its mouth, tasting it with a tongue. **Dream?**

Oh, she was *so* not answering, no matter how clearly the

words reverberated in her skull. Where was she, anyway? Eyes still closed, she turned her head ever so slightly, her senses quivering like a bat's. Her ears pricked to a crackly rustle beneath her belly. Paper? Or perhaps that was cellophane. From a distance came a different sound: hollow and irregular and more formless than a moan or cry. More like a lot of . . . *noise*. Clamor? Voices? Other people?

Yes. A hiss. **Thanks to you, they've put me with the rest of the nutters.**

Nutters. She knew that word. You didn't have to be a rocket scientist to understand that.

Rocket scientist? What are you babbling about?

She didn't know this voice, didn't understand why it was there. *Screw you.* She gave the voice a mental shove. *I'm going to wake up.* She would open her eyes—

Don't ignore me! The voice was an angry red clot. **I'm speaking to you!**

and there'd be her roommate, Marianne, sleeping it off in a tangle of sheets—

Who?

across the room. It would be noon and Christmas break and—

Answer me! A *kick* to her skull, and then an explosive *ker-POW* as the voice boomed, **I WILL NOT BE IGNORED!**

"Uh!" Emma's head rocked back. Her teeth clashed together with an audible click, snagging her right cheek. Bright orange spangles burst over her vision. Her spit was coppery, and she could feel a slow trickle of blood at the corner of her mouth.

YOU THINK YOU CAN BANISH ME WITH A THOUGHT? YOU THINK IT'S THAT EASY?

"Jesus, would you shut the hell *up*?" Her voice came as a low, animal croak, and the effort cost her. A knifing pain scraped her ribs. *Hurt.* She thought she was sick, too. When she swallowed, her throat convulsed around a clog of what felt like broken glass. Yet she still heard the difference: that lighter tone that was a touch more musical—and that *accent.*

At that, it all came rushing back, the images tumbling one after the other through her mind: losing Eric and Casey and Rima in the Dark Passages, her command to the cynosure, and then *blinking* onto the ward. Racing away from Kramer and that inspector and *Doyle* . . . yes, Arthur Conan *Doyle* . . . only to smash into that mirror from which loomed a face, large as life: the delicate oval of a much smaller girl with wild blonde hair and yet one with *her* eyes, that golden birthmark . . .

No, my eyes, my face!

that belonged not to her then but little Lizzie, all grown up.

Oh crap. Emma's eyes snapped open, and her heart turned over in her chest.

She was in blackness.

DOYLE

A Different Girl

"WHOMEVER MCDERMOTT THOUGHT he was—whether Charles Dickens was a nom de plume, a *dédoublement*, flesh and blood, or Jolly King Eddie—is immaterial, Doctor," Battle said. "My interests lie in tracking him down. For that, I require his daughter to be lucid. At this point, I see little value in your methods. The way you and that *thug* of an attendant manhandled that girl . . ."

"Don't tell me my business," Kramer said as he went to work on another lemon slice. God, the smell was driving Doyle mad. He swallowed back a flood of saliva; his stomach seemed to have grown claws that dug at his belly. He didn't know what he wanted more, the phial in Kramer's vest or that bit of fruit. Christ, he'd settle for the rind at this point.

"She was agitated," Kramer said, around lemon. "You may not approve of my tactics, Inspector, but if you want information, if you desire her lunatic of a father before he kills some other innocent in the misbegotten fantasy that he can somehow magically restore his family . . . well." Plucking up a napkin, Kramer set about wiping his fingers. "This is the way. The answers are locked in that girl's brain, and I will have them."

"As you had the father?" Battle observed.

"Yes, *thank* you, Inspector." Every word was hard-edged as a cut diamond. "Would you like me to admit defeat? Very well: I failed. There." Kramer tossed his napkin aside. "Satisfied?"

"It is not a question of satisfaction, Doctor, or blame. This is not a competition. This is about catching a madman."

"But you hold me responsible, isn't that right?"

"McDermott was in your custody." Battle's shoulders moved in a slight shrug. "If he'd escaped my station, I'm sure there'd be a hue and cry."

"So you *do* blame me. Brilliant. We've descended to name-calling and finger-pointing." Sitting forward again, Kramer selected a lumpy scone studded with what might be raisins but looked suspiciously, to Doyle, like dried rat turds. "I'd complained to the Lunacy Commission for quite some time about the criminal wings' gas mains. They cleared me of any culpability in the explosions. Besides"—Kramer snapped his scone in two, the sound crisp as the break of a small bone—"you ought to be delighted. All those criminal lunatics immolated at a go."

"I'm glad to see your irony intact. I might share your sentiments if the same explosions hadn't both set McDermott free and destroyed his notebooks and writings, so we've no clue as to his whereabouts. You say you read that last novel?"

"*The Dickens Mirror*? Yes, but it was in pieces, not a proper story at all. More fragments and notes." When Kramer slipped scone into his mouth, Doyle caught a fleeting glimpse of wet muscle. "Why?"

"I wondered if there might be something you recall, a detail or mention of a place that might point us in the right direction."

"Other than it being set in London and predominantly within these walls? It revolved around the man's usual preoccupations: labyrinthine tunnels, structures that transmogrified, doppel-gängers, splits in the personality, false selves, and, of course, his wife and daughter. I *was* struck by how he wove the Peculiar and our current predicament into his mythology. Saw it as energy that might be manipulated. I wouldn't be a bit surprised if he's not holed up somewhere close by its edge, or even worked out a way to wander in and out without becoming lost."

"All conjectural and meaningless if the girl can't remember where she was. Your mesmerism's failed, and I don't see how clouding her mind with your tonics helps."

"Which is why I am the doctor and you are the inspector. Get a medical degree, we can talk. Otherwise, lodge your complaints with the Lunacy Commission . . . but oh *yesss* . . . they've gone the way of Parliament and our good King Eddie, haven't they, steal-ing off into the night?" Kramer dusted crumbs from his fingers. "You say we should work together? So answer me this: why have I not been allowed to examine the bodies?"

"The bodies." Battle gave Kramer a look as if the doctor had just spouted gibberish. "You're not a police surgeon. You've not even a surgeon. You're a *doctor*. An *alienist*." (Doyle thought the inspector might as well have said *quack*.) "You've no standing," Battle said.

"Balls. Who do you think performs necropsies here or inspects the dead before we sack them for the rats?" How Kramer man-aged a noise like a wet fart with a mouth like that was a mystery to Doyle. "I know my way around a body."

"Don't try to sell me a dog, Kramer. Why are you so keen on them?"

"It's not obvious? Battle, for God's sake, a thorough study of the corpses might provide a clue as to McDermott's whereabouts."

"They're not within your purview, and that's final."

"Oh, don't piss on me, Battle, and call it rain. This is about territory. You don't *want* me to examine them, do you?"

"Perhaps not. Frankly . . . I suspect you've other motives."

"Have I? And what might they be?"

"I don't know. But I'm certain to find out." Battle got to his feet. A very tall and broad man, he seemed to inhabit the office, which settled around his shoulders like a cape. "The bodies are not your concern. Now, if you've nothing useful to add, I'll leave you to work on Doyle here. In the interim, I wish to interview some of the staff who've attended the girl. If you'd make them available, I'll speak to them on the ward." Battle tossed a look at Doyle. "How long? For you to tend to my man?"

"Not very," Kramer said, regarding Doyle with eyes that were hard as stones. "I dare say your constable's as eager to be free of this place as you."

Got that right. Doyle forced himself not to squirm.

"What about the girl?" Battle asked. "When can I speak with her?"

"Hard to say. I'll send word when she's stable. But, Inspector," Kramer said, "let's not get our hopes up, shall we? It's not as if she's going to wake a different girl."

EMMA

A Different Lizzie

1

FOR A SECOND, Emma wondered if she'd gone blind. The space was absolutely pitch, as in *no* light, not even a mild wash of silver from a shuttered window. It reminded her of a particularly heart-stopping moment in a defunct iron mine when their guide flicked off his headlamp just for kicks. Jasper had arranged it all back when she was eleven and fresh out of the hospital with her new face. Detouring on their trip back from Milwaukee to the U.P., Jasper steered them into iron country so they could do a little camping and a little illegal spelunking with this gruff, really ancient, chain-smoking miner dude with nicotine stains on his knuckles. Some wheezy old drinking buddy of Jasper's who didn't mind bending the rules, like, a *lot*. They'd followed tracks laid for ore carts down branching corridors with rotting crossbeams, flittering bats, cables sagging from ceilings, iron mesh and bolts holding up the ceiling in some parts. A lot of standing water, ankle-deep in places, the pools still and mirror-perfect. Death traps, the dude said; actually screamed for her to *freeze!* with her boot poised a half foot above what she could've sworn was solid rock. *That's the problem with old mines,* the dude said, thrusting a walking stick into the pool. She kept waiting for his hand to stop and the stick to hit bottom . . . and waiting and waiting. *Lower levels flood. Remember, girl, still waters run deep. One wrong step*—lighting a fresh smoke with the dying butt of another, the miner dude cracked a yellow grin—*it's a long way down.*

Yet this darkness now was also . . . weird. It actually seemed to shimmy and move, the way things did when you had a high fever. Everything trembled and she couldn't shake the sense that the darkness wasn't only air but *something.*

Where am I? Felt like she was underground, or in a deep basement. Her left shoulder ached; something knobby and a little musty-smelling palmed that left hip and her cheek. *Lying on my side.* A pad? Or maybe a mattress? Every movement rustled, like wind stirring dried cornstalks. Something heavy snarled around her legs and feet. *Skirt.* Her hand drifted up and touched the buttons of a coarse, long-sleeved, high-collared blouse. Thick tights. Low-heeled ankle boots with tons of little buttons. What *was* this stuff?

Be grateful. The hectoring voice—Elizabeth, a different Lizzie—was back. **They've always made me wear a strong dress to keep me from tearing my clothes.**

Strong dress. She knew that word from both her *blink* while still in House and from when she'd appeared on the ward. Well, now she knew where they'd put her, too. *Padded cell, below the asylum.* Kramer had her drugged, then put somewhere for safekeeping, probably to keep her away from that inspector, Battle, and . . . *Arthur Conan Doyle.* In this *Now*, he was a constable, and he'd . . . rescued her? From what?

I don't know. Elizabeth faltered. **I can't remember.**

Sometimes, I'm not even sure I was ever in this *Now* at all.

Struggling to a sit provoked a gust of nausea. Emma's already aching head chattered with fresh pain. When she moved, the darkness seemed to curl, then pull back, like a wave over sand.

Oooh, does that hurt? A vicious jag behind her eyes. **It's what you deserve. Why won't you leave?**

Believe me, honey, nothing I'd rather do. The question was how. *Wait.* Her hand drifted for her neck, but she already knew from the lack of weight. *Gone.* Kramer had taken both the galaxy pendant and Eric's tags.

Eric? Who's that? Is he another piece? And what do you mean, *tags*? Those scraps of tin on my necklace?

Ignoring Elizabeth took energy; it was like trying to hold back a wide stream with two hands. *Focus, come on.* Kramer took the pendant but only *after* she'd awakened in Elizabeth, which meant that the other girl had obviously been wearing a cynosure, or a close facsimile. *And Kramer has panops.* Which meant he'd spotted some *change* in Elizabeth's pendant after *she* showed up. Did that mean he was worried she could get out with it again? But wouldn't she need the Mirror for that?

No. That's not how you do it. It's the symbols that matter.

No, little Lizzie had used symbols.

Don't contradict me! The voice *kicked*. **What do you know? You're nothing but an intruder, a PIECE!**

"Jesus!" Emma pushed back with her will. *"Stop!"* A second later, the nattering voice and the feel of elbows and knees trying to punch out real estate in her brain receded. Felt good, a relief. Her head still ached, but at least she could actually think. *Yes, but for how long?* Shivering, she crouched on all fours and listened to . . . okay, this was so weird . . . to the inside of her own head.

Her brain felt as if it trembled like a pot of water just shy of a boil. Was there something else *beneath* this voice? *Other* voices?

Don't go looking for trouble. She smoothed moist palms over rough canvas. Considering she was trapped in a different *Now* and in a padded cell with a nasty bitch in her head, she was in deep shit already.

I'm nasty? Elizabeth faded back. **Try living with so many pieces you can't keep track.**

That stinging red venom was absent from Elizabeth's tone. In fact, Emma thought she sounded a little . . . cautious. *Worried that I was able to shut her up?* Could she do that, permanently? Lock Elizabeth away somewhere? *But she knows this* Now. *If I can get her to cooperate and help me . . .*

"What do you mean, *pieces*, Elizabeth? Are you talking about hallu . . ." She caught herself; *hallucinations* sounded somehow worse. More clinical, like the girl was really sick. *But she is.* There was a pang just under her right ribs, and she dug in the point of an elbow to brace herself. *Something physically wrong with her.* "Are you talking about voices, Elizabeth?"

No, more than that. I hear my mother, sometimes, but I know that's memory. Odd how I never hear my father. A pause, as if Elizabeth were giving herself a shake. **These others are . . . facets, like the different faces of a diamond.**

Aspects of herself, that's what she was talking about, and this actually made a loopy kind of sense to Emma. In the valley, Lizzie said that Emma and Rima and Tony and everyone else were book-people based on *her*. (Well, except if you believed the whisper-man, Emma had written Eric to life, and then Eric had given himself Casey: a creation of a creation of yet another creation. Emma wasn't entirely sold on the whole book-people thing either. She sure as hell felt real.) But if Lizzie/the whisper-man was right, then some book-people, like Emma, had more of Lizzie, and yet they were each their own person, designed to fit and function as distinct characters in separate worlds.

But what would happen if you reversed that? If you tried to put back, say, Rima without erasing everything that made her Rima, and not Lizzie? What would happen to your mind? Wouldn't you feel like you were in pieces? Crazy? Nothing would fit together. She thought back to what she'd read in abnormal psych. Elizabeth would be . . . what . . . a multiple,

dédoublement de la personnalité

a dissociative, in this *Now*?

Oh boy. Emma felt her insides ice. That made *her* just an alter? *In psych, the teacher said a strong personality can take control.* And *she* supposedly had more of Lizzie than all the others.

I asked the cynosure to take me where I'd find Eric again, and the others. The device had done exactly what she'd asked, too, slotting her into a different Lizzie, tortured by the voices of characters McDermott created based on his daughter. *I know that at least Bode is here, because I saw him, on the ward.* So Bode was a real person in this *Now*. What about the others? Did this mean that Rima and Tony and everyone else had their doubles in this *Now*?

Did she?

Wow. That thought hadn't occurred to her. What would happen if she came face-to-face with herself? Could multiples of the same person exist in the same *Now*? In the valley, Lizzie said that too many *finished* book-people, ones whose stories were set, could destroy a *Now*. But if she believed the whisper-man, *she* was unique: a creation that had either escaped or been set free.

Except Elizabeth's heard me, as a voice. Why was that? *She called*

us pieces. Which meant they—Bode, her, Rima, and all the rest—
were also *in* Elizabeth, and she experienced them all as voices. So
where *was* everyone else? Why could she hear only Elizabeth? *Is
it because I* am *strongest and shut them down?* Could she find them?
Talk to them? Yes, but how would that help?

"Look, Elizabeth," she said, pushing unsteadily to her feet.
Her head swirled a woozy second, and her lips tingled. What was
wrong with this girl? Coughing again, she brought up something
gluey that she gagged back. Phlegm, she hoped, but her mouth
went brackish again. Panting, she put a hand to the ache in her
right ribs. "Help me out here. Where am I?"

You're in me.

"I understand that, okay? You know what I mean." She aimed
her words into this weird, shimmying darkness. *What* is *that?* It
hit her then that she had no idea how big this cell was, or . . .
Jesus, are there other people in here with me? She'd assumed there were
none because all the cries and bellows were so distant. *But what if
there's someone else, tucked in a corner, just* breathing, *waiting for me to
stumble into it?* She felt her lids peel back as her eyes bugged. How
would she know? *Only if it talks out loud or touches me.*

At that, she felt a faint whisk over the back of her neck. *What?*
Spinning around, she stumbled and almost fell. "Wh-who?" Her
breath came ragged. "I-is somebody . . ." She clamped her lips
together. It was just air, the wind, a draft. Shrugging her shoulders around her ears, she shivered. *Imagining things.*

Or you're only mad.

"You shut up." She swallowed around a snarl of fear. "Instead
of fighting me, let's work together so I can get out of here."

No. Elizabeth's response was viper-quick. **I won't. Every
second you're in control is one more I'm not.**

Damn it. "Elizabeth, I only want to go home."

Home. You say that as if it's real, but it's only make-believe, the energy of thought fixed to White Space, and nothing more. As soon as I find a way to put you back where you came from, energy's *all* you'll be.

Put her back? Emma felt a sinking in her gut. The other girl was talking about putting *her* back into the Dark Passages. Could she do that, without the Mirror? Obviously, Kramer thought *she* could, or he wouldn't have taken Elizabeth's pendant. "How would that work, though?"

How would what work?

"The necklace." *Okay, that's really interesting.* They occupied the same body, but Elizabeth couldn't read every thought. Maybe she could use that. "Kramer took it. But that makes no sense."

Why not? Elizabeth sounded curious despite herself. **Of course it does.**

"No, not really. Think about it. Let's say my *essence* came out of the Dark Passages because it was attracted to you, okay? Like a moth heads for a candle?"

Yes, that's obvious. I'm the original.

Okay, she wasn't going there. There was also a serious flaw in Elizabeth's logic; she saw that right away. Honestly, with so many pieces of Elizabeth and the possibility of an infinite number of *Nows*, who knew who came first? What would that make little Lizzie? Just another piece? *That* little girl thought *she* was the original.

"Kramer took the necklace *only* after he saw it through the panops. I think that means that he believes it'll work now, which means that it didn't or couldn't have before. Why else would he take it?"

You don't know that. Uncertainty, now. **Perhaps** *he* **didn't want you using it.**

"But there's no Mirror. So what does it matter if I have it or not?" Silently praying, *Please don't freak out.* Because wasn't she pretty much saying that Elizabeth wasn't as special as she thought? "Don't you see how it doesn't make sense?"

No. It's only that I don't understand which symbols I need to make the right *Now.* **I might not even require the Mirror.**

All right, that could be. Little Lizzie used symbols to create new realities, and hadn't used the Mirror at all.

Whoa, wait a second . . . Until this instant, Emma had thought Lizzie was a *real* kid. Yet Elizabeth was obsessed with symbols as the way out of this *Now*, carving them into her arms—and so far as she knew, only Lizzie could use symbols that way.

So does that mean a piece of Lizzie's in Elizabeth? And if that was true . . . *Lizzie was a creation, too?* Everything—the explosion, McDermott's death, Meredith crashing the car—hadn't happened in the real world, but in a book? As part of . . . what . . . *her* story?

Jesus, that can't be right. Because what could it mean? That *this*, a London where people fell apart . . . *this* was the only *real* place?

Wait, wait, slow down. Lizzie had died still trapped in her forever-*Now*, the Peculiar in which she'd imprisoned the whisper-man. But did that mean that what happened to little Lizzie then was the same as when Tony had died, or Chad? *Back in the valley, Lizzie said that Tony wasn't really dead and neither was Chad; that if you died in a* Now *that wasn't yours, you went back to the one in which you belonged.* Or maybe the whisper-man, who'd inhabited Lizzie all along, had been lying. Honestly, keeping all this straight was giving her a headache.

Headache. A ping. She gasped. *Jesus.* "That would *prove* it."

What? What proves what?

She'd forgotten all about them. *But they were there.* She'd felt them. *Graves asked if I had a headache.* Trembling, she walked careful fingers to the ache at the center of her forehead. She felt stitches, regular as a train track, but . . . *No.* Panicked, she pressed harder, ignoring the protests from her freshly stitched flesh. But there was nothing.

Of course not. What else should there be?

Nothing. No metal, no lacy filigree. Maybe she was wrong about this, the whole direction her thoughts were tending to here. But if that was true, she was really screwed, because then she had no idea what Kramer could possibly want from her.

"They were *there*," she said fiercely. "*Damn* it, they were!"

All at once, under her probing fingers, she felt a firm and familiar edge surfacing from beneath those fresh stitches. It was just suddenly there, like one of those stop-action films where a tulip

How are you doing that?

goes from a tiny green nubbin to full flower in the blink of an eye.

"Ohhh." The word came in a dribbling little moan that was equal parts relief and awe. *Oh, thank you, God.* She moved her quaking hand to explore Elizabeth's scalp, which was smooth. *But I have plates and screws and scars.* She'd let Eric feel them, and she never let anyone do that, but Eric, she trusted.

Who is *Eric*? Is that another monster my father created, another piece? I don't recognize the name.

She paid Elizabeth no mind. Beneath her hand, her scalp wriggled. "Oh, holy shit!" All the tiny hairs on her neck went stiff as spikes. "Please, make this be real, please." Yes, beneath her fingers, her scalp was squirming, actually writhing and clenching and *heaving*

How are you doing that?

as her many scars wormed to life,

Stop.

tunneling from deep burrows to the surface,

STOP STOP THIS STOP!

where, an instant later, they knit into a familiar quilt of healed skin.

HOW DID YOU DO THAT?

Because of who I am; because I am *stronger.* Her scars were like her skull plates. *They can't* really *be there.* But she felt them. *And this is proof.* She traced an index finger over a fibrous filament on the crown of her head, then walked her fingers to the base of her skull. The mate to the titanium plate screwed to the bone between her eyes was there, too. *I was right about why Kramer took the cynosure.*

STOP! A mental punch to the jaw. **Stop trying to change me into YOU!**

"S-stop! L-listen to me. I don't want to be you." Another kick between the eyes, and now there was blood in her mouth from where she'd bitten herself. "I'm only t-trying to show you why Kramer—"

You've nothing to show me! Get out of my body! Just DIE! Another mental slam, and now there was blood streaming from her nose. **DIE!**

No! Shut UP! Emma hurled the thought, heard it actually *snap*, a very hard stinging sound, like the smart crack of whip. Inside, deep in her head, she felt a kind of stutter step on an icy mental slick as Elizabeth faltered, and Emma thought, *Can't give her a second chance.* She *snapped* off two more, like a boxer throwing a left jab and then an uppercut with his right. "*Stop* it, Elizabeth. Go away! *Go away!*"

No. But there was another of those strange mental staggers. **I w-won't . . .**

"*Yes,* you will! You won't help? Fine. Then leave me the hell alone! Go away, go away!" She was bellowing now. Anger helped, and so did her fear, because this could not go on—and she'd just proven something to herself, too. *It's me; it's the essence of who I am. I'm the one—the piece—the devices will recognize. I* am *the power, the key Kramer was talking about.*

And she thought: *Key.*

2

SHE'D ONCE READ a book where some psychic kid put all the monsters that scared him into mental lockboxes, turned the key, and shelved them in a back closet of his mind. They weren't real boxes, just as the closet was only in his imagination. But the point was to build it all in his head, to give it a reality there.

Down cellar. It was the first thing that occurred to her, and the image came fast, down cellar unfurling in a rush from some dark vault of memory: the long wooden stairs, concrete floor, whitewashed cinderblock. That second room, where secrets and all things best forgotten hid. To all that, she added a single change: instead of a wooden door at the top of the stairs, she made one of iron.

No, please, don't don't lock me in there let me out this is my body this is my . . .

She was right again: to the Elizabeth that existed in her mind, this would be a real prison. "No," she shouted, "*I'm* in charge now!" But she was getting tired. Pushing against a formless presence was very difficult, like bullying fog that clotted to soft sponge before dissipating in the next second. That bizarre knee-and-elbow sensation intensified as Elizabeth flailed, and Emma thought she would lose this fight if she didn't think of something, and fast. *Have to hurry. What if she locks* me *away?*

I won't. Still frothing and kicking. **You're right. Let's work together.**

"Forget it." Then Emma did the only thing she could that would help her end this. This all existed only in her mind, but she had to give herself something *solid* to push against. So she gave the Elizabeth in her mind a body, *her* body: same blonde hair, same delicate oval of a face, and eyes that were also Emma's, dark blue with that golden flaw—

"No, they are *mine*," Elizabeth snarled, "and you've just made a fatal error." Features twisted into a mask of hate, Elizabeth flew at her with a screech.

The mental impact—the force that was Elizabeth plowing into her—slammed the breath from Emma's lungs. Anyone looking at her from the outside would've seen only Emma, in her cell, eyes tightly shut, body quivering and straining, fighting a battle that was going on in her mind.

Rocked onto her heels, Emma grabbed the shrieking girl by her blouse and bullied her in a blundering backward stagger for that open cellar door. It was then that Emma realized that she'd made herself a mental body, too, as she was: taller and stronger, and back in clothes she recognized. Jeans, the turquoise turtleneck she'd found in House, and boots, because it had been snowing when she and Lily climbed into that van just that morning . . . or more than a hundred years from now, take your pick. She'd even given herself back her own face. Felt it mold to her skull like cling wrap. Maybe, in this instant, she'd finally grown into herself.

"Please," Elizabeth said. "Don't lock me away, please." Her smaller hands clung to Emma's wrists. "I'll die in there. I can help you. I know the asylum. I know *London*. You won't know where to start."

This was true. Could they work together? All Emma wanted was a way out of Elizabeth's body. If Kramer was looking for the Mirror, then didn't it follow that it existed in this *Now*? Maybe not; lost artifacts were the stuff of legends and stories. *But even if it* isn't *here, could there be another way?* She felt that snag, a little tug, as if she might be onto something. Jasper had down cellar, which she thought must be another way into the Dark Passages, or something close. *So what if there's a back door here?*

Maybe her mental grip—her fists knotted in Elizabeth's blouse—loosened because she was distracted. As it was, she almost missed it: the moment that Elizabeth's lips skinned from her teeth.

"No!" she shouted, a second too late.

In the next instant, Elizabeth drove for her neck.

EMMA

Mistake

1

THIS WAS LIKE the valley; at the moment it was all happening, illusion or not, mental image or not, it was real and she had no choice but to react that way.

As Elizabeth lunged for her throat, Emma got an elbow up just in time. The point caught Elizabeth in the mouth. There was dull *chuck* as the other girl's teeth clashed. Elizabeth's head rocked as blood leaked from her mouth. Her eyes, darkly blue and glittery, rolled in their sockets.

Emma was no fighter, had never taken kickboxing, but she liked books, and the zombie apocalypse was big. So she knew: *Go for the hair.*

With one hand still firmly clutching Elizabeth's blouse, Emma knotted her other fist in blonde curls. Elizabeth screamed. Body bowed, she tried locking her fingers around Emma's wrist, but Emma pushed the girl back, and then there was the iron door.

"You'll *never* get out without me." At the very brink, Elizabeth scrabbled for purchase, her hands flailing for the jamb, heels digging in for all she was worth, like a struggling cat fighting against being shoved into that carrier. Beyond, the basement steps seemed to plunge down a dark throat. "You're *trapped*," Elizabeth said. "You need me, you *need*—"

"Shut *up!*" Planting her feet, Emma shoved, hard. Wailing, Elizabeth stumbled but didn't tumble out of sight, and Emma saw why. She'd made down cellar too perfect; had even included handrails. Before she could think, *Go away*, and erase them, something happened outside her head.

In the real world, there was an enormous buck and then a heave as the earth trembled.

2

The feeling was like the time she'd been stupid enough to stand on the flatbed of Jasper's truck when he'd started rolling without shouting a warning first. The sudden jerk had sent her off-balance. She'd nearly jackknifed over the side.

The lurch now was strong and immediate, a kick she felt in her knees and hips. In the formless space, right above that open door, she felt a hard twitch and shimmy under her feet. On the steps, Elizabeth suddenly fell backward, arms windmilling.

All at once, the space deformed in a wrinkle, as if puckering its lips to spit her out. In the blink of an eye, the door to down cellar vanished, and Emma was outside her head again, in her cell, sprawled on her lumpy mattress. *What the hell?* The earth vibrated and quivered beneath her hands as the cell's walls rumbled. There was a pop, like the bang of a cork shooting from a bottle under pressure. Something cleaved the air above her head with a fast *whirr*. Bits of rock or maybe brick showered all around with a sound like rice on stone.

An earthquake? Above, there was more cracking and smashing of rock. Teeth bared, she threw her arms over her head and waited for the ceiling to come down. Under her belly, the earth rose and then dropped, shivered—and went still.

What's going on? The air tasted of cold grit. She couldn't hear anything above the roar of her pulse.

Then, she became aware of a jostle in her skull and thought, *Oh shit.*

3

IT WASN'T CONSCIOUS so much as reflex, a snapping of her attention the way you might jerk your head to catch movement at the corner of your eye. A quick wink and she'd returned to that formless space, the open cellar door. Less than three feet away, the iron door gaped, and there was Elizabeth: storming up the cellar steps, her face distorted with rage, her hair a gorgon's wild cloud.

"No!" Springing back, Emma hooked both hands around the iron door and heaved it to. The door was only a construction, a mental barricade, and yet she slammed it so hard she felt the ghostly clang in her teeth. An instant later, there was a *thud* as Elizabeth bulled into iron.

The door to the down cellar prison she'd built in her mind held.

4

ALMOST GOT PAST *me.* With a sliver of her consciousness, she knew that, outside her head, she still lay on her stomach, gripping a mattress in a cell choked with grit and rubble. Yet, inside her head, Emma stood in the formless space on her side of a mental door. In the past, when she'd *blinked*, she still carried on with her life: went to school, turned in homework, hung with friends. The doctors had called them dissociative episodes and fugue states, but the principle was the same. You could look completely normal, order a mocha Frappuccino even while, beyond your awareness, there was an awful lot of drama going on in your head.

Pressing her fingers to the cold, unyielding iron door she'd manufactured in her mind, she now thought, *That was cutting it pretty damn close.*

That quake had been so strange, too. It reminded her of what had happened to Rima and the others and that fight where the snow broke apart: too many book-people in one space, and the world disintegrated. *But that can't be right.* This wasn't a book-world or some weird construction like Lizzie's forever-*Now*, but a real place, an alternative London. She just couldn't be strong enough to *cause* all this.

But I am *strong enough to change some things, even if they're only in my own head.* She eyed that door floating in midair. "Build me a floor," she murmured. "Give me walls." Almost instantly, the old pine floor unfurled like a carpet under her feet. Walls glimmered into existence. Probably build the whole kitchen if she wanted, maybe even the cottage.

Another thud and then a hard thump as Elizabeth either kicked or used her fist. *Seems solid enough.* Then thought, *You nut, this whole place exists in your head. It's as solid as you want and need it to be.* But she couldn't leave Elizabeth here forever. If *she* left Elizabeth's body—God, how? and go where?—this down cellar prison should disappear, right? *Only what if it doesn't? I can't do that to her.*

As if conjured from thin air, Elizabeth's voice drifted through iron. *"Please.* Don't leave me here in the dark. At least give me light."

A thought: *No one gives a lunatic a candle.* It felt like a kind of warning.

"Emma?"

"Hold on." No matter what Elizabeth thought, Emma wasn't a monster. She thought about it for a second, letting the image coalesce in her mind, and then put that image where she thought it ought to go. "There." She waited a second. "Do you see it?"

"Yes." Elizabeth snuffled. "Thank you. It's . . . it's blue."

"It's from my birthday." *When I turned twelve, and a week before I went down cellar and found . . .* She closed her mind to that memory. "Normal rules don't apply in a place like this. So it shouldn't burn out. You'll have plenty of light, Elizabeth, for as long as . . ." She let that go. No telling how long Elizabeth might have to remain under lock and key. But she should leave this place. In her psych course, her teacher—a real film nut—said that basements were metaphors for all that was dark and deep and scary. Basements were where the monsters lived. Now that she thought about it, hadn't the psychiatrist she'd seen before her reconstruction said the same thing?

"Emma?" It was Elizabeth, behind her prison door. "What did you mean by proof? Your scars, those . . . plates? They're not *really* there, but I felt them."

But they're me, part of who I am, how I think of myself. Lizzie would've called it an *essence.* No matter the name, it was the power Emma had brought with her, something Elizabeth didn't seem to have. But why not? Because Elizabeth didn't really know who she was? Had no true sense of herself, or spent all of her energy at war with the voices in her head? But that didn't make sense, especially if *she* was based on Elizabeth. They were all tangled together, right? So why didn't the devices know Elizabeth? Why didn't that glass bauble *become* the cynosure for her?

Unless it's no more complicated than that, for whatever reason, I'm the battery, the power source, stronger than the others because I've got that little extra something that lets me jump off the page. It's the only explanation for why Kramer took an otherwise worthless hunk of junk. If she was a book-person, that was—and Jesus, did it matter? It all felt like semantics, and who the hell cared at this moment? She only wanted to go home.

"Emma?"

"I'm sorry, Elizabeth," she said, "but I have to go."

"Wait!" Elizabeth said something else, but Emma closed her mind. *I'm not hearing you, and I am getting out of here right now.* Working fast, she scrubbed at the seams and jamb with the flat of a mental hand. Just like that, the door itself went away and only iron remained. If Elizabeth screamed, she didn't hear.

Emma left and didn't look back.

5

SHE HAD, HOWEVER, just made a very big mistake.

ELIZABETH

Down Cellar

STAY CALM. **HUDDLED** in this bizarre mental trap, Elizabeth stared at that strange little candle Emma had made for her. *Every box has a lid and every cell a door.* She'd only need to find the key to this place, this *down cellar*, that was all.

This place didn't feel like a cell. There *was* a scent, however. *Paper?* She couldn't tell. Although a tiny circlet of light wavered from that one feeble candle, its glow petered out after a few feet. It wasn't completely silent down here either. There *was* something beyond the walls, though not the hollow cries of the mad she knew. The sound was a little bouncy, even jaunty, falling in tiny drops from above . . . and was that a man's voice?

"Music." She aimed a look at the dense, dark bowl of a ceiling. "Upstairs." Was this cellar part of a house? Possibly. She liked that idea, too; it felt right. "Whatever Emma made, she made quickly. This is a place she knows well," she said, listening to the words roll off her tongue. Hearing her own voice above the clamor of all those pieces always had calmed her. Although—she cocked her head—there were no voices here, only that music filtering down from above. Why? Because Emma had carved out this private space? "So how much of Emma will show itself here?"

Well, there was the candle. Never seen its like. Very odd little thing: no bigger around than a slender twig and blue, with those curious little ridges, too, like ribbons tightly curled around a maypole. Gobbets of wax spilled down the sides, and yet the candle was no shorter. She debated a quick moment, then held a finger above the flame. No heat. *Hmmm* . . . Moistening two fingers with her tongue, she pinched the wick. The candle died with a tiny *ssstt*, and on its heels came darkness, dropping like a black shroud. Her heart thumped, and she heard her breathing speed up.

"It's all right, Elizabeth." Was there a quaver? The taste of fresh char drifted onto her tongue. "It will pop right back. It has to, because none of this is real. This is a simulacrum. Be patient and—"

At her feet a yellow rose unfurled as the flame blossomed to life again.

"All right." She released a slow breath. "That's good." Picking up the candle, she studied the floor, running the flat of her free hand over a cool and slightly stippled slab. Was this stone? Now that she was looking, she spotted a metal disk that reminded her of a hob's grate, only bolted over an opening in the floor. No air coming through. She studied the placement. Perhaps a drain of some sort. That could be.

"But it's an interesting piece of detail. Why put that here if it serves no purpose? *I* don't need it." *Unless I'm to piss in it.* A single sniff put that to rest. The scent that came back was dry and cool. So this metal disk had to be something peculiar to this particular place, and that meant she was right: this was a room Emma knew. You didn't just put in a steam grate or drain or whatever this thing was on a whim. You did it because it was part and parcel of the place itself.

This room is all Emma. Her eyes fell on the flame again. "You gave me a candle that won't snuff out. All this is made from the energy that is *you*. Which means that energy is *here*." Her eyes picked out a faint pink spiral scar on her left wrist. "And I am *still* me." Did that mean she had some control in this place?

"I don't like you." She twitched her drab skirt. "I want blue and a nice lace . . ." She broke off with a startled little laugh as the skirt wavered, then spun into loose blue folds; the weight over her shoulders eased as a lace blouse with an elaborate high collar melded to her body. "No corset either." She despised bone stays.

"That's better." She wiggled her toes, now clad in silk stockings and supple calfskin boots. "And you've made a mistake, Emma. You've left too much of yourself behind." Emma's essence shed energy the way a candle bled light *and* heat. Yet you lit a candle for light; you didn't warm yourself with it. But that didn't mean the excess energy of the candle's heat couldn't be used for warmth—or, in here, to make clothes. For that matter, Emma had given *her* a body, meaning she'd inadvertently left a smear, a smudge of herself, behind.

For me to use. It was time to explore and know this place, its dimensions, its weaknesses. Every house had its creaky boards and hairline cracks and faulty joints. So did minds. So must Emma, and she would find this enemy's weakness.

Just wait and see.

PART THREE

RATS

DOYLE

Meater

DOYLE DIDN'T SEE a way out. With Battle gone and his orders to remain behind and let Kramer tend to him crystal-clear, Doyle was trapped.

"All right, Constable," the doctor said, crossing to a glassed-in cupboard, "off with your coat now. Shirt as well. *Both* arms, if you don't mind."

"That's all right. I'm fine," he said, too quickly. "It's my right arm, not the left."

"Come, Doyle." Kramer gave him a bland look. "I'm no fool."

Uh-oh, poppet. But Black Dog didn't sound all that upset. **Jig's up.**

"I . . . I don't . . ." Doyle's eyes bounced to Meme, who had escorted Battle to the ward before returning with basins and rolls of instruments, which she was now setting out. *Damn.* "I'm a touch uncomfortable," he said, and then added, hating himself, "With the girl, I mean."

That's my darling. Black Dog's chuckle was nearly lost in a clash of metal as Meme fumbled. **To hell with chivalry when it's your neck on the line, right?**

Oh, shut up. Though he couldn't muster much indignation. He *was* a monster. But was this his fault? He had to protect himself. "If she's to stay, I'd rather not remove my shirt. It's not seemly."

"*Seemly?* She lives and works in a *lunatic* asylum. People tear their clothes off here, run round naked as jays, and covered in shit. You're such a hypocrite, Doyle. This has nothing to do with protecting *her* delicate constitution and *everything* to do with shielding you." Snorting, Kramer draped the long canvas tongue of a tourniquet on his desk and then, very deliberately, squared a fine morocco case of mahogany and turquoise inlay alongside. "So don't let us pretend to a higher morality we both know you don't possess."

Doyle barely heard. *Oh.* He was practically salivating because he recognized the case, at once, for what it was. The size gave it away: about ten inches long, four wide. There were only so many things that fit a case like that. Draftsmen's tools, perhaps, or pens. Jewelry, he supposed, but he thought not. This was a doctor, and his office. So Doyle knew, exactly, what nestled in velvet plush.

"Now, if you want my help, I need to see your arms. After all, we *do* want this going into a viable vein." Kramer was regarding him with those stone-dead eyes again. "Don't we, Doyle?"

"I don't . . ." He tried swallowing past the boulder in his throat and only choked. "I-I'm not sure . . ." For some stupid reason, he glanced at the girl, but her face was averted. She might be trying to spare him, but that somehow made it all so much worse. He couldn't be more naked now than if he *had* dropped his britches and unbuttoned his placket to pull his pudding, exposing himself in all his miserable glory. "I think there's . . . there's a misunderstanding."

"Oh, shut your cakehole, Doyle." Kramer sounded a little bored. "I'm a *doctor*, for God's sake. Sweats? Agitation? Your guts have been singing quite the tune, too. Oh, and there are the longing glances you've been giving my vest here. I'm sure you've been trying to think of ways to nick that bottle. A fine wirer could manage it, and you look a bit of ruffian. I wager you've dipped into your share of pockets."

There was nothing to say to all that, particularly since it was true. Trembling, his nerves humming—with desire? fear?—he watched Kramer open the box, which was lined with purple velvet. Selecting a brass syringe, Kramer fitted a needle. Then, unlocking the hinges from that wooden box, Kramer folded back the sides to reveal ranks of glass phials. Tweezing out one, he held it at an angle to better scrutinize the amber liquid inside. To Doyle, the phial sparkled like a rare yellow diamond.

"Now, we both know you want this," Kramer said. "So you'll do *exactly* as I say."

He wanted to say no. He wanted to bolt from that horrible office. Most of all, he wanted to explain to that girl, who was still so very careful not to look at him, *No, I'm not what he says. I'm not like this. I'm not a monster. It's just that things are so awful. I'm good, I really am. I could be good to you.* He didn't know why all that felt so urgent either, as if his life really hung in the balance here.

This is a mistake, Black Dog niggled. **Far better the devil you know, even if that is I.**

"What do you want?" Doyle's voice was as flat as Kramer's eyes. "You're not doing this out of the goodness of your heart, or because you're such a humanitarian."

"No, I'm not." Kramer gestured with the syringe. "Other arm, please, the left."

He was very conscious of Meme, only a few feet away, and the faint scent of lemons on her skin. It was bad enough to have the girl as a witness. It wasn't even about dignity. He didn't want her to see what a wreck he truly was. For some stupid reason, he cared what she thought of him, and wasn't that pathetic? "I'd really rather not."

"It's not a question of what you'd rather do. I doubt you've been scrupulous. I'll not have you die of blood poisoning." The half of Kramer's forehead capable of a frown wrinkled, and he threw a quick look toward Meme. "Ah, your embarrassment's misplaced, as is your pride. Meme is my assistant. You're an addict, Doyle. She understands that. Don't you, Meme?"

"Yes, Doctor." A monotone. The girl's face was so still, almost waxen, yet when her dark blue eyes touched his, Doyle thought he saw something soften. "But perhaps," she said to Kramer, "I might be of service elsewhere?"

"Nonsense. I've no more time to waste, and several more patients require my attention. So, decide, Doyle: either do as I say, or Meme here can stitch and then send you on your way. Not to worry; she'll do a fine job. But that is my last offer."

He almost told Kramer to do something anatomically impossible. Instead, wordlessly, he shrugged out of his jacket.

"That's better." Inserting the needle into that phial, Kramer said, "Any fevers?"

"No." Doyle watched his fingers work the buttons of his left cuff. His neck was hot. "Just the shakes."

"Excellent. No blood poisoning then." Loaded syringe in hand, Kramer rounded his desk. "How long since your last . . . ah . . . well, whatever drug you favor, or cheap gin and tin-pot beer?"

I'll take whatever I can get, damn you. "Morphia, and then a dram of laudanum. Been three days."

"Oh then, yes, you are in a bit of a twist. When was the last time you et?"

A flicker of rage. "You sod." He looked up, conscious of the shimmer of humiliated tears that, even in this bad light, Kramer—and God, that *girl*—must see. "Why do you think I even started? You bloody well know the drugs kill hunger." Although he *did* have food from the police stores, most of which was confiscated: public and private supplies brought under civil control, yet another benefit of joining the force. What he'd carefully gathered was hidden. He took only what was necessary for him to put one foot in front of the other. Even now, he had a small paper packet of real toffees tucked in an inside pocket, and another parcel of peppermint humbugs at his hip, though he suspected his craving for sweets was because of the drugs. Nonetheless, tuck a candy into his cheek or slide a toffee to slowly dissolve under his tongue, and the sugar kept him going for hours.

"Yes," Kramer drawled. "Of course, the devil of it is that once it's got its talons in you, you're feeding quite a different hunger. Before you go, though, you will have some tea, with plenty of sugar, and biscuits. It will calm your stomach." Taking hold of Doyle's left arm, Kramer twisted it this way and that in the light. Doyle didn't have to look; he knew every scab and scar, each swath of inflamed flesh, that rock-hard sclerotic vein he'd used ten times too often. Kramer paused over the pale zigzag of a thick scar that jagged over Doyle's elbow and halfway to his shoulder. "What's this? Quite the rip."

"Knife. It's old." His throat bunched again. "Kid stuff."

"Mmm." Arching the only eyebrow he could, Kramer let that

go. "How is it you avoid detection? I assume the police doctor or surgeon holds routine inspections."

"He does. But he also has his needs." When Kramer only stared, Doyle snapped, "He likes *boys*, all right?"

"Boys." Kramer said it as if speaking a foreign tongue. "And you find them . . . ?"

Any street corner. Pick the scrawniest, promise a biscuit, and ya can go at the doggy back way as many times as you like. Doyle's left leg jiggled. He was swimming in sweat. What was the girl thinking? He wished he could read her face. Her dark blue eyes were steady, though her cheeks were hectic. She must think him a monster.

"Why you want to know?" His voice was brutal and hard as Kramer's eyes. "Ya fancy one?"

"No, but I like to understand what manner of man you are, just how far you're willing to go. Very far indeed, it seems. Splendid." Returning his attention to Doyle's arm, Kramer ran the pad of a thumb over that petrified vein. "Are you injecting between your toes? Or under your tongue?"

"No." Try as he might, he couldn't stop the tremble of a tear that welled over his lashes to wet his left cheek. "Why you doing this? Ya want me to grovel, beg? I never asked you for nothing."

"But you're willing to take. Unless you wish to walk out of here with only stitches, and an unfortunate desire to soil your trousers. Or you could tell Battle. It would be my word against yours."

"And *stupid*," Doyle spat. "Battle'll want to know why you bothered. I'd be cutting my own throat. There's no way to win this."

Unless you refuse to play. Black Dog had been silent so long he almost started. **There are deals to be made with worse**

than the devil you know, far more ruinous than you can imagine.

Really? Oh believe you me, I can imagine quite a lot. He had, after all, been fourteen once and bearer of a secret that even now burned his brain like the vengeful eye of a lunatic god.

2

HE LISTENED, CAREFULLY, as Kramer told him what he wanted. When the doctor was done, he only stared a moment, then said, "You're mad." He glanced over at the girl, but Meme's face was a fixed and steady neutral. He looked back to Kramer. "Steal *evidence*? I can't do that. I don't know where they even are. No one does."

"But you could find out. Then you bring them here," Kramer said.

"But why? What good are they to you?"

"Playing the detective? It don't suit. You're no bricky boy, Doyle." Kramer leaned so close Doyle could smell the sour tang of horehound on his breath. "You're a meater, a coward, and weak. Now, you want what you want, and so do I."

"If I'm caught, I'm sacked, on the street." He wanted to add that he was dead, because there would be no more money and, therefore, no more morphia or cocaine or opium. He could barter food for more drugs, but one way or the other, it would all catch up with him. He couldn't live *on* drugs, and he couldn't live without them.

"Then don't get caught. A shame that only a few years ago, this would all be quite legal. You seem quite resourceful, Doyle. You've managed this long with your little . . . habit?"

It was on the tip of his tongue to ask again: *Why, why this? What you want something like them for? What's so important about them?*

Want is want. At the end of the syringe, a golden drop swelled. For an insane moment, Doyle yearned to take that honey-colored drop on his tongue the way a lover catches the tear of a beloved. The color was very different from what he'd expected, but who bloody cared? Kramer needed him, and this was payment.

"Here." The tourniquet, a Petit's, was one with which he was familiar, but you were talking about someone who'd have jerry-rigged a rat's tail to plump up a vein if needed. As Meme came forward to help, Doyle stopped her with a look. "No," he said. "You shouldn't be made to do this."

"I do not mind, Constable," Meme said. "I want to help."

No one can help me. He wouldn't let her sully herself over the likes of him either. "Thank you, no." Turning aside, he used the bloody fingers of his right hand and then his teeth to fix the tourniquet's canvas strap through the steel buckle. He tightened the winged brass screw, then pumped the fingers of his left hand. *Ahhh, there you are.* A fat blue vein wormed at the base of his thumb and crawled over his wrist.

"That's a good one." He thrust his arm at Kramer. "Hasn't failed yet. I try to rotate and rest it because . . ." He stopped talking. What an idiot, going on like a couple of boy apprentices comparing notes on which brick ought to go where. *I'm a person. I must count for something.* But he couldn't think what.

Then don't do this, poppet. Black Dog, again. **Walk away.**

"Ah." Kramer's ravaged mouth parted in a surprisingly boyish grin that made him look only half a monster. "You know what we call that? The intern's vein, because any fool can hit it."

And which of us is more the fool now? Doyle honestly couldn't tell if that was his thought, or Black Dog's. It probably didn't matter.

"Shut up." Doyle closed his eyes, mostly because he couldn't bear to see the pity in the girl's eyes turn to disgust. "Just get on with it, can't you?"

3

IT WAS NOT what he expected.

For a few, long moments after Kramer depressed the plunger and he felt the cold thread of liquid stream into his vein, nothing happened. Kramer was silent, though his gaze, bright as a raven's, scraped over Doyle's face. *Studying me.* Then, a more horrible thought: *As if I'm a specimen.* He had to throttle back a scream. Black Dog was right. Kramer was using him for some mad experiment . . .

And then the drugs hit. *Oh God.* A warm and liquid rush filled his chest and ballooned in his head. *God, this is good, so gooood.* He heard himself sigh.

"Better?" Kramer's voice sounded far away.

"Yes." That was true enough, but at the same time—Doyle swallowed against an odd taste on his tongue—something wasn't quite right.

Normally, his mind went a little fuzzy, quite quickly, as the drug, carried in his blood, swirled through and around his brain. Now, he was comfortable, but only just. Teetering on the brink was more like.

"What's in this?" He watched Kramer dismantling his syringe. "This isn't . . . *ahhh!*" A sudden icy fist slammed his chest. His head snapped so violently he heard the crack of tendons and bone in his neck.

Distantly, he heard Meme: "Doctor?" And then Kramer: "Leave him. It will pass." Evidently, she didn't listen, because the next thing he felt were her hands on his cheeks. Her face swam out of a red haze. "Constable," Meme said, "what is happening?"

"Hurts." The word rode a hiss through clenched teeth. "Not *right*. Not supposed to . . . Oh *God*." Another blistering shudder, and he plugged his mouth with a fist to keep back the scream.

"Doctor." Meme turned a pleading look. "*Help* him."

"This will run its course," Kramer said. Then, more sharply: "What the devil do you think you're doing?"

"I know you must have an antidote." Through a fog of pain, Doyle saw that the girl was hastily rummaging through Kramer's phials. Selecting one, she held it out. "This reverses the effects of morphia, does it not?" When Kramer didn't reply, she said, "Doctor, *please*. I have never defied you, but—"

"Then do not begin now." Kramer's voice shook with rage. Extending a hand, he snapped his fingers. "Give me that." When she made no move, he said, "Do *not* overstep. You are my creature, girl. I made you, and I can just as easily—"

"N-no, l-leave her out of this." He couldn't let her risk her position. *He'll turn her out to die on the streets.* Doyle pressed a fist to his chest. "S-sometimes, it happens."

"I do not understand," Meme said to Kramer. "The lies, what you told Battle, and now—"

"I said *give* me the *phial*!" Kramer's hand flashed. The blow caught Meme just below her left eye. Staggering, she let out a sharp cry. Cursing, Kramer wrenched the bottle from her fingers. "How *dare* you defy me!"

"*N-no!*" Panting, Doyle struggled to his feet, but he was off-balance. Swaying, he clutched at the tea cart. Cups and china saucers slithered to the floor in a bony smash. Trembling, he latched onto a wingback to keep from falling. "Don't *h-hurt . . .*"

"Remember, you are *my* creature." Kramer shook the girl violently enough for her head to snap on the thin stalk of her neck. "You serve at *my* pleasure. Do you hear?"

"Damn you, *leave* her!" Doyle's arms shuddered under the strain of his weight. *When I'm past this, wring your neck, tear your head . . .*

Patience, poppet. A snarl in his left ear. **There is a time and place. This is not it. Choose your battles. You gain nothing by playing the white knight here.**

"Yes, Doctor." Except for the fist-sized splotch under her eye, Meme's face was pale as porcelain. "I apologize. It is only that you taught me to do no harm and yet—"

"And I've done none. It is a serum of my own making, and believe me, I have no wish to harm the good constable." Cutting her off with a tone as cold as the slush passing for Doyle's blood, Kramer thrust her aside. "You, Doyle, sit down before you break anything else. I wouldn't poison you. How would I explain that to Battle? Oh, so sorry, your constable dropped dead whilst I was stitching his arm?" He tossed the syringe's needle and tube in a basin of carbolic acid. "I've remedied the constable's physical symptoms and the worst of that craving. It's passing even now, isn't it, Doyle?"

It was true. His heart was only racing, not trying to blast out of his chest. "Yes." He knuckled sweat from his forehead. "But what's in it? I've a right to know."

"A *right*?" The half-mask rode up a little as Kramer arched his good right eyebrow. "I told you. It's a combination of morphia with a touch of seven-percent—and a little something extra for clarity and to scrub your mind clean."

"Clarity?" *Something extra? Wash his mind until he was, what, a blank slate?* Meme had drifted closer. Her hand brushed his back: a gentle touch, but it helped center him. Why was she being so kind? "Whatcha mean?" he asked Kramer. "You're talking riddles. I'm a person, not a piece of parchment."

Poppet. Black Dog, at his ear. **Think of the girl. Don't give him an excuse to take it out on her.**

Black Dog was right. "I'm sorry." He straightened enough that the girl's hand fell away. *Be strong. Think of her.* "You caught me by surprise. I've only had that happen once before, when what I got wasn't . . . pure."

"Oh, my cocktail's pure, but you wouldn't understand the chemistry behind it." Kramer nested the dismantled syringe back into purple velvet and closed the morocco case with a decisive snap. "Bring me what I want, and I assure you: if you wish, you may spend the rest of your life in an opium fog."

4

HERE WAS THE surprise: then, wreathed in the scent of lemons— and later, when he'd rejoined Battle in the asylum's vestibule and turned to find the girl watching him from the top of the asylum's wide marble staircase—Doyle wasn't sure he wanted that at all.

BODE

The Other Side of the Screen

1

"BOY!" THE CALL came from the asylum's vestibule. Half run off his feet, darting between the men's ward on second and the women's ward on first, Bode threw a glance down to find Battle, elbows akimbo, steel-gray bowler tipped back. "Could you see what's keeping my constable?" Battle called. "Haven't got all bloody night, you know."

"Yes, sir." Balls to that. *Not paid to be your errand boy.* "Right away."

Except it wasn't right away, because that quake hit, and he was a good long time putting patients back to rights before he remembered the inspector. *God.* Bode hurried for Kramer's office. *Probably already done with the constable.* But if word got back he'd not relayed Battle's message . . . he didn't need any more drama.

Kramer's door was ajar; the room, empty. A wool overcoat hung from a coat tree, along with a bloodstained jacket and vest. (Kramer was a prig, but all doctors worked in formal attire, dressed to the nines.) From the light of an oil lamp and what filtered in from the window, he could see that used instruments were still strewn atop a wood stand, though some had clattered to the floor; a curl of black thread looped through a needle's eye; and there was a basin half-filled with murky liquid, the remainder of which had slopped to the carpet.

He should've left right then and there. No Doyle meant that the constable was probably on his way back to the inspector at this moment. Besides, Tony and Rima would be here soon, and he had to make sure they got what victuals he'd squirreled away and none the wiser.

Yet he was curious. Something untoward had happened here. His eyes strayed over smashed crockery on the floor, an overturned cup. The quake? Probably, quite possibly, but still he couldn't shake the sense that there was a touch too much disarray.

Then his eyes fixed on the cart and those biscuits and that plate of sliced lemon and a whole one besides, all *begging* for a home—and he felt a talon tug his gut.

Walk away. Spit pooled under his tongue. A fast look over either shoulder showed him an empty hall. He toed the threshold. *Don't do it.*

But he did. Darting inside, he worked fast, cramming two biscuits into his mouth at the same time that he grubbed up a double handful for his pocket. As soon as he bit down, he nearly choked. The biscuits were tasteless and stale, like sand. No wonder they'd been left. He looked for a place to spit them but saw nothing. *Christ.* Maybe some lemon would help . . .

It should've registered before he even put the slice in his mouth. No scent, no tangy aroma. Too late, he remembered that the juice would burn his cut mouth something fierce, except it didn't. The lemon had all the taste and punch of poor water. His throat convulsed in a swallow. Could not eating well put you off your food, make everything taste bad? Unless the lemon had turned. Probably should leave the other one. *Biscuits are enough.* Well, presuming that they tasted better to Rima and Tony than him. He felt the hard knuckle of his mouthful of biscuit and lemon sliding slowly down the middle of his chest. *Nicking the lemon is so much butter on bacon.* Still, it *was* food, and Kramer was always going on about scurvy.

Pocketing the lemon, he thought, *All right, get out.* He would have, too, and maybe nothing else would've happened, except his gaze strayed back to Kramer's jacket and vest. He wasn't like Weber; he'd only ever stolen food. But his mouth throbbed from those nasty slaps, and his chest burned with the memory. A toff like Kramer probably had something nice. No watch chain he could see—no use anyway; nothing kept proper time—but maybe a nice penknife?

The jacket wasn't soiled, but the vest was crusted with dried blood. One pocket was empty, but the other showed the conspicuous bulge of something long. *Might be a knife, or a pen, a pencil.* Whatever it was, he suddenly just *wanted* it. Payback. Reaching into the pocket, he felt something angular . . . *metal* . . .

He'd just drawn out a pair of brass spectacles with queer purple lenses when his ears pricked to footsteps and then Kramer's angry, slithery hiss seeping through the open door: ". . . in my *office.*"

Shite, SHITE! He was so startled, his heart nearly rocketed out the top of his skull. Clutching the spectacles, he darted his gaze round the room, looking for a hiding place *anywhere.* God, God, Kramer would be here any second! Then his gaze hooked on the foot of the doctor's exam table, and that folding screen.

"You will explain," Kramer was saying, just as Bode scurried into a dark wedge between the screen's edge and a standing ward-robe. The smart clap of the office door made him wince. His heart was thumping. His knuckles tented white, and he forced himself to relax his grip on the spectacles. Ruin them and he was *really* cooked. Sweat crawled down his neck. If Kramer or who-ever was with him came around to this side, they'd spot him in an instant. But they shouldn't need to. He swept a frantic look over the exam table, which seemed to have been tidied up. No soiled sheets or bandages, only bare wood. All the mess seemed to be on the other side, so that was good.

Holding his breath, he reached a hand past his waistband to the inner pocket. At the slight *tick* of brass against Graves's iron skeleton, his lips skinned from his teeth in a tight, fearful gri-mace. *Damme* if that wasn't loud.

On the other side of the screen: "I'm waiting," Kramer said to someone. "Well?"

"I have already apologized. I know I was wrong"—and Bode thought, *Oh no.* "I do not know what else you want," Meme said.

"An idea of what possessed you?" There was a splash of liq-uid against porcelain and then the louder *chik* of a spoon. "Your complete lack of self-control?" A noisy inhalation as Kramer sucked tea. "You've taken a liking to the constable? Strange. Here I thought you were quite fond of Bode."

"You know I . . . I am fond of him," she said. "Though that does not mean the reverse is true. After today . . ."

"What, you think *Elizabeth* is competition? That was mis-placed chivalry." Kramer made a blustery, horsey sound. There was the tick of porcelain as Kramer replaced his cup and saucer. "Not only is she far above his station; she's *mad.*"

"She is also very beautiful."

"You are just as much the beauty. Perhaps you need to make your *interest* clear to the boy."

"I do not . . . I would not know where to begin."

"Do what comes naturally."

"Naturally?"

"Oh, for God's sake, you're a *girl*; he's a *boy*. You need me to draw you a damn diagram?" Kramer's tone was brutal. "Tell me, do you think about him? Of yourself with him? Of his *hands*, his *body*?"

God. Bode's ears weren't only burning; his entire head was going to spontaneously combust. Weber had been bad enough, but listening to this made him want to rinse his brain with carbolic acid. *Leave her alone, you sod.*

"Myself with . . ." The words came out small. "I . . . I do not understand."

"I mean *this*." Meme let out a sharp gasp, though from where he cowered, Bode couldn't see what Kramer was doing, and probably just as well. "Do you think of his hands on your breasts, his mouth on your neck, *your* hand on his—"

"Doctor!" Through that narrow gap between screen and wardrobe, Bode saw Meme bumble backward until she was stopped by a bookshelf and could go no further. All he could see of Kramer was the hand with which he cupped her left breast, and then Kramer himself moved in closer. "P-please, do n-not . . . ," Meme began.

"I'm talking *this*." With a fierce snarl, Kramer pressed one of Meme's hands to his trousers. "*Feel* that. That is the mark of a man. Do you think of Bode and *this*, and yourself lying with him in sweaty sheets?"

"No, no!" Though Meme wasn't shouting, Bode heard it

that way. Tears streaked her cheeks. "I do not *understand*."

"Yes, I *know*." Kramer said it as he might a curse. Releasing the weeping girl, he stepped out of Bode's line of sight. "*Missing* something, just as he *said* would happen."

"I do not know what you want from me," Meme said, and if he'd the balls he thought he did, this would be the moment Bode should burst out and do something. But the courage he'd felt with and for Elizabeth didn't translate to Meme. *What's wrong with you?* Shame surged in his chest. *You could help.* But show himself now, what was the point? *Talking yourself out of it, you coward.* Weber was right; he *was* a meater.

"I do everything you ask. I work for you. I *lie* for you," she said.

"Nonsense. No one's asked you to lie. We've simply omitted. Here." Through the slit, Bode saw Kramer's fingers, from which dangled a kerchief. "Blow your nose."

"No." Meme put up a warding hand. "I do not wish to."

"Fine, then smear snot all over your blouse if you've a mind. At least that would show some *spark*."

"Is it not that which angers you? My *spark*? What I did with Doyle?"

"There's a time and place. But since we're on the subject . . . yes, what you *did* could've been ruinous. What was that? Whatever possessed you to *defy* me for someone like Doyle? Don't delude yourself: addicts are *not* to be trusted. Pity him all you want, but he's not a baby bird fallen from his nest for you to rescue."

"I told you." Turning aside, Meme drew a hand over streaming eyes, a curiously childlike gesture that made Bode's shame all the worse. "I felt *sorry* for him." She was facing his way now.

"The way you badgered and humiliated . . ."

That was when Meme looked up and through the gap, and their eyes met.

2

BODE'S HEART SKIPPED a beat. His guts iced. On the other side of the screen, Meme's dark blue eyes shimmered even as her face stilled. They stared at each other for a long beat and then two, and Bode had time to think that if it had been anyone else, he'd have been out the door, on his ear, in the snow so fast your head would spin. A complex welter of emotions seemed to cross her face, though he doubted Kramer could see. His own emotions were much simpler; he was terrified.

"Humiliated him." Straightening, Meme turned away from Bode. "The way you humiliated me just now. What I think of Bode or any boy—"

"But you don't, do you?" Kramer's tone was flat.

"That is my own affair. Is that not correct?"

"Perhaps." Pause. "You felt something, though, didn't you? Just now? When we were talking of that young buck?"

"Is that the point? For me to feel something for Bode? Or are you speaking now of Doyle? Because you also hurt *him*."

"I already told you. That injection was for his own good."

"Really. I thought it was all part of your experiment."

"Do not bait me. You know that this work is necessary. That serum will strip him of artifice. Think of him as an onion, and now I shall peel back layers until what passes for his essence reveals itself."

"It was not right to trick him."

"Who said anything about subterfuge? He got his precious drugs—"

"And *your* serum. What's in it?"

"What, you want a blow-by-blow chemical breakdown? The formula? And what will that tell you, eh? The specific composition is unimportant. What is more, of all people, you are the *least* equipped to understand what I'm after."

"And what is that?"

"I told him. I told you. I am after . . . clarity, his essence. A clean slate. I want Doyle freed of what little memory he may possess, and illusion. A tabula rasa, if you like, upon which I might write something new . . . no, more than that: I want to *restore* what's been denied us, what *we* lack."

"Lack? Write something new? Doctor, he is a person, not paper you scrape with a knife when you have made a mistake."

"No, you see, *that* is just it. The serum will rid him of mistakes."

"Mistakes? What kind? And then what? You remake him? Give him a new personality?"

"No." A pause. "Something much more specific than that . . . No, don't ask me to explain. You truly wouldn't understand. It would all seem quite foreign, words spoken in an unknown tongue. To be frank, I'm not sure I really have a grasp of it myself, but I will know it when I see it."

"But how will manipulating Constable Doyle help us? Why make the constable steal those—"

"Enough." Kramer made an impatient sound. "You are my assistant, yes, but I do not owe you an explanation for every single move I make. I know what I'm doing, and you are not to question me and most certainly *not* indulge in ridiculous, ruinous outbursts. Do you think it's wise to call me to task for *lying* in front of a bloody *constable*?"

"Then why have you?" If Bode had been in her shoes, he'd be pissing his drawers. How could she be weeping one moment and so calm the next? Why hadn't she turned him in? *Because she cares for me?* "You lied to Battle's face," she said. "You know where McDermott is."

"A man like Battle will never understand what's at stake, that I do what I *must* to try and save us. I am doing this to save *you*, Meme, though you do not seem to see this at all. My God, girl . . . you are unique amongst us, my pearl without price."

"Unique? A pearl? I do not understand what you mean."

"Yes." Kramer sounded suddenly tired. "I know you don't. But I think we are very close to the moment when you *will*. That constable will be our control subject."

"Say that you can do what you want: erase what he is and then . . . make him again, or whatever you've in mind. Can you reverse the process?"

"Perhaps. But he might not wish that. In fact, if this works, he might consider that I've done him a great service. I will repair this world, Meme, no matter the cost or sacrifice. Now, are we quite finished with your interrogation?"

"Not to be contrary, but you called me, sir," Meme said, and Bode thought she *did* have balls. "But I do have one more question. Earlier . . . why did you call Elizabeth by a different name?"

"What?" Kramer's imperious note seemed to waver. "What the devil are you going on about?"

"You called her *Emma*." She said it in a straightforward way, without a hint of accusation or guile. "Please do not deny it. I heard you."

Wait, Emma? *From the dream?* Bode's pulse gave a little kick.

"You misheard," Kramer said.

"No, I did not." A beat of silence, and then Bode heard what he thought was a new, shrewder note: "No one else did, if that worries you, sir. Bode was well behind me. I know he did not catch it."

"I am *not* concerned," Kramer said. "*If* I said that, it was a slip of the tongue."

"I do not believe that is true either, sir."

"You call me a liar? You are my creature. Mind your place!"

"And I do, sir. I would have discounted it as well, if that boy down below, the one arrived today, had not called me by the same name."

"What?" Kramer's tone was sharp. "He *did*?"

"Yes, sir. He was quite emphatic."

"What about the other? Did he?"

"No. But they both talk about a . . . a *dream*." She said the word as if uncertain how to move her mouth around the letters. "They compare notes and common threads about some . . . about a very bad dream, what they call a . . . a *nightmare*?"

What? Bode's focus sharpened. *Others have had the same dream?* He wondered who these other two boys could be, and where they were. In an asylum as large as this, Bode didn't keep track of every admission and certainly had no idea who every single patient was. What was *down below*? Did Meme mean the padded cells?

"I was not sure what those boys were going on about," Meme said.

"What about *them*? Have *they* spoken of this same phenomenon, this night—" Like Meme, Kramer's mouth seemed to examine the word before letting it go. "This nightmare?"

Them? The way Kramer said the word, Bode thought these other patients must be very different. Special? Patients whose care he entrusted only to a chosen few, like Meme? *Probably held beneath the asylum somewhere, and if they're dreaming, had the same nightmare, are we all connected somehow to Elizabeth? To each other?*

"No, *they* have not. Although I believe *he* understands what the boys are talking about. I can see it in his face, and that he is very keen on hearing more. His wife only seems . . ." Meme stopped short at a knock.

"Blast," Kramer muttered. To Meme: "Not a damned word about any of *them*, all right?" Then, more loudly, "Yes?" When the door opened: "Yes, Mrs. Graves, what is it?"

"I apologize for the intrusion." Graves said it with all the mealymouthed sincerity of a parliamentarian. Bode could imagine her curiously peering down the parish pickax of that nose, first at Meme, who now stood with her back to Bode, and then Kramer. "But I've word from the gatehouse that the rats are here, and I can't locate Bode, sir, and I'm short-staffed and—"

"*So?* Have Weber meet them then."

"Well, I can't do that, sir. Mr. Connell confined him to his rooms and—"

Kramer cut her off with a blue string of curses, quite a few of which Bode hadn't heard, and being a foundling, he'd heard *plenty*. Running down, Kramer shouted, "I don't bloody care if he's in bed, pulling his bloody *pudding*, you get Weber this instant!"

"I . . . I . . . I . . ." Bode could imagine Graves opening and shutting her mouth like a flounder. If he hadn't been so spooked, he might really have enjoyed this moment. Graves finally managed, "It's not my place, sir, to drag Mr. Weber out of his bed, and most especially if he is engaged in, as you say so euphemistically, pulling his *pudding*."

"Then send someone else! Send a man!"

"That's why I've come, sir. Since I can't locate Bode and the others are all occupied—"

"God*damn*! Very well. Meme, clear this mess while I'm gone. Come along, Mrs. Graves, and let us track down the elusive Bode."

3

A FEW SECONDS passed, during which time Kramer's voice receded, then disappeared. Then Meme's voice reached him from beyond the screen. "You can come out now."

Cheeks burning, he did. "Meme." He wasn't sure what to say next. *Thank you? I'm sorry? I wish I'd not heard any of that? Why do you let him treat you that way?* He surprised himself. "I should've helped you, done something."

"Absurd." Her face was an unreadable mask, those dark eyes so like sockets it was like looking at a beautiful stone statue. "I am not Elizabeth. You would have been a fool to interfere."

"But if he'd"—*tried to have his way with you, gone further*—"I would have."

"If that makes you feel better." When he opened his mouth to reply, she shook her head. "You need to go. They will be down a floor by now. You can say you were on the incurables ward." She turned aside. "Anyway, I have a mess to clean."

"Meme," he began . . . and then left it. What was there to say? Only when he turned to go did he remember the damned glasses still tucked in his secret inner pocket. *Leave them go for the time being.* He'd sneak them back later. For now, he had enough problems.

DOYLE

Bricky

"SEE THOSE HAIRLINE fissures?" Battle tilted his head at a column supporting Bethlem's stone pediment. "A few more strong quakes and this building comes down."

"Yes, sir." Thinking, *Oh, can't you shut yer yap for five minutes, ya nob?* He was irritable, on edge, though all should have been right with the world. After stitching Doyle's wound, Kramer had Meme give him two cups of very strong, very sweet tea laced with something to settle his bowels, and several biscuits. As a result, Doyle's guts had ceased yammering; his belly was full, and he'd had a powerfully satisfying shit.

It was the girl that bothered him. He wondered if she'd be all right. Hadn't liked when Kramer hit her. *Shoulda done something.* What he really wanted was to chuck it all and go back there, knock Kramer in the teeth, and take that girl away.

Bricky Sir Lancelot. He tightened the strap of his constable's helmet until his tongue mashed against the roof of his mouth. *As if I'm such a prize.*

"Doyle." Battle gestured at thigh-high drifts along the drive that led to the Lambeth Road gatehouse. "Be a good man and blaze our way, would you?"

I've an idea: whyn't you take that bull's-eye of yours and blaze a trail up ya bunghole, ya mutton-shunter? "Oh yes, sir. Right away." Strapping his own lantern to his belt, Doyle slid back the shade. A beam of fuzzy yellow light punched the gloom, illuminating slants of falling snow. As he broke trail, snow immediately worked its way into his heavy police-issue boots and began to melt into his socks. *Oh, I hope someone commits a crime.* He bent against cuts of wind that hacked his cheeks. Icy grit pecked his eyes. *Give me an excuse to be off and leave this nob.*

Now, now. Black Dog chuffed its strange hound's laugh. **Contain yourself, darling. If you're determined to do as that doctor wishes, you need Battle.**

He didn't bother with a reply. Of *course*, he knew that. But oh, what he wouldn't give to allow his tongue free rein, say whatever popped out, duty—and *Kramer* and *Battle* and *all* of them—be damned.

"Oh, good God, would you look at that?" The inspector lifted his chin to point toward the guardhouse. "Shall we lend a hand, Doyle?"

Ahead, Doyle saw that at the entrance gate immediately adjacent to the guardhouse, a pushcart blocked the way, having sunk under its own weight. The cart now listed to the right at such an acute angle that several burlap sacks had slithered to the snow. A few had split to spill their contents. One of the two . . . men? boys? . . . he couldn't tell—one must have taken a fit or fallen, because he lay in the snow, his back resting against a wheel, while his companion crouched by his side. A smaller figure hovered uncertainly by the cart. A few feet away, the asylum guard only stood at the threshold of his gatehouse, lantern in hand. He made no move toward the cart at all. Considering what was in those sacks, Doyle wouldn't have been eager to lend a hand either, if not for Battle.

Oh, bloody excellent. "Of course, sir." He'd learned: when a superior says *we*, he really means *you*. Jogging up to the cart, he called, "Police. Do you need help?"

"Oh," said the one boy still on his feet, and that was when Doyle realized that he was looking down into the gaunt, hollow-eyed visage of a girl. Backhanding a coil of honey-blonde curls that had come loose of her green muffler, she tried to fix a smile on blue lips that trembled. "Thank you, yes, a little." She cast a dismal look at her strewn cargo. "I guess we didn't stack them very well and then that earthquake . . ." A helpless look at her companion. "He slipped," she said, then added, quickly, "It's not rot, I swear."

"Stop fussing. I'm fine," said the boy, who looked to be the same age and equally thin, with a fringe of kinky brown hair showing beneath a fraying wool cap. He daubed the back of a hand at a rivulet of black blood oozing from a nostril. "A little dizzy, that's all. I'll be . . . *No.*" Cringing, he warded the girl off. "*Don't* touch me."

"Here, she doesn't mean any harm, I'm sure." Doyle frowned. "I think she only wants to help." He cast a glance at the smaller figure and now saw that it was a much younger girl. From her size, he thought she might be . . . ten? Twelve? Dark eyes wide above a thick shawl, the girl hadn't opened her mouth or moved a muscle. Well, judging from that large, rough plaster on her chin, probably got herself a nasty gash there. Perhaps the little girl had already been knocked about enough, and knew to hold her tongue.

"Begging your pardon, Constable, but what do you know about anything?" Working his jaw, the boy hawked up a foamy gobbet that glimmered a dark purple in lantern light. "All of you," he said, breathlessly, "can't you leave me be a moment?"

"Tony," the girl began, as Doyle, suddenly alarmed, backed up a step and said, "Just a moment, are you *certain* he doesn't—"

"Oi!" At the sight of the boy's bloody spittle, the asylum guard suddenly came alive and brandished a stout club. "I knew it, I *knew* it! You got the rot, boy, doncha? You turn round right now, march yourself—"

"I don't have rot." The boy gestured at the sacks on the snow. "And look for yourself: none of those sacks is marked with a red *X*. We don't truck in infected."

"*I'm* not checking those." The guard waggled the club. "Go off with you now."

"No, *please*," the older girl said. "He's telling the truth. Tony doesn't have rot, just a bad cough, and the sacks are safe. Please, let us pass so we can collect—"

"The only things you're *collecting* are these dead 'uns and taking them and your arses off asylum property," the guard fumed. "No *cough* or *cold* makes a boy *that* sick."

"It does if you're *starving*," the girl said fiercely. She gave the guard's belly a pointed glare. "Of course, *you* wouldn't know much about that, would you?"

"Leave it, Rima," said the boy, Tony.

The guard drew himself up. "Listen, ya little dollymop, don't you be mafficking with—"

"Oh, shut your yap, man." It was Battle. "Can't you see the poor boy's thin as kindling? If you're too much the coward to check for squirmers, I'll do it." Ignoring the spluttering guard,

Battle unbuckled his bull's-eye lantern and crouched.

"Mind your face, sir." Doyle shifted his weight as Battle fished out a telescoping pencil. Nothing was worth risking a squirmer drilling its way through your eye. The only bright side: if a squirmer started munching away at the inspector, that certainly solved the problem of going around the man for what Kramer fancied. He held his breath, ready to run.

"Nothing." Battle gave the mess a thorough stir. "Not a single squirmer." Stabbing his pencil into snow to clean it, Battle butted the silver case to size and looked up at the guard. "Put that club down, man. The sooner we put this cart to rights, the faster they can be on their way, and so may we."

"It's not *my* place," the guard grumbled. Taking himself back to his gatehouse, the man folded his arms over the hump of his belly. "I got my duties, and they *don't* include lending a hand to no rats."

Ignoring the guard, Tony said to Battle, "It's all right, sir. We can manage. We didn't mean to cause trouble."

"And you haven't. Up you go." Offering his hand, Battle helped the boy stagger to his feet, then bent to rummage in churned snow behind a wheel. "Hold on. Don't imagine you'd want to leave this behind," he said, coming up with a smaller sack. "You know this drawstring's no good. Gaping wide open."

As Battle gave the sack an experimental bounce, the youngest girl, the one with the plaster over her chin, let out a sudden, small, mousy sound. Doyle saw that her eyes had gone so wide they looked like holes in a white sheet. "Is she all right?" Doyle asked.

"Oh yes." The older girl, Rima, dropped a hand on the girl's shoulder. It might have been a trick of the light, but Doyle could've sworn Rima's fingers dug in the little girl's arm, as if in warning. "She's fine."

"Thank you for fishing out that sack, sir." The boy made a move to take the burlap sack from Battle but stopped short as the inspector pulled open the bag.

"What you got in here?" Battle said, peering inside. "Victuals?"

"Uh . . . you know, nothing special," Tony said, tucking his hands in his coat. "The usual."

Oh yeah? Doyle watched the boy fidget. *Musta stolen something. Bad luck, running into the police.*

"That so?" Frowning into the sack, the inspector paused, then said, "This is all you've got to eat? A morsel of bread, a scrap of cheese?"

"Uh . . ." The boy blinked, as if this was something he hadn't expected Battle to say. A look of surprise spread over his face. "Yes, sir."

"Well, you'll need more than that. A good drawstring would do, for starters." Cupping the bottom with a massive hand, Battle handed the sack over with some care. "Do be cautious. If that's all you've got to last the day, you wouldn't want that bag to grow legs."

"No, sir." The boy quickly but carefully tucked the sack into a corner of his cart. "Thank you."

"Indeed. Well, let's get you loaded and on your way." Battle turned to Doyle. "Don't just stand there, Constable. Snap to."

"Yes, sir." *Oh, thank you so very much.* He threw a look at a long sack draped over the snow. The bony twig of a leg and bare foot protruded from a split seam. *A trio of rats moving dead meat . . . just the topper of a perfect day.* He snapped his fingers at the younger girl. "You there. Come over, give me a hand here." When she only stood, he said, "What's wrong with you? You soft?"

"Constable," Battle began.

"Never mind about her." It was the older girl, Rima, the one with the honey-blonde hair. She came to stand between Doyle and the younger girl. "We've only just taken her in. She's mute. I'll see to her. Come on." Rima steered the girl away. As they passed, the younger girl's eyes jumped like scared little rabbits from Doyle to the snow. "Mind where you're going," Rima said, though she didn't sound cross. "You stay by me. I'll put what bodies have spilt back in, and then you sew."

By the cart, Battle said to the boy, "You don't think you're a touch overloaded?"

"No." Arming blood from his lips, Tony trudged to a sack from which an arm spilled. When he bent, Doyle caught the yellow glint of steel from an enormous blade secured to the boy's waist by a leather strap. Damn if that boy's chopper wasn't as long as a dirk. "They're really not all that heavy," Tony said as he inspected a long tear. "We try to stick to them that's no more'n bones. Easier that way, what with us two. Well . . ." He glanced at the mute girl, who'd hunkered down next to Rima. "Three now."

"Perhaps." Frowning, Battle fished out a long spiked tool Doyle recognized and touched a gloved finger to a thick iron hook with a downward curve. "What is this?"

"It's a pike, sir," Doyle said. "We used 'em for rolling seals, hooking slabs of whale blubber. Sometimes the odd, very large fish."

"Yeah, we got two," Tony said. "Easier than your bare hands."

"Really?" How was it Battle managed to sound both surprised and suspicious? "Refresh my memory, Constable, I forget: how many years at sea were you?"

"Only the one, sir. Right afore I came down to London.

Shipped out of Peterhead." God, he hoped that was what he'd put down on his application.

"Fascinating." Slipping the pike back onto the flatbed, Battle said to the boy, "Let's try repositioning, shall we? With your permission?" When Tony waved his hand, *be my guest*, Battle took hold of a corpse that was a touch longer than its neighbor and hefted it as easily as a broomstick.

"Come here now," Rima said to the mute. The older girl was crouched over a sack from which the entire upper half of a woman, mouth agape, had slithered like a limp flounder. Crossing the corpse's arms over deflated bags that had once been breasts, the girl used one hand and a boot to keep the body from moving as she tugged at the burlap the wind kept snatching from her free hand. At the mute's stricken expression, Rima clucked. "She's *dead*. Can't do you no harm."

Doyle, come on. "Let me," he said, hanging his bull's-eye from a cart handle and then stooping to take hold of the corpse. The dead woman's skin was colder than marble, her eyes sunken, milky pellets. "You work the burlap, all right? Careful, it's quite worn."

"Yeah, most people can't be bothered to patch them. No one wants a corpse hanging round long, rot or not." Pulling a roll of string from one pocket, Tony threaded two large needles he'd stuck through the lapel of his thin coat, then handed a needle to both girls. "You sew, too, Rima. These bodies are too heavy for you."

Yes, and you're the one spitting up blood. Still, he half-admired this Tony, the way he looked out for the girls. Brother? Or perhaps he fancied himself Rima's lover? "Let me," Doyle said. He saw that Battle had already hoisted a sack to a shoulder. Bending over another body, Doyle looked at Rima. "You're sure there are no rotters."

"We don't traffic in rotters." Rima was sawing at the twine with her teeth. By her side, the mute was busily throwing in large, looping stitches to seal a rip. "But it's not worth the risk."

Rima looked like a savage, working away with her teeth like that. Doyle reached for his *sgian-dubh*. "Here. Use this."

"Oh. Thank you," she said, as her hand closed over the stag-horn handle. "That's very . . ." Eyes snapping wide, Rima started. The knife tumbled from her hand, and she actually jerked her head to one side as if to avoid a slap.

"Ah . . ." The mute's mouth snapped shut as color flooded her cheeks.

"I'm all right." Rima patted the girl's hand, though her voice quaked. "I'm fine, it's fine."

"Are you sure?" What was wrong with her? Her cheeks were so pale, her eyes were holes. Retrieving his knife, Doyle asked, "Are you hurt?"

"N-no." She pressed red, rawboned fingers to her lips. "Just a . . . it's nothing." Waving away his knife, she fished her twine and needle from her lap where they'd fallen. "No, thank you, Constable, but there's nothing I need so much it's worth *that*."

2

WHAT THE DEVIL *was that about?* By the time they were done, the slash on his right arm was beginning to sting. Whatever sense of well-being he'd felt after Kramer's injection had fizzled. *But I still feel quite strong.*

"Thank you." Tucking a curl the wind tried snatching away behind one ear, Rima worked at knotting a rough knit shawl under the mute girl's chin with stiff, chapped fingers. When she saw Doyle looking, she mustered a crooked smile. "Been out for hours. You get accustomed to it."

"Where are your gloves?" It was not what he'd planned on saying. For an instant, he'd had the insane urge to tie that poor mute's silly shawl himself. "Can't you . . ." He made a vague gesture at the cart.

"If there are any." Blowing on her fingers, Rima said, "Most are already stripped. The ones that ain't, the clothes are so soiled you don't really want them if you've a choice. Although you never get used to any of it, know what I mean? The bodies? Stripped or not? They're . . . eerie."

"I'd worry they'd open their eyes," he said, wondering where that came from.

"So do I." Her gaze slid to one side. "Couple times I've thought the sacks might be moving. You know, that they're come back from the dead for their revenge?" She stopped, a flush of embarrassment creeping up her jaw. "Stupid talk," she said, placing a hand over a cheek. The gesture was oddly childlike, something a little girl would do to comfort herself at night when she finds herself alone with ghosts. "It's all right."

No, it's really not. Rima was so small. Not delicate; this wasn't a girl from a romance novel. But she was thin and not very tall. "Have you et today?" Before she could answer, he was reaching into his coat.

Poppet? Black Dog had been so quiet, Doyle near about jumped out of his skin. He felt the hound give his mind a curious sniff. **What are you doing? First Meme, and now this girl?**

He'd no idea. "It's toffee." Withdrawing that paper packet, he held it out. "Only four pieces, but they're real cream and butter.

Go on. Take it." He reached to his hip for his sack of peppermints. "I've humbugs, too."

The mute moved as if to take the parcel, but Rima pushed the other girl's hand away. "No," she said, roughly. Her dark blue eyes glistered. "He wants something. Isn't that right? An exchange, a little barter?" Rima's tone was flat and much harder. "You think I'm some tuppenny upright? Because that's all I've got. I've no family, no trade. It's just me and Tony and this girl. I've nothing else to barter for it."

"What?" *Doyle, you idiot.* Of course she would think that. "No, no. I don't want anything. I just et, really. Tea and biscuits and real sugar, a few slices of lemon." He was babbling. *You're pathetic, Doyle. What, you'll save this girl with a nice sweet? You really want to help, you'll put a bullet into her brain, another into that boy and the mute, and save the last for yourself.* Embarrassed, he proffered the packets. The wind whipped, lashing a coil of aromas: butter and sugar and sharp peppermint. "You and this poor girl and your . . . your brother? You look as if you need them far more."

"Tony's not my brother." He could see the warring emotions chasing over her taut features. "We grew up together, that's all."

"Ah." There were any number of reasons why. He chose the safest, hoping he might be saying something right for a change. "An orphanage?"

She nodded. "Foundling Hospital. Coram . . . you know, near Gray's Inn. Tony and me and a boy works here."

"Works here . . . you mean, Bode?" He remembered Kramer thrashing the boy, calling him an ungrateful foundling. "Met him. Seems a good sort."

"He is. We're all chuckaboos . . . you know, family. Got out of Coram's soon as we were old enough. Fog was well north then, but when it made it as far as Crouch End, we took ourselves back and across the Thames. We kept wondering if we ought to go further, only we've heard the way's blocked." Ducking her face, she swallowed. "I don't know why I'm telling you this."

"It's all right. I'm glad you have. Look here . . . wouldn't you like a sweet? Or the little girl here? I don't know any child doesn't like a humbug. Here, if it makes you feel better." Tucking the toffees under an arm, he shook out a small number of peppermints that he pocketed. "There," he said, resealing the parcel. "Now I've some of my own. Better?"

"A little." Rima smiled. The younger girl was transfixed. Doyle wouldn't have been surprised if she started slavering like a dog. "Much, in fact. All right, thank you."

When he handed over the parcels, her chilled fingertips lightly brushed his own. At her touch, he felt a little shock, like the sort of spark that scuffing wool stockings over a silk carpet might produce if you grabbed a brass knob. Before he could process that, he felt something . . . *whisk* away, as if his entire body had suddenly exhaled a steamy breath. Something actually *left*— and in his center, right in that black terrible place where the claw of his need always raked first, he felt the knot of his heart loosen.

"Sorry!" He tried turning his gasp into a weak laugh and only came out sounding bewildered. "I must . . . I'm sorry. A little . . ." He pressed a hand to his chest. "Dizzy."

"Yes." Her skin was glassy, and her voice nearly transparent, more air than sound. Eyes shimmering, she slicked her lips. "Constable? Are you . . ." Her voice dropped out as the ground suddenly stuttered.

Good God. Doyle gasped as the jolt, swift and sharp, rippled through snow and into his bones. "Hold on!" Swaying, Doyle managed a snatch, hooking Rima's left elbow. With his left hand, he grabbed onto the mute and reeled her in. As soon as he touched Rima, that same *whisking* sensation swept him again, but he was too surprised by the rumble of the earth to pay it as much attention. Drawing both girls to his chest, he set his feet against the bucking snow. Driving up from deep underground, vibrations rattled through his boots and into his hips. Through the guardhouse window, he saw the stout guard actually tumble out of sight. A flash of bright orange fired the window and died fast as the guard's oil lamp guttered. Platters of snow skated off the guardhouse roof to hit the ground with dull thuds. A portion of the supporting brickwork along the base of the asylum's front gate grumbled with a series of pops and hollow bangs as stone, under too much pressure, ruptured.

"The gate!" Battle cried. Having stumbled back, the inspector was now braced against the rickety, squealing cart upon which their two bull's-eyes, dangling from the cart's handles, danced and threw wild yellow arcs. Tony was skittering like a nob of butter on a hot skillet, and perilously close to the gate. There came a long, high-pitched groan of fatigued metal as, less than ten feet away, the gate's iron supports began to buckle.

Rima cried out, "Tony! Look out!"

"Watch it!" Launching himself from the cart, the inspector barreled into the boy, knocking him just as there was a large, loud crack of metal. An iron spear shot over snow, its point burying itself not two feet from where the boy and Battle sprawled. If Battle hadn't shoved Tony aside, the boy would have been impaled.

There was another gigantic jolt, like the last kick of an exhausted child—and then the shivering stopped as suddenly as it had begun.

3

FOR A MOMENT, everything stilled. Doyle stood hunched, his arms clasped tight around the girls. "Are you all right?" His voice was a stranger's. "Are you injured?"

"No, but . . ." Through his own harsh breaths, the girl's voice seemed thin and very far away. The mute was white as bone china. "You're . . . you're hurting me."

"Oh." Embarrassed, he loosened his grip and shambled back an uncertain step. Catching his heel in a clot of dislodged snow, he swayed and would've fallen if the girl hadn't grabbed his coat. "Thank you," he said, then tried a laugh that came out as raucous as a Tower raven. "And here I thought to save you. Are you all right?"

"Yes." Rima looked a question at the mute, who nodded. Then she turned and called, "Tony?"

"He's fine." Caked with clots of snow, Battle looked like a mummy breaking out of its wrappings. "Making a habit of this," he said, pulling Tony upright. "Not hurt?"

"No, but . . ." His eyes widened when he saw that broken iron arrow jutting from the snow. "We'd have been kebabs."

Beyond the now-teetering front gates, Doyle caught the clamor of the ever-constant crowd. The note was higher, and frightened, a gabble. Somewhere far to his left along Lambeth Road, there came a growling rumble of stone against stone.

"What is that?" Rima put a comforting arm around the mute, who cringed into her. "Is it happening again?"

Battle shook his head. "Sounds like a wall collapsing, or perhaps a tenement."

The rumbling subsided. In its wake came shrill stiletto notes of surprise and fear. With the thick swirling snow, it was impossible to tell exactly where the collapse might be. Doyle hoped Battle wouldn't succumb to a burst of civic-mindedness. If another tremor struck, the last thing he wanted was to be clambering around rumble, searching for survivors. On the other hand, his own rooms were on the second floor; if the police barracks came down in another shock, all they'd find of him would be a blood smear and squashed guts.

"Rima!" Tony stood by their cart. "We should go. Don't want to get ourselves caught out in another of those."

Battle retrieved their bull's-eyes. "Maybe you should leave off for the day."

"Can't." Stumping around to the head of his cart, the boy ducked under the traces of an ox's harness. "And we're here now," he said, seating the leather collar and straps over his shoulders. "If that happens again, we're safer in the open anyway."

Doyle couldn't argue that. As both girls started off, he said to Rima, "Do be careful."

"As we can be. Thank you for . . ." She gestured with the packets. "Constable . . . ?"

"Doyle." Then blurted, "Where are you staying? At the gasworks near Battersea?" She must; the Battersea furnaces were the only ones still in operation. When she nodded, he said, "I'm at Lambeth Station, you need anything." *Need anything? Doyle, what are you thinking?* If his performance with Meme was any indication, he could barely care for himself. Still, it felt good to say it to her. "Anything," he said again. "Whatever you need, I'll help."

"Oh, Constable." She gave him a direct look. "I think we're all of us past help, don't you?"

RIMA

Watcher

1

THE QUAKE HAD split the snowpack into wide fissures that made the going even rougher. Tony concentrated on picking a stable path past the row of doctors' houses that were now so many faint smears of light only just visible through the snow. They'd just begun to skirt the front steps to walk along the asylum's west wing when Tony paused and craned a look back. "You girls all right?"

"Are you kidding?" Their "mute" let out something halfway between a shaky laugh and a grunt. "An *earthquake*? In England? I didn't know you guys even *had* them. And then the sacks sliding off, the *bodies*, we had to actually *touch* them, and we can't even wash our hands or anything? You know how *gross* that is? Does this happen a lot?"

"First I can remember," Rima said, and felt a tiny tickle of disquiet. How many actual *days* doing *this*—going about their rounds, collecting bodies—did she really recall? Nothing firmed in her mind.

"What about the police? Could we have gotten in trouble?"

"Only if you'd not kept your mouth shut," Tony said. "That constable upset you?"

"*Yes*. He was really *weird*. Like, he was all *over* you, Rima." The girl suddenly scowled. "And what was all that *crap* about me being, you know . . . *soft*? Like retarded or something? Don't you guys know how insulting that is?"

After a short pause, Tony said, mildly, "You know, I do believe I fancied her more when she was mute."

2

FIRST, IT HAD been a shock: not just how she'd appeared, or how the Peculiar had lifted and the snow begun as soon as the girl was spat out, but her name: *Emma*. A name from the nightmare. Except *that* Emma hadn't been a girl of twelve. Yet the eyes were the same, an exact match. So this was *another* Emma, just as they'd seen another Tony, Rima, Bode? For all their questions, there were no answers, and the frightened, confused girl knew even less. So then it had become a dilemma of what to do next.

"I don't think we've any choice," Tony said. "We had the dream and now she's here. Don't tell me it's a coincidence, because we both know better. Thank goodness you were there, though. Those clothes . . . what she called them . . . *shorts*? A *tea* shirt? Whatsat mean? It's woven of tea leaves?" He frowned. "I've seen men in bathing costumes with better cover. She'd have frozen to death in minutes. Frankly, if you hadn't seen it all yourself, anyone else would think she'd escaped from Bedlam. Her story's mad."

We're all mad here. Apt, considering. They were on the retort's first floor, and Rima glanced toward a far corner, where they'd tucked the girl until they decided what to do. Curled in a nest of burlap, the girl was asleep. Nestled against her back, the cat was watching. *That cat . . . maybe it'll vanish and leave only a grin behind.*

She looked back at Tony. "Fine, we take care of her, but to what end? Why *not* try our luck with the Peculiar? She's proof that it's possible to traverse it and come out somewhere else. So perhaps she can get herself back to this *Wis . . . Wisconsin?*" Bizarre name; she'd never heard of the place. "Or show us how it's done, and then we can leave here." When he shook his head, she pressed, "But Tony, she knows *nothing* about any of this: not the Peculiar, the squirmers, rotters. Why *not* go?"

"I thought of that, but there are a couple problems, and you know it." He began ticking off the items on his fingers. "First off, she didn't mean to end up here. She plunged through this . . . this *door*. Who knows if it's even open on her end anymore? I don't get the sense that she understands what she did or how to do it again. Second, I think we'd have heard about any other people popping from the Peculiar, don't you? And third, no one's ever gone into the Peculiar and come back."

"Who would want to come back to this?"

"You're missing the point. With no idea of what we're doing, we're just as likely to end up . . . well, wherever people end up when the Peculiar swallows them. And there's another thing: that woman with the glasses. Emma's story of the window's like what I saw with that other Tony and that mirror in my dream. What if the Peculiar is how that woman gets round? You want to run into *her* or more of her kind?"

"So what do we do?"

"What we've always done. We make our rounds tomorrow."

"What about Emma?"

"I don't see a choice but to take her with us, keep her close, unless you've a better idea. If we don't, someone's bound to wonder who she is, why she's not going out. She opens her mouth, jig's up. Besides, once people start getting back with their loads and she sees bodies going down a chute and into the furnace . . ."

"All right, all right." He had a point. She only dreaded having to explain. Privately, she was also worried about the cat. Someone was sure to make stew of it before the day was out. "For how long?"

"Given our dreams? How I feel?" Tony let go of a weary sigh. "Something's going to break, Rima, and soon. Only a matter of time."

Just so long as it's not you. Yet from what the girl had said, and given what Rima had gleaned when she'd touched Tony's mind, she thought it was only a matter of time before that woman came looking. When that happened, the woman with the purple eyes would find yet *another* Tony, a boy she'd *already* stolen in a nightmare.

And what of *her* Tony then?

3

NOW, SHE SAID to Emma, "I agree. Doyle's . . . odd."

"Was it the knife, or when he touched you?" An instant later, Tony recognized his mistake and made a face. "Sorry."

"What about the knife?" Emma looked from Tony to Rima and back again. When Tony hesitated, she put her hands on her hips. "Come on, you guys, I told *you*."

"Cat's out of the bag." And then Tony gave a startled little laugh when Jack suddenly poked his head from the small sack in which Battle had been so interested. "Ooof, when that Battle started rummaging around, I nearly had heart failure. Thought for sure he'd say something. Decent sort not to. All we need is more attention."

"Actually, I thought that cat transformed himself into the Cheshire," Rima said as Emma ruffled Jack's ears. She couldn't decide who was grinning more, Emma or the cat.

"He kind of does that," Emma said. "Up and disappears. Sometimes it happens so fast, like he can be *right there* and then *poof*, it's like he's found a secret door or something only cats can see."

"Never had a cat except in stew," Tony said. "So I can't comment."

"Gross," Emma said, though it sounded more like a reflex. Her tone had turned contemplative. "It *is* weird, how he does that. Jasper, my guardian, says Jack goes on walkabouts and not to worry, that he'll find his way back. There's this song . . . *Oh, the cat came back, we thought he was a goner, yes, the cat came back* . . . da-dee-da-dee-da-deedee." She shrugged. "I don't remember the rest."

"*The very next day*," Rima sang, then felt her forehead crease. "How do I know that?"

"Jasper said it's kind of an old song."

"I don't think I've ever heard it either . . . but that's odd." Tony's face held a bemused expression. "In the song, don't the cat drop dead and its ghost come back?"

"Yeah." Emma's eyebrows arched in surprise. "You sure you don't know it?"

"Positive," Rima and Tony said at the same time, and then Tony said, fast, "Jinx. There." Reaching back, he gave her arm a light pinch. "Got ya."

"Next time," Rima said, wondering why her throat was suddenly so tight. *Maybe because it's been forever since we've joked or had some fun.* Running a hand along the cat's spine, she smiled when it licked her thumb with its rough tongue. *This is almost normal.*

"So what's with the knife?" Emma said.

So much for normal. "I'll tell you, but you really can't say anything to anyone."

"Yeah, right." The girl rolled her eyes. "I'm mute, remember?"

Despite her anxiety, Rima grinned. *Girl's got spirit, that's for sure.* If *she'd* suddenly found herself shooting out of fog into the past—or a different world altogether—she thought she might be as wobbly as aspic for quite a while. *And how is it that I accept that she might be from a future time? Or another place?* "It's only that I sense things." She gave the girl a brief explanation, omitting her ability to draw sickness. No need to go into all the gory details, and besides, better safe than sorry. If word leaked of her talent, the scientists and doctors would never let her go. She'd spend the rest of her days chained to a post in some hospital, forced to draw sickness and rot until the Peculiar swallowed them all. *Or maybe lets us through, the way it did Emma.* What she wouldn't give to go somewhere, *anywhere*, else. Their shared daydream of a cottage on Mull by the sea—she would be content with that. "I got something from Doyle's knife, that's all."

"Wow." The girl looked impressed. "Like, you're a psychic? So, did he kill someone with it?"

Given how her fingertips still tingled, she thought that was pretty close. The contact hadn't been long enough for anything as coherent as an image to truly firm. All she'd gotten were impressions: rage, pain. Blood, lots of it. "I got something else, though, when I touched *him*, Doyle. A . . . *presence*. But what popped into my head? Makes no sense. I thought, *Dog*."

"A dog?" Emma echoed. "What kind?"

"Don't know. Big, black." *Red eyes?* "Not a nice dog." Whatever this presence was, its touch had been very strange, complex. She swallowed, tasting only sour bile from an empty stomach. *Doyle's got some sort of hunger, but not for food,*

There, there, my poppet, my dearest darling

and beneath that, there's the dog. The presence was sinister, something that would be at home skulking in a dank sewer. *Maybe that's what's driving him.*

"Well, maybe the dog wasn't so great, but *Doyle* liked you," Emma said. "He was practically falling all over himself. Think he'll come looking?"

"*You'd* better hope not," Tony said.

"We won't be seeing him again." Squaring her shoulders, Rima rearranged her grip on the cart, wincing at the burn. She'd given her mittens to Emma, and now her own hands were blocks of ice. "Come on, let's get going."

"Wait." Emma peeled off her left mitten and held it out. When Rima started to shake her head, the girl said, "Come on, it's not fair for you to freeze."

"I'm fine," Rima said.

"Oh bull." Emma snorted. "If you don't, I'll talk to the next person we see."

Tony's eyebrows drew together. "Is it only you, or do *all* children argue with their elders where you come from?"

"Well, I only know Wisconsin. But"—the girl shrugged—"sure."

4

AS THEY SKIRTED the asylum's main entrance, Rima saw that snow had tumbled from the portico to pile in high mounds along the front steps. In the bad light, she couldn't be positive, but she thought that a chimney stack, immediately right of the dome, had collapsed, and that pediment was off-kilter, too. All this stone and old masonry—pity the poor nutters if the building came down, but at least it would be fast for them.

"Place gives me the creeps," Emma said.

"No argument there," Rima said. "Never have liked coming here." Thinking, *So far as I can remember. If there have been other days.* Such an odd thought, but with the Peculiar, no one's memory could be trusted. "Always brings on the jimjams."

"No, I mean, it *really* freaks me out." Emma sounded a little sick. "Like I've been here before. But . . . that can't be right. I mean, I've *never* left Wisconsin."

At the girl's tone, Rima exchanged a look with Tony, who only shrugged. As far as Rima could remember, there was no building like this in her nightmare. "Do you recall something that stands out?" she asked.

Emma paused, then tilted her head back and pointed. "The dome. Can't hardly see it, but . . . it's got a lot of glass, right? And it's a church or something?"

"Well, it's got glass. Whole asylum does." At that, what she thought was a true memory—or maybe only an impression— wavered into focus: how those windows looked, swarming with faces, as they did when the nutters crowded up. Perhaps it wouldn't be so bad if they *looked* mad; if they'd only raved and screamed and reached through the bars with hands starred to claws. But most often it was like trudging past a colonnade of expressionless corpses with black holes where their eyes ought to be. "Lots of domes do, I'm sure."

"But is it a church?"

"We can find out," Tony said. "You think it's important?"

"I don't know," Emma said, and it was then that, over the girl's head, Rima caught a wink that solidified into a steady, brassy glow, as someone with a lamp moved within a second-story room. The glow stopped, and then grew brighter and swam closer to a window, like a curious fish in a bowl—and became a man's face. A spiderweb of cracks marred the glass, and at first she thought the unevenness of his features, the way the man's face fractured, was an effect of the ruined panes. A second glance, though, and she realized that the man himself was a ruin. Half his face was absolutely still, as frozen as cold candle wax. *God.* He looked like a walking corpse. Rima felt his eyes. He might be only curious, but she didn't like that he wasn't moving on. *He's interested.* She read it in the inquisitive cock of his head to the right, like a terrier trying to decide if that rat was worth the trouble. *Why?* They *were* just rats, out to gather the dead.

"You okay?" She looked down to find Emma studying her. Turning her head, the girl followed her gaze. "It's just a light," Emma said.

Which I don't like. Something about a window was important. Perhaps someone she'd spotted there? Who? "It's nothing," she said, against another tickle of unease.

"Uh-huh," Emma said, and turned to face forward. "Come on, let's go. Place gives me the jimjams."

BODE

Lost the Fork

AFTER HE LEFT Kramer's office—and Meme; God, he'd bolloxed that—Bode thought he was home free. Surely, Kramer and Graves were on a different floor by now. But then, just before he slipped through the door leading from the ward to the landing, his heart gave an unpleasant lurch. Directly ahead, big as life, were Kramer, lamp in hand, and Graves, at a window that looked onto the front lawn.

Damme. Bode slowed and, for a split second, thought about doing a quick about-face and bolting into a side room. But then Graves turned, spotted him, and called, "Bode, come here at once!"

"Right away, ma'am." His right pocket felt heavy, and too late, he remembered the lemon and Kramer's odd purple spectacles. By now the landing was as deep with shadows as most of the rooms, so he hoped the doctor wouldn't notice the bulge. Dropping his hand to his waist to better obscure his pocket, he said, "Ma'am? Sir?" He listened as Graves repeated what he'd already overheard. Kramer's behavior, though, was very strange; not bothering to acknowledge Bode, the man moved from window to window as if following someone's progress along the front lawn.

"And when you've finished with those rats, I want you back here immediately, is that understood?" Graves looked ready to take a bite out of his backside.

"Yes'm." Scuttling for the door, he was so anxious to be gone that he was nearly halfway down the hall before he remembered and turned back. *Oh, that was a close one; might 'a gave myself away otherwise.* Theoretically, he didn't have a key and so no way to let himself in and out. If he *had* gone off and then reported that he'd done what she asked, she'd know he had her old skeleton. "Might I have the key for the storehouse, Mrs. Graves? So's I can let in the rats?" While Graves fussed, Bode's eyes darted down the hall to the landing where Kramer paced, lamp in hand, like a light-house keeper waiting to direct a wayward ship to shore. What was he fuming about? The man was an absolute black study. God, he hoped Kramer wouldn't take it out on Meme. The thought prompted another hot rush of shame. *Oh yeah, like I'll do anything about it.*

"There." Graves slapped her key into his hand. "Go. And I expect that back within the hour."

"Yes'm." Ducking his head, he hurried for the stairs. As he circled a newel post, Kramer rapped in a stentorian tone, "Hold on a moment."

Bloody shite. Stifling a groan, he craned back up. "Sir?"

"Those rats." Lantern in hand, Kramer pointed. "That . . . *boy.* Do you know him?"

"Sir?" A spike of alarm. Following Kramer's gaze, he saw three figures. Two, he knew; the third was smaller, though. A girl? "No, they're just . . . you know, *rats.*" The less he talked, the better. *But what's he want with them?* Kramer has specifically asked about that *boy.* Why the interest in Tony?

"I want to speak with them. Bring them. I know . . . promise them a meal. Do whatever you must, but I don't want them leaving the grounds. I would send someone else with you, but I don't want to frighten them."

Uh-oh. Curiosity was one thing. *But Kramer really wants them, has his eye on Tony. Why?*

"Doctor?" Graves looked as confused as Bode felt. "What could you possibly want with—"

"Mind your place, Mrs. Graves." Aiming a finger at Bode. "You, bring them at once."

"Yes, sir." As he took the stairs, though, he thought, *Bloody snowball's chance in hell of that.* A knee-jerk reaction and probably unwarranted, but Kramer's sudden interest was a little scary. Maybe best for Tony and Rima and whoever that new kid was to back slang it off grounds, skirt the old criminal wings. Hurrying through the asylum's darkened kitchen, he headed for the back. Supper was long over, and the cooks were all gone. Prime foraging time, but with Kramer waiting, he had to get a move on. The outside air was so cold he felt the draft through the keyhole. When he opened the door, a balloon of snow swelled on a gush of frigid air. The sky had lightened to the color of tarnished silver, enough so the night was no longer pitch. (He *hated* that. Couldn't take anything for granted anymore.) Tugging the door shut, he wallowed along the cut in the snow from earlier that day, before Elizabeth's fit, when he and Weber humped bodies for safekeeping to the far storehouse. In the distance, the faint suggestions of outbuildings—storehouses, an old greenhouse, staff cottages that were no longer in use—wavered through rippling curtains of thick snow. The rest of the grounds were lost to distance and the general gloom. Everything always seemed . . . muzzy, not quite filled in, something he always chalked up to this ceaseless bad weather. He glanced back over his shoulder. The asylum loomed, a blue-gray hulk, pressing against his back.

Maybe he was worried over nothing. So, Kramer met them, what of it? He was worrying over the frayed phantoms of a nightmare. He'd be a fool to let his chuckaboos miss out on tea and a chance for more food, even if it *was* as bad as those biscuits.

Really: it wasn't as if the world was their oyster and they'd only lost the fork.

RIMA

She's Here

ONCE THEY'D CLEARED the west wing, the back grounds spread in a great expanse studded with dim gray-blue cubes: storehouses, staff dormitories, and other defunct structures. Rima couldn't recall the last time she'd actually seen the buildings in any kind of detail. Very far away and cloaked in snow and gloom, the crumbling edifices of the asylum's derelict criminal wings reared like ancient castle ruins.

As they neared a large storehouse to the right of the main building, the gloom suddenly lightened, the smoky gray sky that passed for night brightening to dirty white. False dawn: true sunlight was as much a fugitive as news of the outside world. Rima couldn't remember now what the sun truly looked or felt like.

"Hate when the sky does that." Grimacing, Tony spat. "You know, my mouth *still* tastes like I've been sucking on a sewer drain."

"Yeah, that toffee was pretty terrible." Emma wrinkled her nose. "Maybe it spoiled. Think the other candy's okay?"

"I wouldn't want to bet on it," Rima said. The constable's

candy had been too great a temptation, and they'd paused along the way to share a bit of toffee. What a disappointment. Her tongue was coated with a taste like dog shite smelled. Eating dirt would be easier.

The storehouse was a sorry pile. A portion of roof had slumped and caved, probably from the quake. Another few tremors like that and this would be just another derelict. As they reached the side door, there came the rattle of a bolt being thrown. The door swung in, and Bode appeared, lantern in hand.

"Good to see you, brother." Bode pulled Tony into a one-armed hug, then nodded at Emma. "Who's the kid? What happened to her chin?"

"Nice to meet you, too," Emma said.

"What?" Then, as Jack's head poked from between burlap sacks, Bode said, "Is that a *cat*?"

"He's mine," Emma said, then added, "And you can't eat him either."

"What, have you all gone nutter? That's *meat*."

"Off-limits, brother," Tony said.

"What's got into you?" Bode gaped. "What you listening to a kid for? What's so special about the cat? How'd she even manage to hang on to it this long? How come you two haven't put it in a pot?"

"It's a long story," Rima began, but Emma interrupted. "What's wrong with you guys? He's *mine*. You want to talk about *my* cat, you can talk to me."

"You got a real mouth, don't ya?" Scowling, Bode looked the girl up and down. "And what's that accent? Where you from?"

"Wisconsin," Tony said.

"What's that?" Bode said.

"It's a *state*. Do you guys, like, *not* study geography or something?" Emma asked.

"Pardon?" Bode said.

Rima held up her hands. "Shall we start over? Emma, this is our friend, Bode. Bode, this is—"

"Emma." Something flickered through Bode's face, but so quickly Rima wasn't sure if she saw only surprise. "*That's* your name?" he asked.

"Yeah." Emma looked disgusted. "*So?* What, you don't like my name either?"

"No. It's . . ." Bode put a hand to his lips as if to stop himself saying more.

"Bode?" Rima put a hand on his arm. "Are you all right?"

"What?" Blinking, Bode tried tacking on a smile. "Oh . . . fine. Sorry. Just . . . name reminded me of something, is all. Sorry. Ah, how ye do, Emma?"

"I've been better," Emma said, darkly.

"I'd say that goes for all of ya." After a last longing look at the cat, Bode eyed Tony. "*You're* thinner, brother. Is that blood on your mouth?"

"Nosebleed," Tony said, briefly, though he knuckled his lips. "I'm all right now."

"Mmm." Leaning in, Bode sniffed and then recoiled. "God, what you just et?"

"Would you believe toffee?" Rima said. "From a constable. The cart tipped at the gate, and he helped, him and an inspector."

"Ah, yeah. The inspector's Battle. Doyle, though . . . he's a queer duck. Twitchy, and the cheesers he let go . . . ohhh." Bode waved a hand before his nose. "Lucky I didn't go blind. Got himself a little tore up, though. One of the doctors tended to him."

Twitchy. Rima thought back to their fleeting contact. *Morphia? Cocaine?* She wouldn't be surprised. "I wouldn't have thought toffee could go off, but they taste terrible. You want some?"

"I thought he was your friend," Emma said.

Bode arched an eyebrow. "Dash my wig, she's got quite the tartur-trap, don't she?"

"And then some," Tony said, but he was trying not to grin.

Definitely not amused, Rima said, "*Fine.* There's humbugs, if you'd like."

"I wouldn't say no," Bode said. "My mouth's rank."

"I wouldn't," Emma said, as Bode fingered up a peppermint.

"Full of opinions, aren't you?" Popping the candy into his mouth, Bode sucked experimentally, then wrinkled his nose. "Well, if there's peppermint, I can't taste it. Not *terrible.* Just . . . nothing."

"Told you," the girl said.

"Emma." After a warning glance, Rima spied a blotch on Bode's jaw. "You're bruised. What happened?"

"Long story. Got myself cuffed, that's all." Tonguing the humbug into his uninjured cheek, he said to Tony, "But that don't answer my question, brother. Why you bleeding?"

"How should I know? I'm fine now," Tony said, pointedly not looking at Rima.

Bode arched an eyebrow as if to say, *Tell me another.* "Well, come on." Bode jerked his head for them to follow. "Just me tonight, but ain't got but four."

"Where's Weber?" Not that Rima was *heartbroken.* The man was a pig. His specialty was sandwiching her to a wall as he passed and calling that an accident.

"Given the night off," Bode said, leading them from this entry and down a short corridor. At a large double door, he fished out a key. "Good riddance, too."

"I'm not arguing," Tony said as they followed Bode into a high-ceilinged storeroom. Once used for putting up what was grown in the asylum's gardens, the room was now empty of barrels of preserved pickles, boxes of potatoes and beets and turnips in straw, clutches of onions, ropes of braided garlic, and dried herbs. The air was cold and smelled faintly of brine and dust. Spooling from a burst pane of the room's one window, a tongue of snow had settled in a long drift over the cobbled floor. In the center of the room, four bodies, done up in burlap, had been laid on a low table. "What happened?"

"Too much to explain." Bode's face darkened a moment. "I'm not sure I understand it all myself, but a patient . . . a girl . . . took a bad turn. I'll check on her later." He shook himself free of whatever he was thinking. "They's a sack in the fourth bag. Some bread, cheese." He hooked a thumb at her. "Mittens for you, Rima."

"Oh." She felt a leap of relief and hurried over to tug open the sack. Reaching in, she pulled out a pair of brown wool mittens. "*Thank* you."

"Wait," Emma said. "You put *food* in with a *body*?"

"Best way to smuggle it out," Bode said. "Not to worry; she wasn't one of the bloody ones. A girl what hanged herself, is all."

"That's *gross*," Emma said.

"Well then, I guess you don't need any of the victuals now, do ya?"

"I didn't say *that*."

"What?" He cupped a hand behind one ear. "Say that again?" Grinning, he pointed. "Got a few bags o' mystery in there, too."

"What?" Emma asked.

"Sausages," Tony said.

"Oh." Emma frowned. "Why don't you just *say* that? What's so mysterious about a sausage?"

"Oh, plenty, my little chuckaboo." Bode waggled his eyebrows, which made Emma giggle. "Cook swore they was dog, so they're likely rat and cat . . . uhm . . ." He gave Emma an apologetic shrug. "Cat's meat really is quite good, you do it up right."

"As long as it's not Jack." Emma looked at Rima. "I'm not saying that this isn't übergross, but can we eat something now, *please*? I'm *really* hungry."

Rima was about to agree to a bit of cheese and bread when Bode cut in. "I can do one better," Bode said. "I'm to bring you for a little sit-me-down. There's a meal in it."

"What?" Rima exchanged a puzzled glance with Tony. "With whom?"

"One of the doctors . . . Kramer?" Bode eyed Tony. "He's *very* keen on you."

"Me?" Tony frowned. "What for?"

"Damfino," Bode said.

That light in the window. Rima's heart gave a sick lurch. "Something's wrong with his face, isn't there? This doctor?"

"Yeah. Rot took half," Bode said.

"Rot?" Emma's nose wrinkled. "Like what you guys said—those worms?"

"Squirmers," Bode said.

"Yeah, those. Like it rotted off? Gangrene and pus and stuff?"

"Worse. Got this tin mask?" Bode cupped a hand before his face to illustrate. "Gives you the jimjams to look at it."

"Yes, that's the man," Rima said. "He kept an eye on us and . . . Oh." A white bolt of shock jagged through her, and she put a hand to her mouth. "Oh God."

"What?" Tony's brows knit. "Rima, are you all right?"

"Yes," she said, trying to quell the shake in her voice. *God, no; now I remember.* There had to be a connection. "Bode, what's this doctor want with Tony?"

"What you worried about?" Bode said. "I'll be right there. What could happen?"

Plenty, if I'm remembering right. "What if we don't go?" Rima asked.

"Rima?" Tony asked. "What is it?"

She only shook her head. "If you come back empty-handed, would you be sacked, Bode?"

Bode frowned. "Me? Dunno. I doubt it. But why would you refuse? I mean, we're talking *food.* Kramer's got himself quite the hoard, I think. So you can be sure of hot tea, biscuits, probably cheese that ain't gone off, plus what I got for you besides."

"But if we left?" Rima slicked her lips. "We have to get back anyway."

"We do?" Tony asked.

"Yes," Rima said. To Bode: "What would happen?"

Bode tossed a look to Tony, who only shrugged. "Nothing, I suppose," Bode said. "But Kramer's no idjit. You're rats, and Battersea's the only gasworks still running. He'll find you one way or the other, he wants you."

"I could eat," said Emma.

"I don't see the harm either." Tony looked at Rima. "He's an alienist, yeah? That's what they do. They talk. So where's the problem?"

"I just don't like it," she said. "Bode, is there another way out of here?"

"Rima, what's gotten into you?" Tony said.

"Well . . ." Bode looked befuddled. "Yeah, you could duck out back, past the old criminal wings, though it's across acres of unbroken snow. I ain't never been."

"Fine," she said. *Just get out, get Tony away from here. Emma too. I don't like this, I don't.* "That's what we'll do. Bode, you should come, too."

"What?" Bode said at the same moment that Tony shook his head and said, "Rima, you're not making sense, and we're not doing *anything* so stupid without good reason . . ."

Her control broke. "You want a *reason*? How about this? That woman, the one with the purple eyes, who came from the mirror? The one from your nightmare?" She looked at Emma. "The one who nearly got *you*?"

"What? *You* had a nightmare?" Bode said, as Tony tried to take her hands.

"Rima, calm down," Tony said. "What about her?"

"Oh, Tony." Tears, large and frightened, coursed down her cheeks. "That woman . . . she's *here*."

BODE

Everyone Dreams

TONY HELD HER hand as Rima talked about odd images: a mother who tried to kill her, a home she didn't recognize. When she got to the part about another Tony and an explosion, *their* Tony paled. "Why didn't you tell me?" Tony said.

"I didn't want you to worry." Rima squeezed his hand. "I was afraid you'd be angry at me for *drawing* from you, but I had to do something. Anyway, I'm telling you now."

"So the woman wasn't in the valley during any of it?" When they shook their heads, Bode moved his in a curt nod. "Right. I don't remember her either. So I guess that's something. What about after?" He heard the newer, grimmer edge in his voice. "After that other Tony died?" As Rima described a bizarre contraption that propelled them through a blizzard—*wheels of India rubber, and it was very loud*—he recognized some of the words: *whisper-man, Peculiar.* A younger Elizabeth named Lizzie.

And Emma. He glanced down at the girl, who sat cross-legged on the floor. The cat curled in her lap. The girl had gone white as salt. *But it's the right name, same color hair. Even the eyes are right.* He *could* see some faint outline of the young woman this girl would become. It bothered him that, to him, she looked a touch like Meme. *Coincidence; you're letting the nightmare confuse you.* "What happened next, Rima?"

"I was . . ." Swallowing, Rima pressed her lips with shaking fingers. "Bleeding. *Dying*. The whisper-man was too much for me to hold, and then that other boy, the one with the gray eyes, he tried to help . . ." She shook her head. "I don't remember much after that, other than darkness and a feeling of *rushing*."

"You didn't get any of this?" Bode looked at Tony. "The cave, the birds?"

"No." Tony's skin was tight around his skull. "I didn't get half what either of you did. That business on the snow, for example. Wolf-creatures, spiders erupting out of a girl's mouth, and then your . . . cart? . . . being drawn down into some black muck. Got none of that. I think the other Tony was dead by then." He peered into Bode's eyes. "You didn't see the end either, did you? What Rima's talking about, what happened in that cave? Because *that* Bode was . . ."

"Dead. Yeah." Exhaling, he gave himself a shake. In the broken window, his distorted reflection stared back, like a freak show curiosity caged in glass. *Glass.* Hadn't there been something about that in his nightmare? He remembered a mirror, but he thought *this* was altogether different. *About reflections trapped in a glass basin?* No. That wasn't quite the right word. Not basin, but . . . *energy sink?*

"What about a sink?" Tony said.

"What?" He looked from his broken reflection to find them both staring at him.

"Energy sink," Rima said. "What's that? Is it for some kind of water?"

"Damme," he said, "I don't . . ."

"Think of it as a place where energy goes when it's released." Emma's voice was very small, almost inaudible. "It's basic physics."

"Physics," Bode repeated. "Science? *You* know what this is?"

"Yeah, what's so weird about that? Of course I know science." The girl looked up from her cat. "Look, when you burn a log, there's fire, right? Once it's burning, though, it's not like you can set it *more* on fire. So where does the heat go?"

"Into the air," Bode said. "The room."

"Right. That's because it's colder. When there's heat, there's more energy, by definition. The molecules are moving faster. When you heat water, it doesn't stay hot forever. That's because the air's cooler. When you get a fever, you're hot, right? Your body works harder when it's fighting? So, that *drawing* thing you do, Rima . . . you're kind of this human energy sink."

"So what you're saying is that this . . . energy, it always goes to a place where there's less of it?" Rima asked.

Emma nodded. "That weird rock you saw, Bode, in your nightmare? Somehow it saps energy. Eventually, if it takes enough . . ."

"It empties the tub." Bode nodded. "All right, I see that. Makes sense. The Emma in my dream was worried we'd be trapped inside, never make it through."

"Odd about the Peculiar," Rima said. "That it's a kind of container in our nightmares but a *fog* here. Strange coincidence."

"Maybe not," Emma said. "It's cold here. You can't go anywhere. Other than this is like, you know, a *place*, a city, and your dreams are about some weird valley, I don't see the diff—" She stopped, her expression intent and inward-looking, as if parsing through a thorny mathematical equation. Watching her think, Bode was struck by how much older she looked at that moment. That finger of disquiet tickled his neck again. *In the dream, I see the child Elizabeth might have been—and I see the girl this Emma might become?*

Then why did he see the ghost of Meme taking shape under this little girl's skin?

"What?" Rima asked the girl.

"Oh . . . all this talk about energy? I was just thinking about what you said happened on the snow in your nightmare. I didn't see that part, but that thing with the wheels—actually, that sounds like what we call a truck, not a cart; you don't need horses or anything and . . ." She flapped an impatient hand. "Never mind. Anyway, how the snow broke?"

"Energy." Tony gave her a sharp look. "You're thinking the quakes, aren't you? A release of energy?"

"Uh-huh. During a normal earthquake, that's why the earth shakes. Do you guys remember *why* that whole scene or setup or whatever it was broke up in the first place? Because it *did*, and kind of the same way ice has to be, you know, thick enough to take a lot of weight. My guardian, Jasper, always told me that if you get stuck on the ice and it starts to break, then you spread yourself out." Emma held out her arms. "You distribute your weight so it's not all concentrated in the same spot."

"So . . ." Rima hung on to the word a moment. "Too many people? In one spot?"

"Kinda?" Emma said. "I don't know how it would work, though, or why it would happen. I mean . . . lots of weird stuff happens in dreams. I only mentioned it because energy seems to come up a lot."

"Well, it's beyond me," Bode said. "What I can't figure is, what's all this got to do with a woman with purple eyes coming through a mirror or window, *especially* if she wasn't there in the valley in the first place?"

"That's the *only* thing you can't parse?" Tony asked.

"What if the *nightmare's* the reason she could?" Rima looked to Tony. "You said something *changed* for the other Tony. What if the *nightmare* was the change?"

"And now we're having it?" Tony screwed up his nose. "But *we* weren't in the valley. Our . . . well, I guess you'd call them our doppelgängers were, and the woman came after *them*. Actually, all we know is she came for the other Tony. Maybe it stops there, with him. Bode hasn't seen her in a nightmare or real life, here."

"Yeah, well, don't forget she came after me. None of you guys saw me in the dream as me either," Emma said.

"Maybe we're seeing what will happen." Bode nodded down at the girl. "*Your* future. Perhaps this is about warning *you*, not us."

"Then why are *we* dreaming it?" Rima asked. "The nightmare's about the *other* Rima, the *other* Tony and Bode, a different Emma, not us."

"I don't know. We're obviously connected somehow."

"To them as well as to each other? How? I understand us, I guess. *We* grew up together," Tony said, then added, "Not that I remember much of that. Odd, don't you think?"

"And then some, but I think it's moved beyond that, brother. We're all tangled up, our lives bound to each other and now to you, Emma. What we're supposed to *do*, though . . ." Shrugging, Bode spread his hands. "Haven't a clue, except I *feel* this urge. Like I got to take care of Elizabeth because she's important, even though I didn't see her *as* her in the dream." *And Emma, too.* He regarded the little girl. The pull to protect her was there, too. It was obvious to him that Tony and Rima felt the same.

"I understand that, but how about we all get away from here, this asylum, for starters? That woman doesn't have to come to life in a dream. She's *here*. I've seen her in a window." At Tony's skeptical look, Rima said, "I *did*. It came to me right after I noticed that doctor watching us. We passed under some windows, and I remember looking up and thinking there was something there I ought to see or once saw that was very important; that felt . . . déjà vu? Been here before? I didn't put it together until you told us about Kramer. That's when I realized that I'd seen her here, *in* a window. Don't ask me when, because I can't tell you. I just know I have."

"A patient?" Tony said.

"No one I've seen." Bode scowled. "I'd think I'd remember a woman with purple . . ." *Oh.* His hand fell to his waist. *Oh good Christ.* "You said, a window," he said to Rima. "You remember if you could see anything else in the room behind her?"

She nodded. "Books. And . . . a folding screen? Some kind of table, I think, but not one you would put flowers on or dishes. Does that make . . ." Her voice trailed away, and her eyes went wide as saucers. "Oh. Bode, where . . . ?"

"Kramer's office, and that's where she was when you saw her." The purple lenses were coal-black in the dim light. "Nicked them just now. Don't ask; stupid reason. This is them, yeah?"

"You look through them yet?" asked Tony.

"No. Give me the jimjams." He tucked them back in his pocket. "Sooner I get 'em back to Kramer, the better."

"So now what?" Rima asked. "Whether this woman was a patient or nurse or relative of a patient doesn't matter. The point is, she was *here*; the glasses prove Kramer knows or knew her. She came through the other Tony's mirror."

"Yeah, but in a nightmare," Bode said.

"Unless I'm dreaming right now and you guys aren't real," Emma said, "she came through my kitchen window. And how do you explain me?"

"Right." Rima nodded. "Now *Kramer* wants Tony. There's got to be a connection."

"Yeah." Eyes brushing over his distorted reflection in the storehouse window, Bode chewed over that a moment. "Let me ask you both something, all right?" As he transferred his gaze back to them, he thought he saw something wink outside, on the snow. Thought, *Reflection from my lantern,* and dismissed it. "Don't stop to think about it. Emma, hold your tongue; this isn't a question for you."

"Okay," Emma said.

"What?" Rima asked.

"Have you *ever* had a dream before now, ever?" Out of the corner of his eye, he saw Emma open her mouth, then quickly shut it. Tony and Rima only turned puzzled frowns to each other. "Come on," he said, "it's a simple question. Have you ever dreamt *anything* before now? Out with it, fast."

"I . . . well, I . . ." Rima's face suddenly went slack, and she gave him an incredulous look. "No?" It came out sounding like a question. "Not that I recall?"

Tony took her hand again. "Me neither."

"Right. That's what I thought." Bode felt as frightened as they looked. "Makes three of us." He looked to Emma, who was squirming, a hand over her mouth. "All right, out with it. You've dreamt, haven't you?"

"Oh yeah, lots of times," the girl said. "Some I remember, a ton I don't, especially when I've been awake for a while. But everyone dreams."

Remembering Kramer and Meme, the way they said *dream* and *nightmare*, Bode said, "Maybe not all of us."

"Yes, and we recall *more* as time goes by," Rima said, "not less. It's as Tony said, the feeling that something's going to happen."

"But if you guys haven't ever had a dream, how do you know what to call it?" Emma said. "Where would the word come from? Why would you think *nightmare*?"

"And why *that* nightmare altogether? Why are we dreaming about *us* somewhere else?" Bode's gaze went back to his reflection, so steady in that broken glass. A strange thought: What happened when he looked away? Did his reflection scratch its nose? Cross its eyes? Take itself away completely? Then he noticed something beyond his ghostly image: that reflection he'd thought was his lantern was brighter than before, and bobbed. *Oh, bloody hell.* "Someone's coming," he said. "They probably rousted Weber. Can't let him get his hooks in any of you."

"What do we do?" Tony put himself between the girls and the door. Clutching her cat, Emma had scrambled to her feet. "Is there a back way?" Tony asked.

"Not so's that cove won't see you before you can make yourselves scarce. 'Sides, your cart's out there. He'll know you're about." Snapping his fingers, Bode held out his hand. "Give me your chopper."

"Bode, no." Rima put a hand on Tony's arm to stay him. "Killing Weber will only make things worse."

"You end up in that asylum, and you'll be singing a different tune. 'Sides, we can't let him get ahold of Emma here, not with what we've all dreamt. Maybe she's not the same girl, but this is just too close for comfort, too many coincidences. Now," he said, dousing his lantern, "give me the damned chopper." As Tony reluctantly handed it over, there was a sudden shift in pressure as wind flooded in from outside. The door to this space chattered on its hinges.

He's inside. Putting a finger to his lips, he pointed the others to a corner thick with slate shadows, then tiptoed to a position in line with the storeroom door. Monkeying up the shelves, he cocked his elbows and brought the square blade above his head. From this angle, a quick downward strike, and the blade would bury itself in Weber's skull as soon as the man opened the door. *One good whack.*

Over the pounding of his heart, he heard the slow clump of boots on stone. In a far corner, Rima pressed Emma behind her, although Bode saw Tony creeping round with the broken handle of an ax or sledge clutched in his fists. *No, what's he doing?* Bode waved him back, but Tony only took a position opposite the door and hefted the stout handle over a shoulder for a swing if Bode missed.

A slim ribbon of yellow fired the floor as Weber came to stand before the door. Bode felt the man on the other side, could imagine him listening for a shuffle, the rasp of a sole on brick. Then his pulse skipped at a crisp rattle as the knob turned.

Wait. Bode's fists cramped on the chopper's handle. *Wait for it . . .*

A fan of light unfurled as the door opened and Weber stepped over the threshold, lantern upraised. Bode thought Weber whispered his name as he came forward, but it was hard to hear over the storm in his ears. Every nerve of his being focused on the blurred hump of Weber's head. Sucking in a breath, he thought, *Now!*

"Bode!" Rima's shriek pierced the thunder rampaging through his skull. *"No!"*

Too late.

BODE

Panops

1

HE'D PUT HIS weight into it. The chopper's blade cleaved air, whizzing down in a fast, hard, whickering arc.

Then Bode saw what he'd missed. Weber might be many things, but this was certain: he wouldn't be wearing a skirt. Or a shawl. There was time for him to register an oval blur, to parse out a face. Realizing his mistake, Bode tried angling the blade— also a split second too late.

Opposite, there was a sudden flurry of movement. Flinging himself forward, Tony got one arm up. There was a hard *chuck* as the chopper bit the stout wood ax handle. Vibrations burred through Bode's palms to ball in his shoulders. But it was enough to deflect the killing blow. Now off-balance and with his own momentum against him, Bode staggered, lost his footing, and crashed to cold brick. At the same time, he heard the smash of glass as a lantern snuffed. He landed with a sickening thud that knocked the breath from his lungs. Dimly, he heard the clatter of steel on stone as he lost his grip on the chopper. Gagging, chest hitching, he managed a shrieking gasp and then another. *My God.* Rolling to his knees, he held himself up on trembling arms. *That was close.*

To his left, on the floor, Emma was still hanging back. Rima had rushed from her corner to drop next to Tony, who was already sitting up. "I'm fine, I'm not hurt," he was saying, although there was a dark rivulet snaking from a nostril. He backhanded it from his upper lip. "Leave off, Rima, I'm not dying. But what about . . . ?" Then Tony gasped as he got a good look at the intruder. "God, Rima, it's . . ."

"Who are you?" Rima's tone cut the gloom as sharply as that blade had sliced air. "What are you doing here?"

"I came to . . . to see." Her shawl was askew, her copper hair come undone to tumble around her shoulders. "For myself. And if it was true, to *warn* you."

Tony opened his mouth again, but Rima jumped in. "True? True about what? Warn us about *what*?"

"What they are planning." She looked to Bode. "I am sorry; I should have called out." Then she blinked as if her brain had just now caught up, because her head swiveled back to peer into the far corner. "Who are you?" she asked Emma.

"She's mute," Rima said. "Can't make a sound, poor thing. We don't even know her name."

"Oh." The other girl put a hand to a cheek. "But she looks so familiar."

"Muh . . ." Finally, after what felt like ages, Bode's balky throat cooperated. "*M-Meme.* What the devil?"

2

"I NEEDED RAGS and followed you out of the office a few moments later, so I overheard when Kramer went on about wanting to meet these rats. The way he was, how insistent, I just knew." Light flickered over Meme's face, steeping the hollows of her cheeks in shadow. She pushed a lush coppery hank of her tousled hair from her forehead. "I had to come see for myself, to be sure."

"Be sure of what?" Bode's nerves still buzzed. Every time he looked at her, he felt the weight of the blade, heard the riffling *hoosh* as it sliced down. If not for Tony, she would be dead now, her skull shattered like a rotten nut. As cold as it was in the store-room, what flowed through his veins was icier still. "What did you need to see?"

"Them." She nodded toward Tony and Rima, who stood close together. Emma still hung back, as if reluctant to draw attention, which was fine with Bode. Tony's pale skin was a shade of weak piss and glistened with fine sweat. He'd rested his hips against that low table, still laid with bodies in burlap. Rima's arm was around Tony's waist, but Bode thought it was more to prop him up. "I had to see it for myself," Meme said. "If you were real."

"Real?" Mouth working, Tony spat dark foam. His teeth were faintly orange. "There, that blood *real* enough for you? I don't understand what's so fascinating. First, your doctor and now you . . . what is it about us? We're nobodies. We're rats."

"True. *Here*." Meme nodded. "But not everywhere."

"What?" Tony and Bode said at the same time.

"What do you mean, *everywhere*?" Rima said, then put a hand to her lips. "God, you've had the nightmare?"

"Nightmare?" A slight wrinkle between Meme's eyes. "No. I have not."

"But you said *everywhere*. You're talking about another Tony; I know you are." Rima bunched her fists on her chest. "Another *me*, and a different Bode. Aren't you?"

"I do not know about . . . about Bode." Meme sounded surprised, and now she darted a probing look his way before turning back. "Or you," she said to Rima. "That is, she could not find your double at all. That world was in ruins. Falling apart, like London, only worse, is what I heard."

"*That* world?" Bode held his hands out. "*This* is the world."

"Yes, *our* world. *Our* London. Meme is talking about a place like the valley. Like where Em . . ." Tony cleared his throat. "Like where the other Tony comes from."

"But how do *you* know?" Rima asked Meme. "If you've not had the dream . . ."

"Dream." Meme said it tentatively. "I told you, I do not know anything about that. But I do know *you*." Her cobalt eyes fixed on Tony. "You are ill, are you not? And getting worse?"

Rima put a protective hand on Tony's arm. "What do you know about that?"

"How long?" Meme asked Tony.

"Can't remember, exactly." Tony made a vague gesture. "Sometimes it feels like this morning's the very first day. So it's either been a while or just started." He gave a weak and breathy laugh. "Specific enough for you?"

"What does it *feel* like?" Meme's hand tightened to a fist over her heart. "Is it something dark *pulling* at you, draining you dry?"

"Yes," Tony whispered. His face seemed to shiver. "That's exactly it. A whirlpool, drawing me down. It feels like I'll drown."

"Stop it, Tony. No one's going to *drown*." Eyes flashing, Rima looked at Meme. "Why are you doing this? Can't you say anything plain?" Rima started for the other girl, but Bode grabbed her elbow. Glaring, she tried tugging free, but he held her fast.

"Whose side are you on, Bode? If she *knows* . . ."

"She's *here*, isn't she? She came to warn us." Bode looked at Meme. "But you *do* know what's happening, at least in part." It wasn't a question. "It's something to do with Kramer, isn't it? What you and him was talking about?"

After a moment, her head moved in a small nod. She held out a hand, palm up. "Give me the glasses." When he didn't move, she said, "I know you stole them. Doctor always keeps them in his vest, which needed cleaning from all that blood. But when I checked a while ago, they were gone." Her gaze was steady on his. "If I wished to turn you in, I would have done so already."

"Why are they important?" Rima asked as Bode, wordless, handed them over. Then her voice changed, rising a notch. "Wait . . . she. You've said *she* several times over. It's that woman, isn't it? The one I spotted in the window?"

Without replying, Meme unfolded the glasses, then hooked the tips behind her ears. She turned a long, speculative look first at Bode, then transferred her eyes to Rima. Emma she bypassed completely—didn't even remark on the cat, still as a statue, in the girl's arms—and turned instead to Tony. Bode saw her face grow taut.

"What is it?" A thrum of fear in Tony's voice. "What do you see?"

"Nothing good." Taking off the glasses, Meme held them out to Bode.

"For God's sake!" Rima said. "Just *tell* us!"

But Meme only shook her head. "You would not believe me."

"Go on." Tony pulled himself straight as Bode reluctantly seated the glasses, pushing the nosepiece with a forefinger. "Out with it, brother. What do you see?" Tony asked.

For a second, Bode thought it was a trick of their one lantern. Then a cry jumped out of his mouth. *"Christ!"* Throwing his hands up before his face, he stumbled back on his heels and might've fallen if he hadn't fetched up against the table with its dead.

"Bode?" Rima's voice was distant. "Bode, what . . . ?"

"Oh God." The round knob of a head butted his hip. His heart boomed. Yet he couldn't look away. "M-Meme, what does this mean? What does it *mean*?"

"Bode . . . *Brother*." Tony's face, the intact one, kept trying to break apart, but that was because Bode's eyes were full of tears. "Please," Tony said. "Tell me."

"Go on." Meme's tone was as detached as any he'd ever heard from Kramer. Or that inspector, Battle. "Tell him."

"I . . . I s-see . . ." The words came in a tremulous whisper. "T-Tony, I see . . ."

3

WHAT BODE SAW was mercifully blurred, as if Tony was composed of overlapping shadows. But there was still plenty of definition. So he saw enough, and realized that this was from that part of the nightmare he'd been denied because the other Bode, his doppelgänger, wasn't there at that precise moment. But Rima had described it in broad strokes, and so he thought that what he saw now was twofold: the friend he had known for as long as his faulty memory stretched, and the other Tony as he had been in the last moments of that other boy's life.

The shadow-Tony was a pulpy mess: no lips, no eyelids, and only dark vertical slits where his nose had been. Awash with hemorrhage, his eyes wept ruby tears. It was as if someone had taken a very sharp knife—or only a razor claw—and cut just above Tony's brow, at his hairline, etching a fine, bloody arc from ear to ear, and then worked his fingers between fascia and muscles, the better to peel Tony's face from his skull the way you would the rind of an orange.

"Bode?" When *his* Tony spoke, the other Tony moved its mouth, and that was how Bode knew *that* boy's tongue had been ripped out by the roots. "It's him, isn't it?"

With shaking fingers, Bode dragged off the spectacles and was relieved when the shadow-Tony vanished. "I think so."

Tony looked at Meme. "So he's really dead?"

"Yes and no," she said.

"For God's sake!" Cursing, Bode shook the glasses in Meme's face. "What do you mean?" He might've thrown them, but Rima's hands closed over his and plucked the glasses from his grasp. He barely noticed. All his frustration and fear were focused on the other girl. "Are you saying that because the *other* Tony died, that's killing *our* Tony? What?"

"Yes and no." When Bode's face changed, Meme put up her hands. "I am not toying with you. I really *mean* yes and no."

"What kind of answer . . . ," he began, but Rima said, suddenly, "Wait, I understand. Yes, the other Tony died in the valley. But then he . . . went back?"

"To his world, where he began." Meme put up that warning hand again. "I do not *truly* understand all of it. Kramer has his theories, but even he has only an inkling. Neither of them understand fully, except . . ." She let that go.

He heard the *neither* and thought, *Who? Who else is there?* Then, a mental tap on the shoulder: *The woman?* She was here, in the asylum, at this moment? Or was Meme talking about those mysterious patients? *When she was speaking with Kramer, Meme mentioned two boys.* From what he recalled, it sounded to Bode as if there were also at least two adults: a man and his wife. "Who? Understand what?"

"How it all works, with the *Nows*, what they call Many Worlds."

"Many Worlds," Rima echoed. "As in many of us? More than one?" She eyed the purple glasses with a look that was half curiosity, half dread. "And these let you see . . . what we really are?" With exaggerated care, she slipped them on and looked up at Meme. "Or who . . ." Rima's throat moved in a sharp swallow. Her face went so pale and glassy, it seemed to Bode that he could see clear through. "Who we . . . we might *not* be?"

"Yes, but I think that is also only a portion of it. Sometimes, I am not entirely sure what I am looking at," Meme said. "To me, they are . . . shadows."

"That's what I saw," Bode said.

After another second, Rima pulled the glasses free and refolded first the lenses and then the arms with exquisite care. Her face was unreadable. "That's why you wanted to see us?" She handed the glasses over to Meme. "Because this doctor knows about another Tony?"

"It is a bit more than that." Meme paused. "I also know they have a device they have been trying to make work for the longest time."

"They have more than just the glasses?" Bode asked.

"The panops? Yes."

"All-seeing," Rima said. Bode could've sworn he heard a tremor.

Meme nodded. "Anyone can use them just as you and Bode did. But not everyone can make the cynosure work."

"What's that?" Bode asked.

"Some kind of guide? Like a lantern? Or lens? It is a way of getting to the right world, the correct *Now*." Meme shrugged. "They have not been able to make it work, and it is of no use to them anyway unless they find another device. Dickens Mirror, Kramer calls it."

"Dickens." Bode frowned. Name didn't ring a bell. "Is that a place? Or some kind of glass?"

"I . . ." It might have been *I*; Bode wasn't sure because Emma quickly closed down on whatever was trying to find its way out of her mouth. *Good girl,* he thought to her. *Mum's the word.*

"No." Meme favored Emma with a long look. "Dickens is . . . was . . . a person."

"What kind of person?" Bode said, hoping to draw her gaze to him.

Her eyes shifted. "A writer from another *Now*. As I said, they do not truly understand either. They think the Mirror is here in London, but they have not been able to locate it. After today, however, they think they are a step closer."

"Why?" Tony asked. "What happened today?"

"We all had the same nightmare," Rima said.

Meme's forehead showed that small frown. "They have not spoken of that."

"Then it has to be Elizabeth," Bode said. "What happened with her. That's why Kramer's so keen on keeping Elizabeth in seclusion, isn't it?"

Meme nodded. "Where he has put her is . . . quite a different place from the rest of the asylum. It is all part of some kind of test."

"Test for what?"

"I am not sure. It has something to do with"—Meme seemed to search for the right words—"the manipulation of energy. Kramer calls her the *key*. Some theory about the strongest piece being the actual entity or spirit or whatever that can access the devices. And he is in a hurry, too."

Entity? Spirit? Piece, he recognized, though. *It's what Elizabeth calls her hallucinations.* "Why's he in a hurry?" Bode asked, then answered his own question. "Kramer must be afraid Battle will step in? Force him to give her up?"

"In part. Frankly, it has all sounded mad as hops. But," Meme said, her mouth moving a grimace, "as Doctor is so fond of reminding me, I am only an assistant he may make or break. After overhearing about his interest in you"—she inclined her head at Tony and Rima—"I had to be sure that what they were talking about was real and not lunacy."

Thank Christ, Kramer didn't know about *their* little Emma here. Bode aimed to keep it that way. *But Kramer calls for an Emma, and then Elizabeth goes nutter and we get ourselves a little girl.* Which did beg the question of *which* Emma Kramer wanted.

"I thought that if you *were* real, it might explain what was happening," Meme said.

"Why?" Tony asked. "What's happening?"

"They have him," Meme said. "The other Tony."

"What?" they all said at once. "He's *here*?" Tony said. "In Bedlam?"

She nodded. "And he's dying . . . just like you."

BODE

That Business with Doyle

"NO ARGUMENTS." BODE dumped the last body into the pushcart. The sack made a dull *puh* when it hit a thick white mantle of new snow. The false dawn had faded and the wind was up, flinging large wet flakes to plaster faces, clothes, and hair. "I'm not happy, you taking these with you," Bode said, watching as the cat leapt from Emma's arms to mince over sacks and wedge itself into a convenient hollow. "You ought to cut and run."

"I'm not excited either," Tony said, stumping around to the front of the cart. "But we need as much food as we can grab. For that, we got to deliver our load. There's method behind the madness, you know."

"Is that supposed to be a joke?" Rima's voice was tight. She gave the body Bode had deposited a hard, unnecessary shove. On the cart, Emma straddled her cat and silently repositioned the body, using one of their long pikes. "Because it's not funny," Rima said.

"I know that." Tony was very calm for a boy who'd just heard his doppelgänger lay dying somewhere; might, in fact, be taking Tony down with him. "But assuming we do get off-grounds, it's stupid to leave them. 'Sides, if someone else comes looking and sees the cart, they'll know Bode warned us. I'll tell you what bothers me, too." Having picked up his harness, Tony looked up from sorting leather traces. "The other Tony. Not right to leave him here. Who knows if maybe we can help? If maybe *I* can?"

"Oh no." Rima shook her head. "Think, Tony. The closer we've gotten to the asylum, the worse you are. More nosebleeds. You're weaker."

"And vice versa." It was Meme, who'd stood quietly by. "That is why Kramer was so keen on getting his hands on *your* Tony. He thinks that the doubles might even cure each other if he can perfect a serum. It is the same as that business with Doyle."

"What business?" Rima asked.

"A long story, and all rather ghoulish, actually." Meme shook her head. "Honestly, there are times I think Kramer is quite mad."

"Oh, *wonderful*." Sighing, Bode scrubbed fresh snow from his hair. "Rima's right, brother. You need to lay down distance."

"That's just it," Tony said. "I don't think any place is far enough. So long as the other Tony is . . . in this *Now*? I'm cooked."

"Unless he dies first," Rima said.

"God, listen to yourself. He's a *person*. Your other Rima . . . she cared what happened to him."

"I'm not her, and Meme said that Rima's . . . world? Her *Now*? It's in ruins. So who knows what's happened to her?" Sidling closer, Rima made a move as if to rest her palm on his left cheek, then checked herself. "You're the only Tony I care about."

"Can you help him?" Out of the corner of an eye, Bode saw Meme give him a curious glance. He wished he'd thought of this sooner, but it needed to be said. "Can you draw it?" he asked Rima.

Tony answered before Rima could. "I won't let her. Now that we know about the other Tony, think of what it might do to her if he gets his claws in."

"What are you all talking about?" Meme asked.

Bode sidestepped the question. "All right then. You three best get on your way. I've never been out that far, but once you're past the criminal wings, there shouldn't be anything else between you and . . ." His mind blanked. "Funny . . . name of the road's on the tip of my tongue, but . . ." He shook that away. "Never mind. What I know is there's open land and then trees, not very thick, and once you're past, you'll be closer to Battersea than if you went out the front." It all sounded vague, as if he were making up a story on the spot. But he suddenly had no mental image of London at all.

"We should all leave right now," Rima said. "You too, Bode."

"Nowhere left to run that will be far enough," Meme said.

"I don't think I was asking your opinion." Rima's jaw clenched. "I appreciate you warning us, I do. But please do shut up now."

"Here now," Tony said.

"I don't *care*." Rima aimed a fierce glance at Bode. "*Why?* Why risk going back for her? She's not one of us. We don't know her. You owe her nothing."

Bode made a sound as helpless as he felt. "Can't explain, Rima. I know it sounds half rats, but I got to try." Running might be the smartest thing. *But I can't. Saving Elizabeth is what I'm meant to do, why I'm here.* Or was it that he was to save Emma? He didn't know. Scared him how final it felt: as if it might be the very *last* thing he did.

"Once we get clear, how long you want us to wait at Battersea?" Tony asked.

"Until morning, I guess. If we're not there, you three cut out. Get as far away from Lambeth as you can. Me, I'd go to the very limits of the Peculiar down south. Once you're there, you might figure a way to either bypass it or get through. So go on now." After wrapping Rima in a quick hug, he threw an arm around Tony's neck and drew him close. "Stay alive, brother," he whispered. "Be there as fast as I can, and then we'll get out of here together, I promise."

"You just hurry," Tony said.

"Right." He dropped to his haunches in front of Emma. "You have a care now. Stick with them, understand?" As her eyes pooled, he gave her a light chuck on a cheek. "No crying. Your face will freeze."

She surprised him, throwing her arms around his neck. "There, there, it's all right," he said, tightening his grip around her shaking shoulders. She suddenly seemed so small, like a bird. "I'll be fine."

She gave his cheek a ferocious kiss, then said in a murmur only he heard, "Watch out for Meme."

"I will," he muttered back, touched that the girl could think clearly enough to care about someone she didn't know.

BODE

Mission

1

MEME'S LANTERN WAS smashed beyond repair. In the storeroom, Bode unearthed an ancient nubbin of candle fixed in an iron miner's pick, not that this meager flame did them much good in the wind and snow. Using their footprints, they navigated back by dead reckoning, a journey that felt like an eternity, though it may have been no more than a half hour before the gray bulk of the asylum glowered from the snow. They'd just crowded in through the kitchen's back door when Bode turned to Meme. "Thank you. For coming, I mean. You didn't have to."

"I know." Meme's hair, frosted with snow, tumbled around her shoulders. Flakes clung to her lashes, and the wind had stung her cheeks ruby-red. "But they are your family." Her mouth moved in a wistful wisp of a smile. "Sounds quite nice."

"It is. I'd do anything for Tony and Rima. I'd die for them, if it came to that." Looking at her made his throat tighten. "But what I mean to say is . . . after what happened in Kramer's office . . ."

"It is all right." Her dark eyes darted away. Snowmelt

glistened on her shawl and made her lips gleam. "Let us not speak of it."

"But I want to. You deserve a better friend than I've been. I'm sorry I didn't help . . . no." He put up a hand. "I know I said it before, but you took a risk for us. What I got to do for Elizabeth . . . it's this *pull*, like I got no choice. You had one."

"You do not know that." Her eyes sought his again. "The . . . pull?" She pressed a palm to her chest and then to his. "I feel it."

His heart shuddered under her touch. He remembered Kramer's questions, the near-taunting quality of his tone. Meme had risked this for him. He looked down into the girl's open face and thought, *I could kiss her.* He wanted to; the urge was a sudden ache in his chest; the tug of his attraction, a liquid fire in his thighs. Elizabeth, he had to help and protect. But with Meme, he might press his mouth to her chill lips and kiss her slowly and thoroughly until they warmed; draw his lips along her neck to linger over the throb of her pulse as she gasped and threaded her fingers into his hair; slip his hands beneath her coat and blouse and then . . . then her flesh. First his hands—roving, touching, stroking so lightly her back arched and strained to meet him—and then his mouth might feather her skin, the soft pillows of her breasts, his tongue pulling a moan from her throat, and then . . .

You are *mad.* "We should go." Stepping back, he tore his gaze from hers, though not before he saw a flicker of some emotion: not disappointment or hurt but confusion, which was almost as bad. He felt a surge of self-loathing. *What are you thinking, toying with this poor girl?* But had he been? He thought of the thousand small signals and Meme, always and forever there, with a word, a slight touch. But he'd been so focused on Elizabeth, his . . . God, it sounded so stupid . . . his *mission,* he'd discounted them.

Worry about this later. Still, it was all he could do not to press her up against a wall, surrender to his desire and her need, and the hell with consequences.

"You ready?" he said.

"Yes," and she even managed a small smile. "Always."

2

THEY DIDN'T SPEAK again until they'd made their way down a darkened hall to the rear of the front vestibule and an iron door that opened onto wide stone stairs leading down to the first series of tunnels. As he socked in Graves's skeleton, he said, "There's something I been meaning to ask. Something about what Kramer said."

"Yes?" The word was as void of expression as her face.

"Doyle. Kramer did something to him."

"An injection. Yes." After a pause: "He's an addict. Kramer provided."

Ah, well, that did explain Doyle's raucous guts. A few times there, he'd have liked to die from the stink. For Kramer to go behind Battle's back, circumvent the police, he must want something very badly. "Why? Kramer's not exactly the charitable type."

"No. But Doyle can lay hands on something Doctor cannot."

"And what's that?"

Her eyes were steady. "Bodies."

PART FOUR

BLACK DOG

DOYLE

Madding Crowd

1

"MOVE ASIDE . . . police . . . make room." Working his stout billy club in a steady tick-tock, Doyle forged a trail through the general crush of foot traffic and handcarts. The air was a stew of curdled smoke, thick snow, and the unintelligible burr of voices. Slicked by icy patches and fresh snow, the cobblestone road was treacherous. With the quake, whole portions had buckled and caved whilst others had been thrust up a good six, seven inches. The way was a positive horror. "Move along . . . police. Make way." *Tick-tock, tick-tock, right-left, right-left.* "Have a care . . . police . . ." The crowd, only so many anonymous blobs, jostled and shouldered past. Why, you could run this same madding crowd past him night after night and he'd never know the difference.

Yes, but if not for Battle, would I know the way? What street is this anyway? Are we still on Lambeth? He didn't think so. They'd taken turns, rounded corners, passed doorways and snickets and ginnels. Somewhere past the crowd, he'd the impression of hulking tenements, narrow alleys, crumbling fronts curtained behind snow and a thick gray veil through which no light of any sort oozed. These warrens, these passageways and secret back court-yards, were their own worlds. Who knew what creatures lived there? There was talk around the station: certain constables gone missing, never to be seen again. Anything could live in that soup, *anything*, and here he was, breathing it in. They all were. The Peculiar hadn't smothered them, yet he felt its tendrils kneading his brain, poking and prodding the way you stuck your finger in a Christmas pudding to search for a silver coin.

Or perhaps it's Kramer and his injection. Black Dog gave his arm a tiny nip. **Think about it, how quickly your mood's soured, how irritable you are. Touch a match, you'll explode. Don't you feel it? Kramer's out to poison you.**

He couldn't deny how he felt: nerves jangled, entire body on alert. His skin fairly fizzed, like vinegar and bicarbonate. All of a sudden, he wanted to tear his clothes from his hot, flushed skin and race bare-arsed into the night. Let the fog and whatever waited inside take him and be done with it.

Stop, Doyle, stop. He ground his teeth until his jaw complained. *What you thinking, you lunatic?* He had to remain steady. Kramer wanted something only Doyle could procure. Cove wouldn't cross him, not yet.

I didn't say the drug doesn't work. I'm suggesting that you've fallen for the oldest con in the books, poppet. Black Dog actually seemed sympathetic. **Shoot you up enough to take the edge off but leave you chasing your tail until you make good.**

No, that was ridiculous. All he had to do was tell Battle. But wait . . . no, he couldn't do that either, could he? Then what was he going to—

". . . mind, Doyle?" Battle, alongside, tap-tapping his shoulder.

"Are you there? Is something the matter, Constable?"

"What?" He looked over, then realized that he'd gone on several paces. Turning, he found Battle, with his bull's-eye lantern held aloft, giving him a curious stare. "Uh, no, sir." *Stop it. Focus. Do your job.* He darted anxious glances right and left, his neck swiveling, *tick-tock-tick-tock,* trying to look at everything at once. "No. Just . . . thinking," he said, finally. It seemed as good an answer as any. It was also true.

"Yes." Battle managed to make it sound as if Doyle had decided to drop his drawers and relieve himself on the bare cobbles. "You've been preoccupied since we left the asylum. What's on your mind, Constable?"

Too many people; hard to breathe. His face dewed with fresh sweat. The snow stinging his face actually felt good. *Getting sick.* He was distracted, feeling the pressure, this whisk of people brushing close, and the *noise,* this incessant burr of many voices and, beyond, the squall and creak of pushcarts. Another shiver grabbed his neck. *Get back, wrap myself in a blanket, sweat this out.* Suck his humbugs for the sugar; that would make him better, too. Then he remembered: he'd only the few left that he'd dropped in his coat pocket. *Idiot, giving them away to that girl; you're a fool!* Well, he'd make do. Then what? Back to Kramer, beg for another shot? Then he thought, *Kramer. Right. Come on, Doyle. Keep your eye on the prize.*

"Well, sir, yes, there is something." Having rehearsed this as he'd made his way off the ward and then down the long marble stairs to the asylum's ground floor, he understood that what he said next had to flow naturally. "It's that Miss Elizabeth. A shock, how she came out of it. And her parents . . . I didn't know any of that."

"Well, you wouldn't. It's not your investigation or business to know." Battle favored him with that copper's dead-eye. "And? Come now, speak up. It's cold, and I've not had my supper."

Oh, riiiight. As if *he* had. But *nooo*, the great inspector had to be properly fed and watered at regular intervals like a damned nag. (*God*, he would gladly murder his own mam for a nice horse's haunch.) "Right. Sorry." What was wrong with him? "Ah . . . it's nothing, sir. Not for me to say, that is. It just seems to me that—"

From the gloom, something suddenly shot to hook his injured right arm. "Fancy a bit of boiled leather, dearie?"

"What?" Jerking round, he looked down into the snaggle-toothed maw of an old hag, with a left hand made of tin and a huge divot carved from her skull just above the place where she ought to have a right ear. It looked as if a giant had taken a large, sloppy bite of bone and brain. "Christ! Get *off* me!"

"Now, now, no need to get upset." Showing all three of her teeth to their best advantage, the hag said, "I asked if you wouldn't fancy a nice mouthful 'a boiled leather." The fingers of her good right hand tightened to claws on his arm. "Only a farthing."

"God, no." This close, he could see the pulse of her brains against a thin tent of grimy scalp. "Move on. Go back to your cart." And sod Battle; they could talk once they were back at the station. Without waiting for the hag's reply, he plunged forward, brandishing his billy. "*Police!* Move your bloody arse out of the way!" A startled cry jumped from the murk as his club met something soft. Man, woman; he didn't care. Butting the person aside, he bawled, "*Get* your—"

"Doyle!" Battle grabbed the hinge of an elbow. "What are you doing, man?"

Touch me again and I'll cave in your teeth. Then what Battle had said caught up with him. Blinking, he looked around and realized with a start of dismay that he hadn't moved an inch. As far as he could tell, he was in the same spot as five seconds before.

Oh hell. A fierce trembling swept him. *I wasn't walking away? I* imagined *it?*

"Doyle?" Battle seemed genuinely concerned. "Are you ill? One moment, we're talking, the next you're swinging your truncheon about. Nearly knocked my head in."

"Oh." *Christ, Doyle.* He armed his forehead with a sleeve. "Sorry. Not quite up to dick. Might be taking a bit of a fever."

"Then let's get you to the station." Battle gave Doyle's arm a small tug. "Come on. Some hot tea . . ."

"Dearie." Something twitched his coat, and then he heard it—her—again, as the hag continued, "Either of you nice coppers in the mood for a good hot piece 'a boiled leather?"

2

HE MUST HAVE stood, paralyzed, a good few seconds. *No.* The pressure in his chest was so immense, he should've blown apart. *No, I just saw you; you can't be real.*

"Dearie?" Another twitch, and then he could smell the noxious fumes of her sewer's breath. Her scalp throbbed. "You all right?"

No. He was bathed in sweat. He wouldn't be surprised to find steamy curls wafting up to mingle with the smoke and murk. The cut of snow and wind on his face felt muted, insubstantial. *I'm losing my mind.*

"We're fine, thank you, mum." Battle, that stiff, actually touched the brim of his bowler. "I don't believe either of us require a morsel of leather, boiled or otherwise."

Either Battle didn't remember, or this was happening for the first time. *But it felt so real.* "Right." Slicking his lips, he extricated his arm from Battle's grip. To the hag, he said, "Be off with you. Go on."

"Doyle," Battle began, as Black Dog whispered, **Poppet, no. Stop.**

"Oh, but wait, wait," the hag said, "I've ever so nice a mess of—"

"Didn't you just hear? Didn't I just *say*?" Planting his billy in her chest, he gave her a shove. "Out of my *way*."

"Doyle!" Battle snapped.

"AAAWWWK!" Mouth snapping open in a surprised O, the hag wheeled, sticklike arms circling, before falling back. She was lost from sight in a second as the snow and crowd closed over her once more.

There, stay gone! Turning, he roared, *"POLICE!* Make way, make way! Come on, *move!"* Brandishing his club: *right-left-tick-tock-tick-tock-right-left-right-left-right! "Movemovemove!"* Thinking, *Get back, fast as I can. Wrap myself in blankets.*

Poppet, stop, listen to yourself.

He paid Black Dog no mind. Plowing forward, he hacked right and left with his club. *Sweat this out, it will pass. Have a few humbugs . . .* "Oh *shite*," he said, the whimper worming between his teeth. *I just thought that.*

That's right, poppet, that's right. Take a look round. Go on. What you see?

Right. He felt his mind grasping onto Black Dog's voice, which reminded him of his mam's, how she soothed when he took a high fever. Close his eyes, Doyle could almost taste milky, sweet, weak tea. But now he did what Black Dog said and looked about.

Same spot. Same cobbles. Same smoke and mist. The incessant snow, and of course, the crowd. *Haven't budged an inch.*

"Doyle." Holding his lantern high, Battle was studying Doyle with the avid intensity of a scientist gawking at an eight-headed hydra. "My God, man, you're positively swimming in sweat. Are you feverish?" Using his teeth to pull off a glove, Battle pressed a hand to Doyle's forehead. "Burning up, boy."

"Sorry, sir. Just a little . . ." *A little what? Oh, it's nothing, sir; just a touch of the old shakes, the jimjams, that bloody fucking withdrawal. Never you mind that I'm suddenly mad as hops because I've no idea where in hell we are, or what's really going on. Only damme if I don't keep reliving the same few moments over and over again.* "Might be taking ill," he said, with remarkable calm. "A touch on edge. That's all."

"Yes, so I've gathered. You've been preoccupied since we left the asylum," Battle said. "What's on your mind, Constable?"

3

OH. SAME WORDS, same question. *You watch; the hag will appear next.* He *was* like a dog after its own tail, chasing round and round. If he hadn't already been living the same day over and over again. Maybe this was the only real moment of his entire day.

Kill Battle. Yeah, that might work. Certainly change things up now, wouldn't it? He threw a wild eye over the gray steel bowl of Battle's hat. *Split your face with a single blow, then melt into the night with these others.* That would be a way. *Or . . .* He looked away from Battle and into the snow. Out there was the Thames, and the patient veil of the Peculiar. Lose himself in that and no one would ever see him again. Who knew? Once he passed inside, perhaps he'd dissolve completely, like bones in strong lime.

"Doyle?"

"Nothing, sir." His lips strained with a lunatic's grin. "Nothing on my mind, not a thing, not *any THING*." *Shut up shut up shut up!*

"Well, you look rather peaky again, Doyle." Battle frowned. "Are you quite sure?"

Yes. No. God, he had to stop this. Get off this particular flying horse on this particular carousel. *Round and round I go.* His tongue skimmed wet salt from a bottom lip. Black Dog was right. *It's whatever's in that cocktail Kramer's dreamt up.* Get himself to his rooms—that was the ticket. Swaddle up in blankets, sweat this out a bit, pop a few humbugs, the sugar would help, and . . .

Some person—male, female, he didn't know—brushed too close. Startled, he wheeled, arm coming up and a cry leaping from his tongue: "Don't *touch* me, ya *gob*!" Swinging, he cursed. "Move aside, make way, *police* . . ."

A tap on his shoulder made him whirl and draw back, elbow cocked, club half-raised to strike. "Doyle! Easy!" Wreathed in snow and mist, Battle put a palm out. "What are you doing, man? There's no need for that."

He was going to kill Battle; he would pulverize that face, split the man's skull if they didn't get moving, out of this snow, away from this damned crowd! "Just clearing the way, sir." He could hear his voice climbing the registers of hysteria. "On our way . . . yes, on our way, on our way to the station, that's right!" *If you'd only mind your own sodding business and move your bloody ass afore that hag . . .*

"*Dearie.*" On cue. "Would either of you fine gents care for—"

Bellowing, he rounded and cut the hag a vicious blow. *"NOOO!"*

Her face caved. The space between her eyes burst wide open in a fume of blood and tissue and broken bone. Ballooning from the pressure, her scalp ruptured, spewing wormy pale-pink brains. Without uttering a sound, she collapsed, but Doyle was already following, this time with his heavy policeman's boots. Raising a foot, he drove down, square on what was left of the woman's skull.

"Doyle!" Battle was screaming. "Stop, *stop!"*

"Fuck no, *fuck* no!" The shrieks cut like knives but felt good. He stomped down hard. There was a loud wet sound midway between a crunch and the *thuck* of a melon smashed on brick. The hag's skull gave. Gore and bloody gobbets spattered cobbles and splashed his trousers. When he pulled his boot out, it came with a sodden sucking sound. And yet no one stopped; the crowd continued on its murmuring way, and he was mad, going mad, gone gone gone! *"Fuck me, oh fuck me!"* Screeching, stomping hard, hard, harder! His spit flew like foam from the mug of a mad dog. *"Fuck FUCK!"*

Then, all at once, the hag's head—this mash of pulped meat and bony shards—quivered and *heaved.*

"Christ!" Panting, he stared, aghast. The mess pulsed once, twice. A large bubble grew and then ballooned in a red membranous sack—and within, he could see them: a teeming, roiling, gelatinous clot of squirmers.

"N-no," he said, backing up a slithering step. Hands out, *pleading.* "D-don't. Stop, s-stop . . ."

The sack burst.

DOYLE

Squirmers

1

THE HAG'S BLOOD expanded in a halo of pink mist. Doyle screamed as wet, wriggling slop sheeted over his face, and then he was choking as squirmers shot for his open mouth, spilled into his throat, nosed his ears. There were sharp pricks at his eyes as they bit in and then burrowed into the whites.

"No, no!" Clawing at his face, gargling blood against an undulating tide down the center of his chest, he staggered. The thin-walled grapes of his eyes pulsed; he could feel squirmers rippling, see their slithery bodies shoot across his vision. His bull's-eye smashed to the cobbles as he screamed again. "Get them out!" Digging at his eyes, he felt his nails rip skin, and now blood was pouring into his sockets, or that might only be the squirmers thrashing through soft jelly, drilling their insatiable way into his brain, and in the next second, his eyes would rupture in a torrent of snotty jam . . .

"*Doyle!*" Snatching at his shoulder, Battle whipped him round. Staggering, his boots slimy with brains and blood, Doyle nearly went ass over teakettle. Battle grabbed his coat in his fists.

"What's the matter with you, man?" Bulling his face only inches from Doyle's own. "Have you gone mad?"

"I think I told you not to touch me again, sir"—and then, with a roar, he swung that billy as hard as he could . . .

2

. . . AND IT connects, the sound of his club against bone like the bite of an ax into a stout log.

Battle's head whips right with a sharp crackle like dry rats' bones ground underfoot. Black blood jumps from his left ear. Going limp as a rag doll, the big man drops as Doyle—with no squirmers now but only murder on his mind—goes with him.

Been waiting all my life for this. Gripping his club with both hands, he brings the billy down again in a vicious chop. *Die, you bastard, just die and leave us in peace!*

This time, there is a swift, smart *crack*. Battle's scalp splits in two, from crown to the hinge of his jaw, revealing a glimmer of smeary bone. Blood begins pouring, pulsing in a red torrent. Another chop and Battle's skull opens in a sodden crunch, the crack of a gourd or rotted pumpkin under a stout heel.

Oh, this feels good, this is good! Huffing like a blown horse, Doyle stares down, gored billy in hand, blood singing in his veins.

Crumpled on soiled cobbles, Battle is, incredibly, moaning. Through the purple, swirling muck of torn skin and battered bone, Battle's head pulses and heaves as the pink worms of his brain struggle under a milky, membranous shroud. Battle's jaws suddenly unhinge, and what comes is a groan—and a word. Actually, a name.

"Ar-Ar-Artieee." Battle drags in a ragged, wet breath. *"Arrrtieee."*

What? Still blowing, Doyle gives himself a shake. On his arm, Black Dog's gone silent, and for once, Doyle wishes the thing would speak. *WHAT?*

"Arrrtieee," Battle moans again, and now Doyle is positive. The inspector's lying there with his brains dashed all over snow-covered cobbles going bright red with the seep. But this is not Battle's voice. No, this is lighter, a little plaintive, with the burr of a brogue. *"Arrrtieee."*

Shite, no. Gasping, Doyle tosses a wild look. There is suddenly no crowd or mist or smoke or snow. If he were to take himself to the Thames, he's positive the Peculiar would've vanished. The cobbles have disappeared, too. *No . . . NO . . .*

But the view does not change.

3

THE KITCHEN IS small, dingy, dirty. Ancient grease splatters stain the wall over the hob. A large splotch of soot, black and oily, smears the ceiling above a weak gas flame that sputters and spits. Off-true, the room's one window lists to the left, and there is daylight through the chinks. Yet the room is close and hot and stinks of rotted eggs, fried onions, greasy potatoes. The floor's awash in blood and smashed crockery. A shimmering white slick of oatmeal and leek soup vomits over tired wood, because it's Lent and his father . . . his *father* . . .

Oh, good Christ. Doyle wants to fall to his knees. *I'm back.*

DOYLE

Dogged by the Devil

1

IT'S THE LENTEN holidays, and his father—that sot, that drunk, that bastard—has swept everything from the table. In one corner, his mam cowers, belly huge, hair come undone to drag around her face, a blood bib on her blouse. Clustered round like chicks are his brother and seven sisters, all weeping and cowering. On the wall opposite, there's a large, drippy red arc. A longer, brighter smear paints an exclamation mark all the way to the floor, where his father lies in a red-black pool.

"*Arr . . .*" His father's got both bloody mitts wrapped around that stag-horn hilt, and he's managed to pull the blade out a gory inch. A mistake, that, like unstoppering a bottle, because now his blood's pulsing in great spurts, *splish-splish-splish.* "*S-sonnn . . .*"

So he's never left? *I've traded one horror for another? Blink my eyes and I'll be back in London, standing with Battle in the snow . . . round and round . . .* Or maybe all the rest has been nothing but a vision provoked by bad gin or cheap beer, both of which he has developed a taste for by now, because he is fourteen and dirt poor and so hungry some days cockroaches look good. The Jesuits, those prunes, feed him, but the meals are meager and there's no money or nice packages coming out to Stonyhurst for Artie to buy treats and sweetmeats in town like the rest of the boys, no. He's charity, and everyone knows it. How his mam wheedled a spot there is beyond him. But that's what she's always done, *push-push-push*, because Artie is her favorite, her savior, her jewel.

As this is, perhaps, his. He senses this. This is the pivot about which all the rest of his life will turn, round and round and round.

His face smarts. Working his mouth around a taste of copper, he spits blood, but more trickles down his throat from an aching tongue his teeth have snapped. The sight in his right eye's bleary, the focus soft. With blood-spattered fingers, he gingerly probes his cheek, wincing at the knot. Above the ring in his ears, he can hear the ceaseless din of voices from their many neighbors below this top flat because the walls of this squalid tenement are so thin. For once, though, he's glad of the noise, because it's likely covered his father's bellows, and what's one more drunk in Sciennes Hill Place anyway?

"What have you done?" His mother's eyes bulge in horror. "What in God's name were you thinking? You *killed* him!"

"He's not dead yet," he says, hoarsely, in a voice he barely recognizes. "Are ya?" Toeing his father with a boot provokes another long groan, a plaintive *Arrrtieee*. The flow of his father's blood is beginning to weaken, the *splish-splish* dwindling to a dribble as thin as the tail end of a good long piss. "Won't be coming after anyone now, will ya?"

"Have you gone mad?" The fear in his mother's voice makes all the girls weep even harder. (God, so many damned yammering sisters; that's one thing he's not missed being off at school.) "Are you a lunatic?"

This is a very good question. *Not now, but I shall be?* "He was hurting you."

"And I've stood it for years. He's my *husband*."

"Yeah?" His fingers are tacky. He stares at his fists flexing and clenching, studying the deep rust-red crescents under his nails. His palms are red traceries, and he sees how one line, quite short, is fairly broken in two on either hand. *Life line?* He should ask a gypsy. "Not for much longer. Then we can get clear of this, of Edinburgh. Find us a nice cottage in the country, with clean air. Keep chickens and a cow and pigs."

"You've gone off your head. How? With what? They'll take you away," his mother whispers. "They'll put you in jail. They might even hang you, and then who'll take care of us? We've no money, no one I can ask." Her tone shifts, becomes a wheedling accusation. "I'll be reduced to taking in boarders, you know that. Strangers in my house, bringing in their filth, their women, doing God knows what . . ."

Oh yeah, he thinks as he eyes the bulge of her stomach, *like you're a stranger to what goes on behind closed doors.* The idea that his mother's let his drunken pap into her bed time after time makes his head turn a giddy wheel. *Steady. See this through.*

"No one's taking me away. We call the coppers, and we tell 'em. Here's what's happened, all right?" His gaze sweeps their faces. He enjoys how they all dodge their eyes. *Good. About time someone was afraid of* me *for a change.*

"He was beating you," he says to his mother. By the time the police come, this stranger's voice will be gone. He will be fourteen again, snot-nosed and scared out of his wits, and oh so beside himself with grief over what's happened to his dad: *But I couldn't help it. I was afraid. He was hurting my mother. I didn't mean it. It was him, not me.*

Though he will see this man again, many times over and for years: over his bed, risen from the grave, the body green and bloated with decay and innards rotted to jelly. Always, the thing will fade before it can say his name. A good thing, that. To name is to control. To name is to possess.

"He had that damned knife, too. When I tried to stop him hurting you, he turned on me, and I got my arm up only just in time." He is now aware of blood coursing down his left arm to drip from his wrist, a wicked slash with that fine scalloped file-work and a scar he will wear for the rest of his life. "And I hit him with a skillet. Self-defense, it was, and he slipped, and that's when he fell on his knife. That's the story."

"But that's not what happened." Her eyes, large and frightened, remind him of a mouse quivering under a cat. "He slashed you, and he slipped, and then *you* grabbed up the knife and . . ."

"Shut it," he says, in a voice that is a whip and more brutal than he thought possible. Certainly, he's never used this tone with his mam. What worries him, but only a little, is how much he enjoys seeing her flinch. "Wipe that right out your head." His eyes touch first her face and then each of his siblings in turn. "This is the story. This is what happened. He fell on the knife, and that's all."

There is a short silence, one that even the *splish-splish* of his father's blood does not break. That pump's run dry. Mouth open in an airless gawp, his father's face is gray, his eyes already glazing. The edges of that bloody slick are growing turgid as grape jam.

"But . . ." His mother's voice is meek now, and this pleases him, too. "But Artie, you didn't hit him with a skillet."

At that, he grins, and from her reaction, he wishes he could see his dial for himself: orange teeth, ruby lips, bruised face. He must look a positive horror.

"Well." Striding to the hob, he fetches up the skillet. There are still curls of oily leeks and crusted onions stuck to the blackened cast iron. They'll make a mess, but all that's to the better. It lends that little bit of credence: *He came at me. I was scared, and the skillet was right there on the hob.* Gripping the heavy pan in both hands, he cocks his elbows and sets his feet. "Not yet I haven't," he says to his mother.

And then he brings the skillet down with all his . . .

2

"DOYLE?"

"What?" He blinked back to find the hag, with only half a skull and one good hand, still on his right arm. Doyle cleared the rust from his throat. "Yes?"

"I asked if you were all right." Battle cocked his head like a spaniel. "Your skin's flushed, and you're sweating again. Are you ill?"

Round and round and round . . . "Me? Ill?" He shook the cobwebs from his mind, and the hag's hand from his arm.

"A touch green, you ask me." The hag tipped Battle a knowing wink. "Bit of the old puffer'd set him to rights, you don't mind my saying."

"Thank you," Battle said, icily, "but I *do* mind."

Oh, speak for yourself. The image of his moaning father was a red cinder between his eyes. *Look away, look away, Doyle, before you go blind. This is one god you dare not gaze upon for long.* But he couldn't. It was as if this memory was the only star in all his black sky.

"Fill your bellies then," the hag persisted, latching onto Battle. "Got me good leather. Cost ya just a fadge. For you gentlemen, I'll part with double. Five pieces if you've an appetite."

"No, thank you," Battle said.

"*Hate* then," and it took Doyle a second to realize that she was upping the number by three. "Can't spare no more."

"Didn't you hear?" Angry and more than a little frightened now, he wedged the knob of his billy in the hag's chest. "Aren't you listening? The inspector *told* you . . ."

No. He took back his billy. *No, don't start this again. Walk away, Doyle, walk . . .*

Yes. Well said, poppet. From the corner of his left eye, something smoked so closely Doyle felt the whicker of its passage. **Let us walk this shadowy valley together.**

What? Heart flipping, he jerked round, billy raised to strike. Nothing. *Where are you? What ya playing at?*

Playing? A shadow steamed to his right. **Darling, the time for games is past.**

"Oh, really?" With a wild yelp, he whirled, eyes wide, muscles quivering . . . but there was still nothing. "Then stop *playing* them!"

"Doyle?" Battle said.

He paid no mind. Another glimmer unfurled, right to left. This time, he spun so fast, his feet tangled on icy cobbles and he nearly fell. "Show yourself, ya Devil!"

"Doyle, for God's sake, man." Battle turned a look right and left. "What is it?"

"Jimjams," the hag opined.

Behold, I stand at the door and knock. Whisking to his side, Black Dog drew its long, moist tongue over his left ear. **All**

you must needs do is open the door, poppet.

"God!" He was so startled he actually bit his tongue. "Christ!"

No, dear. Black Dog chuffed its dog's laugh. **Hardly.**

Good Lord, first the hallucinations, the memory, and now this! *It's never touched me, not like this!* His ear tingled. Black Dog's hot, sulfurous breath steamed into his nostrils. *I've never smelled it or* almost *caught a glimpse.* What did that mean?

Mean? Black Dog chuckled. **Didn't you just ask me to show myself? Haven't you conjured the very god you seek? What is that memory of your dear pap but the monster burning bright in your soul?**

"Doyle?" Battle, curse him. "Constable, what in God's name . . ."

"Tole ya." The hag sounded smug. "*That* one's in need of a good pipe; touch of the old smoke set him to rights. Maybe even a needle."

Christ, no, no more needles! He had to hang on. God, this was the drug, had to be. But what was Kramer's game? His mouth filled with liquid, and he spat—and that was when he realized: his blood had no taste. None at all. *What, what?* He knew his tongue bled; he felt the ooze down his throat. But the taste was less than water. *This isn't right; it can't be . . .* He suddenly bit the tender flesh of his lower lip as hard as he could, wincing as his teeth gouged soft skin. *All right, good; I felt that.* He thought Battle said something—he caught the burr of the man's voice—but it was Black Dog he heard most clearly: **Poppet? What are you doing?**

Testing something. Eyes closed, he sucked at this fresh cut, rolling moisture on his tongue. Nothing—and that wasn't right. Blood had a texture and taste, and it was . . . *Salt. Salt and . . . rust.* But there was nothing.

What's that prove? Black Dog was positively clinical. **What's your hypothesis?**

He didn't know, but he felt naked, shucked. He thought that this might be what it was like for Saul, blinded by God and struck down from his mule, once the veil was lifted and the scales began to flake from his eyes, and the old world, all Saul had known, fell away. *Except I'm dogged by the Devil, and there is no light, no god.*

"Doyle." Lantern held aloft, Battle stepped into his line of sight, ducking his head down to grab Doyle's eyes. "You're bleeding. Bit yourself when you slipped?"

"Yes, sir," he said, simply, wincing a bit at the stab of light from Battle's bull's-eye. What else *could* he say? *I'm dissolving; I'm unraveling, a layer at a time?* "Lost my footing there a second, sir, is all."

How metaphorical, dear.

"I can fix 'im," the hag said to Battle.

"No," he said, before Battle could respond. Pulling himself straighter, he smeared blood—*not even sticky*—then stared at his palm, dark with strange ink. His life line was as short and broken as before. *The earth is utterly broken; the earth is split apart.* He wanted to weep and laugh at the same time; here, his mother always wanted what the Jesuits stuffed in his brain to be put to good use. "I'm all right, sir. Just a . . ." He let that die. "Shall we?"

"Indeed." Turning, Battle held his lantern aloft and strode into the faceless, madding crowd. "Follow me, Constable."

Yes, follow Battle, darling. Black Dog whisked like smoke around his legs. **Follow that light, for as long as you can.**

"Yes, sir," he said, wiping his not-blood on his uniform coat. "Right behind you."

DOYLE

Window Dressing

1

WHAT FELT LIKE hours later, Doyle finally spied a bright gray blur above a doorway that resolved into the blue lantern marking Lambeth Station. He followed the inspector into the station and then across the short entryway to the front desk as Black Dog slithered behind.

To Doyle's right, a clutch of constables chatted and held their cold-roughened hands over a low brazier mounded with orange coals. As he passed, the faint scorch of hot iron drifted past his nose, and he felt a cushion of warmer air.

I felt that. Relief made his knees weak. *I'm back. It was just the drug, that's all.* If he bit himself again, would he taste his blood this time?

At the desk sergeant's counter, he waited, trying not to fidget, while Battle leafed through a bedraggled day ledger. To his left, just out of sight, he felt Black Dog settle onto its haunches. Doyle listened with only half an ear as the desk sergeant reeled off the day's happenings.

All right. Doyle thought back to the faceless crowd. *An*

aberration, that. This sergeant, for example . . . he might be a real man. Glancing askance, he registered an impression of eyes behind spectacles and a grizzled tangle of ginger beard, the faint gleaming crescent that extended a hair beyond the collar of his uniform shirt because the man had a tin chest, belly to just below the Adam's apple. So far, so good. *But is that because I'm filling it all in, or because the desk sergeant really sports a beard?*

Excellent question, poppet. A massive paw dropped to his left shoulder. **Your capacity for observation has grown more acute.**

STOP that. He gulped back a shout. It was one thing for Black Dog to nip and lick and speak, but another entirely to actually clap him on the shoulder and—my *God*, was that hound *larger*? Had to be near man-sized. From the corner of his mouth, he said, "Take your bloody paw off my shoulder this instant."

Or what? Black Dog laughed its silent dog's laugh. **Make me.**

"Keep your voice down." His eyes slid round in furtive little darts. From around the station came the clap of boots and the buzz of desultory, unintelligible conversation. It never had bothered Doyle before, all that background noise. Really quite soothing, like the flow of a river or wind through leaves. (Wait, did he actually *know* either? Where had he last heard a breeze through trees? Or flowing water that didn't come from a bucket of melt?) Now, though, he felt the noise as an annoying drag of a claw along his spine. And shouldn't he get snippets, whole sentences? Had he ever called out to any of these men by name? Had a conversation, gone for a pint, had a smoke, warmed his hands over those coals? And would they give off heat?

Stop it. Of course, those coals were hot; he'd felt the temperature change himself. His constable's coat sparkled with fresh snowmelt. Smash his fist into stone, he'd break a knuckle. There'd be blood.

Ah, yes, poppet, but would it have taste and texture?

Shut it, ya mongrel. Those men clustered over that brazier were no illusion; they had *mouths* set in actual *faces*. (But still . . . so faint, every visage a smear.) He spied one with a tin hand, another with a limp that suggested his wood leg needed adjusting. As Battle and the sergeant talked, he heard a door creak, felt a balloon of colder air expand against his back (*and see,* see, *it's snowing, freezing outside*), and stole a glance. At the bottom of the steps, two constables were shaking snow from their shoulders and stamping slush from their boots. He recognized the uniforms and the brass buttons; the numbers—pinned to high collars—were right. But as the men climbed the second, shorter flight of steps, Doyle realized that the numbers were only brassy blurs and a jumbled impression of symbols set right in the spot where you'd expect to find them.

Well, Black Dog said, positively chummy, **are you sure this isn't so much window dressing?**

No, he wasn't. The two constables were chatting each other up and laughing; one slapped the other on the shoulder. He got the basso timbre of their notes but none of the substance. They might as well have been uncredited actors on a stage, standing well back and muttering nonsense: *Peas and carrots, peas and carrots, she's a tart, she's a tart.*

He had to hold on. He pointedly transferred his gaze to his bunched knuckles, white and tented with tension. *Get Battle to tell you what you need to know, and then finish this with Kramer.* Slice the doctor's throat from ear to ear with his *sgian-dubh* considering how Kramer admired it so.

Yes. Black Dog chucked him on the arm. **That'll be a sight now, won't it? Looking forward to it, are you, dear?**

Yes. His lips stretched in a maniac grin. Yes, he really was.

"Something amusing, Doyle? Why, you look more up to dick there, almost jolly." Before he could reply, Battle clapped the ledger shut. "Come. Follow me."

2

"HAVE A SEAT, Constable. Take off that coat, if you wish," Battle said as he hung both his own coat and gray bowler on a corner tree.

"That's all right, sir," he said, watching as his breath steamed in the chill. *I see it; that's from me; I'm real.* Battle . . . well, the man must have the internal temperature of a flounder. Behind, he heard Black Dog pad to flank the office's only visitor's chair while Battle fussed with an oil lamp. The office, which was left of the front desk and down a long and empty corridor, was nondescript. A gas lamp that probably hadn't been lit in months hung from the ceiling. A rank of mounted and locked pigeonholes lined the far wall. Besides Battle's desk and chair, there was a clothes tree and a mirror suspended over a low washstand.

"So." Drawing down the wick, Battle eyed him over the round rim of his lamp's slightly sooty shade. "That was quite the experience. Have a drink with me, Doyle. Take the chill off." When he hesitated, Battle's mouth turned in a grin made a touch ghoulish by the dance of light under his chin. "Come now. You're in need of a restorative."

"Why, yes, I'd be pleased, sir. Thank you." At the thought of a nice mouthful of whiskey or brandy or gin—*anything* would do—his mouth watered. He waited as Battle withdrew a silk pouch, secured with black ribbon, from an inside pocket of his suit jacket. Untying the ribbon, he unrolled the pouch to reveal an impressive array of iron and brass keys, many of which were long gray skeletons, and all secured on silk loops. *God.* His eyebrows crawled for his hair. He knew every inspector had such a collection, though Battle's was huge, at least a dozen keys. He wondered what they all unlocked. *Man could get through every door in Lambeth with those.* Hospitals, chemists' shops, doctors' offices. Every door in this station, too, he imagined.

Inserting a small, ornate brass key into the lock of his topmost desk drawer, Battle slipped a hand inside his desk. There followed the crisp *click* of a hidden catch, and then the inspector was plucking a bottle, three-quarters full of amber liquid, from a lower drawer on the right. "Don't know why I bother with that secret latch," Battle said, pouring liquor into shot glasses. "Every man in this station could pick this lock."

"If he knew where to look." From the color, he thought the alcohol might be rye or brandy. *Don't care what it is, so long as it actually tastes like something.*

Black Dog nosed his left boot. **Don't let's get our hopes up.**

"There is that. I suppose the compartment appeals to my sense of the dramatic." Battle pushed a shot glass across the desk. "We've all got secrets."

Was Battle implying something? "I suppose we do, sir."

"Yes." That silver squint never wavered. "Well, here we are." Battle raised his own glass. "To your health, Doyle."

"The same," he said, though he felt his smile suddenly tighten to a dead man's rictus. *It don't smell like nothing.* There was no sting of alcohol to nip his nose. *Shite, no, can't be!* At the first taste, he thought colored water was probably better, and he could feel the well of a sob in his chest. *This isn't fair, it's not right!*

It is, Black Dog murmured, **what you deserve.**

"Something wrong, Doyle?" Battle peered over his glass.

"No, sir." Tossing back his tasteless drink, he inhaled through his teeth against a phantom burn, purely for show. *And damn you, Kramer.* "Very nice, sir. Thank you."

"Not at all. So, this case," Battle said, easily, as he refilled both glasses and then pushed to his feet. Crossing on a metallic jangle behind Doyle, Battle unlocked the drop-down cover of a pigeonhole and proceeded to riffle through slots. "What's on your mind, Constable?"

"Well, sir," he said, straining to keep the inspector in view. It was odd, and a little disorienting, having the man hover behind his back like that. A tad like Black Dog, come to think of it. "I don't pretend to understand why you won't let the doctor examine those bodies, but what about the girl?"

"What do you mean?" There was a creak and then the sound of a pigeonhole mount being locked. Wandering back round to his desk, the inspector picked apart a twine bow and began to unroll a thick tube of papers on his desk.

Was that a case file? *Must be; desk sergeant's ledger records incidents, but the reports are filed in pigeonholes.* "She says she don't remember exactly what she saw afore she went tearing out of . . . well, wherever she'd been held. But I was thinking that maybe those bodies might jog something loose."

"Interesting idea, but out of the question. Only three of the corpses are recognizable, and to be truthful, they're really quite upsetting. A touch macabre, actually. The fewer to see them, the better."

"Oh." The bodies must be horrors. How to find out where they were? "Well, perhaps a photographer? Make some pictures that we could take around for her to—"

"Are you pumping me for information, Doyle? You've never demonstrated such initiative before. Someone put you up to this." Battle leveled him a look. "Kramer, wasn't it? Come now, don't lie. I'll know if you do. The man's obsessed."

"No, sir." *Shite.* He was smarting, too. No initiative? *Arse.* "That is . . . yeah, Dr. Kramer *did* ask. He's very keen on those bodies. I guess they must be quite a puzzle." He paused to allow for Battle to interject, but when nothing came, he pushed on. "I said I couldn't help him. But his interest made me curious."

"I see." Battle's mouth worked as if against a bad taste. Tossing back his drink, he played with his empty glass. "What did he offer you in return?"

"Offer?"

"Oh, don't be coy." This close, the light from the oil lamp washed Battle's skin the color of bone. Only the man's silvery eyes showed any life, and they were mirrors the lamp fired. "Kramer wants the bodies, and he'll use whatever means necessary." Battle ran a pensive finger over three interlocking metal circles that made up the intricate bow of a brass key. "He'd be prepared with a reward. So what did he promise you?"

"Food." It was the first thing that came out of his mouth. Thank Christ, it also had the benefit of being plausible.

"You lack for victuals?" Battle's gaze raked his body. "Yes, you're a touch hollow-eyed, but aren't we all. How did he take your refusal?"

"Wasn't happy, but what's he going to do? You might have a word with the desk sergeant, though, in case he takes it on himself to come down to the station, maybe with that surgeon . . . Connell? Try and wheedle his way into the morgue."

"He can wheedle until he's blue. The bodies aren't in the morgue. Too cold."

"Oh." *Really? Not in the morgue? Then where?* And why *not* the morgue? Should he ask? *Too cold . . . what did that mean?* All these questions would be natural enough, but . . . *No.* Realizing he'd not yet touched his second tasteless drink, he threw it down, went through the motions. *No, shouldn't press it. Could bribe the desk sergeant, though; he might know.* Yet the idea of engaging a man he wasn't sure truly had a face gave him the jimjams. Besides, the sergeant might spout to Battle.

"Well, Doyle, if that's all. You look better. Get some rest now." Battle corked his bottle to put the period on their conversation. "I've work ahead."

"Yes, sir." He pushed out of his chair, thinking, *Shite, shite, shite.* If he could get a look at Battle's papers, or his rooms, perhaps. As he turned for the door, with Black Dog circling in an ebony blur just out of sight, he said, "Thank you for the drink."

"My pleasure. By the way, Constable, how is your arm?"

Uh-oh. Black Dog prodded his arse. **Careful.**

He didn't need a hallucination's warning for that one. Rearranging his face into a suitably neutral expression, he turned back. "As you said, much more up to dick, sir."

"Ah. Excellent." Battle waggled a finger. "Let's see how our doctor did."

Poppet . . .

"Certainly." His mind was already flying through the necessary calculus. He would have to remove his uniform coat. That, in itself, was no disaster. So long as he took care with his left cuff. . . . Tugging his right arm free, he draped his coat over the back of the visitor's chair, then began rolling up his sleeve.

"Here." Coming round his desk, Battle gestured. "Let me work those pins for you. Difficult to do one-handed . . . Ah." As he unrolled the linen bandage, Battle nodded. "Nice job for a doctor. Stitches are even, edges are very clean. Here." Battle jerked his head toward his desk. "Let's take a look in the light, shall we?"

What's your game? His heart was a sledgehammer against his ribs. He felt Black Dog rear up to place a paw on either shoulder, as if wishing to peek round for a better view. The ladder of Kramer's stitches climbed the bruised skin of his right forearm. His death hound tattoo looked on with a silent, frozen snarl.

"Yes." Battle smoothed Black Dog with a thumb. The gesture was curiously gentle, as if he really were caressing a beloved pet. "Kramer was right. This is quite exquisite. That mate aboard ship was very skillful. Justifiably proud of his work."

"Yes. Well, you know . . . long days at sea, nothing to do. No seals or whales, or we're locked in ice and . . ." He was babbling.

"Yes, and this *date*." Battle still had a hand around his wrist. "On your arm? The year? You know what's truly mystifying, Doyle? It don't tally." He nodded toward the papers on his desk. "According to your application, you were in school, not at sea."

The surprise was so sudden, his brain went empty. He couldn't think what to say.

"I probably wouldn't have noticed, except I'd pulled your papers when you found Elizabeth. So you can see why I'm so puzzled."

He said nothing.

Battle tapped the death hound with a forefinger. "Six years

ago, you were fourteen, and your letter of reference says you were a student at Stonyhurst, not a deckhand aboard a whaler. You can't be in two places at once, Doyle. So the only logical conclusions one can draw are that you're spectacularly forgetful, which seems unlikely, or that either the letter or the tattoo's a forgery. Now I can't fathom a single reason why you'd forge a tattoo."

Beg forgiveness, Black Dog said. **This is a time when half a fiction is best.**

"You're right, sir." Setting his shoulders, he pulled himself straighter. For the briefest of moments, he thought that Battle might not relax his grip, but then the inspector's fingers slackened. "I lied," he said, taking his arm back. He rolled down his sleeve with extraordinary care, buying himself a little time. "I needed the job, but sailors haven't the best reputations. I *did* go to Stonyhurst, but I had to leave."

"Why?" Battle's tone was flat.

"Money. My parents were dirt-poor. My mother had to beg for a space, and that shamed me, it did. I didn't like being a charity boy, but I stuck it out for my mam."

"And?" Battle's face betrayed nothing. "What happened?"

The one thing every excellent liar learns is *when* the right time to look away presents itself. That old saw about an honest man looking you in the eye? So much shite. Only a bad liar locks in, because that's a man always nervous he won't be believed. Want a lie to work? Look away.

"My father." Doyle held Battle's gaze a split second, then let his eyes fall. "He drank the family to ruin and then disappeared. That left my mam, seven sisters, a brother with nothing. So I quit school and went to sea. Sent all my money home. My mam took in lodgers. When I was sure they were provided for, I left ship and came here and . . ." Shrugging, he buttoned his cuff. When Battle was silent, he said, "Am I sacked, sir?"

"For this?" Battle shook his head. "I'm not a monster, Doyle."

In all this madness, Doyle thought this was true. "Thank you, sir."

"Don't thank me yet," Battle said. "Let me see your left arm."

His lungs went airless. "Sir? My . . . ?"

"You must think me a fool. I know the symptoms of with-drawal. Sweats, nervous twitches. Your guts have been playing quite the melody all day, *and* you're right-handed. Besides, liars are like murderers. The first time's always the hardest. So I must insist, Constable."

"Then what?" Doyle said, a little surprised. But then again, he was nearing the end of his tether. In a few more seconds, noth-ing he said would matter. He stood, loose-limbed, hands by his sides. "You get your gander, and then . . . ?"

"You may be a liar, Doyle. You may, in fact, be many other things. But you're not stupid." Battle offered him the first fleet shadow of a smile. "What do you think?"

"You're right, sir," Doyle said. "I'm not stupid."

And that was when he killed the inspector.

DOYLE

Murder Most Foul

1

FOR SOMEONE AS eagle-eyed as Battle, the man never saw it coming. Only a single pace separated them, and Doyle moved fast. Whipping his black knife from its sheath, angling it just right, Doyle pushed off his right foot at the same moment that his left fist snatched a handful of Battle's shirt. The inspector had done him a favor, shucking that coat and unbuttoning his vest. Jerking Battle closer, Doyle drove the knife forward and up. He felt the slight tug as the *sgian-dubh's* fine scalloped filework snagged on wool and then the give as the blade sliced through Battle's undergarment to slip into skin and muscle at the notch of Battle's rib cage. Stiffening, Battle pulled in a fast, small gasp.

No, no shouts, no screams! Clapping his hand over the man's mouth, he bulled forward, steering Battle into his desk. Feet tangling, Battle fell back, and Doyle followed, forcing the knife in and then up up up! He heard the clunk of glass as Battle collided with the heavy whiskey bottle, which toppled and rolled, butting up against the oil lamp. Battle flailed, and there was a smaller *tink-tink* as he swept their shot glasses to the floor. Eyes bulging,

Battle battened his hands around Doyle's right wrist. Battle's cheeks puffed like balloons, and Doyle could feel the man's shout ball in his left palm.

There was the tiniest hitch, a small shudder as the knife's tip grazed Battle's heart. They were face-to-face, only inches apart. Battle's eyes were wide and full of terror.

He wished he could say he was sorry for that. But killing Battle—knowing he was about to do the deed—felt so good it was like the rush of an injection.

Pinning Battle to the desk, he rammed the knife home. Battle's body moved in a great, convulsive jerk; Doyle heard a faint *uh* that might have been either a last gasp or an attempt at a scream. A huge shudder that Doyle felt in his belly rippled through Battle. The man's feet jittered a death dance, his expensive clamshells scuffing stone. Releasing Doyle, the inspector's hands fluttered, briefly, then went limp. Still gripped in Doyle's right hand, the black knife quivered, a kind of spasmodic flop, the *sgian-dubh*'s pommel lifting once, twice, three times . . . before stilling. A second later, the air filled with the pungent aroma of Battle's bowels and bladder emptying.

Well, well, he thought wryly, *talk about murder most foul.*

2

So, now what? Black Dog's nails ticked over stone, and Doyle could swear he caught a glimpse of the hound's long pink tongue lapping at Battle's pinky. **You're committed. Or perhaps you *ought* to be.**

Oh, shut up. He was still stretched atop Battle. Their faces were so close, Battle was one massive eye, silver going to murky gray. "You *stupid* gob," he hissed at the dead man. "You made me do this, ya fool. You just *had* to ask. You just *had* to know. Let's check your tattoo, Doyle. Let me see your arm, Doyle. *God,* if you'd only let it *go,* none of this would've happened, ya nit, ya *idjit.*"

All water under the proverbial bridge, my dear. You'd best start thinking about your next move.

"God, I do wish you'd choke." His voice was a low, angry mutter. But he really did need to get out of here. Letting go of his knife, he planted his palms on either side of Battle's body and levered himself to a stand. There wasn't much blood, only a tumbler's worth of a splotch soaking into Battle's garments and a snail's smear on the back of his own hand that Black Dog cleaned away with a drag of that long, hot tongue. That dark blotch over Battle's groin was quite large, though. A quick glance down at his own nethers, and Doyle was relieved to see that he was dry. Not that it mattered much; without proper baths, they were all a bit ripe, though he'd ceased smelling himself. Because there was nothing of him *to* smell, just as whiskey and his blood had no taste, the crowd, his fellow constables no faces?

Stop this. Battle's body was real enough. *Think.* The day's work was done. No one would come looking for the inspector, although the desk sergeant would remember that Doyle had accompanied Battle to his office. By the time that became an issue, Doyle had better be long gone. It hit him then that he really *was* committed, no turning back.

Wait, wait, don't panic. Because maybe not. If he *took* the knife, got rid of it—hell, trotted out to the Thames and tossed it into the fog—there'd be no evidence that *he'd* anything to do with Battle's murder. Why he'd want to stay . . . he wasn't sure. Perhaps it was because there really wasn't anywhere to run. He might lose himself in what remained of London, sure. That might not be too difficult. Go as far south as he could manage. No one would come after him. Or he could brave the fog. Pack provisions and take the proverbial plunge and . . .

Oh, who are you fooling? Black Dog gave him a playful nip in his right buttock. **You're simply not that brave, my darling. Besides, you're forgetting Kramer. Don't want to get yourself fixed up right?**

A good point. His eyes roamed the office, touching on the glasses, that whiskey. Battle said no one knew where he kept the bottle. *Oh no, Sergeant*—sidestepping the dead man's splayed legs, he silently rehearsed what he might say to the desk sergeant once Battle's body was discovered—*I didn't see anyone go in after I left for my rooms and . . . what's that, Sergeant?* He retrieved their fallen glasses from the floor. *No, I'm afraid not, Sergeant. We never did have that drink.*

Thankfully, the drawer in which Battle kept his whiskey was still open, and there was a rag there, too. Drying both glasses, Doyle seated them and then the bottle inside and shut the drawer until he heard the latch click. Standing in front of the desk's kneehole, Doyle stared down at the papers Battle had taken from their pigeonhole. Should he destroy them? No one would notice. Still . . . he fingered that forged letter of reference, thinking how ironic it was that the fictitious Brother James had declared Doyle to be *quite inventive; perhaps he would consider a career in letters*, and now he would be the last person to see Battle alive. Someone might come looking for these. And just who else might bother to square the date of a tattoo?

After carefully inspecting the papers for blood, he retied the twine and then scooped up Battle's keys. Slotting the papers back where they belonged, he relocked the cover. How many minutes gone now? Probably only five since killing Battle. *Time to go.* His eyes lingered on Battle's keys. The pouch felt good, heavy in his hands, and he hefted it, listening to the muted tinkle of metal, appreciating the weight. *Still Kramer to deal with, the bodies to find.* Himself to make right. "And what the hell did you mean, they're not in the morgue?" He glared at the dead man as if he expected Battle to come out with it already. "If *not* there, where?"

You'll never know if you don't move your baby backside.

Yes, yes, all right, stop yer nagging. Rolling up the pouch, he reached to douse the lamp. He was about to take another calculated risk. *I've got his keys.* They lived in the same dorm. *So . . . get to his rooms, light a candle or lamp.* Then no one would look in the office, not at first, and they'd have no reason to do so until morning anyway. If he was lucky, discovery was *hours* away.

Battle's rooms were his next logical stop for another reason, too. Perhaps a clue as to where the bodies were?

But he told you, Black Dog said. Weren't you listening?

"He only said where they weren't."

Yes, but he said it was too cold.

"Show me a place in London that isn't."

Poppet, you're being literal again. There are many ways of *telling* a story. There is what he said . . .

"And what he did," Doyle said slowly. *The key. He kept touching it.* So the key must be for a very specific lock. Have to hope the answer was obvious, in plain sight somewhere in Battle's rooms. Wasn't that where things were best hidden? God, he hoped he was right. He really had no time to play detective.

Shoving his arms into his uniform coat, Doyle tucked Battle's pouch with its keys into a left inside pocket. Wrapping his hands around the hilt of his black knife, he worked it free, cupping the blade with the rag with which he'd dried their drinking glasses, wincing at the scrape of bone where the scalloped filework sawed at the underside of Battle's rib cage. The body was already growing cold, the skin smooth as chilled candle wax. The lips of the cut sucked and pulled as the knife gave by degrees. When the tip finally slipped out with a moist smacking sound, there was no more than a trickle of thick, dark blood. Wiping the blade clean, he slid his knife into its leather sheath.

Then, after lighting his bull's-eye and sliding the panel closed, he retrieved his helmet, doused the office's oil lamp, and slipped out, carefully locking the door on the dead man he left behind.

DOYLE

Through the Looking Glass

1

SLITHERING OUT THE back way, Black Dog on his heels, was almost too easy. Only a few steps took him out of Battle's office, around a corner, and into a rear stairwell. He spared only a single backward glance. Orange light glimmered at the far end of the hall, and there might have been a muffled voice or two. He met no one. At the back door, he hesitated and looked at the basement stairs that led to the morgue. Why take Battle's word that the bodies *weren't* there?

"You can go round this all night," he murmured. "You've got a plan. Stick to it. If you find nothing in his rooms, then you go look." And if he still found nothing?

Cross that bridge when and if. He let himself out, wincing a little as the door creaked. The police dormitory was across an enclosed courtyard. To the left, an arched cloister marked the entrance into the police stables, and through the muffling mantle of snow, Doyle caught the snort and nicker of the station's remaining horse. No other sound save the whistle of wind scouring the roof, the dull patter of falling snow, and the chuff of Black Dog's breath. Ahead, he saw gauzy light from candles and oil lamps seeping through thin draperies in several rooms. Now and then, shadowy silhouettes drifted across individual windows. The only fairly bright light was a splash of orange spilling through a window to his far right from the desk sergeant's lantern in the station at his back. Under his coat and attached to his belt, his own dark bull's-eye was warm against his belly. While the courtyard was trammeled, there didn't look to be fresh prints.

He started across the yard. The dormitory had three entrances: right, left, center. His own rooms were on the second floor and on the right. He realized with a start that he'd no idea where Battle's were, other than a vague recollection of them being somewhere on the first floor because all senior staff were assigned to the lower floors. *You idiot.* He skidded to a halt so quickly he felt his boots try to fly out from underneath on a thick layer of compressed ice and snow. He'd have to go back. Or abandon this plan altogether; simply go to his own rooms, throw what belongings he wanted into a sack. Or . . . *Think, think.* He stood, snow salting his coat and helmet . . .

Keys, my dear.

"Right. His key." In order to precisely know, though, he would have to read the number. Couldn't risk lighting up the courtyard with his bull's-eye. Shuffling sideways, he edged as close to that wedge of orange light, and now the shadow of a man's head and shoulders, as he dared. Leaning forward, he brushed a quick gaze up toward the window. The sergeant was facing away. Good. After another look across the empty courtyard, he tugged his right glove off with his teeth and dug out his own room key, which he kept on a ribbon pinned to his trouser pocket. Running an index finger over warm iron, he felt along its length, from the rounded and very thick bow and down the shank to a notched collar. Nothing. *I know it's here.* Flipping the key, he repeated the process, carefully dragging his fingertip from the throating just below the collar . . . *Got it.* He felt his heart kick as his finger ran over a tiny plaque upon which there was a minute engraving: *2-2-1-b.* Which was correct: second floor, room 21, right side of the hall.

Returning his key to his pocket, he withdrew Battle's pouch. In the light, the iron and brass keys inside gave off an almost nacreous glow. Finger-walking the many loops, he found the inspector's room key, then felt for the room number: *4-2-1-b.*

Fourth floor? *Odd.* He could've sworn Battle's room was on the first. In fact, he knew that the station wasn't at full capacity, and only the first three floors of the dorm were occupied. He double-checked by angling the key into the light. No mistake. Battle lived on the fourth floor, in number twenty-one. The *b* signified that he occupied the rooms on the right side of the hall. All this meant that Battle had virtually the run of the fourth floor, if he chose. Doyle massaged the engraved numbers with the ball of his thumb. *Very strange.*

To his right, the orange glow wrinkled. Startled, he tossed an instinctive look and then had to clap his hand over his mouth to keep in the scream.

The desk sergeant was there, another lantern in hand, peering out into the snow. Doyle was sure *he* wasn't visible. Even if he had been . . . what stood there, framed in orange light, couldn't possibly see him.

Because the sergeant's face was blank. Completely. Totally. No eyes, no nose, which made that frill of wiry ginger whiskers all the more ghastly, because there was also no mouth or chin.

The sergeant's face was as flat as unformed clay.

I don't see this. But he couldn't look away. *This isn't real. This is Kramer. This can't be.*

Above and from inside came a burr of sound that Doyle recognized, belatedly, as laughter. Transfixed, he watched the desk sergeant's shoulders convulse and that clay-blank of a face rock back. There was a flash of tin at his throat, and Doyle realized that he—it—was *laughing. It's laughing, but it's got no mouth, no eyes, how can it . . .*

Steady, darling, steady. Black Dog nuzzled his ear. **This is Kramer and his drug, nothing more nor less . . . unless it's not.**

"Whatsat mean?" Without waiting for Black Dog to reply, he wheeled about, lurching away from the light. In another minute, he was across the courtyard and into the dormitory. Slivers fired under many of the doors, and he heard the occasional rumble of conversation. But he didn't stop, and for all sorts of reasons, he prayed to God he wouldn't meet anyone either.

2

A BALL OF cool air sighed past as he pushed into 421b, which was at the very end of a long hall. Pulling the door shut, he stood a moment as the darkness, thick as wool, settled. The room was still and chilly but not frigid. Battle's rooms were a corner suite that faced a narrow, blank-walled alley. If the suite's layout was similar to his own rooms, he now stood in the parlor. That meant the windows were to his right. Dead ahead would be a second door leading into Battle's bedroom.

Turning to his left, he cautiously unbuttoned his coat. Warm air, smelling of singed tin from his bull's-eye, wafted out, and he was absurdly grateful. *You're real; I smell that.* Still facing left to avoid the windows, he unbuckled the lantern, then slid the panel aside a half inch, enough that light dashed out in a bright ribbon. Sweeping right but keeping the angle low, he picked out only spare furnishings: a table and two chairs, a mahogany writing desk with a great many drawers, and a standing wardrobe. No pictures on the walls, no decorations, nothing personal on the table, and the desk was immaculate. To his extreme right, very dark, thick curtains were drawn tightly over the room's windows. He felt his shoulders relax. Certainly not in danger of anyone seeing in.

Crossing to the desk, he played his light over the surface. The stained quill nib was dry. Of course, the pen drawer was locked. Take a look inside? He chewed his mustache. Might be papers, case notes, some clue where the bodies were. Yes, but best to look around first, and wasn't he there to light a lamp? *Steady, Doyle; don't get distracted.* Straightening, he looked up and across the room and into Battle's bedroom.

Someone was there, watching him.

"Guh!" His scream might have been louder if his throat hadn't frozen. He jumped, and across the room, he saw light dancing a fantastic jig. Then he realized: he'd been frightened by his own reflection in Battle's bedroom mirror.

Touch on edge, aren't we? Black Dog glided into view, which was to say that the reflection of its eyes, red as hellfire, glistered in the mirror by Doyle's reflection.

He knew better than to look down on *this* side of that mirror. Black Dog would not be there. (Was it progress that the hound was in the mirror? Probably not. Christ, he needed a proper drink.) He stood there a full ten seconds waiting for his heart to slow. Across the room—in Battle's bedroom—the other Doyle stood with a hand over his chest and a wild look on his face as a huge black death hound with bloodred eyes showed its fangs in a grin. What a damned bad place for a mirror. He couldn't paw through the man's desk with someone, even his own reflection, looking on. Swallowing, he took up his lantern and crossed to close the door. At the threshold, he could see the whole of Battle's bedroom. The inspector's bed, neatly made, was tucked below two windows. A bedside commode squatted nearby. An odd placement for both because of the cold spilling through the windows, even with the shades drawn. Two floors below, he'd moved his bed to an inside wall for warmth. But along Battle's inside wall, there was a large standing wardrobe, a mat with another set of shoes and boots, and a hefty shaving stand with a basin and picture.

What a bizarre arrangement. Doyle stood there a good few seconds, sorting it out, then crossed to the wardrobe and pulled open the doors. Inside were trousers, a few suit jackets, two vests. Ties on hooks. No mirror, though. If Battle wanted to check his tie, he either had to step back to his shaving stand or cross all the way to the far wall and that mirror. So why not move the mirror alongside the wardrobe? There was plenty of room.

"What are you getting your knickers in a twist about, Doyle?" he muttered. So what if Battle's personal habits were a little odd? Did he *care* that Battle bared his arse cheeks to the winter wind? No. *But this is just so . . . off.*

It wasn't until he got closer to the mirror, an ordinary oval set in a wood stand, that he realized it was much warmer here, and the scent of wood smoke was stronger. *What?* He pressed a palm to the wall alongside the mirror. By his side, he heard Black

Dog snuffling with interest. Glass wasn't toasty but not freezing either. *And that ought to be an outside wall.* Unless there were other rooms behind this one? Possible; he'd never been up here. But then who was Battle's neighbor? The hall had been completely dark.

"Strange." Lifting his lantern, he examined the mirror. The wood stand was a reddish-orange wood, teak or light oak, and carved: flowers, vines, bizarre symbols.

The symbols, dear. Black Dog nudged. **Look at them. See something familiar?**

Black Dog was right. Leaning forward, he squinted at a design along the right-hand side of the mirror that he recognized: three interlocking circles. Setting his lantern on the floor, he withdrew Battle's pouch of skeletons and searched until he found what he was looking for. Unhooking the brass key from its fabric loop, he held it before his bull's-eye. *Same design.* It was also the key Battle's finger kept straying toward. What had he said? They weren't in the morgue because . . . "Too cold," he said.

Yes, and the wall is warm, poppet. So what if . . .

"The mirror's really a door, or masks a door." There would be no reason in the world for anyone to check unless he had the key. Opening his lantern all the way, he aimed the beam. The light washed shadows flat, but he saw that the symbol was raised a touch higher than its background. Either more deeply incised or . . . "It's a flap, like what you use for a Judas hole." *Or in this case . . .* "No, it can't be this easy," he said, even as he used the tip of a finger to lever the flap out of the way and expose the keyhole hidden beneath. Socking in the key, he gave it a twist. Deep in the mirror, he heard the tongue slide and the lock disengage. The mirror popped out, enough to hook his hand around an edge.

Be very sure, my dear. Black Dog's voice held an edge of warning. Once you cross through the looking glass, this can't be undone.

"Ya joking? I've murdered a man," he said. "I'm already committed."

He slipped inside, with Black Dog close behind.

3

THERE WAS ONLY one window, cracked to allow for ventilation, and a corner hearth in which the remains of a fire were beginning to burn low. The room was close and comfortably warm. The only furniture was three low cots over which sheets were drawn.

My God. He felt all the hairs on his body bristle. Moving slowly, he fanned his dark lantern over each cot and saw how the body beneath tended the sheet. Two seemed roughly the same size, though one was a bit slighter than the other—a woman or a thin boy, he just wasn't sure. The other was small. A child, he thought.

He stood at the foot of the cots, turning his lantern from one to the other. "What were you doing, Battle? What are you hiding here?" It was strange hearing his voice.

Go on. Black Dog nosed his left hand. This is what you came for, after all. Pick a card, any card. Don't you want to see, poppet, don't you?

The child, he wasn't ready for. So he selected the one on the left, which was the slighter of the two adults. Heart throbbing, he lifted the sheet.

4

WHAT HE SAW was bad enough that if he hadn't jammed his knuckles between his teeth, he would have surely screamed. Yet that still wasn't the worst of it.

The worst of it was when it opened its eyes.

PART FIVE

BEDLAM

EMMA

The Liquid Dark

STEPPING AWAY FROM the down cellar prison she'd made for Elizabeth, Emma opened her eyes to find herself where she'd first come to: huddled on a lumpy mattress in darkness as inky as the bottom of a mine shaft. Formless sounds threaded through the air like a continuous loop from a grade-B horror movie. That weird, wavering, rippling air teased gooseflesh from her skin. If she didn't know better, she'd have thought she was in a movie special effect, something science fiction-y where the heroine wandered into a crackling plasma field. Weird. Like fingers kneading her skin.

Wobbling to her feet sent a bolt of nausea surging up her throat. Gulping, she swayed on lumpy mattress as the liquid dark sloshed from side to side. Her chest grabbed again, and she started to hack, grunting and tucking in her elbows. Pain sliced her ribs. Rusty-tasting fluid splashed into her mouth and made her gag. Coughing hard, she staggered, lost her balance on the uneven mattress, and tumbled back onto her butt.

"God." Her hand was all gluey and . . . were those *clots?* Or

was she bringing up something worse? Hunks of lung, maybe? Shuddering, she ran her bloody palm over her skirt. She wished she had something to spit into. She snuffled against another nose-bleed. Her lungs felt congested. Every breath gurgled.

"I think there's something really *wrong* with you, Elizabeth." Her mouth tasted like a crushed can: flat beer and old aluminum. That shivery, weak feeling was seeping through her limbs again, and her joints ached. "Like you're *sick*-sick." Jesus, what if Elizabeth had something terminal, like TB or cancer or something?

Well, I sure as hell can't be here if she dies. She armed away sweat from her face. It bothered her a little that she didn't feel guilty about that thought either.

Maybe eating something would help. Had they left her some-thing? What if no one had? Then what? Shout until someone came? Could be why everyone down here was screaming. She had visions of patients trapped like flies between windowpanes. Shouting probably wouldn't help either. From what she remem-bered, all this was a faraway gabble on the main floors, only so much aural mist steaming up through iron grates. But shouldn't someone have checked on her by now? Or even before? Didn't they care about sick patients?

Maybe they don't do rounds down here. You know, out of sight, out of mind. That brought on another wave of panic. *Calm down. Your hair's still damp.* She touched a finger to her bandaged forehead. Only a dime-sized crust of blood. *You haven't been here that long.* Or someone might have come in while she was out of it to get her cleaned up, check her dressings. Would they leave food or water?

Squatting, she reached to her right where her head had been when she woke up and began carefully walking her hands over rough, lumpy fabric to a seam. As she moved, the fabric seemed to undulate under her hands the same way the air wavered. After what seemed like a long time but was probably no more than a half minute, her fingers butted another mattress set on a perpendicular to the one she was on. *Right; you'd expect that in a padded cell.* Finger-walking to her right, she found the vertical seam of a corner and another mattress. Using an index and forefinger, she cored into the seam. Her finger sank to the second knuckle before her nail ticked against . . .

Not brick. "Rock? Like a *cave?*" She held her finger there a minute, feeling how the rock also seemed to . . . well, not *give* exactly, but deform ever so slightly. "You know what this reminds me of? Down cellar, when I first touched the square." *That* had felt icy and had burned, but the minute *give* was similar. What kind of place was this? She thought back to the whisper-man's prison: a black-mirror cave, an energy sink constructed of odd volcanic glass. Could explain why Kramer took the cynosure. *He's really afraid I* could *use it down here.* Which meant that wavery, undulating sensation she felt, the way the air seemed to move was free energy?

Wow. What if *she* was in a Peculiar? It was possible. Kramer had panops, but it was *Meredith* who used them and understood about energy sinks and Peculiars; she'd made them. So Kramer knew Meredith, or maybe both McDermotts?

Moving to her left now, she inched forward, fingers quivering like antennae. They'd done some unit on the juvenile justice system in a sociology class once, and she remembered that most of the prison doors had slots and peepholes and . . . *Ah.* Her hands brushed cold, rough iron. She couldn't feel all the way to the top of the door, but that was all right. Lifting her arms, she walked her hands slowly right and then left, searching the door as methodically as she could, mapping out the grid in her mind. Perhaps two inches above her left eye, her hand brushed a round disk soldered in place. There was a small, quarter-sized depression in the center. When she stuck her finger through, the tip bumped up against more metal.

Bet that's a peephole. She was tempted to look through, but Elizabeth was too short. Besides—an eerie frisson tickled her neck—she'd always been a little afraid of peepholes. In movies, when people looked through to check out which bad guy might be waiting, she always wondered why no one put a stiletto through . . .

Something rustled off her right shoulder. *Shit.* That had been behind her. Small hairs prickling, she turned a very slow half circle, held her breath, and listened. Nothing . . . nothing . . . that strangely turgid air bunched and gathered . . . and nothing . . . nothing. Her pulse was starting to thump now . . . and noth—

A rustle. Again. Very light, but very definitely there and *closer* . . . And now another very fast flick as something—a finger, a hand—whisked along her neck.

"Guh!" Her heart rocketed into her skull, and then she was wheeling away from the door, turning a crazy, drunken one-eighty that was way too fast. Gulping, she steadied herself. *I heard something, I* felt *that.* But what had it been? What if it was a rat? This was an underground cell, for God's sake; rats and all sorts of things lived in the dark, in sewers and tunnels and . . . *Stop it, stop it, stop* . . . But *something* had touched her, *twice. Unless it's just this weird space, something about the air.* Maybe it's not *clear;* could there be fog down here, or mist? Or spiderwebs?

Cut it out. Next thing you know, tarantulas will drop from the ceiling. That was also just too damn close to Bode and those scorpions.

Her mind kept looping back to *energy waves, energy waves, careful, careful; don't* make *something happen; don't jinx yourself.* But she couldn't assume anything. If there really was someone or something in here, then it wasn't crawling or slithering around. *It's tall. It touched me on the neck, the cheek.* The darkness felt as if it had changed somehow, too. More . . . solid?

Yeah, like when you wander into a room and you feel *the bureau or bed before you run into it.* Raising both arms and reaching with both hands, she took a cautious, sliding step forward and then a second, and a third. *So I might be sensing furniture or another wall or . . .*

Something eeled from the liquid dark and closed around her wrists.

ELIZABETH

Second Room

1

EMMA'S DOWN CELLAR prison was both a spectacular bore and quite singular. The walls were a kind of lumpy gray brick she'd never seen. Some twenty-five paces wide and as long, the room turned out to be bare of anything other than a squat mechanical contraption with a profusion of square metal pipes, perhaps a foot across, running away into the walls. A few feet away, there hunkered two white cubes—again, both metal and with hinged doors. The air inside one smelled a touch mildewed, like damp wool. The other released a puff of scorched linen.

Interesting detail. Elizabeth let the smells roll on her tongue. *Emma really has left quite a lot of herself here. Quite a bit of personality.* Holding that strange blue spiral candle aloft, she turned a circle. "I need a way out, Emma," she murmured, her gaze touching on that squat contraption with metal tentacles and those two cubes, then drifting on. "Show me a . . ."

The far wall was no longer solid—and now, there was a second room.

"Oh, Emma, what is this place? What are you up to?"

Elizabeth took a few hesitant steps toward the inky square of an opening, then gasped as a raft of thick, gelid air sighed out to raise the hackles on her neck. In her hand, that steady yellow flame suddenly bent nearly horizontal, as if some giant had decided to blow it out. She quickly shielded it, worried that if the flame went out this time, it wouldn't spring back.

Beyond, the blackness seemed to breathe, the air to fizzle with a sound that was like bits of ice crunched under a boot, and she thought, *Voices?* On an impulse, not even understanding why she was doing it, she extended her arms, thrusting the candle before her. The blackness ate the light. She couldn't see inside at all. Dropping to a crouch, she played the light back and forth over the floor. The demarcation between this room and the one beyond was stark: one side grainy but gray with reflected light, the other completely dark as if veiled in black velvet.

What if there is no floor? With her free hand, she reached into the dark: first a finger, just the tip—the air was cold but not so bad she couldn't stand it—and then the first knuckle and then all the way up to the third.

"Oh God," she said, almost without inflection. Her finger just . . . disappeared. She could feel it and, beneath, some sort of surface that was not the same as this gritty stone floor. No, this was smoother, like glass. She let her entire hand drift in, watching as the darkness beyond closed around it. For a giddy moment, she imagined something might make a grab, but nothing happened. Exhaling, she retrieved her hand and thought about it a moment longer. This space was now here where it hadn't been before. Would she be able to find her way out once she was inside? *What if this is a trap?* Somehow she didn't think Emma was that skilled. *She might not be that devious either.*

But this *was* here because Emma wished it so. If she was going to beat her, she had to know all Emma's secrets. Carefully, she placed the candle on the floor as a beacon, something to keep an eye on so she could find her way back.

"Go on now, Elizabeth," she whispered, "before you lose your nerve."

She stepped . . .

2

. . . **AND ALL** at once, the black rushed for her face. There was no transition. One moment, she was in that first room; the next, she was muffled in a thick stygian mantle.

Can't see a thing. This was like stumbling into a cave and then losing the guide. Panic filled her chest, and she could hear herself starting to gasp. *Slow. Slow down.* Clamping her lips tight, she forced even, steady breaths. The darkness felt . . . *crowded.*

Someone in here? God, now she wished she'd taken the candle. Craning a look back tugged a gasp from her throat. That wavering flame was still there, but only as a thin yellow sliver she could barely see. She had taken a single step and gone miles.

What *was* this place? Why was it so important to Emma? Should she go back for the candle? *But I'm here now, and Emma's* responded before. *I think* way out, *and this place conjures a room.*

"If only it wasn't quite so dark," she said, raising her voice a little. "A lamp would do. Or some way of letting light in. Something with a view to the outside world. A window, perha—" The rest dissolved in her mouth.

All of a sudden, the blackness before her eyes *clenched.* It was a sensation more than anything else, but just as the room felt so crowded, something shifted and pulled together. And was that . . . she squinted . . . no, it wasn't her imagination: the darkness was *graying* ever so slightly, as if what lay before her was a . . . yes, a *window*, so sooty with grime and grease as to be completely blacked over until someone thought to give it a good scrub. The black faded by degrees, brightening in first a very narrow sliver before widening to a long oval, pointed at both ends like a diamond fashioned in a marquise cut.

It's an eye standing on end. Or the slit of a lizard's pupil. Reaching out, she felt the glide of smooth glass. "My God, it's a window," she said aloud, and then let out a breathy laugh. "It's a mind's eye."

Yet the eye seemed to function only one-way. Virtually no light at all leaked through, other than a weak, faint, yellow-green wash. So long as she pressed it to this barrier, she *saw* her hand as a black daguerreotype: the *shape* of her hand, but nothing more—no nails, no knuckles. Take her hand away from the window, this mind's eye, and her hand seemed to dissolve.

Then it occurred to her: this room was hidden. *Yes, remember where you are; this is a place Emma needs to keep in the dark? Not let herself see? Or* . . . "Forget?" she whispered. "Is that it, Emma? Is this a place you've tried very hard to forget but can't? Somewhere you hide your deepest secrets, even from yourself?"

And what was she looking at? Beyond her body, out *there*, the world was pitch. But there *was* something happening. Was Emma *reaching* for . . .

A hand slid to her shoulder.

EMMA

Hands

EMMA SCREAMED AS cold fingers wound around either wrist. "No!" Tearing free, she stumbled back. Her left boot banged something heavy that she could've sworn wasn't there five seconds before. She heard a sloshing gurgle and then a crisper clang as metal banged against metal. *What the hell, what the hell . . .* Swaying backward, she kept her eyes fixed on the darkness. "Who's there? Who are you?"

Nothing answered. Other than her own ragged breaths and the faraway shouts of the mad, there was no other sound. She heard herself whimper; the screams she would not let go stacked one on top of the other, from her gut all the way to the back of her tongue like candy in a PEZ. She ached to let a few good shrieks go, but that was a terrible idea. Start screaming and she probably wouldn't stop. Worse, she might provoke another coughing jag or burst an artery or something, and then she'd bleed out and die here, trapped in Elizabeth's body. Or whatever was in the room might just eat her and call it a day.

Stop it. You felt hands. She thrust her own under her arms and squeezed herself smaller. Every muscle felt as coiled as a spring under too much pressure. When she was a kid and school was just so much Chinese water torture, she sometimes daydreamed about what Lara Croft might do, most of which revolved around beating the snot out of that day's bully. She was always more afraid for her face, though, and so didn't get into many fights. If she was truthful, she also worried that if she did, the monster under her skin would show itself and not stop pounding until the other kid was jelly. Now, though, she wished she'd gotten into a few more brawls. A weapon would be good, too. That metal bang . . . that almost felt like she'd put her boot down on a plate. The gurgle might be a water jug.

"Come on," she said. "I know you're there. You *grabbed* me, you asshole."

Seconds passed. Nothing came slavering out of the dark. *Because there's no one. There can't be.* Maybe this was a hallucination. *Crap.* So not only was she physically ill, but now Elizabeth's mental problems were leaking out? She couldn't stand here forever. *If only there was a little light.*

At that, the darkness seemed to ease. Not a lot, but the air above her head went a little murky, as if all this was really black fog now beginning to dissipate. Her eyes tracked up to a ceiling that . . . was glowing? Yes, with a weak, greenish-yellow light. *Like that dead end we ran into back in the valley.* That *had* been an energy sink and the outside of the whisper-man's black-mirror cave. She didn't think this was the same, though.

I think about light and the ceiling glows. Her gaze swept down. The light was still very dim, diffuse, and grainy. It reminded her of twilight, just before the day disintegrated.

Still, she could see well enough. *No one here.* Not ahead or to either side or behind. No slavering monster, no one with grasping hands. No observer equipped with funky panops or night-vision goggles. She was alone, and there was enough light to see that the cell was about the size of a large bedroom. What was more, the air really did waver. Her first thought: *Heat shimmers*. Like what radiated from a highway on a really hot day.

Huh. Her gaze dropped to the floor and a metal plate half-covered with a cloth napkin and a corked, narrow-necked jug. Well, that solved the mystery about what had made such a racket, but . . . She frowned. Had this been here all along? Possibly; she couldn't be sure she'd walked a straight line.

"This makes no sense," she muttered. *I think about a light and the cave starts to glow.* She'd wondered about food, and now there it was. She lifted her eyes to the far wall directly before her. *I think there might be someone here and I reach and . . .*

And through the shimmering dark, she saw the mattress suddenly wobble and ripple. A second later, first the tips of fingers and then a forest of hands sprouted.

Crying out, she blundered across the room until she felt the opposite wall, and its squirming mattress, jam her shoulders. On the far wall, the hands spread and waggled their fingers like a carpet of flowers or bizarre anemones, and then arms appeared, unspooling in spindly stalks. They began to snake toward her face at the same time that, against her back, the mattress and the rock beneath swelled and then deflated as if something had just blown out a breath. A second later, she felt the creep of fingers along the back of her neck and in her hair. Something spidered onto her shoulder.

"No! Stop!" Shrieking, she stumbled to the middle of the room. On the wall she'd just left, more hands swayed, like top-heavy tulips, on arms thin as stalks. The cell wasn't large, and ebony fingers swept through her hair and tugged at snarls. A hand slithered over her shoulder, and then all the hands grabbed to stroke her face, creep over her arms, twine round her waist and legs.

"Please." She was gasping. "Go away, go back to wherever you came from."

The room shuddered. The many hands undulated like seaweed in a slow tide, keeping time with the ebb and flow of this uncertain air—and then, with a shiver, they drew back the way chameleons recall their tongues, to melt back into the walls.

"Ohhh." Whatever string had held her up seemed to snap, and she sank to the floor. Propping herself up on her hands, she focused on simply breathing for a few seconds. What had *that* been about? That was too damned bizarre. Eyeing the way the walls and this entire space glimmered and heaved, she thought, *It's energy for sure.* Energy that . . . *responded* to her? Was that why Kramer put her down here, to see what would happen?

Her eyes fell again to that platter and jug. "To see what I could *make*?" But why? It wasn't as if those hands had truly responded to *her*. She eyed the glowing walls, that swell as wave upon wave of energy flowed through this space. *This is like the barn, taking what scares me and making it real. It's all potential energy, waiting for a strong enough . . . what? Mind? Organizing principle?*

Her ears pricked to a new sound, not one in her head or in this room. In fact, it was very far away but distinctive enough: a long, metallic *creeee*.

What was that? She held herself very still. God, it had gotten so quiet all of a sudden, too. No shouts or bellows. *Like someone muted the soundtrack.*

Then, again: *creeee* . . .

Hinges. A door? Images from dozens of horror movies flashed. The grate of iron on stone, the *creeeak* of rusty hinges. *And now, you watch, there'll be . . .*

A *clop.*

God. She balled her fists. If she was making this happen, she had to cut it—

Clop-clop-clop.

Footsteps. With echoes. She sure as hell didn't just *ask* for someone to come on down and keep her company, had she? *Wait, I wondered about doing nothing until someone came. I thought about whether or not someone would check up on me.* "Okay, then you can go away," she whispered.

The footsteps only grew louder, which meant they were also closer. *Hell, I think someone's coming for real.* That background clamor had also started up again, too.

A flicker of something to her left. Her head snapped that way, and then she sucked in a breath as a bar of light suddenly appeared under the cell's door. *Oh boy.* A yellow glow bobbed and brightened over uneven stone. She could hear the clap of shoes as the long tongue of a shadow dragged from right to left—and she had the queerest sense of déjà vu: *I've seen this before. When?*

The shadow stopped moving. Silence. *Someone listening out there.* Checking if she was awake, probably. Should she say something? *No, let whoever's out there make a move.* Someone with a legitimate reason to be here would say something. Maybe.

Boy, I could really use a bat about now. She pitched the thought at the rock. *Sawed-off shotgun?* But nothing glimmered into existence, and she thought that probably the rock itself might morph, but she couldn't simply *will* something to appear. Then what about the plate of food, that jug? *Could've been here all along, and I just missed it.*

A loud rasp of metal against metal. At the center of the cell door, a small pinprick of yellow-orange light appeared and then blacked out as whoever was there put his eye to the peephole. A scrape of iron as the cover dropped back over the peephole.

Come on. Emma bit her tongue to corral a shout. All the tiny hairs on her arms and neck stood on end. Elizabeth's body was weak. If Emma fought, she'd be put down again, given more drug, made to go nighty-night. The footing here was crap, too. *Oh yeah, and you're just so coordinated. A real Lara Croft.* But she had to do something.

Slowly, she dropped to a crouch and made her way to that jug, the plate. Brushing aside the napkin, she saw only a heel of bread and some petrified-looking cheese. No utensils. *Of course not; no one gives a lunatic a knife either.* She hefted the jug. It was good and heavy. *Have to time it just right.* If she even got that chance. As quietly as she could, she pulled the jug and plate behind her: jug on the right, plate on the left. For an absurd moment, she wondered if Elizabeth was a righty and then thought, *Screw that. I'm in charge.*

A brassy jingle. *Keys.* Her calves tensed at the scrape of metal as a key socked into place. A crisp, loud, *ka-thunk* as the lock was disengaged. Then that iron *groooannn*, a dungeonlike *squawww* of hinges, as the door swung open and light bloomed. So she got a really good look.

And thought, *Oh shit.*

ELIZABETH

Shadow

1

AT THE TOUCH of that hand, Elizabeth shrieked. Spinning, she tried to run, but her long skirt grabbed her ankles. As she began to fall, something swarmed from the black. She felt strong hands snatch her arms and wrest her upright.

"Stop. Relax." A voice, young and male, but *very* strange, the tones overlapping and buzzing like the notes of a Jew's harp. "Don't be afraid, I'm not going to—"

"Let me go, let me *go*!" Frantic, she tried wrenching free, but whoever this was, he was tall and his grip was sure. "What are you? *Who?*"

"I was going to ask you the same thing. Look, I'll let you go, all right? Just . . ." The hands relaxed but didn't release her completely. "Just calm down, okay?"

Calm down? That voice gave her chills. *But think.* Her own good common sense was sometimes a godsend. *Remember where you are. This is a secret place.* People hid their true natures all the time. Her father had used the conceit more than once. She couldn't quite remember the name of the book—something to do with battles and tunnels in some endless jungle war—but she did recall that a character had been haunted by a ghost, a kind of shadow-man. *Emma might not know it's even here.*

She squared her shoulders. "Who are you? Where did you come from?"

"That's just it." The boy sounded confused and, she thought, a little frightened. "I-I don't remember. I know I was falling . . ." The boy seemed to swallow that back. "Your accent. You're English."

"Yes." Was that disappointment in his voice? She thought so. *Was he hoping I was someone else?* "We're in London."

"London? This? Here? H-how . . ."

"In a manner of speaking." Now that her fright was past, she was losing patience. "Do you understand *where* you are?"

"You said London."

"Does this *look* like London to you? And don't say you don't know because you've never been."

"Well, I haven't." The boy sounded a little angry now. She could tell from the direction of his voice that they faced one another, but he was too far away for her to make out much more than the faint oval of a face. Those eyes were queer, though. They glittered like a raven's. A little unnerving. Was he more fleshed out, or simply an idea?

Then she noticed something else: an impression of a *group*, a *gathering* of others behind the boy, but far away and indistinct, like spectators in the very last seats of the very highest balcony. *Who are they? What has he brought with him?* Another thought: *Dear God . . . what has Emma done?*

"Listen, I've been here in the dark for . . . for . . ." That strangely burring voice wavered. "That's just it. I don't *know* how long. It feels like forever and only a second. I know that sounds crazy."

Not really. She stepped closer to the mind's eye she'd fashioned, this one-way mirror into the real world. "Come over here. I don't like talking to a shadow." When the boy didn't move, she said, exasperated, "For God's sake, I'm not going to bite. May I remind you that *you* grabbed me?"

"That's not . . . it's not what you think." The overlapping tones of his voice roughened with emotion. "I thought you might be a . . . a friend. Someone I . . ."

"A friend." She played a hunch. "Emma?"

"Yes," and she thought he might be working very hard to rein back hope. He seemed on the point of grabbing her again—just a feeling; she couldn't see him well enough to note every flicker—so she slid back a step. "Do you know her?" he said. "Have you seen her? Is she all right? Is she here?"

Well, that depends. It hit her then, too: *He cares for her.* So perhaps this really *did* belong to Emma. Could that girl have constructed something all on her own? How had she managed that? *Only my father has that skill.*

Yes, but think. I'm the original. I'm the template after which Emma's fashioned. Theoretically, this boy must also be a piece of *her.* She cast a quick, appraising glance at those faraway others, so many anonymous blanks, clustered in the background. So must they, more or less. Could this shadow have become manifest only because Emma was so much stronger? The thought was chilling. First this basement; a secret room . . . and now this creature, with its faceless companions hovering at the margins.

"Come here," she said again. "I'd like to see to whom I'm speaking."

She read that instant's hesitation again. "I don't know what I look like," he said. "*Now*, I mean. Last I remember, things were pretty bad. I might be kind of . . . torn up."

What an odd expression. "Do you mean hurt?" This was getting more and more interesting. She'd always imagined that the various pieces spent the whole of their miserable little lives in her father's books; that what crowded her mind were only afterimages. Unpleasant, of course. Taking inspiration from her meant her father reached inside, and that always left a stain.

But this is a secret space in Emma's mind. So . . . is this boy a subplot? Something fallen between the lines? A chapter in Emma's life? Or something else altogether? She eyed the blanks. How many more characters in Emma's little drama were down here anyway?

The boy gave a humorless grunt. "That's one way of looking at it, I guess. Before I blacked out, I know it got into me. Really hurt. Started ripping me apart." He paused. "I don't think I let go soon enough. I think some . . . some leaked into Emma."

She didn't like the sound of that. "It?"

"Yeah. This . . . *thing* from the Dark Passages. Lizzie called it the whisper-man." He gave a strangled laugh. "Sounds crazy even to me."

Oh, not necessarily. At the mention of Lizzie, her stomach tightened. This shadow knew that piece? While she knew her father fashioned worlds and characters from energy stolen out of the Dark Passages, she'd always imagined them as separate. Now *this* creature made it sound as if it and Lizzie might have been in league. *Can't fight them all, and certainly not here, where I'm not in charge.* She caught movement behind the boy, very slight, as the blanks shifted and one, smaller than the rest, seemed to ooze that much closer. *God. If it takes on a shape, definite features . . .* Yet *that* shadow might not be all bad; she thought about the symbols scarred into her arms. If this new shadow *was* Lizzie, then *she* might use the girl to her advantage..

"What happened?" she asked.

"Long story. Emma got us out and into the Dark Passages, but the whisper-man was in . . . in my brother, Casey. It had already pretty much torn Rima apart. I let go to save Emma, but . . ."

"Casey," she repeated. "Rima?" She realized her mistake only after. Again, more movement, a kind of milling behind this shadow-boy, as two more silhouettes oozed closer. *Naming gives them substance. Telling his story brings them into the light.* The thought sent a jitter of alarm through her chest. *Can't let them take over.* She sensed it already might be too late. While still mostly shadow, *this* thing was very detailed, already well formed. It had *personality*, like Emma.

He said the whisper-man got into her. That had to be it. *Emma carries the stain of the Dark Passages; she's more powerful than she knows. I probably couldn't have stopped this even if I wanted to.* Did Kramer have an inkling? Given the fact that the man had panops, she thought he might.

"Yeah, my brother and this girl we met. Casey . . . he really liked Rima," the shadow-boy said, and now, behind it (soon to be a *him* at this rate), she could make out the slope of a head, a froth of hair, the humps of shoulders, as those other shadows—the brother and this Rima—took on substance. "We were in this weird valley. Lizzie called it part of her special forever-*Now*. Emma and I think it was an energy sink. Lizzie's idea of a Peculiar, really, designed to contain the whisper-man and . . ." Another desolate, burring laugh. "Sounds nuts, and I lived through it."

"A valley." Didn't ring a bell; her father likely hadn't written that. "And before that?"

"Wisconsin."

Wisconsin? The word felt both odd and somehow familiar. Perhaps a place in Emma's imaginings? And *energy sink?* The shadow-boy had called *where* they'd been a Peculiar. So, not the same as London's? *Sounds like a structure.* "Are you hurt now?"

"I don't know. Until you showed up, there was no light. But when I feel my arms and legs, my chest . . . my hands tell me I'm messed up."

"Look, I know you don't understand this"—actually, she wasn't sure she did either; here she was, an essence, talking to a shadow—"but I think what you're feeling is the . . . the *memory* of where you've been."

"You mean, like post-traumatic stress? A flashback?"

"Yes," she said, having absolutely no idea what he was talking about. "It's like they say about rose-colored glasses? Memories are the same. Strong ones color what you see and feel. I'm sure that *here*, in this place, you're right as rain."

"How can you know that?"

"My father. When my mother was sick, he tried explaining that what she'd experienced tainted her feelings and perceptions, what she saw, and where she . . . she could *go.*"

"Where she could go? You mean, in the future? From that time forward?"

"I'm not sure." She really wasn't. Why had she even brought it up? She hated those memories of her mother, lethargic one moment, hysterical

(Meredith, no, stop)

the next. What her mother had done to herself with knives and

(please, put it down, sweetheart, don't . . . DON'T)

broken glass. She wasn't even sure *where* she'd been or lived when those memories were formed.

"Come into the light," she said. "I want to see you."

"Okay. Just . . ." He inched closer. Darkness peeled from his features. He must've heard her gasp, because he stopped short. "What?" His voice was tight with dread. "It's bad, isn't it?"

"No," she lied. *Steady.* To her relief, the blanks hadn't moved with him. *Not yet, but now that* he's *in the light, they will.* "Not at all."

2

HOW TO DESCRIBE this? For better or worse, what her mind jumped to was a person seen through a veil of swirling mist and dense shadow: a cloudy silhouette with blurred margins, whose contours shifted and eddied, came together and then drifted apart. As if what was being drawn here was indefinite and still in the process of becoming and as likely to dissolve under a strong bolt of sun as to cohere into something solid.

This creature was like that: fog and shadow and incomplete. A suggestion of a boy. What she could see of his shifting, blurred body was tall, lean, and taut. A knife's edge of shadow cut across his forehead, yet she could see that the face, though muzzy and shimmery, was relatively well defined: high cheekbones, a strong jaw, a careless tumble of very dark hair that she thought must be black.

But his eyes were what transfixed her. It might have been a trick of this bizarre greenish light, but she didn't think so.

In the glimmer and waver of that face, his eyes were gleaming ebony stones. Completely and utterly. As in no whites at all. They were dead eyes, the glittery glass eyes you gave to a doll. These were eyes that stared back at you from the abyss.

He's infected, half himself—or what Emma's spun—and half shadow.

"You're not . . ." She paused and cleared away the wobble. "You're not *torn up* at all." *No, you're a monster from the Dark Passages.*

And what about Emma? If she'd traversed the Dark Passages and the infection spread from this creature's brother—*brother? how many of these things has Emma created?*—she had both her innate strength and this boy's now, and that of any other shadows she'd pulled with her: the boy's brother, Casey; that girl, Rima. That shadow-Lizzie.

Even without the stain of the Dark Passages, these must all be very powerful pieces. Her father had always said a name separated a true character from an anonymous blank: *Honey, have you noticed that only the important characters get names and descriptions so you know what they look like? Same thing with places.* It was the detail. Otherwise, the world between the covers of a book was vague. *Tree, house, building*: all convenient shorthand. Streets might be *teeming*, but the people themselves were ciphers.

"I'm Elizabeth," she said. "And you . . . ?"

"Me?" The margins of the boy's head clenched and then frayed as he pulled a frown. The effect reminded her of a spider frantically trying to reel in and repair the torn strands of a fragile web. "My name?"

"Yes." *Come on, you're so detailed; you've got to know who you are. You have a brother. You know where you lived. You care for Emma.* "What's your name?"

"Name." Turning it over the way you might look under a

rock, and then his tone brightened. "Right. My name's—" He suddenly broke off, and when his head moved and his face tilted up to stare at a point over her head, his contours lagged behind, pulling apart only to reform once he stilled, like vapor from a block of black ice. "Jesus, what is that place? Who the hell is *that*?"

Damn, just give me a name. "I made it." Turning, she said, "I think of it as my mind's eye, a kind of window—"

And then she froze. For a second, she truly didn't understand what she was seeing. But then, she did.

"Oh, dear God," she said, "that's . . ."

EMMA
Weber

THE OIL LAMP was what farmers or railroad conductors had in movies: a squat glass globe in a metal basket frame with a reservoir for oil at the bottom and a carry handle at the top. The flame smelled bad, like the goo they used to pave roads in summer.

"Oh." Surprise in the man's voice. When he held the lamp a little higher, she saw that the entire left side of his face was visibly swollen and painted with vivid splashes of purple and blue. All except his eyes, that is, which the light turned into yellow sparks. "You've come out of it," Weber said.

She kept quiet. What was there to say anyway? *Yeah, I'm awake. And?* She wasn't stupid either. Weber shouldn't be here without Graves or some other female chaperone. Which meant he knew he wouldn't be disturbed. Question now, though: what the hell was she going to do? Scream her lungs out, no one would hear. Weber must know that, too.

After a brief silence, he unhooked a canvas bundle from his left shoulder. "Brought you some blankets and a good coat. Thought you might be taking a chill."

No, you thought I'd be in la-la land and figured you might as well be comfortable. Wasn't like he could dial up his sleep number on this ratty mattress. "Why am I down here?"

"What ya talking about?"

"Exactly what I *said*, asshole." Man, she sounded braver than she felt.

"What ya mean?" Weber actually sounded insulted, like she was criticizing how the asylum was run. "Ya nutter, ya snatched a knife! Ya chucked that damn jar, damn near broke my head." He touched a splotchy bandage over his nose. "Then you run into that mirror, and we're expected to hop to whilst they's some of us hurt just as bad."

"I remember what I did. I was scared. But I'm not violent now."

"Yeah, well," Weber drawled, "if'n I had as much laudanum down my gullet as you, I might be a little limber. Surprised you're awake, actually." He seemed to remember something, and his eyes snapped around the cell before coming to rest on her again. "You musta been thirsty. Where's your jug? How much you drink?"

Well, *hello*: water had to be drugged. Good thing she hadn't found it before this. But what he'd said begged another, more interesting question: if Kramer had given her such a large dose, how *could* she have come out of it so soon?

Because . . . I'm not really from here? This felt almost right. *I'm like Meg Murry. Unless I buy into IT, nothing quite works the way it should.* And why hadn't Weber said anything about the cave glowing? Or the energy waves? Did he even notice? *Maybe he's seen it before. This might be normal for down here.* She wondered what he'd do if she could make those hands appear again. *Or . . . maybe he can't see the glow?*

"I don't need to be here anymore," she said. "I want to go back to my room."

"You want, you want." Weber's mouth worked. "Doctor wants you here, and here you'll stay. So shut your trap and don't make trouble."

"I want to talk to him."

"When he's good and ready."

"What about Mrs. Graves? Can I see her?"

"Not now. She's gone to her rooms, I suspect. She's got better to do than worry about you. You're stuck with me. Now you mind, or I'll be happy to make sure you *do*."

She didn't doubt that. "Fine. You've checked; I'm alive. So . . . go away."

"Not so fast. Remember, I'm responsible; I'm to bring you meals, make sure you've not perished from thirst. You'd do well to think about what *I* might want. What *might*"—his eyes roamed her body—"grease the wheel. Save us all a lot of fuss."

She thought he'd probably like it if she fought. The problem with only hurting him was that he'd hurt *her* more. *Although he would have to explain why to Kramer.* So maybe he wouldn't dare. *Can't take that chance.* She felt the jug pressed up to the small of her back. The heavy metal might crater his skull, but she'd have to get it right the first time, or at least stun him enough to give her time for another swing.

"If you touch me, if you d-do anything . . ." She squelched the stammer. "I'll tell Kramer, I will."

"*Oooh.*" He injected a mocking quaver. "I'm *sooo* worried. I'm *sooo* frightened." His tone turned hard. "It's my word against yours, and you're mad."

No. I'm Emma, and Kramer knows it. He'd believe her, but she had to deal with Weber *now*. "Forget it." Still crouching, she inched her right hand closer to her hip. "Don't even try to touch me."

"'At's where you're wrong." Weber hung the lamp on a short wall hook. "Now move away, so I can see the jug and plate." Her dismay must've shown, because he let out another nasty, nasal bark. "Stand up or crawl, I don't care which, but *move*."

"No," she said, "I wo—"

Without warning, Weber came at her, fast, crossing the room in two giant strides.

Still, she almost got him.

EMMA

I'm Not Elizabeth

ELIZABETH WAS A much smaller girl, and weaker. Used to her own body, with its longer reach and greater strength, Emma miscalculated by only a second or two, but it was enough. Too much, in fact. She might still have made it, if only Weber had been just a little slower or stumbled on the uneven mattress, but he wasn't and didn't.

The jug was also heavier than she'd thought, and her swing was awkward, the jug's weight actually pulling her off-balance. Gasping, she tried to correct but staggered on that damned lumpy mattress as Weber loomed.

"Oh no, dear, none of *that*." Trapping her wrist in his left hand, he brought his right around in an openhanded slap.

The pain was enormous, an explosion in her head and something she actually *saw* as a white flash. A cry jumped off her tongue as she felt Elizabeth's body—*her* body now—crumple. *No!* Bucking, she aimed a kick for his groin, but her legs tangled in that stupidly long skirt. In the next moment, Weber had straddled her chest, tacking her shoulders to the mattress with his knees.

"Got any fight left in you, huh?" Weber slapped her again, hard enough that her head whipped to one side. He leaned down, his face only inches from hers. "I can do this all night. You ready to mind?"

"Kr-Kramer . . ." That last slap had driven her teeth into her cheek. She sucked a ball of blood. "Dr. Kr-Kramer will be-believe me." Breathing hurt. Her ribs felt ready to snap under Weber's weight. "He *w-will*. You keep hitting me, there'll be bruises."

"Oh, but he *won't*." Weber ground his knees into the balls of her shoulders and laughed when she groaned. "You may be his pet of the moment, but you're also a nutter, and look what you done to yourself, slapping yourself silly."

"You're *wr-wrong*." Panting now, she tried staying with it, but it was hard. Weber was so damned heavy. Bright red spangles burst over her vision. If she didn't get air, she thought she was probably only seconds from passing out. "He'll b-believe me b-because"—she pulled in a cawing breath—"because h-he knows . . . I . . . I'm n-not . . ."

"What's that, dear?" Cocking his head, he cupped his left ear with a hand and leaned in closer. Mimicking her: "H-he knows y-you're n-not . . ."

She pulled in as large a breath as she could. "I'm not Elizabeth"—and then she struck, fast as a snake.

Weber let out a shrill, high shriek. He reared, screaming, and she went with him, jaws clamped tight, teeth digging into his cheek, sawing, *grinding*. She felt stiff stubble on her tongue and oily grime, and then something wet—Weber's blood, strangely tasteless—burst into her mouth.

"Let go, let *go*!" Bawling, Weber swatted with his right. The angle was awkward, and only the heel of his hand connected, bouncing off the back of her skull. Still, the hit was hard enough that stars exploded before her eyes, and her jaws slackened for no more than a nanosecond—just long enough for Weber to pull free.

"You . . . *you* . . ." Cursing, Weber loomed. A flap of skin hung from his cheek, and blood streamed from his jaw to drip into her face. His huge hands clamped around her throat. When she bucked, he tightened his grip. "You've done it now, ya blower!" he roared. "You've done it *now!*"

She couldn't have answered even if she'd wanted. Her lungs were on fire. Her fingers tried hooking over his hands, and she could feel her nails as they tore and scratched, but his grip only tightened, the pressure, the pressure, the *pressure* crushing, her throat collapsing as the pain in her chest came alive as something with hands and claws that dug and scratched and tried to rip her open from the inside. When he shook her, her head flopped and bounced, limp as a rag doll's. He was still shouting something, but she only knew that because spit and blood sprayed her cheeks. Every sound—his shouts, the dull thump of her feet against canvas—faded in the louder, frantic throb of her pulse. In another moment, even that was gone, as an insidious, remorseless blackness leaked into her ears and over her vision the way an overturned jar of ink spreads over white paper.

No more sound now. No more light. Only the agony in her chest remained: that, and a weird . . . hesitant . . . intermittent awareness . . . like the sweep . . . of the beam . . . from a lighthouse . . .

. . . and there was . . . something . . .

. . . something . . .

. . . in her head, someone . . .

BODE

Dungeon

"WELL?" BODE SAID. They'd come to a standstill at a four-way junction. "You know which way?"

"I think so," Meme said, tossing an uncertain look from one opening to the next. "Give me a moment."

Oh, perfect. Though he wasn't angry at her. Each time this evening he'd unlocked and dragged open a door, cringing at every metallic *clank* and *squawww*, he half-expected Kramer and an army of faceless minions to suddenly appear. Nerves, that, and the noise: that continual ghostly yammer of the mad seeping through iron doors.

It was also the weirdness of the place working on him: these very bizarre tunnels and the way the air *moved*. So different from the tunnels through which he'd taken patients to other cells beneath the asylum. Tipping the iron pick in which he held their one candle, he watched as molten wax dripped to cold stone and instantly solidified. He'd done this the whole way, laying a trail of wax bread crumbs just in case they got turned around. Which they might be at the moment.

Where in God's name are we? You didn't need to be an engineer to know that these tunnels came from before Bedlam as he knew it now had been built. Those more familiar structures echoed the buildings: bricked and lined with cells, with each section gated off with an iron grate and wood door, like an old castle keep. These passages were very strange, as if they'd detoured into a much older, almost ancient portion of the asylum. The strangeness was in everything: the moist air that pulsed with a weird, faintly phosphorescent aura, emanating from walls that were no longer brick but carved, glassy stone. The light was just bright enough that there was almost no need for their single candle. He dragged a tentative finger over glowing, carved stone. *Cool.* And had he caught the slightest suggestion of a reflection?

Yet there were still cells: whole series of iron doors, one right after the other, with patients behind each one, if the noise was an indication. So eerie, though. *More like a dungeon.* What would lie out this way? He tried to imagine where they were in relationship to the surface, but there'd been so many turns and doglegs and crosscuts, he'd lost track. Had they veered off toward the back grounds? Perhaps the derelict criminal wings? But if there were still patients here, who looked in on them?

A sudden muffled shout sounded from somewhere close behind. He near about jumped a foot. Hot wax spilled onto his index finger as the candle trembled and tried to snuff, but he barely felt the burn. All the fine hairs on his neck were stiff as pikes. God, these poor buggers—how often did they actually see other people? *They all sound alike.* It was hard to think of them as people.

"Hate that sound." Meme shivered. "You know, I sometimes think they don't have faces at all? Just . . . bodies screaming sounds. No matter how many times I've been down here, working with Doctor, I never get used to it."

He only nodded, a little spooked to hear his thoughts come out of her mouth. He peered into the tunnel on his right, at three o'clock, which seemed different from the passage they'd just exited at their six, and the other two at nine and twelve. Shadows swarmed, but he saw how the light from Meme's candle bounced back from walls that faintly glittered. The tunnel's mouth exhaled air that was much colder and laced with a sour and slightly noxious fume, like what the Thames smelled like on an ill wind: gassy as a sewer. Shite, probably the real thing: either human or animal droppings. Bats, maybe rats. He edged closer.

"Where are you going?" Meme whispered. "That's the wrong way."

She knew that for sure? "Just checking." Another step, and now his nose tingled with a nip of icy air. Interesting. A draft? He wondered where this cut went. *Not back to the main building, that's sure.* If there *were* bats, then there had to be an exit aboveground. *Maybe once I grab Elizabeth, we go this . . .*

A sudden, sharp scream pierced the air.

Christ. His heart seized, fisting to a knot that pushed into his throat. Startled, he blundered away from the tunnel's mouth and stumbled back to the four-way junction. Had that been a patient? Someone in a cell, or out in a corridor? "Which tunnel did that come from?" he asked. The scream had dwindled to hollow echoes. "Could you tell?"

"No." Meme looked as terrified as he felt. "Do you think it was her?"

The scream had certainly been *high* enough, but the edges were rough, mannish. He just wasn't sure, and there'd only been the one scream. The sound had been so sudden that even the nutters had quieted. He could picture them, quivering in the dark, ears pressing against iron, listening above the thud of their hearts. Yet the scream had also been very loud. Must mean an open door somewhere.

Oh, come on. He turned a complete circle. *Which tunnel, which way?* Excluding the one they'd just left and the tunnel at three o'clock with its glittery stone, that left two: nine and twelve o'clock. Cocking his head, he stilled his lungs and listened so hard his ears rang. *Come on, one more scream. Just one. Help me find you . . .*

As if in answer, the shriek came again, and this time, he heard, very clearly, that brutish bellow. His head whipped left, to the tunnel at his nine.

"Bode?" Meme sounded suddenly tentative. "I think that was a man."

"Think you're right."

"Then it's probably not her," Meme said.

"Yeah, but it was loud, and loud means an open door," he said—and then slapped a hand to his forehead. *"Shite."*

"What?"

Weber. He's got keys, and he's not in his rooms. "Stay here, stay *here!"* Moving fast, he plunged into the tunnel. The candle snuffed instantly, but there was enough rock-glow for him to see. His boots clopped; he couldn't help that, and from the sounds of it, whoever had screamed was probably beyond listening for footsteps. He passed the blank rectangles of one cell door after another. The nutters had started up again, their wails rising and falling in waves. But he was headed the right way. The screamer had switched to shouts now, and no doubt about it: this was a man.

As he turned a tight dogleg right, he spotted a pale yellow rectangle in the distance. *Light. Open door.*

"You've done it now, ya blower!" a man roared. "You've done it *now*!"

God, that was Weber. And *blower . . . He's talking about a girl.* He vaulted down the tunnel. Air raked his throat. *Got to be Elizabeth, but then why isn't she screaming?* Wheeling around the open cell door, he saw two things, both of which stilled his heart.

Weber, swollen face smeary with blood, astride her body, his meaty paws clapped round her throat . . . and Elizabeth, eyes starting from her sockets, as her feet twitched in a final, feeble judder.

And stilled.

BODE

Last Gasp

1

"NO!" HORRIFIED, HIS blood roaring in his veins, Bode ducked his left shoulder and launched himself. He crashed into Weber, a solid body blow that knocked the man sprawling to his left. Weber banged into padding, the impact forcing the breath from the man's lungs in a loud *oomph*. Bode scrambled after, trying to work his way from his knees to his feet on the uneven mattress. He managed to set his right foot and was just beginning to push to a stand when Weber rolled onto his back and scythed a leg.

The cut was vicious, the angle perfect. Bode heard the whisk of air as something huge and blocky whickered for his head. In the next second, his face exploded as Weber's boot clubbed the underside of Bode's right jaw. A fraction of an inch lower and Weber would probably have crushed his windpipe. As it was, his head snapped back; bright orange flashes popped before his eyes. Pain erupted in his face, and there was suddenly the metallic cut of blood in his mouth.

Gagging, Bode tumbled left. The top of his head slammed

against a thin spot in the canvas and, beneath that, into solid rock. A lightning bolt of pain shot down his spine and spread through his limbs. For a second, he went stone-cold limp.

Where . . . where . . . Stunned, his thoughts balling in a snarl, he couldn't bring his head around. Gawping, pulling for air like a suffocating fish, he tried to bring up a knee, but his boot slipped and he flopped facedown on the canvas. A second later, Weber's stubby fingers were crawling through his hair. For a moment, Bode thought Weber meant to wrench his head around and snap his neck. *No, no!* Panicked, he flailed, slapping at Weber's hands, his arms. Cursing, Weber swatted Bode's already yammering jaw with a fist. Gargling a scream, he felt Weber's hand crush the scruff of his neck.

Then he was airborne as Weber heaved him clean off the floor. Bode was taller, but the thickset Weber had more weight and meanness besides. With a bellow, Weber drove Bode into the wall the way he would a battering ram.

No! A split second before he hit, Bode turtled his shoulders around his ears and got an arm up. There was a sickening thud, and Bode choked out a scream as pain, hot as lava, raced up from his wrist to ball in his shoulder.

Weber loosed his grip. Bode flopped to the floor. His right arm was one long, bright shrill of agony. He could feel his mind beginning to slip, the way boots did on sheer ice. *Get up, get away, fight!* He would die here if he couldn't get to his feet. And he'd failed, he'd *failed* her; she was dead, she was *dead!* Squirming, he pedaled, his boots sliding in an awkward scutter over worn canvas. It was like trying to work his way up a steep incline of naked stone. *Weber, where's Weber?* Grunting, he planted his left hand. His arm trembled, weak as water. *Get up, come on!* If he could only make it to the door, pull it shut, *lock* this monster in here, he could get help, he could . . .

A huge, crushing weight dropped onto his back, beating him flat. He let out a strangled, nearly breathless shriek. Weber was riding his back, and he was heavy as an anvil, his bulk driving Bode down. Bode's face sank into a rank pocket of mildewed canvas and moldering horsehair. *Can't b-b-breathe, c-can't . . .* Twisting to the right, he managed to clear a small corner of his mouth for a sip, but it wasn't nearly enough.

"Enjoy that." Perhaps no more than a minute had passed since Bode stormed into the cell, but these were the first words Weber had spoken. When his mouth moved, the slick exposed muscle beneath that torn flap of skin bunched and glistened. "You picked the wrong person to fight. 'Member, *I* know you got Graves's skeleton. It's how you got down here, and then Elizabeth rebuffed ya, and you snapped. I'm sure Doctor will understand that I had to defend myself." Weber's lips parted in an orange grin. "Too late to save that poor girl, though. Pity that poor Meme. To think she was so sweet on you, too. I might have to comfort her."

Meme. Had she gone for help? *Too late; they'll never get here in time.* "N-n-no!" Bode gasped. He had a sudden horrible sense of what Weber meant to do. Gathering himself, ignoring the yammering of his hurt arm, he tried bucking Weber off, but Weber's weight was on his shoulders, and Bode had no leverage, nothing to push against. "W-Weber," he said as the man clamped both hands to his head. "D-don't!"

At the last second, his arms already pinned, Bode managed a quick grab of air, but that was all. Jamming Bode's face into the mattress, Weber leaned in with all his weight. *Smothering me, pushing me into the mattress, got to get air, got to get air!* Struggling only used what little air was left in his burning lungs that much faster. For a wild second, he thought, *Play dead, go limp.* That idea lasted five seconds. The ferocious pressure in his chest exploded in a fireball that swamped him in a red blaze and scorched away reason. Fueled by pain and panic, his body didn't want to give up, but nothing can fight forever. His thrashing was turning feeble; his boots drummed canvas. His mind was closing down, collapsing in a heap, like poorly balanced bricks tumbling from a rickety cart. There was a bucking, heaving sensation at his belly, but he was too far gone to understand if this was anything but his body mustering all its remaining strength in a last gasp.

And then everything was lost as his starved brain let go of a single, coherent thought: *Done for.*

2

THEN . . .

From very far away—so far that if the sensation were sight, he'd have been peering down the wrong end of a collapsible spy-piece—he felt Weber jerk. An instant later, the pressure on his head let up as Weber moved again, more violently and in a herky-jerky dance, like a marionette whose puppeteer has given his strings a sudden yank. The crushing weight on Bode's back eased as Weber began to list in a slow swoon.

Bode didn't stop to wonder or think. Pushing up on his good left arm, he bounced Weber from his shoulders. The man toppled like a burlap sack of potatoes and without a sound. Bode was beyond caring what had happened; what he needed was air, and now he dragged in mouthful after screaming mouthful. Over the pounding of his heart, he heard something like the solid *chock* of an ax biting wood and then a sodden crackle.

What? Still blinking away black spiders, he pulled his head around. *Who?* Then he thought, *Meme*—

But it wasn't.

3

WEBER WAS DOWN, on his stomach. The entire left side of his head looked like a boiled egg that someone had mashed with a heavy boot. His blood was dark as tar, and a slop of something gelatinous—probably brain—glimmered a dusky, faint purple. The only part of him still moving were his hands and booted feet, which jerked and fluttered, but Bode thought that would probably stop soon.

She was there, on her feet, swaying a little. A necklace of black bruises ringed her throat, and blood oiled from both nostrils and a corner of her mouth. She was staring down at Weber. Her expression was unreadable. But there was something about her that was . . . off, at odds. *The way she's standing.* Or maybe it was the cock of her elbows, the set of her shoulders, and the way she gripped that metal jug.

"Elizabeth." The word came out coarse as gravel. He swallowed, grimacing as pain lanced his throat. "Are you . . ." The words died as her gaze inched up from the twitching, dying muck that was left of Weber; and he actually felt himself flinch. Her eyes . . . so *dark*, darker than ever. "Elizabeth?"

"No," she said.

BODE

The United What?

HER VOICE WAS very strange, much lower and as raspy as a file on stone, but then again, she'd just had the life nearly crushed out of her. Her gaze sharpened, scraping over his features, as if going through a mental checklist, ticking off items that matched. Releasing a breath, she nodded and then straightened. Her posture relaxed, the tension draining from her shoulders. After a long, speculative look at the jug in her hands, she tossed it aside, then came to stand over him.

"Jesus, man, are you hurt?" Her eyes ticked to his arm. "Shit. Is it broken?"

"I . . ." Had she just cursed? Flabbergasted, he stared up at Elizabeth, who seemed now to tower. For the briefest of moments, he *almost* saw the ghost of a different face taking shaping beneath her skin. "What is this?" Though what he wanted to scream: *What are* you? *You realize you just caved in a man's skull?* "Your neck . . . I thought . . ."

"Hurts, but she'll be okay, I think." Elizabeth gestured with her chin at his arm. "If you need it, I can bind that for you, but you have to listen to me, man. This is important, and I don't think I have a lot of time to explain."

Bode blinked. "Explain what?"

"This girl?" She pressed a hand to her chest. "I know what you think, but she's not Elizabeth."

"She . . . she's not," he said, carefully. *Christ, what have I gotten myself into?* She was mad; she really was. Beyond, at the threshold, he heard boots, and then saw Meme at the door.

"No," Elizabeth said, still in her rougher, deeper voice. "And this is the thing, man. Neither am—"

Meme cut in. "Get away from him." Before Elizabeth could reply, she darted in and came up with the jug. "Now," she said, cocking her elbows. "*Stand* up and move away from Bode, or I swear to God, I will stave in her head and you will *all* be finished."

"Easy." Holding her hands out, Elizabeth slowly rose from her crouch. Her chin and neck were streaked with blood. "Take it easy. I'm not going to hurt any . . ." Then Elizabeth broke off as if she'd gotten a good look at Meme for the first time. "Oh Jesus."

"You're not going to hurt anyone? *Really?*" Meme actually laughed. "Tell that to Weber."

Elizabeth's lids fluttered. "Listen," she said, still in that rough, odd voice, "he was *killing* her. He'd have killed Bode. I had to—"

"Shut it." Meme used her chin to point at the cell's far right corner. "Over there. Back up, hands out where I can see them."

"Meme." Bode goggled. "What are you doing?"

"Meme?" Elizabeth said, not moving a muscle. "That's your name? Is that someone's idea of a joke?"

"You find this funny?" Meme hefted the jug higher. "Move, *now*."

"What if I don't?" Elizabeth eyed the other girl. "What are you going to do? You really going to beat my head in? You think you can take me?"

"Do *not* try me," Meme said. "That is still another's body, and a weak one at that. I am taller, and have better reach. You would not be taking me by surprise as you did Weber."

"Meme?" Bode struggled to his feet. "What is this? Someone, please tell me what's going on."

"I just did, Bode." Elizabeth's gaze suddenly seemed to turn inward. "She's waking up anyway. Listen, Bode, I don't think she knows I'm here. Tell her it was Eric. Bode, remember the name: *Eric*. Tell her. She needs to know."

"Who?" Bode asked.

"Did I say you could talk to him?" Meme shouted. "I said *quiet!*"

"Eric. Casey too." Hands up, face intent, Elizabeth kept an eye on Meme and another on Bode. "Rima and even Lizzie, we're *here* . . ."

"*Rima?*" Bode said, as Meme cried, "Last warning!"

"We're *here*, we're *stains*! *Shadows!*" Elizabeth shouted. "Tell her, Bode! She has to know, she has to—"

"Not another word!" Starting forward, Meme would've swung if Bode hadn't sprung up to snatch at her waist with his good arm. "How *dare* you?" Snarling, Meme rounded, jug upraised to strike. "Take your hands *off* . . ."

"Then *stop!*" Bode shouted, his face an inch from hers. "Ain't there been enough killing?"

"But you do *not* understand what *that* is! *I* am not even certain!"

"Then *tell* me what ya *think*." He gave her shoulder a small shake. "But no more without just cause, no *more*! We've a dead man here and more trouble to come without turning on one another."

"He's right. Look, look, it's okay. I'm going, all right?" Palms still up, Elizabeth shuffled backward. "But I'm no threat to you. Believe me, I'm here to help. I want to help all of you if I can."

"Oh, and I am supposed to believe that? The panops, Bode, in my right pocket." Meme slid him a quick sidelong glance. "Take them out."

Elizabeth reacted to that. "You've got panops?"

Meme ignored her. "Bode?"

"What? Why?" It was as if the two girls were talking *over* him somehow. What the bloody hell was going on? "What do you want with—"

"For *God's* sake, will you stop asking so many stupid questions?" Meme snapped. "*Get* them, quickly, before this . . . this *piece* loses its grip!" When he just stood there, she readied the jug for a swing. "You want me to bash its brains in? Get them!"

"Hold on, hold on, all right!" Awkwardly, he slid his left hand from her waist and patted until he found the slit of a pocket. Wriggling his fingers inside, he felt the curve of her hip. Embarrassment fired his cheeks, and he thought, *You nob, ya worried about modesty* now? "Just give me—"

"*No.*" A snarl—but not from Meme. Elizabeth had gone rigid, her lips skinning back to reveal teeth that were a murky orange in the light of Weber's lantern. Her delicate features were harder than he'd ever seen. Her eyes were so wide, the whites shone with a kind of feral brightness, and that golden flaw glittered like a star. "*No,*" she said again. "Don't . . . don't *fight* me!"

Was she taking a fit? Odd voice or not, he had to do something. She'd saved his life, for God's sake. "Elizabeth?" Specs in hand, he started forward. "Are you in—"

"Blast!" Snatching the panops from his slack fingers, Meme dropped the jug and jammed the glasses into place. "I need to *see* which piece . . ." She gasped. A hand flew to her mouth. "Oh, dear God, it *is* true. You really *are* . . ."

"Stop!" Back arching, Elizabeth's head twisted right and left as if trying to break free of invisible hands. "D-don't *fight* . . . let m-me *explain* it to them! Bode can *help*!"

"Meme?" There was something very *wrong* with Elizabeth's face, Bode thought. It had to be the light or the strange, shimmering air, because it seemed to Bode that her features . . . *glimmered*. As if Elizabeth was soft clay and unseen hands were pinching and rearranging the shape of her lips, the angle of her jaw. *Or squirmers.* His arms stippled with gooseflesh. *Like they're under her skin, burrowing, eating her alive.* He actually backed up a step. "Meme, what is it? Is it squirmers? Is she . . ."

"No," Meme said.

"B-Bode?" Her features had settled, and it was Elizabeth: truly, this time round. He saw at once that she seemed smaller somehow, and weaker. Her lips trembled. "Oh, Bode, thank God you're all right. I was *so* . . ." Sudden alarm swept her face. "No!" In the cell, her shout echoed back from the walls. "No, please, stay asleep a while longer, just a while . . ."

"God," Meme breathed. "What *is* this?"

"What?" Elizabeth's entire face seemed to wrinkle, to shift— or maybe, again, it was the air. Elizabeth *glimmered* and then she was someone else again. "What is what?" Blinking, she cast a look round, then spied the mess on the mattress. "Oh." Lifting a hand to her lips, she threaded an arm over her stomach. She looked ill. "Oh God, oh *shit*. Did I do that? I *did* that?"

It's as if she's just come awake. Bode clearly heard it now, too: the change in the timbre of her voice, the cadence. And *shit*, not *shite*, though the Elizabeth he knew would never say either. At least, he didn't think so. But just which Elizabeth *did* he know?

"No." The word sounded broken. It might have been the strange shimmy in the air, but it seemed to him that Meme's face was fracturing, too. Behind their purple lenses, her lids fluttered, and then he saw the glister of tears dashing down her cheeks. "How can this be?" Meme said, a hand to her mouth as if she might be ill. "How can you be first a shadow-*boy* and then—"

"Boy?" Elizabeth snapped to attention. "What did he look like? What color was his hair? What . . ." But then Elizabeth stopped, and Bode thought it was because she'd finally gotten a good look at Meme. "Oh my God. That . . . you . . . that's not possible."

"What?" Meme shook both her fists. "You dare say *I* am impossible? It is *you* who cannot be. This is not *right*, it cannot be right! He said that *I* was the only . . ."

The glasses. The realization broke over Bode like a dash of icy water. *When I looked through, I saw the other Tony. Now Meme looks at Elizabeth—and she must see someone else: first some kind of shadowy figure—a boy—then Elizabeth, and* now . . .

"Who are you? What is your name?" Meme shook her fists. If she'd a knife, Bode thought she might have used it. "Where do you come from? Why are you *here*?"

He saw the moment the other girl weighed all her choices; saw them flash through her fine features. He saw the instant she decided, too.

"I have an idea of why I'm here," she said to Meme, and Bode heard just how tightly she reined in that quaver, as if she were a hair's breadth from losing control. Her voice was still harsh, though he thought from the way she grimaced that was because talking must hurt. Weber had nearly crushed her windpipe. "I came to find my friends. I was . . . between, in the Dark Passages."

"I know *that*." Meme spat the word. "I saw that boy, that *shadow*."

"I don't know about that," the girl with Elizabeth's face said.

"But he knows you," Bode said.

"Do not tell her!" Meme snapped.

"Why? Where's the harm?"

"What?" The girl looked from Meme to Bode. "Tell me what?"

How calmly I'm taking all this, like a girl tells me she's a boy every day. "The boy. He said to tell you that his name's Eric. That Casey and R-Rima," he stumbled, "and Lizzie? They're all there, but they're *stains*. He said you would understand what he meant."

"What?" The girl's jaw dropped. "He's *here*? Eric is . . ." She put a hand to her chest. "Inside?" she whispered. "He's *inside* me?"

"So it would appear," Meme said. "He must be strongest of the lot, but he is not what you think anymore. He is part of *it*, more of the Dark Passages than any *Now* you knew. They are *in* you, bound to your blood."

"Where *did* you come from?" Bode asked. "Do you live in the Dark Passages?"

"No." The girl swallowed. "I'm from Wisconsin."

"Wisconsin." *Same as little Emma.* "Where *is* that? North of London?"

"Well, it's *north*." The girl looked taken aback. "Um . . . in the United States?"

"The United *what*?" Bode frowned. "What you yammering about?"

"It must exist in her *Now*," Meme said.

"Wait, you mean there's no United States here? No America?" The girl blinked. "What . . . what about Germany? Europe? Russia?"

The names were so much gibberish. "There's only England," Bode said. "There's only *ever* been England, and now just this part of London, thanks to the Peculiar. Why? Is it different in your . . . your *Now*?"

"Way," she said. "*Way* different." Then she seemed to hear what he'd just said. "Peculiar? What Peculiar? Are you telling me we're inside one?"

"Only in a manner of speaking. It's the fog what's eating up the world."

"Stop encouraging it to believe its own fictions," Meme said. "She is not even a real person, only a fragment wearing another girl's body."

"Not where I come from," the girl said.

"You are *nothing*." Meme pounded her chest with a clenched fist. "I don't care what you think you see in the mirror. *I* am a person, not you!"

The girl cast a look down at her body as if she'd just now tried on a skirt and blouse several sizes too small. "Well, considering *where* I am, I see why you'd think that. But if you know about the Dark Passages and other *Nows*, then you must know that there are multiple versions of everyone: as people, ideas . . . whatever."

"*I* don't know nothing about that, but I seen myself in a nightmare, and doubles of my friends, too," Bode said.

"What?" Meme said, at the same instant that the other girl said, "Nightmare?"

"Yeah, of a valley," Bode said. "A lot of snow. And my friends, Tony and Rima, they saw themselves, too."

The other girl gasped. "You know *Tony*? He's *alive*? He's here? What about Rima? Is she okay?"

"Here? Yeah, my Rima is fine, but she's not the girl from that valley, that dream." Bode's throat tried to close. "The bloody thing's real, isn't it? The valley, the fight, that monster, those . . . *scorpions*. All of it. I die to save you and the others," Bode said to the girl in Elizabeth's body. "Don't I? *Didn't* I?" He bunched his fists over his heart. "I *felt* it happen. But if I saved you, why are you *here*? If I already did this once, what am I to do now? Why am *I* here? Why are *you*?"

"She is here because she has been drawn to Elizabeth and what she carries. She is nothing but a piece, a fragment, and so are these others of whom she speaks." To the other girl, Meme said, "You have nothing to say to him. He belongs here, and so do his friends. They are not like you. *Your* Rima has vanished. Her world is in ruins, and *your* Tony is dying, and good *riddance*; he should, he *should*." Meme sounded on the verge of tears. "I should never have interfered. Doctor is right. We are better off rid of you all."

"Meme." He was suddenly very tired, his head crammed with information. *Just a few minutes' peace and quiet to sort all this out.* "Hold on. Can't lose our heads. We have to think about what to do next."

"I know precisely what I must do." She glared at the other girl. "What is your name? I need to know."

"It's not what you think," the other girl said.

"What does she think?" Bode asked.

"Not this." The other girl didn't take her eyes from Meme. "I know what you want to hear, but . . . my name's Emma."

What? Bode goggled. *Two* Emmas? *One grown, the other not? Which one do I help? Which is the right one?*

"No." All the color drained from Meme's face. "No . . . *no.*"

"Meme?" When she looked at Emma through those glasses, what had Meme seen? Was Emma some monster, or a bloody ruin like poor Tony? That entity, Eric, had said *stain, shadow.* "What did you see?" Bode asked. "*Who?*"

"Bode," Emma said, from her corner, "you can't let her leave."

But it was too late. Meme shrieked something guttural and inarticulate, a high, animal keening that filled this space until it seemed to Bode the world was made of nothing else but that sound.

And then Bode felt the floor, the walls, the *cave* . . . begin to shake.

RIMA

Lost

WHY YOU COMING *so low, and why now?* Hunching her shoulders against the wind, Rima gave the sky a sidelong glance as she and Emma horsed the cart another half foot while Tony strained at the yoke. No, it wasn't her imagination. The snow was still falling in sheets, almost in a deluge like a heavy rain. Yet through this strange half-light, she saw that the fog was much closer. So either they were wandering into a thick roll of errant mist, or the Peculiar itself was drawing down over them. *Or*—she aimed another uneasy look—*you're about to spit out another visitor.*

"No use," Tony said, teeth chattering. Weighed down with bodies, their cart had sunk until the axles were completely submerged. "Don't look anyone's been out this far in years."

One look, and Rima felt a sick stab of dismay. "Tony." She touched a hand to her nose. "You n-need to . . ."

"What? *Sh-shite.*" Swiping at his lip, he studied the scarlet chunks of frozen blood, then brushed his hand against a thigh. "N-no help for it," he said brusquely.

"So wh-what do we do n-now?" Snow lathered Emma's

eyebrows. Her shoulders were mantled with white. On the cart, a sack rippled as Jack wormed his way to the neck and popped out for a look. "Hey, b-boy." Emma rested her forehead on the cat's head. "Don't you know curiosity k-killed the cat? You need to stay warm." To the others: "Do we g-go back?"

"No." When Tony opened his mouth to protest, Rima pushed on, "You heard Bode. You can't risk getting closer to the other T-Tony."

"Don't think it makes much difference." Shrugging out of his yoke, Tony stumped around to the cart's rear and held out his arms. "Come on, girls, get warm."

Sinking into his chest made the icy lump of fear in Rima's throat melt a bit. Burying her face in his coat, she inhaled his scent. Despite her new mittens, the pain in her hands was ferocious, like hundreds of knives hacking her flesh. "Why haven't we made it off-grounds y-y-yet?" Talking was hard work. "How far back do you think the asylum is?"

"Don't know." His right arm tightened around her shoulders. "Last thing I remember seeing was those ruins. I thought I kept them to our l-l-left, but . . ."

But you're not sure. Neither was she. She felt her stomach drop. They'd gotten themselves lost somehow. *Gloomy, and the snow's so thick, easy to get turned around.* Then, of course, there was the Peculiar.

"Was it like that when I showed up?" Emma's eyes slid from the glowering fog to Rima. "That th-thick?"

She nodded. "But lower, too. Like a curtain or sheet of paper."

"Think there's someone else coming? Maybe"—the little girl swallowed—"that crazy lady? She might know we're here b-by now."

"Regardless"—Tony snugged them close—"we won't let her take you."

"May not be up to you." Emma was paler than the snow. "Can I ask you a question, Rima? About drawing?"

"What do you want to know?" Rima asked.

"Does it work both ways? Can you put back?"

"Why you asking?" Tony jogged the girl's shoulder. "What you thinking?"

"What about *what* you take?" The girl skimmed her tongue over lips that were dead-white. "Is it always . . . you know . . . when someone's s-sick?"

"Emma?" Rima ducked down to catch the girl's eyes. "What are you . . ."

"You take energy. So . . . that means eventually things even out, maybe even tip the other way, and you can't h-hold on to all of it. You don't know that you can't draw other things, too. Like that other R-Rima?"

"She took what was left after death," Tony said.

"A whisper," Rima said. "A watermark."

"Isn't that just another name for residual energy?" Emma asked.

"What are you driving at?" Tony asked.

"I'm not sure, but . . ." Emma's mouth worked. "Tell me this: when you take s-sickness, can you let it go where you want?"

"I don't know." Despite the cold, she was mystified, a little interested now, too. "Why are you . . ."

"Could you hide me?" The girl blurted it out, the words under pressure. "Take who I am, my . . . my watermark or stain or whisper or whatever, and b-bottle me up or something? Could you hide me inside of you and then let me go? Put me b-back?"

"What are you saying?" Snow tumbled from Tony's eyebrows as they folded in an alarmed frown. "You mean, you want Rima to steal your . . . your *soul*?"

"If it's energy." Eyes pooling, the girl nodded. "Yeah. Could you?"

"I don't . . ." Rima faltered, looked to Tony for help. "Emma, why would you even think . . ."

"Because what if she *does* come?" Tears swelled over the girl's cheeks. "If I'm . . . you know . . . *dead*, then maybe she'll leave me alone!"

"*No.*" Aghast, Tony crushed the weeping girl close. "*Never.* We have you, Emma. You're our charge, yeah? Our chuckaboo? 'Sides, you heard Meme. They never once mentioned you. Don't even know about you."

"They have to, if they're working together. Only a matter of time before they figure it out." Ice-tears pebbled the girl's jaw. "And I don't trust Meme. Bode d-does, but *you* know he shouldn't."

Blast, why does she have to be so observant? Doesn't miss a trick. Rimes of hoar frost clung to Rima's muffler where her breath had first condensed and then iced. Now that she'd stopped moving, her many layers of clothing, saturated with sweat, were already beginning to freeze. "What are you talking about?" she asked, knowing full well what the girl was saying. "Why would you say that?"

"Come on, Rima, I'm not dumb," Emma said. "I saw your face. When you l-looked through the panops?"

"She's right." Small bits of ice rained from Tony's lashes and eyebrows when he scrubbed his face. "I did, too. The name's wrong, but you know it was her. I r-recognized her from the dream." He paused. "And we let Bode go, no warning."

He'd have done it anyway. What was more, Rima suspected Bode must know, even if the name was wrong. *Why would that be, though? Ours were all the same: two Rimas, two Tonys, two Bodes.* "Once he's got his head in harness . . ."

"He don't back down. I know. But Emma's right. Wh-why did you keep cutting me off, not let me tell him?"

Because so many other things are *right.* She didn't understand this Many Worlds business or *Nows,* but there were the glasses, and she believed in doubles leading their own lives. There was the nightmare they all shared, after all. "Since you're both so observant, did either of you see the way she looked at him? She likes Bode. Cares for him. Her coming out wasn't never for us or the other T-Tony." *And what of the other me? She said that Rima's world is a shambles. But why? Because that Rima's not there?* "She did it for Bode, pure and simple."

"So what did you see?" Tony asked. "When you looked at Meme through the glasses?"

"Nothing," she said.

From the way the little girl's eyes narrowed, she thought Emma understood at once, or at least had an inkling. Tony only frowned and blinked away ice. "Yes, you did," he said. "I know you. You went white as salt. So what did you see?"

He really didn't understand. "Exactly what I just said: I saw . . ." All at once, her skin prickled, the hair standing on end along her arms and the back of her neck.

"Oh boy." Emma jerked a look not at the sky but the ground. "You f-felt that, too?"

"Yes." She followed the girl's gaze. *Something about to happen.* The premonition was very strong, a physical ache like the dig of a claw at her throat.

"What?" Tony's head swiveled right and left. "Felt . . . oh." Eyes wide, Tony released them and chafed his arms. "I'm all pins and nee—"

Beneath her feet, Rima felt the sudden slip and sideways shift of the earth, and then the sound again, the one she'd heard at the guardhouse: that low grumble as the ground shook. *Another quake?* Cutting above the wind's howl, their cart let out a high squeal. To her horror, a spiderweb of fine fissures and cracks sketched themselves over the snow, and she saw the right wheel begin to lurch and tremble.

"Get back!" Launching himself, Tony threw his arms round them both, pushing them back into the snow just as the cart's wheel plummeted in a precipitous drop with the roll of the earth. To the left, a huge block of compressed snow lifted at the same moment, thrusting up like an iceberg in a white sea. The cart went down at a slant, the bagged bodies they'd roped down slithering like fish on a wet deck. Whether it was the sudden weight or the unbalanced load, the wheel shattered, its spokes buckling in loud cracks.

Then, as suddenly as it had begun, it was over. The shuddering stopped. A plume of pulverized snow quickly dissipated in the wind.

"Are you all right?" Tony's voice was as broken as the snow. Rima could feel his heart banging against hers. "Rima? Emma?" Tony looked to his left where Emma had come to rest about a half foot away. "You hurt?"

"I'm okay." Emma sounded breathless. "You guys?"

"Fine." But she was also afraid to move. Whether it was their combined weight or the fractured snow, they'd come to rest a good foot below the surface. Looking up, she thought, was like getting a corpse's-eye view of the world.

"That's two tremors," Tony said. "Why n-now?"

"Maybe it's the end," she said.

"No." It was Emma. "I think it m-might be something else. Remember your nightmare? What happened when that other R-Rima got into that big fight on the snow?"

"Yes, it broke. You think . . ."

"Yeah, same space. Too many of us bunched together, like a crowd on thin ice. This *Now* can't take the pressure. I bet there's more than just the other Tony here now. Maybe"—Emma slicked her lips—"maybe another *me*. You know . . . grown up? Like the girl in your dream? Or maybe they found the other Bode?"

"Whichever it is, we *really* need to go." Rima didn't know if Emma was right, but two quakes in one day and in roughly the same spot were bad no matter what. Belatedly, she realized that she'd not heard the collapse of bricks or the squaw of metal. No shouts either. So they really must be quite a distance out from even the derelict criminal wings, unless the storm muffled all sound.

"Come on." Struggling from the divot they'd made in the snow, Tony extended a hand to pull her out. "Snow's stopped," he said.

"What?" She felt a kick of hope that quickly faded. Their cart had come to rest at a forty-five-degree angle. Its left wheel had popped clear of the snow. Most of the bodies had tumbled out, though a few hung over the cart's lip like partially opened jackknives. *But we're all right.* The sky had brightened to a muzzy gray, and no one had come for them. "I think the cart's ruined," she said, then frowned and scrubbed at her eyes. "Must have hit my head. Snow's all wobbly."

"No, look at the cart, it's . . ." Tony touched it with a finger. "Solid, but do it look to you like it's underwater?"

That was exactly it. "A glimmer," she murmured. "I saw the same thing right before the cat—"

"Jack!" Gasping, Emma floundered to her feet. *"Jack? Ja—"* She stopped. "Guys." She backed up a slow step. *"Guys?"*

"What . . ." And then Tony pulled in a sharp breath. "Oh *shite.*"

"Uh-huh." Emma's voice had almost no substance at all. Air was weightier.

"Dear God," Rima said—because, yes, the snow had stopped. But now the fog was there.

BODE

Emma's Blood

THE CELL WAS eerily bright, the rock high above pulsing and shimmering with that bizarre, phosphorescent glow. Dangling from an iron hook, Weber's lantern jounced, splintering the gloom with wild shafts of light. There was a loud crack, a series of glittery *smashes* as, somewhere beyond this cell, rock splintered. Metal shrilled, and a huge bellowing grumble sounded as stones suddenly gave way to clatter to rough-hewn rock. At the door, Meme was still screeching, but whether from terror, he didn't know.

"Meme!" He managed a single floundering step. All at once, the ground jerked sideways. By the door, Weber's lantern hurtled from the wall like a spent comet. There was a glassy shattering sound, and as the flame guttered, Bode had a single moment to be glad that lantern oil didn't spontaneously ignite the way it did in novels.

Beneath his feet, the mattress padding twitched and heaved. He stumbled, his arms shooting out for balance as his feet shuffled in a queer stutter step. The toe of his left boot stubbed one of

Weber's legs, and he felt himself totter and then fall. A sharp yelp jumped from his mouth as his shoulder slammed into a puddle of gore. As he pushed up, something very large *whirred* past his left ear to thud into Weber's chest. There was a series of snaps as Weber's ribs crumpled, and Bode thought, *Shite, the ceiling!* As if to drive home the point, a chunk of stone plowed into his left thigh. If he'd been thinking, he might even have dragged Weber's body over his, let the dead man absorb any more rockfall. As it was, he drew up his legs and then threw his arms up to protect his skull, turtling his head into shoulders. Another slam of the earth knocked him flat onto his belly. What tasted like centuries of grime and grit rose from the mattress's guts to clog his throat and nose. Choking, spit pooling under his tongue, he cowered, listening to the bang of stone against stone. He realized he'd lost track of Elizabeth. God, what if part of the wall had come down on her? And was that still Meme screeching, or was that only the high scream of stressed rock? Why was this happening altogether? *Like the city's ripping itself apart.*

A moment later, the shuddering began to wane, dwindling to a kind of shivering as vibrations rippled and juddered into his bones, only more and more weakly, until they finally stopped. For a long second, he couldn't move and only lay listening to his own harsh pants. His ears were ringing. Finally, he dragged up his head, blinking against dust and grit. There was a jumble of that glassy stone all around. When he moved his arms, chunks clashed together as if he'd stirred large shards from a broken vase. A single look at the ceiling showed cracks and fissures where the rock had shaken free. In the dim greenish glow that hadn't died, he could see the mattresses had ripped free of their bolts and now lay in heaps along with boulders big around as his head.

Elizabeth—Emma?—had vanished. The corner in which she'd cringed had partially collapsed in a slurry of rubble, torn canvas ticking, and clots of ancient horsehair.

"E-Emma?" His voice was rusty. He also didn't know if that was the right name, but damme, he had to call her something. No answer came. *Shite.* As his ears cleared, he could still hear Meme's high keening screams echoing from the corridor beyond. Pushing up on hands and knees, he wobbled to a stand, then picked his way around fallen rock to the door to look. To his right and left and all the way down as far as he could see, piles of stone spilled from where the walls had slumped to rubble. Meme was nowhere.

"Meme?" Chased by echoes, his shout raced away down the tunnel. No one answered, though that curious high wail continued. Then he realized this wasn't Meme at all but the mad clamor of patients behind their iron doors, all joining on that single manic note as if they'd taken up the chorus where Meme had left off. But where was she?

From inside the cell, he heard a grunt and then a bony slithering of rocks. "Emma?" he said, ducking back. "Where are you?"

"Here." Her voice was muffled. In that far corner, a mound of stone heaved as first a hand and then her arm snaked from a pile of rubble. "I'm buried, can't . . ."

"Wait. I'm here. Hang on." Hurrying over, he grabbed her groping hand. Her fingers closed over his, and he gave them a squeeze. "I'm right here, but you got a load of rock on top the mattress. Are you hurt? Can you move at all?"

"Not much." Her voice was reedy and labored. "Hard to breathe."

"I'm here, I'm here. Don't panic." *Oh no, I'm panicked enough for us all.* Heaving stones aside, he uncovered the mattress that had torn loose. Beneath, she lay in an awkward heap, one booted foot pinned between two large rocks. "You all right?"

"Foot's jammed." Her bandage was gone. An oily black trickle leaked from where her stitches had pulled apart. Her nose was either still bleeding or had started up again. Big ruby drops swelled on her jaw before pattering to her chest and onto stone.

"Give me a second." Hooking his hands around one of the boulders that trapped her foot, he heaved it up a few inches. His shoulders popped with the strain. "Go," he grunted. After she'd wriggled her foot free and crabbed back on her hands, he let the rock bang back into place. "Damned heavy. How about your foot? Can you walk?"

"I think it'll be okay." She gave it an experimental roll, first one way and then the other. Her face was pinched. She used the back of a hand to smear away blood from her upper lip. "Another nosebleed. Is this . . . do you know if Elizabeth is sick? More than her . . ." She gestured toward her head. "You know."

Sick? His chest was boiling over with bright red panic. "Yeah, I've always thought so, though no one's said. You . . . is she *bad* off?"

"I think so, yeah." Pressing a palm to her right ribs, she winced. "Hurts more than it did before."

She sounded wan and worn out, and he remembered what Meme had said about the other Tony. *My Tony has nosebleeds, too.* Christ, what if they were all sick with the same thing? *Yeah, but then why am I all right? Why isn't Rima ill? Because our doppelgängers aren't here?* But Rima's *was*: her . . . her *shadow?* Existing inside this girl. "Your stitches is torn open. You're bleeding." *And I'm going mad.*

"Yeah." Using the side of a hand to wipe her brow, she stared at the blood on her fingers. "Are you okay? Where's Meme?"

"Gone. Probably to warn Kramer. But listen to the others now. It's like they're screaming *for* her." *Why* had Meme become *so* hysterical?

With her pale skin and dark eyes and the blood, it was like looking down at a skull in this weird, grainy light. "How long do we have?"

"Not very." His voice was terse, and then his control broke. "So what *was* all that? *Huh?*" God, he wanted to hit something. "You *realize* you killed a man, yeah?"

"Thanks. You think I don't *know* that? What the hell was I supposed to do?"

"Not . . . bloody . . . *that!*" he roared.

"Bode . . ."

"Shut it! Let me *think!*" Fists bunched, he wheeled away fast. *Got to get out of here, got to get out now!* His eyes fell on Weber, whose torso was half-covered with debris. *Yeah, but Bode, you got to think. You're running now.* Cove probably had pockets full of useful things. Dropping to his haunches, he averted his eyes from the mess and quickly ran his hands over Weber's trousers. Left pocket was crammed full: keys, a penknife, a candle stub jammed in a small brass holder, a brass match safe that was half-full, Connell's silver flask, and a small brown bottle. *Oh, wonderful. Just what we need.* He replaced the laudanum, though he laid the flask aside. Weber's candle stub reminded him of the one he'd dropped. Tossing a look around, he spied a straight iron finger. Miraculously, the candle was still there. Stuffing his haul into a coat pocket, he patted Weber's right pocket and realized why the nob had transferred everything to the left. *Weber, you thieving arse.*

"So, who are you now?" Carefully tugging Connell's scalpel free of that right pocket—at least Weber had wrapped the blade in burlap, probably so he'd not skewer his balls—he said, "Who am I talking to? You Elizabeth? Ya *Emma*?"

"Bode, you know I'm Emma. Calm down."

"Ohhh, that's rich." Whipping round on his heels, he stabbed air with the scalpel. "You're telling me to be *calm*? You *killed* a man. One hit, *one* hit woulda done, and you *know* it!" He was raging, foaming at the mouth. What was he doing, yelling at this girl? So much water under the bridge, wasn't it? *But what did Meme see? Who?* "But no, you *beat* the man's head in!"

"He would've killed *you* and . . . *damn* it!" She dragged an arm over streaming eyes. Dark blood oiled down the side of the girl's face to drip from her jaw. That forehead was a mess, like a weeping third eye. "It wasn't *me*!"

"No? So then Meme is right, yeah? This Eric *is* a monster, and now maybe that's what you are? Nothing but a mon—" His voice failed. What he'd been about to say evanesced from his tongue.

"Bode?" she asked. "What?"

"Emma." Oh, but he suddenly sounded so strange. Why couldn't he breathe? When he pointed the scalpel, the blade shook. "Look. Your blood. Emma, your blood, look how it's . . ."

He heard her gasp. "Oh my God. It's . . ."

She couldn't say it either. But he saw all right. Oh yes.

Emma's blood—that trickle of black oil from her forehead that had dribbled onto shattered rock and torn canvas—her blood, all of it . . .

Was moving.

RIMA

Spider to the Fly

1

"WHY ISN'T IT moving?" Tony's fingers laced through Rima's. "It's just . . . hovering."

"All around us." Emma was crowded back against them. "Like it doesn't want us going anywhere."

Why? The Peculiar was perfectly still and quite dense. *Like milky glass.* Against the white snow, Rima found the effect disorienting, as if they were encased in a white sphere.

"Is this what it was like before I popped out?" Emma asked.

"It was much darker then, b-but . . ." Shivering, Rima nodded. "Essentially."

"How far away you think it is?" Tony's tone was curiously flat, too, as if the space inside this fog dome, however large it was, deadened sound.

"Can't tell." Maybe a hundred feet? Twice that? Until one of them actually tried walking up to the barrier, it was impossible to say. "Listen." Rima cocked her head. "You hear that?"

"Like crackle ice, when you smash it under your boot," Tony said.

"Or Rice Krispies. Snap, crackle, pop. Or static between radio stations. Or . . ." Emma's face trembled. "I've heard this before. From down cellar."

"I think it's coming *from* the fog. Not right at the surface but inside. You know how you can look at a pond and the surface is still but underneath there are currents and things swimming? There's a layer keeps the fog in place," she said.

"*Ohhh,*" Emma breathed. "You mean, a force field. Wow, yeah, why didn't I think of that? It's like on *S-Star Trek.*"

"What?" The girl was a mystery. Rima had been thinking more of hoar ice over a shallow puddle: that she always knew there was water beneath because of the bubbles and the way the water moved when she put pressure on the ice.

"All right," Tony said. "So the fog is soft and squashy as custard and needs something to hold it in place. How does that help us? We can't just stay here."

"The only other choice is to see if we can walk through it."

"Not with a force field in place," Emma said. "Probably get zapped. But . . . how come you guys don't know about this already? I mean, the Peculiar's been here for a while, right? Has anyone ever tried walking into it?"

"From what I've heard," Tony said, "yeah. They make it inside but doesn't nobody ever come back out. Until you, that is."

"I didn't go into a Peculiar," Emma said.

"That you know of," Rima said. "Maybe, in your . . . *Now* . . . it's different. You said there was a barrier between you and that square you came through."

"You mean that the Peculiar changes depending on where it is?" Emma's eyebrows tented. "Well . . . water does that; goes from liquid to solid to gas. I can buy that." The little girl cocked her head. "So what if the force field's like . . . a one-way mirror? Whatever's inside can see out, but you can't see in?"

"Meaning that there's something or someone there, watching us now?" Rima ran her eyes up and down the fog. *Perhaps Emma's right; it's like a carriage, a way of transporting energy from one place to another.* There was a way to know, too. Maybe.

"What?" Startled, Tony looked down when she took her hand from his. "What is . . ." Then he saw what she was doing and battened around her wrist before she could tug off her other mitten. "You taken leave of your senses? That is *not* an option."

"Tony." She said his name calmly enough, but her pulse was jumping in her throat. "You know it is. I'm the only one who can do this. If there's something inside, maybe I can . . . I don't know, *talk* to it. It's not hurting us, just *waiting* for something." She gave her hand, still imprisoned in his, a pointed look. "Tony, we can't stand here forever and wonder."

"You don't know if it's not the same everywhere else in Lambeth. Maybe this is the way it goes. How it . . ." He swallowed. "How it all ends."

"Bet not," Emma said.

Tony scowled. "Whose side are you on?"

"Everyone's. But Rima's right, and you know it."

"Think, Tony," Rima said. "You're saying the fog isolates each and every person in London like this? Then what? Starves them out? Waits for them to die?"

"It could." His jaw thrust in a stubborn jut. "Not like anyone knows for sure."

"That's ridiculous." She gave her wrist a small tug. "It's waiting, Tony."

"Yeah? So do spiders. Spin their webs and wait for a stupid fly to bumble in before moving in for the kill."

"I'm not a fly." But she could actually see a strange, unearthly spider at the center of all this: *Come to my parlor* . . . "You *want* to stay here? With them?" She waved her free hand at their tumble of sacks. Her old fear was back, too, rising in their throat. *You watch; they'll get up and walk next.* She muscled that down. "Eat up whatever's in our sad little bundle, and then what? Wait? Dig a cave? Eat each other? Tony, we're cut off and on the *snow*. I fail to see how *I* can possibly make this any worse than it already is."

"There's always worse."

"*Tony.*" Emma gave him an exasperated look. "Let her *try*."

"What is this? Five seconds ago, you're the one worrying about getting *zapped*."

"But we can't just hang around, *waiting*," the girl said. "I'll do it, if you want. Maybe it should be me, anyway. I came from it. When I touched the square down cellar, it opened up. So maybe we're looking at this wrong. What if it's come back for *me*? What if this is how I get home?"

"Neither of you knows anything for sure," Tony said. "You're both spitting in the wind and hoping it don't come back in your face."

"But you don't have a better idea." When his eyes skipped away, Rima ducked her head to capture his gaze. "I'm the one knows how to draw. If nothing happens, we let Emma try. Tony, we have nothing to lose."

"*Rima.*" His lips were so tight the skin around his mouth was white as the fog. "If something goes wrong . . . say, it grabs you or . . . I don't know. Don't you understand? I might not . . ." Emotions chased across his face. "What if I can't stop it taking you? I don't want anything to happen to you."

"That makes two of us," she said.

"No." Emma slid her hand into Rima's chilled palm. "Three."

2

HE DIDN'T QUITE give up. "Shut it," Tony said when she objected. "It's either me or the rope. Choose your poison, but you're not getting close to that without me having hold of you one way or the other." He looked down at Emma. "Without *us* hanging on."

"Got that right," Emma said.

"What if it doesn't like you hanging on?" Rima asked.

"Bugger that." He untied the rope from their cart. "It can suck wind for all I care."

"Fine," she said, "but no rope. I'm not the prize in a tug-of-war."

"All right. Then it's me and bare hands." Tossing the loops onto the fractured snow, he yanked a pike from where it had buried itself in snow and then took up a loose fistful of her coat between her shoulders. "Arm's length. First sign of trouble, I pull you back, no arguments."

"I'm not going anywhere," she said, though she wasn't at all sure about that.

"Guys." Fishing out their second pike, Emma took up a position by her side, like an armed guard. "Let's just do this, okay?"

Judging distance was hard. But if the cart was the center of whatever odd dome or sphere they were in, then she thought they clambered, perhaps, fifty or sixty feet in a slow, uncertain shuffle, feeling for softer snow through their boots and bypassing jagged chunks. When she was five feet away, she looked back over a shoulder. "You feel that?"

"Yeah." Emma made a face. "Tingles."

"All my hair's standing on end, like I scuffed over a carpet," Tony said.

That was exactly right. She shot a glance at the cart. Why, she wasn't sure, but nothing had changed: the sacks hadn't budged. *Idiot. No one's getting up for a stroll.*

"What is it?" Emma asked.

"Nothing." *Then why do I feel watched?* She faced forward again. The fizzy sound was louder, too, and more like the buzz of an excited crowd. *People?*

"This is what it sounded like down cellar." Emma held the pike like a spear. "You should be *really* careful. When I reached in the first time, something grabbed me."

"*Now* you're telling us?" Tony said.

"All right," Rima said, when she'd come within arm's reach. "Far enough."

"Wait," Tony said. She heard the soft crunch of snow and felt Tony set his feet. "All right, go on. Ready as I'll . . . No, Emma, you get back here, stay behind me."

"Why? God, get over yourself. It's not like it's going to explode." The girl made a disgusted sound. *"Fine."*

"Here goes." Pulling in a breath, Rima stretched her hand. The next moment, she let out a small cry.

"What, *what*?" Alarmed, Tony gave her a tug. "Rima?"

"I'm all right. It was a spark. Like . . . a shock, but sharp like needle pricks? Cold too, but not terrible. Just a surprise."

"Is it freezing cold?" Emma asked. "That's what it was like down cellar."

"Yes." She *haahed* on her numbed fingers. "Surface is a little gummy, too, like aspic left out too long that's started to dry."

"Do you hear anything?" Emma asked. "Like a click or something?"

"No." This time, when she touched the fog, she was ready for the sting and waited to see if it would stop. It did, but her hand wouldn't go any further either.

"Anything?" Tony asked as Emma said, "See? Maybe she's not the one it wants."

The girl might be right. No *whisk* of anything leaving her, and nothing coming back from the fog either. A stab of disappointment. *I was so sure there was something or someone . . .* She gasped as a sudden frisson raced up her spine.

"What?" When she didn't reply, Tony tightened his grip. "Rima, what . . ."

"I feel something." An understatement: she wanted to turn around but couldn't. It was as if invisible hands had shot out to grasp either side of her head.

"What do you feel?"

"I think . . . No, Tony, *don't*." Panic thrummed through her chest as she sensed him gathering himself to give her a good yank. "Don't move. Don't do anything."

"What's happening?" Emma asked.

"It's . . . it's . . ." She gasped as the fingers of these unseen hands seemed to pierce her scalp and melt through her skull. At once she could feel the creep through her brain, the snuffling, probing action of a dog sussing out exactly what all those exotic scents might be. "I think it's"—she almost said *tasting* or *testing*—"trying to get to know me." A bizarre thought, but it also seemed correct. "Figure out what I am."

"Wow," Emma said. "It's *alive*?"

Perhaps. She felt a slight tug, as if an invisible hand wanted to pull her a little closer and into the light. The feeling was . . . familiar, as if someone had said her name in a crowded room. Her focus sharpened, and the sense she got back was recognition: *Aha, there you are.*

All at once, that *tasting, testing* sensation slid away, and in the next second, she felt the pressure on her head ease. She took a hesitant step back, and then Tony was turning her around, wrapping her up.

"You all right?" His eyes were bright. Blinking, he skimmed a light hand over her forehead. "What was that?"

"You get anything?" Emma asked. "Did it talk to you or something?"

"I d-don't know." She was shaking from the contact as much as the cold. Her hands were white as bone. As the fog. Even with the contact broken, her brain squirmed at the memory. *Sliding into every nook and cranny.* The fog seemed unchanged. She had no idea if that was good or bad. "I'm not exactly sure. It felt like when you've got a pamphlet, a magazine? You're not sure it's to your liking, so you . . . you read a few pages or thumb through to another spot . . ." She broke off at the expressions on their faces. "Don't look at me like I'm a nutter. You asked what it felt like."

"So it was *reading* you?" His tone was skeptical. "Trying to decide if it wanted to know more of the story, or if it was satisfied with only a few choice bits?"

"I *know* what it sounds like." A tiny flicker of anger now, though not much. What he'd just said snagged like a burr in her mind: *a few choice bits.* That fog had been actively searching for something very specific, and she thought it had found it. But what? "Well, no matter. Nothing's happened. It either doesn't understand me, or I'm not that interesting. I didn't get anything from *it*. There was nothing to . . . to *draw*." *It wasn't doing that to me either.* The fog hadn't *taken* anything; it was only browsing.

Emma said, suddenly, "Does the snow look funny to you guys?"

"Funny?" Tony peered. "Yeah. That . . ."

"Rippling," Emma said. "Like when you look through water."

"I *do* see that." Bending, Rima squinted at the snow's slight shimmy. "What is that? Not another quake, surely. I don't feel anything."

Emma shrugged. "Kind of reminds me of heat shimmers. You know, when you see mirages and the air looks like water? But the temperature hasn't changed."

"Regardless, we've the same dilemma. We're trapped, and—" Rima stopped so suddenly that Tony, following close behind, blundered into her. She barely felt him snatch her arms and hardly heard his question over the hammering of her heart. But she did hear what he said next: *"Christ."* And Emma: "Oh boy."

So they saw it, too. Despite the slight shudder in the air, this was no mirage or fantasy stroked from her mind by the fog— although she did think that *this* was the juicy bit those phantom fingers had prized free. Perhaps it hadn't been all that hard either. After all, she *had* thought of both: one image had come to her that very morning, as Tony thrashed awake from a nightmare she'd also had, and the other had flashed into her mind not all that long ago, thanks to the very strange Constable Doyle.

3

FROM THIS VANTAGE point and now that Rima had a chance to think about it, she realized that the fog had come down like a bowl or bell jar to carve a wide circle, the kind you might find in a circus. (Or—considering Emma's uneasiness—the asylum's dome.) If the cart was dead center, then they were along the edge, at roughly five o'clock.

On the far side of the cart, the woman was not quite opposite them. Say, nine o'clock, and probably because she'd decided this was the best place from which to observe. At this distance, Rima could tell only that her ankle-length skirt was jet. Her hair was coiled in a perfect chignon. Her face, angular as a skull's, was just as white, and the sockets were very dark. But for the shape— rectangular lozenges—and that glint of gold, you might have imagined her eyes were gone altogether.

Purple spectacles. She saw how, in contrast to them, the woman's boots hadn't even dimpled the snow, and then she realized with a twist of sick dismay that the woman's shoes weren't even touching the ground.

"It's her," Emma said. "That's the woman who tried to get me."

"Yes." *It's the same woman I saw here, in the asylum, in Kramer's office.* Her heart was beginning to hammer. *She came for the other Tony.* She'd come for them all, it seemed—and yet, perhaps, that woman was the lesser of two horrors.

Across the snow, by their cart, those sacks of dead . . . were moving.

EMMA

Infected

SHE'D FELT IT as this odd *worming* sensation along her neck, her jaw, the gash on her forehead. Not the usual *drip-drip* but an unctuous *squirming*. Now, she stared as a small, fresh red puddle suddenly shuddered on dusty canvas as if the earth was gearing up for another quake. The blood-pool stretched, elongating to a teardrop, then a finger, and finally a muscular red rope . . . and then it headed for Weber.

House showed me this in that blink *to Madison*. She could feel her eyes bugging from their sockets. Beyond this cell, out in those halls, the other patients were still wailing, and the pressure to start screaming herself burned like fizzy pop in the bottleneck of her throat. *My arms started to bleed and then the whisper-man pulled himself out of a book. Meme's right.* She watched her blood undulate as it snaked for the dead man. Weber's head was a mis-shapen jigsaw. Everything above the right cheekbone was gone, nothing left but a pudding of brain tissue, pulverized bone, and pulpy meat that looked black in the cave's greenish-yellow glow. His left eye had popped like a cork under too much pressure and goggled, gray as dirty ice, on a sliver of dusky nerve. The empty socket, wide as an ice-cream scoop, stared in wide-eyed wonder. The man's jaw was out of joint, his bluing tongue lolling, held in place by a shred.

I'm stained, infected. She had no idea what had happened after she lost consciousness; there had been no awakening to find Eric and her mind joined. But her blood was proof: he was in there, and so were Casey, Rima. A dark piece of Lizzie. Horrified, she watched the red eel of her blood nose Weber's blued tongue the way a curious puppy pokes at a squished snake, probing and then drawing itself along Weber's dead flesh in a slow, very thorough lick. *I can't go back home, not carrying this in my blood.*

On the floor, Weber's tongue twitched.

"Oh!" Emma caught the rest of that scream in her hands as Bode flinched, dropping the scalpel he'd just tugged from the dead man's pocket, and yelped, "Wh-what, *what?*"

Weber's blue tongue shivered. Thick globules of Weber's dead black blood quickened. The mattress was alive with writhing flesh and undulating ropes of blood and whips of tissue. In the hollow bowl of Weber's skull, a jellylike slurry of curdled brain and oily fluid heaved and rolled in a slow, gelatinous surge as if someone had just given a pot of thick oatmeal a good stir, and there was sound now: an unctuous, wet *splot-sploosh-fwap-splat* that reminded her of Jasper gutting a nice fourteen-incher, digging out intestines and liver and lungs with his fingers to slap into a guts bucket. On his left temple, Weber's lone eyeball was slowly creeping back toward its socket, the nerve spooling onto an invisible reel the way a sinker spins on a tangle of fishing line. As it seated itself, the eye—lidless and fat as a boiled egg—roved in hitches and jerks as if trying to get a fix. Then it fetched up, the eyeball quivering, the iris *tick-tick-tick-ticking*, as if there was an operator on the other side, some guy in Mission Control keying instructions: *No, pan left, go back.* After another second, the eye twitched back a millimeter at a time—*tick-tick-tick*—and then froze . . . on her. A split second later, Weber's neck worked, and then there came a guttural, lowing, gagging moan: *"AAAAH-HHH . . ."*

"Christ!" Bode was by her side in two great leaps. Snatching her wrist, he yanked her away from her corner and slung her around, crowding her toward the door. "Come on, come on!" he bawled. "We're getting out of here now! Run, *run!*"

RIMA

Rotters

"**MOVE, *MOVE!* GET** back!" Grabbing her arm, Tony shoved her behind him. "Emma, you too. Let's just . . . we'll . . ." He didn't finish that thought.

The fog took nightmares from my head. That's what it was parsing. It wanted what scares me. Horrified, Rima could only watch as the sacks bunched and wriggled. These fears were at the tip of her tongue, foremost in her mind. *I dream about a woman with purple eyes who takes Tony. I talked to Doyle about the dead coming back to life.*

Now, her worst and freshest nightmares were coming true. But what was the *woman* waiting for? Rima saw how still she was, like a statue. Meme said that Kramer already had a Tony. This woman had come after Emma, and if Meme was to be believed, this woman had also visited the other Rima's world. Even if Rima herself was of no use, the woman must want Tony and Emma at least.

"Then *take* them!" she suddenly screamed at the woman. "Please! Do it now before these dead come back to life!"

"Rima!" Tony grabbed her arm. "What are you doing?"

Trying to save you both. Maybe it was insanity or only desperation, but she was screaming now, shaking her fist at the woman. "That's why you're here, isn't it? Then please, please, take Tony away. Take Emma! Get them *out* of here! This is *my* nightmare, not theirs!"

"No!" Emma pressed close to her side. "I'm not going *anywhere* with her, and not without you!"

She paid no mind. "Get them out!" she shouted at the woman. "Please, I'm begging you!"

"Rima!" Grabbing her shoulders, Tony gave her a shake. "Are you mad? Stop, *stop!* We're not going anywhere."

"You won't have a choice." That woman hadn't budged, she saw. Probably settling in for a good show, but why, *why?* "If she wants you, she'll take you, and when she does, don't fight her, Tony. Stay alive. Please, promise me you'll stay alive. You too, Emma."

"What are you talking about?" Tony shook her again. "We stay together!"

No. That was precisely what she didn't want. *God, please, help us.* Her eyes hopped from the woman to the cart and those sacks. She could see the sudden bulge of a head in one, the thrust of an arm and hand in another. The outline of a foot. With only the low hum and higher fizz from the fog against which to compete, the scrape of nails over fabric was very plain. *Sacks are so thin, you can see daylight through the weave.* They'd tear through that burlap in seconds.

"Lord." Tony's voice quavered. *"Listen* to them."

The air swelled with a loud, long chorus of moans. She couldn't tell if they were suffering or these were the only sounds a dead man or woman, with either a bloated tongue or no tongue

at all, could make. *Or maybe it really hurts to come back from the dead.*
There came a very distinctive, very loud ripping sound of cold,
dry cloth, and she saw the lips of that one sack jackknifed over
the cart's edge suddenly gape. Two skeletal arms battled their way
through its mouth, and then a girl's head appeared through the
rent. Her face was gaunt, the cheekbones like knife blades, her
flesh green with decay. Rearing, the girl set her bony hands on
the cart and levered herself until she was looking right at them.

God! A scream boiled at the back of Rima's throat. A large
swath of the girl's scalp drooped free of the skull, like the corner of a sheet from an unmade bed, to curl over what remained
of her left ear. What hair was left, that which hadn't fallen out
in clumps to nest on her shoulders, dragged in long gray clots.
Rust-red purge fluid streamed from the woman's nostrils to coat
her neck and chest. Bulging green vessels, filled with dead blood,
wormed under her translucent skin. The wicked stripe of a blue-
black bruise snugged her neck like a satin choker.

*It's the girl who hung herself. Bode put our food in her sack. But she
can't be this rotted. At most, she's been dead only a day, not a week or
month.* This was the work of the fog: not simply reanimating the
dead but giving them the nightmare visages Rima had imagined.

The girl was pushing her way out of the sack now, jamming it
down around her hips as if stepping out of a dress. The girl's belly
hung, the muscles that should moor skin to bone slack, and the
guts inside bloated with gas.

Rima's eyes danced away. On the snow, other sacks were ripping as the dead pulled themselves free. She watched as one old
man, flesh sagging from his jaws to reveal the scattered brown
pegs of rotted teeth, turned them a single baleful, milky-white
eye. The other socket dripped a mucuslike jelly, and when the old

man scraped his fingers over his cheek, his entire face suddenly peeled away in a sodden flap. Groaning, the old man discarded his face, letting it plop to the snow like a soiled kerchief not worth washing. Where his nose had been were only two vertical tear-shaped slits. Dangling scraps of shredded, putrefying muscle bearded his lower jaw. His belly was also heavy with bloat.

"I got the pike and a penknife." Tony's voice was shaky, far away. "Rima . . . *Rima*, look at me!"

"Y-yes?" Her neck was stiff as a rusted hinge. "What?"

Tony's eyes were intent. "Take my chopper. Careful; just sharpened it. And I'm sorry, but you'll have to move out. Go to my left, and remember, short chops. Only got the one edge, and you don't have a lot of reach, so you'll have to wait until they're close. Don't swing so wild it pulls you around and off-balance, all right?"

"What?" It was as if he spoke in a foreign tongue. Her mind didn't want to understand. "I don't . . ."

"*Damme!*" Hefting his pike, Tony flashed an angry look. "Rima, do what I say. Emma? Move away to my right. If I swing, I don't want to risk hitting you. Listen to me, both of you: you get a chance, you see an opening, you run."

"Where?" Emma's voice was quaking. "There's nowhere to g-go."

"Unless the fog lets you through. It did once before."

"It won't, not now." Emma sounded both angry and scared. "*She's* here. I don't understand. She wanted me before. Why not just take me now and *stop* this?"

A good question. *Maybe she wants to see what will happen.* Or perhaps the woman would enjoy watching them being torn to bits. *Makes no sense.* Rima slid the chopper from Tony's hip sheath.

The blade was much more knife than she was used to, and heavy. She gripped the chopper's bone hilt until her knuckles whitened. *Why torture us?* There had to be another game here, something she didn't know yet.

"Tony," she said, moving to flank him on the left, "how do you kill something that's already dead?"

"I don't think you can."

"Chop off their heads." Tears were streaming down Emma's face, but the girl choked up on her pike. "Shoot them in the brains, or burn them. It works in books and on TV."

"Pity, chuckaboo, but this is real life, and I could use some ideas," Tony said. "Not going to stop me trying . . . Oh God." His skin went pale as glass. "Rima, look at their bellies. Look at *all* their bellies."

And so many of them. There were twenty in all—easily twice what they'd actually gathered on their rounds, as if the fog wasn't content with only bringing these monstrosities to life but wished to stack the odds against them. Most of the bodies were more or less intact, though some were in much worse shape. The stomach of each and every one of the dead bulged, but she now saw that instead of bloat, their tented skin heaved and rolled. In a way, it was as if they'd knotted the sack of something undead around their waists.

Her mouth dried up. Behind, not more than ten feet away, the fog's fizz and crackle seemed to grow louder, as if an excited and eager crowd was elbowing its way closer to the edges of a boxing ring—all the better to see.

Kicking their way free of the sacks, the dead—the girl who'd hung herself, that old man, a woman with fair hair who might even have been pretty once—began coming. When they moved, bits and pieces shed and fell: flaps of skin, tangled knots of hair, an ear, half a nose. But the dead didn't seem to care. They kept coming, and fast, puffs of ice rising like the steam of coal-fired engines as they kicked across the snow. As they ran, their heaving, writhing bellies bobbed and bounced. Those stomachs were so heavy, they ought to have burst.

But Rima thought that would happen only when these reanimated dead were closer. One would've done, too, but whatever was in charge here—the fog itself or only the woman with the purple eyes—was evidently leaving nothing to chance.

This is the reason she's waiting. She and Tony and Emma could fight, but a thrust of Tony's pike or chop of her blade into precisely the wrong spot . . . *This is what she wants to see.*

"I don't understand," Emma said. "What's it mean?"

"Infected, chuckaboo." Tony's tone was grim. "Each and every one."

He was right.

These dead were rotters.

EMMA

Why Meme Freaked

DESPITE THIS STUPID skirt and horrible boots and a bum ankle—despite the searing pain in her ribs and new blood in her mouth—she was keeping up, though every breath felt like talons raking her throat. It was true, what they said about fear and adrenaline, though Elizabeth's body was starting to ache, break down. They were going fast, racing through passages, with Bode in the lead, doubling back on his trail of wax drippings. The tunnels were so still it was like moving in that airless, motionless space between heartbeats. The only sound was the scuff of their boots on rock. On the way out of her cell, she'd swept up both the flask and that scalpel. In her right skirt pocket, the flask banged in time with every step. (Though why she'd bothered, she couldn't say; just thought it would be useful. She wasn't a drinker, but if ever there was a good time to start . . .) The scalpel she'd tucked into the left pocket on purpose, because she was right-handed and worried that even with the strip of burlap wrapped around the blade, she'd forget and end up slicing fingers. Now she reached and felt for the long bone handle through a layer of wool. Felt good to have a weapon, not that she figured it would be of much use. A while back, they'd passed a four-way junction, and they were still moving fast, pelting past closed cell doors, every one of which looked the same. So did the rock, and the tunnels themselves reminded her of long snakes eeling for the asylum.

Tunnels and Bode: the echo wasn't lost on her, and it was easier thinking about that than what had happened in her cell. *Her* Bode had spent an entire lifetime between the pages of a book fighting horrors in enemy tunnels. Even though this was a different boy, tunnels might be just a Bode-character hiccup, something constant between *Nows*, like eye color or the shape of his nose.

"Hush." Bode suddenly pulled up. "I thought I . . . *there*." He darted a look down the corridor unspooling ahead of them. "*Damn*. You hear that?"

"Hear?" She was panting hard, coughing a little, swallowing back blood. But then she caught it: a distant *clank*, followed by a far-off rumble. *Uh-oh.* "What's that?"

"Door. A lot of the tunnels are blocked off with iron grates. That's what you're hearing. But you need a key, and if somebody's got one . . ."

"That means we're out of time." *And heading right for them.* Her stomach sank. "Do we turn back?"

"And meet up with Weber?" Bode grunted. "Not in this lifetime. But there's that four-way. We duck into a side tunnel. I think one leads out to the old derelict criminal wings. It was colder and wet-smelling, so it might open to the surface."

"What if it's only Meme coming? Maybe she changed her mind. Maybe that's why the screaming stopped."

"Could be." Bode didn't sound convinced. "We wouldn't know until we come face-to-face, and I don't much like that plan, do you?" When she shook her head, he said, "Tell me something. When she looked at you through those panops, what'd she see? *After* you got to be . . . Emma, that is. You know what she saw, yeah?"

"Let me ask *you* a question. The Emma in your nightmares: who's she look like?"

"'At's just it." He gnawed at his lower lip. "I never have been able to figure it."

"Figure what?"

"How you can be two people at once. Sometimes, in the nightmare, I think you're Elizabeth. Others, I could swear you're . . .'"

"Who?"

"When I think about it?" He held her gaze. "I could swear that you're Meme."

"That's right," she said. "So now you know why Meme freaked."

Bode stared a good half second. "Oh holy God. You're saying Meme is who you really look—"

A voice, hollow with distance, interrupted. "Bode?"

Emma jumped. Starting, Bode snapped his head toward the far corridor ahead, then grabbed her arm and pulled her behind him. *Not a word,* he mouthed, and she thought, *Wasn't planning on it.*

"Bode." Meme's voice was getting closer. From the sound of it, she wasn't creeping along either, but coming pretty fast. "You know what she is," Meme called. "I need to take her to him, and I have to do it before it is too late for us all."

Him. She meant Kramer, who had at least one version of Tony that didn't belong and either had or was trying to find all of them who'd shared in that valley and its nightmares: Lily, Chad,

Lizzie. *Must not know about Bode yet or he'd be with the other Tony.* Unless Kramer thought he had plenty of time; after all, Bode worked here, and—until only a little while ago—had no clue what Kramer was doing. She wondered, too: *If I'm the strongest piece, and a little bit of me was in Elizabeth all along . . . shouldn't Meme be sick like the Tonys?* Unless Meme was different somehow. And how was Kramer or this woman with the panops gathering *anyone* without the Mirror or cynosure? Unless . . . *Another way in? A back door?* Something similar to what a computer programmer put into operating systems and software that allowed him to bypass security protocols and infiltrate the guts of a system? Would McDermott have wanted a back way into his book-worlds? To what, *visit*?

God. The realization was like the detonation of a firecracker in her mind. *Something like down cellar?*

"Come on. Back the way we came. Here." He pressed a candle on an iron miner's pick into her hands. "And take Weber's match safe, too, in case we have to separate."

"Oh no, Bode, we're not splitting . . ." She gasped at the sudden, unmistakable clash of metal on metal that reverberated through the tunnels. "You hear that?"

"Yeah." Bode turned a complete circle. "That's *locks*," he said. "Those are *bolts*."

Not being shot from *the case*. Heart pounding, Emma looked right and left. *Being run* back *on every cell,* every *door . . .*

Then, to her horror, came screams—but not from people. These screams shrilled from hinges that probably hadn't seen use since these tunnels were born.

All the cell doors, each and every one, were beginning to open.

RIMA

Swarm

THIS WOULD BE over in seconds, not minutes, and they all three knew it.

"The fog. Can we get into it somehow? Will it let us through?" When she didn't reply, Tony snapped, "Rima! Don't look at them! Look at *me*. The fog . . . can we *cross*?"

"No." She tore her gaze from the ravening swarm nearly on them. "That is, I . . . I don't know. Emma, maybe, but . . ."

"No way," Emma said. Then, almost to herself: "Where's Jack?"

"Watch it!" At Tony's shout, Rima jerked round just as that girl—the hanger—launched herself on a rusty screech. Gasping, Rima tried for a chop, but then Tony was sweeping the butt end of his pike in a sharp uppercut. The wood handle caught the girl under the jaw. Her neck snapped back, and as the girl blundered back into three other rotters, he whirled the pike around and drove forward. The point punched through the girl's breastbone with a dull *thuck*. No blood spumed, but the girl's mouth gaped in a howl, and ichor, sticky and foul, boiled in an inky torrent.

Still yowling, the sound like a file dragging over metal, the girl staggered onto her heels as Tony yanked the pike free.

"Back up, back up!" Tony jabbed with the pike, batting at hands right and left, trying to keep his swings short and controlled. To his right, Rima saw Emma sweep her pike low to the ground so it snagged a young boy at his ankles and sent him sprawling. "Good girl!" Tony yelled. "Both of you, get as close to the fog as you can!"

Rima saw why he wanted that, too. The dead flanked them in a rough semicircle, but they couldn't or wouldn't pass into the fog either. It wasn't ideal, but that meant no dead could come round behind them. She felt the prickle of the fog's energy along her neck and back. She chopped in swift cuts, first right and then left, trying to vary the rhythm. *Please*—she had no breath to shout at the woman—*please, help them, help us!*

To her right, Tony choked up on the pike and raked it in a fast, sideways cut so violent Rima heard the whistle as the point sped through the air. The iron shaft smashed into a woman whose left arm ended in a jagged tooth of bone. Careering sideways, the dead thing flailed with one good hand, bringing down two more as she fell, the three of them toppling like pins.

That was when whatever good luck they were going to get ran out. As soon as Tony's pike cleared, more dead piled in, hands outstretched to grab.

"Tony, to your left!" Darting forward, Rima brought the chopper around in a wild swing. She felt when the blade clipped the arm of a bedraggled man with muttonchops, shaving skin and then stuttering over bone to skip away.

But she'd also done exactly what Tony warned her against. As she finished the follow-through, her center shifted. Pulled off-balance, she floundered into a staggering half turn to the left. In the next instant, she felt hands scrambling up her back, fingers whisking at her neck. Something knotted in her shawl and pulled tight. The thick wool inched down, and then a wave of panic crashed into her chest as her air cut out.

No! Dropping the chopper, she clawed at her neck. There were other hands on her now, and they bore her to the snow, smashing her facedown the way you might bludgeon a large fish you'd just hooked. She felt cold sheet over her face. Snow clotted in her mouth and plugged her nose, not that it mattered, because she couldn't breathe anyway. Above the pound of her pulse, she thought she heard Tony bellow something, and then Emma's shout. An instant later, whatever had hooked her shawl jerked and then the pressure eased: not a lot, but enough that she was already blindly surging up from the snow.

Coughing, she wrenched the shawl from around her neck. *Tony . . . Emma . . . the chopper, where's . . .* She spotted the chopper's bone handle two feet away to her right. To her left, Tony had impaled her attacker in the neck. The pike had pierced clear through, and the hook was now snagged under the dead woman's right ear.

"Hurry, Tony!" Emma had her back to him, and now she swung her pike, jabbing at hands and bodies. A boy—most of his chest gone and only shreds of muscle clinging to jagged ribs—clamped both hands on the pike's handle and gave the girl a mighty jerk. Crying out, Emma stumbled, then loosed her grip on the pike. Without her weight, the boy lost his footing and staggered to one knee. Racing forward, Emma aimed a kick for the boy's jaw. There was a sodden crack, and suddenly, half the boy's jaw ripped free to career away, like the broken handle of a jug, into the snow. Gargling, the boy clapped both hands to his ruined face. Seizing her pike, Emma levered the iron spike upward. Another crack, and this time what remained of the boy's head split in two. The girl danced back. "Tony, come on!"

"Can't!" Try as he might, he couldn't wrest his pike free. "Clear out, Emma, back up!"

"No, let it go!" Emma shouted. "You can have mine!"

"She's right!" Rima croaked, as the dead woman wrapped both hands around the pike's iron shaft. "Let go, Tony! Leave it!"

Too late. As the woman fell back, her momentum dragged Tony forward and off his feet. Rima heard Emma shriek as grasping hands shot out to latch onto and then swarm up Tony's pike. A leering boy with no lips opened his naked jaws—

Tony began to scream.

EMMA

Domain

"BODE." BLOOD SLUSHING with terror, Emma put a hand on his arm. Up and down this corridor, each cell door was slowly swinging open. "Bode, the doors . . . how . . ."

"I don't know, but . . . *Christ*." His eyes bulged. His hand closed over her elbow, and he began taking slow steps backward, tugging her along with him. "There are cells ahead *and* behind. We got . . . we got to get out of . . ."

Yes, but go where? As they drew back, she saw that the doors were wide open now, each coming to rest with a resounding *clang* of metal against brick wall. Her heart squeezed down with dread. In the nacreous green light, each open door was a blank, a yawning void. She could hear *them*—the scrape of Bode's boots and the tap of her heels—but from the open cells, there was nothing. No one wandered out. For a split second, she let herself think, *They're all empty. No one there. Just props, like in a horror movie.*

"Meme!" Bode shouted, still moving away but slowly, his head swiveling from side to side. "Meme, what are you doing? Why are you doing this?"

"I told you." Meme's voice came back, instantly, not only from the tunnel before them but all around: misting from the ceiling, steaming up from the rock floor, sighing from the many cells' black mouths. "She has to come with me. *She* is the reason we are all dying."

"That's not true, Meme, and you know it." Bode was already crowding her back the way they'd come. "We were dying before Emma got here. London's been falling down forever."

"I am not speaking of Emma but Elizabeth, too. Kramer is right. She is the key, the nexus. Stop Elizabeth—stop *Emma*—and all this goes away." Meme's words were a mournful sough, like wind through bare branches. "I do not want to do this, Bode. But you leave me no choice."

"You've got choice, Meme," Bode said. "There's always choice."

They were about halfway down the tunnel from which they'd just come. Still a hell of a lot of open doors between them and that junction, too. That crazy, chain-smoking miner dude from years back said that miners left behind blind tunnels all the time, places where they'd started to core out rock and then stopped either when the vein petered out or when what they were getting wasn't worth the effort. Maybe there were other, smaller openings and corridors here, too, or a shallow room, something with an entrance that was kid-sized, low to the ground. That would work if it wasn't too obvious. She thought of the dark square down in Jasper's cellar, which looked pretty damned good right now, back door into her *Now* or not.

"I am his creature," Meme said from ahead, above, behind. From the open cell doors. "I must do what he wants."

"But you haven't." Bode pulled up. "You helped me. You helped my friends."

"Bode," Emma warned, in a low voice. "You're not going to convince her."

"I knew her before you and that damned nightmare." His words quavered with anger. "Why'd you have to come? Why'd you spoil it all? I was better off *not* knowing, *not* dreaming."

"She is not your friend, Bode," Meme said, and now Emma heard the rustle of a woolen skirt coming from her left. *Shit, she sounds close.* Emma peered into an open cell door. *Like she's right beside us.* She thought of House and that barn in the valley, both of which had been manifestations of Lizzie's parents. *It's like this is Meme, or her domain: it responds to her. When she screams, it screams and . . .* That rustle came again—and her blood froze. *Oh shit.*

"Meme, I know what . . . *who* you saw in those glasses," Bode said. "That don't matter to me. There has to be an explanation, a reason, a—"

"Bode." Emma's hand shot for his arm. "Bode, shut up. Listen."

"What?" Rounding, teeth bared, Bode snapped, "I don't *care* what you say; Meme will listen to . . ."

The sound came again.

"Oh holy God." Bode's eyes went round, and then jerked to the open cell door on her left. "Do you hear?"

She tried to say *yes*, but her throat wouldn't let go of the word.

The rustle coming from the open cell door was not wool, because, she thought, this wasn't Meme. Instead, what came was a rhythmic *shush-shush-shush* of feet over worn canvas, and not *just* in that cell now. That steady *shush-shush-shush* was everywhere, as whatever was inside each cell kept coming on and coming on and . . .

Shush. Shush-shush-shush.

She didn't think she was even breathing. If her heart was beating, she didn't hear that either.

Shush-shush-shush . . .

Then, the thick, impenetrable darkness of the cell on her left peeled back, like a heavy curtain being raised on a stage, as something within slowly slid into view.

2

IT WAS A man—and it wasn't. It had the right form, like a man-sized silhouette on a target range. It wore clothes, but they were nondescript: a general impression of a shirt and trousers and boots, but with no detail or color or buttons or lacings. It was like looking at the *idea* of clothes on the *idea* of a man: a cardboard cutout with just enough detail for her mind to fill in the blanks and register *shirt*, *pants*, *boots*, the same way she might read *tree* or *mountain* in a book and let her imagination give the tree color, the mountain height and definition.

What drew itself from the dark of each cell had a head and shoulders, arms, a torso, and legs. There were hands and fingers. Ears . . . she wasn't sure. Really, she was too stunned by the rest of its face to worry about that.

The face was a swirling, churning, amorphous mess. No eyes or mouth. Nothing, not even the blade of a nose. The face was flat and blank, though it simmered like the surface of a pond in a heavy rain.

She'd just seen Weber's head, reduced to paste and pulp, begin to stitch itself together. Somehow, though, this was worse.

For a stunned instant, she was paralyzed, a deer caught in the headlights. *You watch.* She stared at the thing with the swirling, seething blank of a face. *It'll settle; it'll be a mirror or the whisper-man.* Or her face, swimming up to spread and mold itself to this thing's skull. She could practically hear her doctor from so many years ago: *I can give you any number of looks . . .*

"Come on." Bode gave her arm a hard tug that made her stumble and nearly fall. "Come on! We don't got time for this! We got to go, we got to go, we got to *run*."

He was already turning, yanking her along. All up and down the line, blank-faced things stepped from their cells—then turned, en masse, and started for them.

It's the scorpions again. But she thought this might even be worse, and not only because *they* had no weapons at all—and God, what good was a lousy little scalpel against things like these?

Grabbing her skirt in both hands, she floundered after him. Keeping up with Bode was torture; he outpaced her in an instant. She wanted to shout at him to slow down, but she had no breath in reserve. *It's Elizabeth's body wearing out; whatever's making her sick is eating her up from the inside.* Her lungs were on fire, and every step jarred and ripped at the muscles around her ribs. That crushed-tin-can taste was on her tongue again, and she could feel blood splash her lips and trickle from her gaping mouth. Every inhalation was like pulling air through a throat jammed with broken glass. Elizabeth's body was rail-thin, but Emma felt heavy and clumsy, as if wading through concrete. Her vision was going fuzzy, too. Far ahead, Bode was graying out, seeming to disappear before her eyes.

Don't pass out. Keep going. Hands whisked through her hair, and she gasped, whipping her head to one side. More hands seemed to sprout from open cells to snatch at her clothes. If she'd had breath, she might have screamed. God, it was like that sea of hands and fingers in her cell, only this she couldn't command or wish away, if she even had before. *Can't be that much farther to the junction, can it?* Unless the tunnels were changing, too, like one of those movie special effects where things telescoped away in a swoop. *Maybe there is no junction anymore, and these things will keep after us and after us, run us down, tear us apart . . .*

Then, like a mirage, the end of this particular tunnel swam into view. Bode was already past. To her left, the last cell was coming up, and then she was even with it, though nearly spent. *Need to rest.* She slowed without really meaning to. Reflex, that was all, and Elizabeth's body wearing out.

Then, out of the corner of her left eye, she saw a smudgy blur. *What?* She looked, but in slow motion, her mind as gluey as her body, and by the time her brain ticked through what she was seeing . . .

It was already too late.

RIMA

These Ravening Dead

"TONY!" HER PARALYSIS lifted. Sweeping up the chopper, Rima screamed to Emma, "Back up, back up!"

She brought the blade straight down. The chopper's keen edge buried itself with a hollow crack, splitting the boy's skull. A gray slop of decaying, jellied brains gushed from the split, and more dribbled from the boy's ears and eyeless sockets. The boy's jaws slackened, but now there were other hands on Tony and he was screaming, the snow under his torn arm going crimson, as they swarmed him like ravenous rats feasting on carrion.

"*NO!*" Emma was stabbing at backs and buttocks, but it was like spitting into the face of a hurricane. "Let him go, leave him alone!"

Rima sprang for the roiling mass of bodies. Tony's pike still jutted straight up, waggling like an obscene masthead void of its sail, but she couldn't see him for all these ravening dead. Slashing in a sweeping cut, she drove the chopper into the side of a neck— man, woman, she couldn't tell—and watched with sick horror as the head swooned until the right ear rested on its shoulder . . .

and still, the thing did not turn to face her but jabbered and tried clawing up the back of another blocking its way.

"Stop it!" It was Emma, fists balled. She shrieked at the woman. "Don't hurt him anymore! I'll come with you! That's what you want, isn't it?"

"Rima!" Whipping round, she saw Tony rearing up, smeared with his own blood and the viscous tar of foul ichor and decayed guts. A girl with no nose or lower jaw had twined her arms round his neck and now clung to him like a lover. "Rima!" he shouted, and then she spotted a flash of steel in his right hand. "Emma! Girls, run, get away, *run!*"

No, no, no! "Tony, *stop!*" she shrieked as Emma screamed, "Kill her, Tony, *kill* her!" He was already driving, ramming the blade home, his penknife burying itself in the girl's swollen, churning belly.

That's it, Rima thought. *We're done for.*

The girl arched. Her mouth unhinged, and what came was a wordless, ululating bellow. Then, in the blink of an eye, her stomach erupted, tore itself apart, releasing a mist of red fluid and black squirmers.

No. Her breath stoppered in her throat. The mist bloomed over Tony, who was already coughing and choking, clawing at his face as the ebony whips wormed down his mouth, up his nose, and into his ears. Dumb with horror, Rima watched as they thrashed and cored into the whites of his eyes, and now there were ruby tears streaming down his cheeks, as Tony, back bowed in agony, collapsed to the snow, gargling blood, his skin rippling as squirmers bored and chewed.

"What are they?" Emma shrieked, eyes bulging with terror. "What are they, Rima, *what are they?*"

They are our death. She couldn't move. Really, where could she run anyway? The fog, perhaps, if it would've taken her. Less than two seconds had passed, and they were coming for her now, hundreds of them corkscrewing, eeling, riding a seemingly endless red river of the girl's blood. She felt the moist flick of something on her cheek and then dozens more, and all at once, they sprang for her exposed flesh and writhed over her face. As soon as she opened her mouth to scream, they leapt into her mouth and she felt them instantly swim down her throat, fan out through her lungs. Agony detonated in her chest. Her knees buckled. Somewhere, in the far distance, she heard Emma screaming and knew the squirmers had found the girl, too, and then that knowledge winked out and there was only pain and the constant burrowing, slithering, chewing.

Rima barely registered when she hit the ground, though she saw white rush for her face; felt the crawl and rapid slither up her cheeks. Black filaments swarmed before her vision, and as they reared to strike, she saw them, up close, for what they were: bristling maws and glaring red pinpricks for eyes.

She managed a single, last scream.

EMMA

Way Out

FROM THE LAST cell on the left, an arm shot out.

Shrieking, she stumbled, her boots skidding over stone as a hand wrapped itself around her left arm and gave her a single, powerful *yank*. A short distance ahead, she saw Bode begin to turn, but he wouldn't get there in time. This thing was already reeling her in like a hooked fish.

"No!" she screamed as that churning, roiling blank of a face loomed. Elizabeth was small, and this thing was taller by a head. In her right hand, she still had the candle in its iron holder, and now she pistoned her arm in a hard punch, an uppercut to the jaw. Whatever else this man-thing was, it had skin, and she felt the moment of impact, the slight hesitation as the spike pierced and then skewered flesh and drove into denser tissue.

For a split second, there was nothing. Then, the thing's face bloomed and became a mouth—or maybe only an opening; she couldn't tell, and it didn't matter. What erupted was a bristling maw. No eyes, no nose, no other features: just that mouth jammed full of spiky teeth. Clawing at its neck, the thing bawled, a loud, guttural blast of a bellow as a torrent of black ichor, hot and sticky, spurted from beneath its jaw. It blundered back, the spike of the candle holder still jittering, and shrieked again, except the sound was multiplied, a clamor that rose and doubled on itself. Despite her terror, she looked back down the tunnel and saw why. *All* the things were screaming, each and every blank's face peeling back like lips to reveal open mouths, sharp teeth.

"Come on! Don't *look*!" It was Bode, face cramped with horror. Whirling her around, he jammed a hand between her shoulders and crowded her on ahead in the junction. "Go go *go*!"

"Which way, which way?" Her chest was heaving. Sweat glued hair to her forehead and cheeks. Behind, the creatures' screams were climbing in a Doppler crescendo. As they rushed into the four-way junction, she snatched another gasping breath. "Bode, which way?" Then she stopped short as her stomach bottomed out. "Bode?"

"They're gone." Bode spun around so quickly he'd have fallen if she hadn't grabbed his arm. "All the passages are gone, even the tunnel with your cell! But how can they be *gone*? We just passed them; they were just *here*!"

We're at a dead end, just like in the valley. She threw a wild eye over blank, glowing rock. Without the cynosure, she was certain she'd never get through this. She wasn't sure this was even the same type of rock. *But you did it once.* She pressed her hands against a cool blank of glassy stone. *Come on, you stupid rock. You grew hands before. Now, give me . . .*

She felt it happen: a slight push and swell. Then the rock glimmered, rippling like thick mercury under her hands as the stone wavered and began to melt.

"*Christ!*" Bode stared. The entire rock was in motion,

undulating and churning in the same way as those blank creatures and Weber's face. "How'd you do that?"

"I don't know." *This can't be the Mirror or this* Now's *version of it, can it? Or down cellar, my back door?* That felt too easy. It would mean the answer had been under Kramer's nose the whole time—and he was part of this *Now*. This had to be like House's library door and that bathroom mirror. *They were all illusions designed as . . . tests? Training? Blank faces, blank rock . . .* The creatures' screams were a swarm, growing louder, bigger, swelling to fill the junction as, low to the ground, the suddenly liquid margins of the stone pulled up and apart in a black inverted grin: the mouth of a low tunnel. *If this was a test, though, that means someone's pulling the strings*. Probably Kramer. But why? Simply to see what she could do?

Or to see what Meme—her doppelgänger—might?

The cells opened because of her. Those things came after us . . . because of her.

"You understand they're driving us." The voice wasn't hers, but she almost didn't recognize Elizabeth's either. "*She's* driving us. Yeah, I opened that, but it might not really be *me* doing anything."

"A trap?" Bode had already dropped into a crouch. "Don't think it much matters. This is a way out. You want to stay here, wait for those things to catch us?"

Meme cares about Bode. She won't hurt him. She hoped. In the back of her too-quiet mind, she wondered if Elizabeth knew how Meme felt about the boy. *And where are you, Eric? Rima?*

"Go." She crowded in behind Bode. *"Hurry."*

EMMA

Still Waters

1

AS SOON AS they'd scrambled through the entrance, she felt space above them, though not that kind of expansive soaring away she'd sensed in those first few moments in the barn, before her Bode's nightmares of VC tunnels had sprung to life, or when she'd gotten them through that energy sink into the whisper-man's mirror-cave. This ceiling was simply higher, and her first thought: *Like a mine.* Then, a second thought: *Oh crap.* Clamping down, reining in her thoughts, she waited, skin fizzing, for the space to shift around her, but nothing happened. *Okay, so it's not responding to me.* Or maybe it was that the whole mine thing hadn't been that big a deal. Except for the moment that dude turned off his light and she'd almost killed herself stepping into an old flooded shaft . . . mostly, she'd had a good time. Hell, she'd already lived through the valley, and if that hadn't been a nightmare, she didn't know what was.

At least she didn't have to keep running. She wasn't sure how much longer she'd have lasted before Elizabeth's body just up and quit. *Take a breath.* She backhanded sweat from her forehead and blood from her mouth. *Take it easy and think about this a second. Whether this is Meme or you, you're here for a reason.* That's the way it had been with House and in the barn: every scenario designed to get her to act in a certain way—or learn a skill. *This wasn't just good luck.* On the other hand, this really might have nothing to do with her. Then . . . with Bode? Did he have some ability, like Rima? Like Casey?

Behind, she felt something close down. There was no sound, nothing dramatic. It was only a feeling of the rock drawing down and in. *Shit.* Before she even turned, she knew what had happened, because she didn't hear the creatures anymore. The entrance was gone. That diffuse glow faded, too, drawing down like the wick of a dying candle. Within seconds, it was black as pitch. They were sealed inside, like flies in amber.

For a second, neither spoke. The moist air was musty and stale, as if they'd cracked the door on a basement room no one had visited in years. She could hear the slight *plik* of water dripping onto stone and more pattering onto her hair to trickle along her scalp. Otherwise, it was so quiet she heard Bode swallow.

"What happened to the rock?" Bode's voice spooled from the darkness. "Why's it not glowing no more?"

"Good question." This was as bad as when that chain-smoking miner dude switched off his lamp. Her heart kicked, and she could feel fresh sweat pop on her upper lip. Maybe she'd been wrong about the rock here. If Meme or Kramer had more control than she did . . . Extending a hand, she leaned left until she felt her fingertips brush stone. *Light would be nice,* she thought. But the cave stayed dark. *Why is that? This worked before.* Had this space been responding to something else going on below her awareness? Maybe . . . Elizabeth, deciding she needed light or a way to see out of my head? Just because her mind was quiet didn't mean there wasn't an awful lot going on in there. *So those hands in the cell might have appeared because* Elizabeth *thought about touching something.* But Elizabeth couldn't have that kind of power on her own. If she did, she'd have gotten herself out of here long ago.

Wait a second. Her breath caught. *Meme said I brought shadows, Eric and Casey and Rima and God knows who else. I know they're in me; Eric and Elizabeth actually* fought *for control. So what if what happened in the cell is because something touched Elizabeth?*

God, could it be that this space—the rock—responded only to the shadows? Then what about Meme? *She's my double, what I would look like if I were in my own body.* And if McDermott truly had drawn energy from the Dark Passages to craft his fictions, mold his characters . . . make *Emma* . . . what was Meme? How close was the other girl to the shadows?

"They's only two things scare me more than those things out there: drowning and the dark." Bode tried a laugh that sounded strangled and too high. "Or maybe it's only tight places. Squirmers, too, actually. You know how they punished us at Coram? If we nicked food because we were hungry, and the thing is, we was always hungry? Put us in a pit for an old privy. Damn thing filled up when it rained, and I couldn't swim or even tread water. Never learned and—"

"Bode, stop talking." He did, instantly, as if he'd been switched off. But she could hear him panting. "Freaking out is what they want."

"How you know that?"

"I just do, okay? Trust me on this. Come on, stop it. You're hyperventilating." From the sound of his breathing, he was ahead of her and a little to her left. Shuffling toward him, she heard the gurgle and slop as her boots splashed through standing water. "Get a grip."

"Oh, *wonderful*," he said, still in that strangled, half-hysterical voice. "All we need now is a flood as the topper to an already perfect day."

"Bode, will you shut the hell up?" She tensed, half-expecting to hear the roar of floodwaters heading their way. Sloshing over to Bode, she waved a hand back and forth until her fingers brushed a sleeve. "Take it easy. Do you still have your candle?"

She had to ask the question again before he said, "Hold on." She felt him move, and then he was wrapping his free hand around her left wrist. "You got that match safe?" he asked. "I'm afraid to go reaching around for my box. Might drop the candle."

"Yes." Drawing out the brass box, she carefully thumbed the hinged lid and tweezed out a single match. "How do I light it?"

"Striker. It's a ridged groove on the bottom of the case . . . yeah," he said as the match spat to life. "'At's better. Here." He touched the flame to his candle. His forehead glistened with sweat in the candlelight. "Sorry. Just . . . had a bad case."

"You're not the only one." She'd coughed up so much blood as they'd run through tunnels, her tongue tasted as if she'd been licking the bottom of her old red Radio Flyer wagon. Her chest was one big ache, front and back.

"So what do we do? We can't stay here."

"Yeah." She suspected that if they tried, something would happen to force them on. She could see about ten feet with their candle's meager light. The water rippling around their feet was maybe a couple inches. If it didn't get any deeper, they ought to be okay, though the rocks would be slippery. "Bode, do you know why it's so wet?"

"Lambeth's marshland. Flooded all the time until they built the Embankment's what I heard." Moving forward a few feet, he held the candle at arm's length and pointed up at crossbeams bolted to the ceiling and at vertical timbers, bloated with water, topped with cap blocks. "Look at that, will you? Never seen anything like that."

"I have. Old mine." She pointed at a length of corroded metal bolted to the left wall. "Is that a ladder?"

"What's left of one, looks like." High-stepping over, he craned a look up. "Yeah, I see the hole. And look here, right alongside." He peered more closely. "It's a hole bored into the rock. Not for a bolt." He made an *aha* noise. "I'll bet it's for one of those iron candle picks, so your hands'd be free. I wondered why the kitchen had them. You know," he said as she sloshed over to join him, "I know worse than nothing when it comes to things like this, though I had chums liked to wallow through sewers looking for coins, dropped purses, combs. They used ladders to get in and out, so this makes sense if it's one of the old drainage spillways. Don't all of them open to the surface, though. Some go to the Thames, but others drain into underground rivers. On the south side alone, they's"—he counted under his breath—"eight or nine, I think."

"I don't think I want to find more water." She could picture them winding through endless passages, going deeper and deeper, the roar growing louder and louder.

"Well, we can't stay here. Just got to hope we find a ladder to the surface, or maybe turn up close to the old criminal wings. Air's cold, so might be a vent or open pocket. So long as the rock doesn't come alive again, I'm good with that." After a pause, Bode added, "Meme let us in here for a reason?"

He said it like a question. "I think so, but I'm not sure. Bedlam is Kramer's."

"And she's his creature." Bode grunted. "Never liked when he said that."

Now that she'd seen what lived in those cells . . . she didn't either.

2

THE CUT WASN'T uniform, but hooked and branched into various side passages as well as larger carved rock rooms that might have been used to store equipment. Whenever they came to a fork, they went right unless there was no choice and marked each turn using Weber's scalpel to scratch arrows. Although the tunnels felt uniform, they must be gradually heading down. The areas of bare rock dwindled, and the number of standing pools, orange in candlelight, increased.

"We're going to be swimming soon." Her skirt, wet almost to her knees, was getting heavier. What she wouldn't give for jeans. No: waders.

"Oh, *balls*. Don't like this." Bode pointed at a bloated-looking crossbeam. Digging in a thumbnail, he pried off a long, soggy splinter. "Wet rot. Lucky this hasn't come down."

Don't jinx it. Her eyes skipped to the view ahead. Water gathered in a wide bowl of rock that stretched to either side of the tunnel. Was there a lip or something, a ledge to skirt that? Jumping her gaze to the right, she spotted a narrow, horizontal, rust-red rill. It took her a second to recognize what this was. "Look. Train track."

"Damme, you're right." Crouching, Bode ran a hand over

worn metal. "Tunnel's a little wider here. Must've used that to move rock out in handcarts." Pushing up, he gestured toward the far wall and the remains of a rusted ladder. "Best one we've seen."

"Think we could climb up? Be nice to get out of this water."

"That's what I'm thinking." Wading across, he edged right around that large pool. "Like a mirror, that is. You can even make out the gouges in the ceiling."

"Still waters run deep," she said.

"I heard that. It's from some story, isn't it? About a cat or something?" A small silence, and then he said, "Speaking of which . . . mind if I ask you a question?"

"Sure," she said, only half-noting how strained he suddenly sounded. She began sloshing her way through to where he stood. The water was deep all right. "What?"

"You know it would go easier if you'd pick up your skirt there."

"I'm about five seconds from chucking the damn thing." Kicking a swath of sodden cloth, she blew out in frustration. "What's your question?"

"It's about a cat." He'd already turned to move on, but now he paused and looked back. "I can't believe I'm asking, but . . . the name Jack mean anything?"

She stopped dead. He couldn't have surprised her more if he'd spit in her face. "I had a cat named Jack," she said, slowly. "When I was a girl. He disappeared when I was twelve. After I'd . . ." Her hand brushed her jaw; without her thinking about it, her tongue pressed against the jagged edge of a bottom tooth. "I had an accident."

"Laid open your chin."

She blinked. "Yes. Bode, what . . ."

"Well, I'll be dratted," Bode moaned, turning aside. He started forward, water rising in sheets. "*Two* of you. I *am* mad as hops, gone completely nutter . . ."

"Bode?" But then the gurgle of water, that hollow *bloosh* as he stumped away, penetrated. Actually, it would probably have clicked sooner if he hadn't mentioned Jack and put her off her stride. Now, though, above the drum of her heart, she also heard that old chain-smoking miner dude: *Remember, girl. . . lower levels . . .*

"Bode!" She splashed after. "Bode, wait!"

"What?" Face still working, he looked back over his shoulder. "What in blazes you want now—"

His foot came down with a loud *sploosh.*

And then, so quickly that he never had time to cry out, Bode plunged through the surface and took the light with him.

ELIZABETH

Shadow-Boy

"BODE!" FOR A moment, Elizabeth forgot where and what she was and lunged, arms outstretched, hands open in a grab. All she slapped was that cold black mirror. While that queer greenish-yellow glow still suffused this space, her view beyond and through the mirror into the world she'd left behind had gone the way of Bode and his light. The darkness was so absolute, so pitch-black, she doubted that Emma could see her hand in front of her own eyes, much less that pool into which Bode had plummeted. "Emma, don't just stand there! Do something, *do* something!"

"What exactly do you expect her to do?" The shadow-boy, Eric, moved to flank her. Gesturing at the mind's eye, his hand lost coherence for a brief second, thinning to wisps before solidifying again. The shadow-boy was, mercifully, behind her. "She can't *see.*"

"*Quiet!*" From beyond, in her real world, she heard a sudden thrashing, a huge, gasping inhale, a spasm of coughing, and then Bode's frantic, choked cry: "He-help, Emma, *help*, I c-can't . . ." At the same time, Emma was screaming, "Bode, can you swim?

Can you grab on to something?" More crashing, the slop of water smashing rock, and what Elizabeth thought was a blubbery gurgle. Then . . . nothing, *nothing*. Still no light either. Only water on stone, and Emma, that stupid *stupid* girl, shouting Bode's name into the dark.

"*Damn* you, Emma!" Elizabeth shouted. "Stop sniveling and go *after* him!"

"And just how is she supposed to do that? There's no *light*. If *she* falls in, then they're both dead." A pause, and then the shadow-boy added, "Us too."

"Then *damn* it all, I hope she *does* fall in, *does* drown!" Tears dashed down her cheeks. From the corner of her eye, she saw only his form, umbral and indistinct as black mist. She was afraid to turn a direct look. After that horrible business with Weber and how effortlessly Eric flowed out of this place to take control before she even realized what was happening, the other pieces she'd only glimpsed as silhouettes, the *sense* of a crowd, were even closer now, especially those three other shadows: the small girl that had to be a shadow-Lizzie and the other two closer to Elizabeth's age. "At least then I could take control again, if only for a little while!"

Although this was not precisely the way it had happened before. She'd felt nothing physical, not Weber choking her or even panic as her throat closed. Yet her chest had grown suddenly heavy with a crushing *doom*. Casting a startled glance down at her hands, she'd seen them begin to bleed of color and substance and grow glassy. *God, I'm going to die; my body's dying.* Even that thought felt transparent, as if she were nothing more than a fading scrawl done in weak, watery ink. As Emma slid into unconsciousness and the weird glow in this space darkened, the walls of this prison wavered. The floor shimmied under her feet, and for a second, she could feel herself moving back into her body the way blood gushes through arteries. In that brief moment, agony suddenly flared in her chest and throat; she was aware of Weber's weight on her body, could *feel* his spit spray her face and the judder of her heels on canvas.

Coming back had been swift, like the sudden flare of a match: awakening to a room only just beginning to reconstruct itself and this shadow-boy beating the life out of Weber. The only reason she'd managed to eke out even a few seconds in control of her body again was because, however strongly this Eric felt about Emma, he *hadn't* planned any of it. His move into the front of her mind had been reflex, and then she'd surprised him, that was all. She was certain he'd never let that happen again.

Now, the shadow-Eric said, "Actually, it's probably good there's no light."

"What? How is that better?"

"Because she'll have to take a breath and think. If she had a lamp or candle, she might've made a grab . . ." His voice trailed away.

"What?" Seething, she aimed a punch at his chest and then gasped as her fist sank in an ebony swirl to her wrist. How did he do that? Solid one second, then so much shadow the next? "What is it?"

"Matches." He moved past her to the mind's eye. "Emma," he called. "Emma, listen to me. You've got *matches*."

A distance behind, she heard the blanks shuffle ever closer, and she hurried to join him at the black mirror. "What are you doing?"

Despite the burr, Eric's words were taut. "Making a suggestion."

"How can you do that? She's locked us up tight."

"No, she's locked up against *you*. But she knows I'm here. I'm not a threat."

"You'll never get through, not while she's conscious and in control. Even if you could, how will she know it's really you? She'll never listen. *I* wouldn't. I would *never* trust a shadow."

"And that's why she's my Emma," he said. "Because she will trust me. She knows I would never hurt her."

The words cut. "Oh no? You didn't just knock Weber out. You beat the man to pulp. What kind of a monster does that?"

"I was . . ." His face seemed to lose coherence a moment before it firmed. "I was upset. I lost control for a second, that's all."

"And killed a man. So think twice about just how much you should be trusted. Besides, you're not strong enough to break through." Actually, with the mark of the Dark Passages on him and the three shadows pressing ever closer—any moment, they would take on some coherence and personality, just watch—she thought she might be wrong about that.

"Do you want to save Bode? Because I do. He was our friend, and if he means anything to you, then you'll stop getting in my way. I'm strong, I *am*, and so is she." His obsidian gaze fixed on the mind's eye. "Come on, Emma. Don't be afraid. Listen to me. It's Eric. You know I'm here. So listen: remember the matches. Remember the *flask*."

"Flask?" she said. "Why is that . . ."

"If you want Bode to die, keep talking," he said, and then paid her no mind as she fumed. "Emma, this is important. Listen: you've got . . ."

EMMA

The Strength Only Shadows Possess

1

MATCHES. THE WORD popped in her mind. Followed by another: *flask*.

"What?" she whispered. The faint echoes of Bode's shouts had only just faded away. When she first heard him thrash, she'd come *this* close to bolting forward but stopped herself at the last possible second. Go into the drink with Bode, they were both cooked. She was on her knees, inching forward, trying to remember what she'd seen before the light went out, feeling through icy water for the edge of the hole.

Then she thought, *Canvas*.

Light. Of course! Her stiff fingers fumbled the button securing her right hip pocket and gave the fabric a vicious yank. There was a *tick* as the button popped and struck stone. She slid in a hand. Her fingers curled around the match safe. She carefully drew out first it and then the flask. She didn't even bother to try the button on the right. Ripping that pocket apart, she found the burlap-wrapped scalpel.

Sitting cross-legged, she unwound the burlap and clamped it

in her teeth. Uncapping the flask, she stuffed the fabric into the open bottle, jamming it in as far as it would go, leaving enough of a tail for a wick. With a quick flick of her wrist, she upended the flask until the burlap got wet. The liquid inside had no smell, which worried her. Shouldn't alcohol smell? *Remember, might be different for you, like Meg Murry and IT. Food didn't taste like anything for Meg either, but it was still food.* She sure hoped that explained it.

Teasing a match from the safe, she snapped the hinge closed, then felt along the matchstick until she nested the head into the ridged striker. She gave it a sharp swipe. The match head flared with a spit and sputter. Quickly, she held it to her booze-soaked wick. A second later, the burlap caught in a sooty shower of tiny sparks.

"Bode?" Returning the match safe and scalpel to her pocket, she held her homemade torch over her head with one hand as she shuffled forward on her knees, feeling along the rock floor with the other. *How much time gone, how much?* Thirty seconds, she thought, maybe almost a minute. In the candlelight, the rippling water was a dull bronze. The remaining iron rungs were black slashes. *Just got to find the opening.* If there'd been ladders bolted to the rock, might there be a rung or something still below? Or a protruding piece of iron he could grab onto?

"Come on, Bode," she said, "here's the light. Look up. *Think.* Bubbles rise." *Where is he? Why hasn't he come up yet?* Flicking her gaze to the left, she looked for the ladder's boreholes, then followed those to where she thought the opening must be. With a start, she saw the water there was a little darker and then realized that what she was looking at were streamers of diluted blood.

"*No.*" She thought about it for exactly a half second, then clawed her way to a stand. Hugging the wall, she balanced her makeshift torch on a rung high enough where she thought a splash wouldn't douse it. She dropped to the rock again, the temperature change stealing her breath. Just one more piece of bad news; she knew that from those CPR lessons Jasper had made her take before he'd let her kayak on Superior. A lot of people didn't drown in cold water; they suffocated because when cold water hit their faces, they gasped. *Reflex.* Their windpipes clamped down at the first wash of icy water, and then it was over unless they got to the surface.

Leaning forward, she thrust her right arm through the hole, stretching as far as she dared, afraid of losing her balance and sliding in headfirst. All she felt was cold water and stone and . . . Something brushed her hand. The contact jerked a gasp from her throat, and she almost flinched away before she registered: *fingers.*

"Bode!" Flopping onto her stomach, she dug the points of her boots into the rock and plunged both arms into the water. Her left fingers scrabbled over the limp back of his left hand and then a wrist, the bunched folds of his coat sleeve, the hump of his left shoulder. *Coat's hung up on something.* Finger-walking around his shoulder, she felt a stout thumb of metal protruding from the wall, and understood at once how he must be oriented: listing to his right, legs falling away from her and to his left, which put his head and chest under the lip on her side of the hole.

You have to go for it. Sucking in a deep breath, she pushed through the surface. She felt her throat convulse from the shock of frigid water on her face. Her eyes burned. What she could see was meager: a pale wash that wasn't light so much as less dark, and then a much deeper shadow that was Bode. When she reached her right hand, her fingers knotted in his coat. While he was still buoyant—*and that means air in his lungs; that's what my instructor said*—he was deadweight dangling from a hook. So *push* his legs away from her, and his upper torso ought to move in the opposite direction, toward her and the opening. *Then, if I can grab his head, get his nose and mouth to the surface . . .*

Walking her right hand down his chest, she pushed as hard as she could, wretchedly aware of how much strength Elizabeth's frail body didn't possess. Nothing happened for a long second. Then, all at once, she felt the slow, vertiginous swirl of his body as he twisted; saw the fingers of his right hand, limp as a dead starfish, swim into view. Fingers scrambling for purchase, she clutched a fistful of coat at the base of his throat and hauled him toward her. Through the water, there came a very dull *clump* as his head met rock, but she couldn't do anything about that. The water darkened even more, stained with a wash of fresh blood. Screaming with strain, her shoulders balled and clenched as she tugged. *Now or never, come on, come on! Just a little more, a little more. . . .* But she couldn't do it. Her lungs were on fire, and he was just too heavy and *damn it!* Rearing back, she coughed out the last of that breath, sucked in another, and shouted, "*MEME! Help* me! This is your space! Do you want Bode to die? Help . . ."

"Help yourself." The voice came from only a few feet away, and she looked up to where he stood at the very limits of her pathetic little torch's light. "You know what to do." Somehow Kramer's serpent's whisper was so appropriate here. "Use the strength only shadows possess. You did before, when that shadow-boy bludgeoned Weber. I know it must have been he. I saw him and so did Meme."

"That was different. I nearly died. *I* didn't do anything." Her arms were shuddering. Still clutching Bode's coat in both hands—his dark hair fanning over the surface, his face just *inches* from open air—she looked at Meme, who stood a little back and to Kramer's left. "You were there, Meme. You know I had no control over that."

The other girl, with *her* face, didn't answer. She might as well have been talking to a department store dummy.

"Of course you do. Drop your barriers. Let them come. That was the point of putting you down here to begin with. This space responds to shadows." Kramer readjusted his panops. "Stop wasting time; Bode will be beyond saving in seconds."

"I don't know *how!*" Although she had an inkling of what needed doing. But what if she wasn't allowed to come back? *Eric killed Weber when he didn't have to. He's half shadow.* Or more than half. *Maybe what's left isn't close to the boy I knew.* What if she ended up like Elizabeth, shut away in some mental prison because Eric, whatever he was now, decided he liked being in control?

In the valley, Bode died to give you time. He's helped you here when he didn't have to. She turned her focus inward. *Do this for him, and do it now.*

2

IN LESS THAN the blink of an eye, she was in two places at once: outside, straining to hang on to Bode's body, and inside, in a suggestion of a kitchen at the blank wall from which she'd erased an iron door. Nothing but an expectant silence on the other side. Who knew what waited in the dark? But she had to go through with this.

Make me a door. All around, at once, the space went from a half-gloaming to a blaze of yellow sun; from an amorphous haze to bright cabinets, a potbellied stove, pans on a rack. In the distance, she could hear the thump and boom of water on sandstone. There was a proper door now, too, not of iron but knotty pine.

Please, Elizabeth. Stretching, she reached above the jamb. Her fingers closed around the wire pick that only Sal and Jasper and she knew was there. *Don't fight him; let Eric through. Let him help me. Let us both stay long enough to find a way to end this.*

Jimmying the pick into the keyhole, she heard the thumb lock snap, and then she turned the knob and stepped back as the door swung open.

"Eric?" she said.

PART SIX

THE
DICKENS
MIRROR

DOYLE

The Woman in Black

1

DOYLE HAD ONLY the vaguest notion of how he'd gotten here. The time between finding what lay in Battle's secret back room and now was a blur, a span of time as blank as the faces of the other constables, the desk sergeant, the anonymous silhouettes jostling through the murk and snow. If he didn't know better—and he wasn't sure he did—Doyle would've sworn he'd fallen into the gap between chapters, where a character ends one scene in a particular locale only to begin on the very next page somewhere else with no idea how he got there and yet is expected to behave as if he knows what's going on. Really, this place was something from a novel; it was truly that bizarre.

The underground room beneath the derelict criminal wings was cavernous, huge, hollowed from strange rock that pulsed with a sulfurous glow as if keeping to the rhythm of a hidden heart. The air wobbled and shimmied. Sensible, keeping criminal lunatics from mingling with the merely insane. Best to box them in: private wings, their own kitchen, this . . . well, was it a clinic? Doyle thought this place must once have been some kind of infirmary or a surgery. Or perhaps an old basement morgue; asylum doctors performed their own necropsies. Whatever this had once been, it now could have passed as the underground laboratory of a madman: chains, manacles, examination and operating tables, worktables chockablock with various scientific instruments.

There were also cells, six in all, three to a side. Of the cells on the right, only the very last held prisoners: a man and a woman. The man was fortyish, with thick black hair and large spectacles set in a queer frame that didn't look like metal. His clothes were odd: not proper wool trousers but some worn blue material. Instead of a high buttoned collar, his shirt had lapels. Yet the man *was* vaguely familiar in the way of someone you might pass on the street every day. The *contours* of his face, the shape of that jaw, reminded Doyle of someone.

The woman—she must be the man's wife; Doyle just had this feeling—was very handsome, with fine bones and a glossy mane loose around her shoulders. Her clothing was equally strange; she wore a man's trousers of the same blue material, and her blouse, filmy and insubstantial, was scandalously low-cut. Still, she'd have looked almost normal but for all those bandages, splotchy with old blood, on her arms. From the sheer number on her left forearm and wrist, Doyle thought she must be right-handed.

Self-murder, just like Elizabeth. If not for her clothes, Doyle would have mistaken her for one of Kramer's patients. To cut oneself so badly, the woman must be deranged, but Doyle didn't think that was the only reason that the man, her husband, had his hand firmly clamped over the woman's mouth. In fact, Doyle understood exactly why the man was doing it altogether. His wife's dark eyes sparkled with horror. If Doyle were she and their places reversed?

Oh, I'd scream. His own eyes traveled from the couple in their cell to a tall woman in black who stood in the alley running between. This woman in black was, besides himself, the only other person in this mad place not behind bars. *Yeah, come face-to-face with you, I'd be pissing my inexpressibles.* (Actually, he was very close anyway.)

Although the man . . . the handsome woman's husband . . . was *concerned*, he wasn't frightened, Doyle thought. More *apprehensive*, but also *interested*. Doyle hadn't missed the sharp look the man gave *him* when Doyle had laid out his burdens, what he'd stolen from Battle's secret room. *Like he knows what's in them, and that's got him worried.* But the man's eyes also kept ticking to the middle cell on Doyle's left and—Doyle thought—one particular occupant.

I agree, poppet. Black Dog nosed his fingers. **He's intensely interested in that little girl, don't you think? If I didn't know better, I'd say he might *even* know her.**

He thought Black Dog was right. He also wondered if he shouldn't do something to help. *But what am I to do?* His eyes roved over Rima, who lay in a heap, awash in blood and horribly bruised. On the stone floor a short distance away from Rima, the mute with the blotchy plaster on her chin sat cross-legged with Tony's head cradled in her lap. (And was that a *cat* crouched alongside?) From the fresh cuts and bruises on her arms and face, the girl had been in quite the brawl. As for Tony, a single glance was enough: the boy was infected. His skin writhed as squirmers burrowed and eeled and chewed. As another spasm shook Tony's thin frame, bright red foam bubbled over his lips and fresh crimson rivulets leaked from his nose and both eyes.

But it's the mute that man's interested in. Black Dog sounded positive. **Oh, don't misunderstand: I think he's keen on everything and everyone here. But her . . . you can see it in his eyes, how greedy they are. Almost . . .**

Proprietary. Yes, Black Dog was right. Doyle's gaze shifted to the closest cell and the two boys there. One was a veritable whippet of a young man, with a shaggy scruff of blond hair and narrow blade of a nose. His clothes were also rather bizarre: a loose olive-green overshirt, with what appeared to be military insignia, and matching trousers. Both garments had many outside pockets simply *begging* to be picked. Doyle had never laid eyes on that boy before.

As for the *other* boy in the same cell . . . well, Doyle knew him. After a fashion. This boy's clothes, rough trousers and a coarse shirt, were much too large, and his feet were bare. Doyle thought the boy must've been caught before he was properly dressed and then given the first clothes that came at hand. The boy was sick, too; that was obvious. His arms were limp, the hands upturned like dead spiders. Glittery with fever, his eyes were large in his pinched face, and he was gasping, his bare chest going like a bellows. His brown hair was a mass of short, damp corkscrews. Although he was cleaner, a bit more meat to his bones, there was no doubt.

Twins? His eyes clicked from that boy to the Tony he knew and then back again. The boys were also somehow fundamentally dissimilar, as if they might be actors: the *same* boy plucked for a different role depending on which play was to be staged. It was in their general *look*; he couldn't explain it to himself any better than that. In one cell lay the Tony of this moment, this particular drama: *his* Tony. In the other was a Tony destined to play a part in some far future.

Darling, I think you've got it. They're from different . . . eras? Worlds? Even Black Dog was interested. *Fascinating, especially given what's in those sacks. What you stole from Battle's secret room. Oh, and take a good long look at that woman in the far cell, and then that woman in black. You're a detective. After you discard the rest, what remains . . .*

No, I don't care. It's not my business. Doyle tore his gaze away. A Tony from a future? *Absurd. Eyes playing tricks. It's the air, the wobble in this place.* He stole a look at his own hand, saw how the outlines—the stubby fingers, the grimy nails, his broken lifeline chalked black with Battle's blood—wavered and undulated in this bizarre air. Made him sick. If he wasn't stone-cold sober, Doyle would've thought he'd shot himself up good, or drunk off a half dozen pints until the world swirled, nothing nailed down, everything gone molten. He was muddled, that was all, and ashamed. It was seeing Rima in the cell that did it. He should help her. Hadn't he *said* he would? What was *wrong* with him? *Kramer was right. You* are *a meater.* But what could he really do?

I want a needle. I want a pipe, a draught. God, hadn't this been where he'd come in? Guts in a tangle, and so awash in sweat he ought to steam with the reek. But of course, he couldn't smell himself anymore. Only his cravings were real now. *I'd take poison, bleach my brain. Anything to go back to the way I was.*

Though that would never happen now, would it? Not unless Battle performed a Lazarus.

Of course—his eyes bounced to those three sacks laid on examination tables—that Battle might rise from the dead was entirely possible at this point. Considering.

2

HE'D ONLY THE dimmest recollection of hitching the station's one remaining nag to a cart—all the while averting his gaze because he could *swear* the horse's face was scrubbed clean, no eyes, no muzzle—loading those sacks, and then weaving through a crowd that paid neither him nor the horse any mind. *That's wrong, that's wrong,* he thought, doggedly plodding along, reins in one hand, bull's-eye in the other. *The horse is meat; they ought to mob . . .*

At that moment, he'd felt a sudden, very familiar tug on his arm. "Oi, dearie." The hag's voice was an iron nail screeching over glass. "Fancy a bit of boiled leather?"

For a split second, he almost welcomed this. *All right, this I know; this is . . .* That choked off. A good look and he'd have screamed if his throat hadn't ratcheted tight. *No no no no . . .*

The hag still wore that absurd, rumpled wool cap parked at a jaunty nautical angle—and yet now her face was as featureless as molten slag.

Shite! His head went airless, and he thought, *That's all right, Doyle. Go on, pass out now, boy-o. Take a bit of a kip. Been a long day.*

"Five pieces for a fadge." When the hag leaned close, the blank of her face churned. "*Hate* if you've an—"

Let me, poppet. Black Dog's massive head flickered out of the corner of Doyle's eye as it leapt. Quick as a lick, the hag was on her back. There came a ripping sound of wet cloth, and then a spume of purple blood.

Horrified, Doyle's jaw unhinged, and he might still have screamed except for something he noticed that gave him pause.

They were in a crowd—and yet no one stopped. The stream went on, with no more care for him or Black Dog or this dead hag than if they'd been boulders around which the crowd had to part in order to be on its way. In this small eddy, this transparent pocket about which the outside world—if this was a reality at all—flowed, time was at a standstill.

There we are. Black Dog held the ragged, dripping meat of the hag's throat clamped in its mouth. Then, with a flip of its head, it swallowed the steaming, bloody chunk in a single gulp as, all around, the crowd swarmed. Turning, Black Dog threw Doyle a wink. **Not to worry, my darling.** It set off, oiling around the hag's still-twitching body, threading the needle of a path through the faceless swirl of bodies. **Follow me. I know the way.**

I see Black Dog, really see *it*. How? Why? Bending against a slash of wind, he plodded, leading the faceless horse. Sweat leaked from his scalp to soak into his high collar. *I* see *it now when I ain't never truly* done *before.* The scream he'd stoppered simmered at the back of his tongue. *Whatsat mean?*

Either Black Dog didn't hear or felt no need to reply. Perhaps all for the good, that.

Time . . . passed. Or maybe it hadn't, and only his surroundings had streamed past in an amorphous blur, like riding a carousel spinning so quickly the world smeared. Whatever the case, at some point they were just *there*, at the asylum's wrecked front gate, with its ruined guardhouse. That, at least, hadn't changed. Then another gap in time, and he was traversing the rear grounds. Ahead, the broken edifices of the derelict criminal wings loomed, and then the wide bore of a subterranean entrance seemed to pull apart like a gigantic maw . . . so he *had* descended . . . and he seemed to *fade* into this place. Because there were no corridors, no door, no openings carved from stone. Everything— walls, ceiling, floor, even the instruments—was indefinite, hazy, out of focus. Unformed, as if some god had yet to fashion them from black mud, like the flat fronts on the street, the blanks of the crowd.

And yet, when Doyle thought about it: aside from the wobble and shimmy, Bedlam now seemed the only real, solid thing.

Well . . . and Black Dog.

3

"DO SOMETHING!" IT was the little girl, the supposed mute. "If Rima draws any more from Tony, it'll kill her." The girl glared up at the woman in black, who stood just beyond the bars. "Do you *want* Tony to die?"

"In this instance, what I want is immaterial." The woman in black was willowy, with chestnut hair done in a neatly coiffed chignon. Rapt as a vulture, she gave the younger girl a keen look. "What Rima *chooses* is what matters. That's the way of *all* binding, child, no matter what you call it. It is about free will."

"Oh, *riiight*." The golden flaw in the girl's right eye flashed. "You came after me with an *ax*."

"Do remember that I didn't use it on you."

"Yeah, you only killed the door."

"As I said." The woman raised a hand to a nasty purple-black splotch of a bruise just beneath her right eye. "I still want to know how you did that, what that was you went through. And that *cat* of yours." The woman angled her head in a speculative look. "Quite an interesting creature. Positively Cheshire. Does it often slip in and out of blind spots like that? Do you know where it goes?"

"Blind spots? I don't know what you're talking about. I . . ." The little girl's grip on Tony tightened as he shivered and groaned. "Please, he's *dying*. Why won't you help him? Do you just want to see what happens when you get too many Tonys in the same place? How'd we even get here anyway? The last thing I remember is those . . ." The little girl's lips trembled as new tears leaked over her cheeks. "Those squirmers crawling all over us and you, floating on the snow, just *watching*. You didn't try to grab me that time, I don't think. It was the fog, wasn't it, because it's energy and somehow you can use it to get around. So did it swallow us after we passed out? Is that how we got down here?"

Ah, poppet, there's a bright one. Black Dog's muzzle brushed Doyle's fingers. **That talk about too many Tonys, she might be onto something. Could it be that the Tonys are making one another ill? Remember how our Tony was when we first saw him at Bedlam's gate?**

Yes, the boy had been quite sick even then. Did that mean this other Tony—*Future Tony,* he decided—had already been taken prisoner? So draining each other, perhaps? Why? Because there was only so much Tony to go around? Or, as the girl said, too many Tonys in one place? Or had spiriting in a Tony who didn't belong here, in London, triggered a slow unraveling in both? Yes, but by that logic—Doyle transferred his gaze to that man and woman in the far cell—that woman ought to be ill, too. So it couldn't be just the mere fact of one too many Tonys. *Has to be something else at play here.*

Perhaps. Black Dog's breath was hot on his neck. (God, the animal was huge now.) **Or that woman's only just arrived, or somehow different from the Tonys.**

"After what happened on the snow, I'm very interested in why you're *not* infected," the woman in black said to the little girl. "Something in your blood, perhaps? Perhaps I ought to dissect you and find out."

"L-leave her alone." Drawing in a halting breath, Rima lifted her head. A crimson ooze leaked from a nostril to drip from her jaw. Her bare arms undulated, rife with squirmers, though it seemed to Doyle that their eel and slither over the cliffs of her cheeks was slower, weaker, not as pronounced. *They're dying?* A part of his mind wondered how she was doing that; maybe some natural resistance?

"You want to s-see how much more I can draw?" Choking, Rima spat, backhanding a gobbet of coagulated blood from her mouth. "I w-will. Just n-need to rest a bit, that's all."

The woman let out a small laugh. "That boy needs much more than *you* can muster, girl." Squatting, the woman brought her face close to the bars. Her mouth curled to an avid half-moon. The way she crouched, the woman was like a hungry tarantula or a black widow spider ready to sink its fangs into that plump, hapless little fly. (And Doyle thought, *Yes, Black Widow.* As good a name as any.) "Although I am as intrigued by that ability of yours as I am about why little Emma seems to have left a bad taste in the squirmers' mouths."

"So this is just some stupid experiment? We're *lab rats* or something?" More tears chased down Emma's cheeks. "You could *help*."

"You give me too much credit, child. Don't you think if I'd discovered a cure for squirmers and rot, I'd have used it? Do you think I *enjoy* living in this *Now*? Trust me, if not for my daughter, I would find my way to a *Now* I could seal in some fashion so I might not be swept back."

"Seal? Swept . . . swept back?" Snuffling, Emma gave Black

Widow a long, penetrating look. "You don't have a choice, do you? You keep getting yanked back here, or maybe the fog . . . the Peculiar . . . can only go to certain places, like a bus with only so many stops on its route. Otherwise, you're stuck, aren't you?"

"Very perceptive. You're partially correct; I can't go hither and thither, and yes, I must return. But there are more . . . stops than before. It is how I finally found you"—a wave of the hand at Future Tony and the rat-faced blond, neither of whom spoke— "and these others and another Rima's *Now*."

Another Rima. Two Tonys, Black Dog mused. Doyle could imagine that devil tapping a paw to its muzzle in thought. *The Nows must be worlds. Given what we've seen—and what's in those sacks, poppet—perhaps there are many more Tonys and Rimas. Since there's only the one Rima here, that might explain why she's not taken ill in the same way that our Tony has.*

Perhaps, but that couldn't be the sum of it all. Doyle's eyes traveled back to the far cell, and that couple. By the same reasoning, *that* woman should be sick, too.

Unless she is put together differently, like little Emma.

Put together? Doyle's eyebrows tented. He really was getting interested now. What an odd turn of phrase. *And what's that about Emma?*

Listen to her, poppet. Her *accent*. So different. Where did she come from? How did she get here?

"Well, let us say that our little Rima *had* a doppelgänger. I can't find her anywhere, and the *Now* is a shambles, the occupants only so much goo. I *believe* this means that *Now*'s Rima was essential. Without her, the *Now* disintegrated and . . . *ohhh*." Black Widow put a finger to her lips. "I wonder, Emma: without you, will *all* you know fall apart?" She tossed a look at the two boys in the adjacent cell. "Or your *Nows*? Tony there, perhaps; you seem quite important. But you"—lifting her chin at the shaggy blond—"could it be that you're nothing but a bit player, a vaude-villian of no importance whatsoever?"

"Who cares what you think?" Thin but knotty with muscle, the scruffy young man was quite, *quite* twitchy in a way Doyle recognized. "You think I'm scared of *you*? Put you in a tunnel with a couple gooks, see how you do." Scrambling to his feet, the young man banged an already torn and bloodied fist against iron. "Who are you? Where am I? Why'd you bring me here?"

"Save your breath." Inhaling long and tortuously, Future Tony said, "You won't get answers that make any sense. Just be glad there isn't another one of *you* here. Goes worse when there is."

"He's right," Emma said. "That's what Meme told Bode."

"Bode?" The scruffy boy's head whipped up. "He's *here*? Last I saw, he was running."

"And he got away." Black Widow's mouth was a thread above her chin. "But I'll find him again, probably more easily than before, now that you're all linked."

"Linked?" Emma echoed. "By what?"

"So if Bode got away," the blond said, "who are you talking about?"

"She's talking about the Bode from *here*, *our* Bode, in this . . . this *Now*?" Emma looked up at Black Widow. "That's right, isn't it? *He* knows Bode's double?"

"Yes." Black Widow glanced askance at the far cell, and Doyle saw how she and the man with the black hair and glasses locked gazes before Black Widow returned her eyes to Emma. From the corner of an eye, Doyle saw the man in the far cell whisper into his wife's ear. When her head moved in a fractional nod, he slid his hand from her mouth to rest on her shoulder. "And quite possibly there's more than just the one double," Black Widow said.

"What?" The shaggy blond scowled. "I don't got no twin."

"I bet you do," Emma said to the boy. "What's your name?"

The young man dug at a sore pocking the corner of his mouth. "Chad."

Stirring, Rima pushed up on her arms. "What?"

"Right. If we're all linked, then it makes sense that you'd know him, Rima," Emma said. "Where's *your* Chad?"

"Dead, oh . . . years back. Drowned by the old Battersea Bridge."

"What?" Chad's frown deepened. "What the hell you saying?"

"She's speaking of your doppelgänger in this *Now*," Black Widow said. "Well, if he's dead, less work for me. Be grateful, Chad. It explains why you've not taken a turn for the worse as the Tonys have."

"Hey." It was Future Tony. Drawing a slow hand across his mouth, he said to Emma, "This *Now* stuff . . . she's talking multiverses, right? We just studied that in school. So she's snatching versions of us from different universes or timelines?"

"Versions?" Black Widow snorted. "A good a term as any. You're not a person. You're a faint replica. You only *think* you're living a life. None of you are even from a proper *Now*."

"A proper *Now*?" Emma echoed. "What's the difference?"

"I feel pretty damn real," Chad said. "This cage is real. What I want to know is, how'd I start the morning in 'Nam and end up here?"

"The fog," Emma said. "Like I said, she travels in it, or becomes part of it . . . I'm not sure."

"But how . . ." Future Tony coughed red mist, cleared his throat, then spat. "How'd she find us?" he said, breathlessly. "How are we linked?"

"Did you have a dream?" Emma asked. "Before she showed up?"

"Yeah." Future Tony's face clenched. "A real bad one."

"It was all about a valley, wasn't it? With a lot of snow?"

"Hey," Chad said. "Wait a goddamned minute."

"And monsters." A shudder grabbed the Future Tony for a long shake. "One of them got me, *hurt* me and . . . *Jesus*." The boy squeezed his head as if trying to keep his skull from exploding. "*This* is the nightmare."

"If only," Black Widow said.

What is *that thing he's going on about?* What was this . . . this *dream?* Was it an illusion, a fantasy? Maybe a mirage, or a product of the mind's most macabre imaginings? Doyle's eyes fell to the examination tables and what lay hidden, cocooned in blankets and snugged in burlap sacks. *Is that what* you *are: nightmares?*

No, a dream is what you live when you sleep. Black Dog licked Doyle's left ear. A nightmare is what you're relieved to find, upon waking, your life isn't.

"Christ, I had the same dream, man. That bat-shit crazy valley; the fog that rolled in out of nowhere, swallowed us up, and then landed us where there were *things* with . . ." The knob of his Adam's apple bobbed as Chad swallowed. "But I don't remember *you*," he said to Tony.

"Makes two of us." Gulping back a strangled laugh, Future Tony coughed more blood. "But I remember Rima. She's about the only person from the dream that I *do*."

"Yes." Rima gave the boy a slow nod. "You gave the other Rima a muffler."

"To keep you warm." Future Tony's eyes rested on Rima's face for a long moment. "You were the only one who felt real to me in that place. After that, I think I don't remember anything else because I . . . I d-died." Blood stained his lips the color of fresh roses. "That's right, isn't it? I s-saw you and then all I could think was . . . *save* her, do it for *her*, and then . . ."

"Don't think of it anymore." Rima's eyes pooled. "It's past."

"Or prologue," Black Widow said.

"I think I died, too." The tip of Chad's narrow nose reddened. "The snow b-broke up and something grabbed me, pulled me down. *Killed* me. God, it hurt." He looked at Emma. "Then I woke up. Is that what happened to you?"

"I didn't have that part of the dream, but now that I see you? I think we met. You and Bode were in a really weird house that showed me stuff I can't hardly remember." Emma looked to Black Widow. "That's how you do it. It's the nightmare. That's why the fog has more stops than it did before. The stops are our *Nows*, and we're linked because we've all had the same dream. It's kind of like we're infected. You use the dream to home in on us. It's why I saw you come through the window, and our Tony saw you come after the other Tony through a mirror. Maybe you *knew* about us before but couldn't *find* us until we had the dream, and then we showed you what we looked like, because Tony looked in a mirror and I saw my reflection in a window. Mirrors and windows are like your eyes into the *Now*. Either the fog travels through dreams—or maybe it's what *makes* dreams—or *you* follow the dream and make the fog go to that *Now*. But here's something

I don't understand. *Our* Tony was sick before the squirmers got him because the other Tony is here. If another Rima was here or a Chad or Bode, they'd be sick, too. If there was another *me* here, I bet I would be. Isn't that right?"

"These others . . . yes. *You*, however, I am not so sure." Head cocked, Black Widow studied the girl. "You are singular, unique in your construction."

"I don't know what that means." Emma actually seemed to grow smaller, the way a flower might wilt under a hot sun. "But if what I said is right, then how come *you're* not sick?" The girl turned a look down at the man and woman in the far cell and then back to Black Widow. "Because *she's* here. So you *ought* to be."

"Well, I must be singular, too." Showing her teeth, Black Widow slid a sidelong glance to the far cage. "Wouldn't you agree, darling?"

"Darling?" Emma repeated.

In the cage, the handsome woman opened her mouth but closed it again when her husband squeezed her shoulder and then turned a stony face to Black Widow. "Where's Kramer?" he asked.

Kramer. Doyle goggled. *Darling? That man* knows *Black Widow?*

But of course he would. Black Dog snuffled at his neck. **Look at his wife.**

"Kramer? You'll get your chance. I dare say he'll be along . . ." Black Widow broke off as a far wall abruptly wavered much more violently than before, as if Doyle were looking into a vat of mercury into which someone had thrown a large boulder.

"What the hell?" Chad said.

The rock wall glimmered, both puckering and yet expanding.

Then, a figure melted into being. A body was draped over its shoulders. At a glance, Doyle knew this figure wasn't Kramer, but there was something wrong with this person's face. Doyle squinted, then gasped, *"God!"* There was a crash of glass on stone. Swaying, Doyle gripped the worktable into which he'd bumbled with quivering arms. "Dear God, what *is* that thing?"

Steady, dearest. Black Dog actually braced him up.

"It ain't got a face." Any wider, and Chad's eyes would plop from their sockets. "It's a nothing, it's a . . ."

A blank, like the crowd. Doyle gulped back a surge of vomit. *Like the hag!* The man-thing was brutish, incomplete, only so much unformed clay. Beyond, the rock shimmered again, and then a clot of dismay iced his chest. *No,* Doyle thought, as he watched the girl, face ashen, emerge. *No no no, you can't be here, Meme, you can't . . .*

"Oh!" Rima cupped a hand to her lips. Next to her, Emma's eyes were wide with shock. "No," Rima said. "*No.* Is he dead, is he . . ."

"Oh, Jesus Christ," Chad said, as the man-thing strode to an examination table and laid out a body with surprising gentleness, cradling the head with a massive hand. *"Bode?"*

DOYLE

All Mad Here

1

"YOU *FUCKS!*" CHAD screamed. Bode's long brown hair had come undone, and a black rill of blood slowly wormed from a rude gash on his right temple. "What'd you *do* to him?"

"He's not *your* Bode, Chad." Emma sounded as if she was trying very hard not to cry. "He's ours."

God, if you're listening, if there's any mercy left in this world at all, please. Doyle watched as Meme slid alongside the man-thing and began to swab away blood from the boy's face. *Please, get Meme out of here.* He should do something, say anything. Sidle over, touch her, murmur, *Leave this place. Come with me, and I'll care for you.*

Oh, my dear bricky little Doyle. Black Dog chuffed. **Then go, quickly, before Kramer returns. Kick the dust from your sandals, rest your head on her breasts.**

"Bode?" Rima clung to her cell's bars. "What's wrong with him? What happened? Is he dead? Did you kill him?"

"Do calm yourself. He isn't, though he ought since he drowned." It was Kramer, emerging from the rock. He gestured at another man-thing just behind him that had a girl held fast by an arm. Like Bode, the girl was soaked to the skin. "You may thank *her* for his life."

"Elizabeth!" Black Widow started forward. "What happened? Is she all right?"

"Stay." Kramer held up his free hand. "She is not what you think."

"What are you talking—"

"Oh my God!" It was the handsome woman in the far cell. Scrambling to her feet, she launched herself at the bars. "My *God*! She's alive!"

"No!" The man was by her side in a second. "You don't understand."

"What's to understand? I always knew she was alive, even after all those months of doctors telling me she'd died, that they couldn't do a damn thing about the leukemia. I knew they were wrong. I told you that all we had to do was get to another *Now* and find her again."

"No. Love," the man said, "it's not as simple as—"

"Yes, it is. That is *my* daughter." She held out her bandaged arms. "Honey? Lizzie? Don't be afraid. It's Momma. You know your mom, don't you?"

Mother? Perhaps it was the way the air wobbled and shimmied, but Elizabeth looked very odd. Her face wavered as if Doyle were peering through flawed glass during a rainstorm. The effect was eerie, as if her features were uncertain how they ought to settle. Yet when Elizabeth looked toward the couple in the far cell, Doyle thought he registered first surprise and then a narrow expression of suspicion, a slight parting of her lips as her eyes settled not on the handsome woman who called herself *mother* . . . but the man. Her *father*? Doyle blinked. *That* was

McDermott? If true, this meant that Kramer had known where McDermott was all along. *Or really had been looking for him and only now found him. But how?* Doyle's eyes snapped back to Black Widow. *The little girl, Emma, said they were all linked by that . . . that thing they call a nightmare. So Black Widow found the McDermotts through the same dream?*

"Sweetheart, listen to me," McDermott pressed. "It's not her. It's a trick."

Sweetheart. Elizabeth's mother and his wife. Doyle swallowed and tasted acid. *That is Meredith McDermott.* But then Black Widow . . .

"A *trick*?" Black Widow rounded on McDermott. "Oh, that's *very* good, coming from you!"

"What are you *talking* about? Of *course* it's her," Meredith said to McDermott. "I *told* you she was alive. Didn't I tell you?"

"No." McDermott tried to gather her. "She isn't who you remember."

"My dear woman, you should listen to your husband. Quite astute," Kramer said. "But then, he always was."

"Shut up, Kramer," McDermott said. "Where's Battle? What have you done to him?"

"Me?" With his half-mask and serpent's hiss, Kramer looked as innocent as a viper coiled about a clutch of fragile baby birds: *Oh, not to worry; I'll care for them while you pop out for a pint.* "I'm sure I don't know."

"Doyle, then." McDermott transferred his gaze to him. "Constable, where's the inspector? I demand to see Battle."

He knows my name. Doyle's insides shriveled. This was like that moment Elizabeth had called him Arthur. How did either that girl or McDermott know him?

"Honey?" Meredith was still calling to the girl. "Sweetheart?"

"Not so fast there." Black Widow gave Meredith a dark look before turning to Kramer. "What have you done?"

"Doyle, answer me, damn it!" McDermott wrenched at the bars of his cage. "Where the hell is Battle?"

Too many people, too much noise; everyone, plug yer damn cakeholes! Doyle gnawed a knuckle to keep from screaming. McDermott, in league with Battle . . . Given what Doyle had discovered, he could see that.

"You're in no position to demand anything, Franklin. If Doyle is here, I'd say that the good inspector's usefulness is past. Although your concern does confirm what I've long suspected: Battle was your creature, wasn't he? Solving murders was never his goal." The doctor tilted his head toward the exam table. "His sole aim was to preserve *them*, wasn't it? What I don't understand is why he kept after Elizabeth so, unless it was to make certain that she couldn't give away your whereabouts, or reveal too much of the process, so that only you would retain the power over life and death? Or . . . was the unfortunate Battle looking for you, too, waiting on his master to return and wondering what was taking him so long, why you'd abandoned him in this godforsaken place? Well . . ." Kramer almost seemed to puff up with pride. "Take a good look. I've been quite the apt pupil, yes? I am close, *very* close to mastery. All I require is the Mirror, and I will set this world to rights—or leave it for another *Now* where we can be whole."

McDermott was shaking his head. "The Mirror wouldn't work for you. It's not in your nature, Kramer."

"Both of you can sod all." Black Widow scythed air with the side of a bladelike hand. "Kramer, what did you mean when you agreed that Elizabeth isn't who that woman remembered? Did you . . ." Black Widow's jaw went slack. "My God, you let one take control. Damn you, we had an *agreement*."

"Things have changed," Kramer said to Black Widow.

"Honey?" Meredith called again.

"Oh? What?" Black Widow bit off the words. "We were to gather these pieces together and *purge* her of them. You said you'd perfected a serum. You promised to get *rid* of them!"

"He can't," McDermott said. "You have to trust me on this."

"Trust?" Black Widow seethed. "*You?* The one man responsible for all this?"

"What's wrong with Lizzie?" Meredith sounded confused, though Doyle didn't think she was really listening to the others. Her eyes were only for the girl. "Honey?"

"What about Bode?" Rima said.

"I told you. He drowned." Kramer aimed a forefinger at Elizabeth. "He was dead until *she* breathed life back into him."

"You know, guys, it was only CPR." Elizabeth's words were toneless yet *burred* a little, as if having the same trouble settling down as her features.

"Don't be modest. You're a slip of a girl, and you hoisted the boy from that pool with your bare hands. I'd say that's a touch . . . unusual?" Kramer inclined his head toward the last person just now materializing from what had been solid stone. "And there is, of course, your effect on Weber as well."

Weber? Doyle recognized the general shape of the man's body, although Weber's head, still in partial shadow because of distance and grainy light, looked a touch misshapen and off-kilter. Doyle squinted as Weber tottered a little closer. Very unsteady on his . . . *Oh*. Gasping, Doyle gripped the worktable so tightly the edge bit his flesh. *What is this? What's happening? Rock that moves, doppelgängers, men with no faces.*

And now, Weber.

2

LIKE THE HAG, a portion of Weber's skull pulsed with the undulation of pink brains beneath as a milky white membrane unfurled over a tracery of red capillaries and blue veins. The edges were a quivering bristle of sharp spicules, like miniature darning needles that nosed toward one another, lacing and darting like fingers, the filaments of moist muscle drawing together like the frayed threads of worn socks.

"Jesus." It was the scruffy boy, Chad. "Look at his face, look at his *face!*"

"It's *regenerating*," Black Widow said, awed. "But how?"

Regenerating? He remembered what Battle had said: McDermott was obsessed with the science of revivification. Then Weber had been dead? His head broken to pieces? *This is madness. It's the fog. We're all mad here.*

"From Elizabeth's blood and what's bound to her from the Dark Passages."

"Bound." Fumbling out her purple spectacles, Black Widow jammed them on. "Good God. Are they . . ."

"Yes, they gave her power. They are her shadows, creatures of the Dark Passages, and with them," Kramer said, "I will remake this world."

EMMA

The First

SHADOWS? DARK PASSAGES? Emma hugged poor, sick Tony a little tighter, though mostly to comfort herself. That new girl, Elizabeth, scared the heck out of her. The way her face didn't want to *be* any one person kind of reminded Emma of when her craniofacial doc showed her what faces fit her own deformed skull: *I can give you any number of looks.*

Until that second, Emma had been convinced she was way different. While the nightmare linked them all together, she'd figured *she* was unique, the one and only. Hadn't the crazy lady said she was *singular* in her construction, whatever the heck that meant? But that was kind of close to the truth, too, wasn't it? Her face *was* a reconstruction. So was her whole head. But still, she thought she was the *only* Emma.

But now she looked at Elizabeth—at the eyes that were an exact match to hers, and what were the chances of that, like ten trillion to one?—and thought, *Maybe not.*

2

ANOTHER THING: THAT McDermott guy, the one with the black hair and glasses, seemed *awfully* familiar. The way he *stared* like he recognized her or something. If she let herself think about it too much, he almost matched the mental image she had of a dad: kind of handsome, looked real smart, seemed calm.

His wife, though . . . In Emma's school, there were a couple cutters everyone whispered about, but everything they did was where you couldn't see. Like under their blouses and on their stomachs and thighs and stuff. There was nothing hidden with this lady. Her arms looked like she'd taken a meat cleaver to them; they were that bad. So she must be really messed up. Like locked-in-the-hospital messed up.

Still, Emma felt a tug of sympathy for that woman, too. Heck, one look at that crazy lady in black, and *she'd* have felt like screaming her head off, too.

3

THAT CREEPY, HALF-FACE guy, Kramer, said he would remake this world with what was in Elizabeth's blood. Seemed to Emma that he'd been trying, like with the rock-morphing bit, although rock was way different than a person. Not as complicated, and you didn't have to get all the different moving parts to work together. He did know how to make some things from scratch— those ooky android-looking guys with Silly Putty blobs instead of faces, for example—but maybe he couldn't get beyond a certain point? Like give them faces and personalities and stuff? *And* somehow *Elizabeth's blood, these shadow-things, will help?* But how? She looked over at the big, ugly guy with the cratered skull. (If all this were a movie, she'd definitely be watching through her fingers.) She bet if she was close enough, she'd hear the high *smee-smee-smee-squee* of all that muscle and junk screwing itself back into place. Beneath a latticework of new bone, the insides of his head still boiled, like his brains needed more elbow room.

The guy's head gets all smashed. Then Elizabeth's blood, what, organizes all the pieces? Like these shadow-things were the final ingredient, or a . . . come on, what was the word? A . . . *catalyst.* Right. Something that sped up a reaction because the catalyst had a lower activation energy.

Energy was super important here, too. Probably why everything wobbled and wavered, like looking through heat shimmers radiating from superheated blacktop on a hot summer's day. Here, people wandered around with tin arms, no legs, glass eyeballs. Creepy old Kramer, with that mask. *But they're breaking down. So is this whole London, and that means there's a ton of free energy down here.*

She wondered if that was why the crazy lady said there were blind spots. Light was energy; the colors were different wavelengths, and people couldn't see every single wavelength, like UV. So what if some spots were *blind* because you couldn't see them without panops or X-ray goggles or something? *Jack's always looking* between *leaves and trees and shadows.* She glanced down at the animal. Standing at attention by her side, his tail twitching in spastic swishes, Jack was staring fixedly at this strange, wobbly energy-air. Boy, she'd pay good money to get a look at what he saw. Because Jack *could* slip into a blind spot. So maybe a blind spot was a way out? Or a . . . a kind of rip you could hide in?

In her arms, Tony let out another soft moan. When she touched his cheek, she felt the slow slither of a squirmer gliding under her palm—and then it hit her.

What if Elizabeth's blood could heal Tony?

4

SHE LOOKED OVER at Meme, who'd finished bandaging Bode's head. To her relief, Bode's head was rolling, like he was waking up. When Bode raised a hand to a temple, Meme took it, then bent to murmur something and even smiled when Bode's eyes fluttered open. The two of them were kissing close. She thought Meme wanted that. From the long look Bode gave her, maybe he did, too, but there was something else in his face Emma couldn't read. Whatever it was, Meme straightened abruptly and let go of Bode's hand.

Neither saw Elizabeth's eyes flick their way, or the way the other girl's face changed into something half suspicious, half . . . well, not *fear*. Like Meme really *bothered* Elizabeth, or was a tough problem that needed figuring out.

Meme bugged the crap out of her, too. Sure, she *seemed* okay on the outside, even if she did have a stick jammed up her bum. (On the other hand, this was *England* after all, and all those guys were into good manners and everything. Well, when they weren't chasing you with an ax or making you fight zombies.) She and Rima hadn't had a chance to talk about it, but when Tony asked Rima what Meme looked like through panops, he hadn't heard her response the right way: how Rima said *nothing*. Not *oh, it's fine, it was nothing*. No. This was when *nothing* meant *something*. Meant, *Holy crap, Tony! When I looked through those glasses, there was nothing there!* Like maybe what Rima saw was a walking android-girl with a Silly Putty face. Or no girl at all.

At that thought, she felt one of those lightning jolts, like when you've worried over a tough math problem for a long time and then the answer just—*blam!*—comes out of the blue.

What if *that* explained why Meme was so bland? So *nothing*? Because she *was* the same as the man-things but more advanced, like a better model that's almost but not quite human?

So Kramer made her, too, but only got to a certain point? Because Kramer didn't have either the know-how or that last secret ingredient to make Meme a real person?

How *Star Trek* was that? But she thought she was onto something here. Meme was missing a certain essential ingredient—call it personality—and she didn't react normally. Like she'd never once noticed or commented on Jack, asked where the cat had come from, or how come they hadn't made stew out of him or something. All kinds of *ding-ding-ding-ding* warning bells went off then. That's why she'd said something to Bode. No matter what Meme looked like on the outside, she wasn't wired like them. In a way, she was the reverse of Elizabeth. There was a whole *lot* going on inside *that* girl.

Going on inside . . . Emma felt her heart jump. Another *aha* bolt. *Whoa, wait just a second.* Elizabeth had saved Bode's life. She said it was nothing. That it was *CPR.*

CPR. In *this* London. Elizabeth *knew* CPR.

Oh, holy crap. Emma stared at the other girl's freaky face, which glimmered and shifted, and those eyes that matched hers—and thought, *Just who is inside you?*

5

"**WHO ARE YOU?** How did you get in there?" Peering through her purple glasses, the crazy lady pointed a trembling finger at Elizabeth. "I don't know *what* you are . . ."

"We're not things," Elizabeth said—and Emma thought, *Oh yeah, right. Your face is all wobbly, like it can't figure out who you're supposed to be now.* "We're what's left of the people we were," the other girl said.

"Leave her alone!" It was that poor woman in the far cell. "Stop badgering her. I don't know what's going on here or what you are, but that is *my* daughter."

The crazy lady whirled. "You ask what *I* am, Meredith? Look in the mirror and ask the same of yourself."

"I *know* what you are. I don't understand why Frank did it, but . . ." The woman named Meredith faltered. "Wait a minute, where did you get those? The glasses?"

"What? These?" Slipping them off, the crazy lady gave her spectacles a look, as if seeing them for the first time. "You mean, *my* panops?"

"Yes." Meredith swallowed. Her fingers knotted. "You can't possibly have . . . that is, *I've* got the only pair."

"Oh. Well." The crazy lady gave a careless shrug. "I guess you're mistaken then, and don't tell Kramer, because he's got a pair, too. What do you use *yours* for?"

The small muscles in Meredith's jaw twitched. "When I make my Peculiars."

Peculiars. Emma sat up a little straighter. So Meredith could *make* this weird and funky fog? Or was she talking about something else?

"And I use them when I check Frank, after he comes back from . . ." Meredith scrubbed air with a hand. "I wouldn't expect you to understand."

The crazy lady's eyes glittered like a crow's. "Understand what? That you use panops to check our dear, darling Frank for hangers-on after he cuts himself to bind one of those things from the Dark Passages? After he's gone off, disappeared, traveled to a *Now*? Because you want to make sure, don't you? Nothing left inside, bound to the blood?"

"Yes." Meredith's voice was really small, like the crazy lady had just slapped her. "But how do you . . ."

"Meredith," the man—Frank—said, and put his arm around her. He shot the crazy lady a glare before smoothing hair from his wife's forehead. "Sweetheart, don't say any more."

"But Frank, how does she know? How can she? I still don't understand. *Why* did you make her in the first place? What possessed you? I'm here." Meredith's lips wobbled, and Emma wasn't sure if she was trying on a smile—which was awful, terrible, like watching a poor dog that just knew it was in deep doo-doo for chewing that table leg—or working on not crying, which was just as bad. "Aren't I enough?"

"*Make* her? Sweetheart?" The crazy lady showed her teeth in a grin Emma had seen on the faces of really popular girls, right before they took out your jugular with a class-A snark. "Isn't that nice. How he must care for you."

"Stay out of this." If looks were lasers, that crazy lady ought to be burnt to a crisp. "Your argument is with me," Frank said.

Frank and the crazy lady know each other. Then, Emma thought, *Well, of course they do, you dope. Look at* Meredith *and then look at . . .*

"But what if I want to hear what she has to say?" Meredith

turned to face the crazy lady. "How do you know about all those things?"

"How do you think? You really believe you're the *first*? The *only*? You've seen all this—doppelgängers and doubles and the malleability of matter—and you still believe you're unique?" The crazy lady spread her arms in a *ta-DA*. "Then how in God's name do you explain me? How do you explain my *daughter*?"

"She's not yours," Meredith said.

"Don't!" Frank snapped at the crazy lady. "Can't you just *leave* it!"

"Do *not* dictate to me." The crazy lady drew herself up like a queen. "You are no longer master here. Or are you afraid? What is it, dear Frank? Isn't she strong enough? No better luck this time around?"

This time around? Emma's eyes fixed on Meredith's bandaged arms. Her stomach gave a sick little flutter. *Sure; of course; that would explain why he did it. Because what if* this *time—the arms, the hospital, her being sick and wanting to die—what if all that isn't the* first *time?*

"What does she mean, Frank?" Meredith said, slowly, though Emma couldn't tell if Meredith had already guessed and wanted Frank to lie. (Because, sometimes, people really want that. Sometimes the truth hurts so much, you'd rather close your eyes and let someone tell you a nicer story, one that feels better to believe.) "This time around . . . what is she talking about?"

Oh boy. Frank looked like he couldn't decide if he wanted to cry or claw his eyes out. Emma actually felt sorry for him. *Meredith, you really don't want to know.*

"Nothing. Darling, sweetheart . . . *please*." Frank's voice was as watery and wavery as the air. "Let this go."

"Let it go? Frank, we're in a goddamned cell. I don't even know how we got here. One second I'm on the ward, in the bathroom, just out of a shower, brushing my teeth, and . . . there was the mirror, so foggy. I thought, well, it's the steam, or my eyes even, not wanting to focus. They'd given me a shot, and I had the strangest dream." Meredith pressed a trembling hand to her mouth. "About *us*, Frank. I was *afraid* of you because you couldn't stop with some damned book, and so I took Lizzie . . . except it wasn't her. I mean, it *was*, but she was so young, a little girl again, and then we're in the car and there's an explosion and this strange fog began chasing us . . ."

Wait a second. Emma clapped a hand to her mouth to keep in the shout. Meredith's words were like a clear white dagger plunging straight through her brain. *That sounds like a story I know. Did I read it, or was it a movie or . . .*

"Meredith, darling." Frank tried catching her hands. "It was just a bad dream. It was the drugs, that's all."

"Felt so *real*. I . . . I *killed* you, Frank. I killed our daughter; I crashed the car . . . and I died, I felt myself die . . ."

Dream. Emma's insides curled like snails frightened into their shells. She recognized this now as part of her nightmare. She also had a sense she was the *only* one of them all to have had it, too. *Rima doesn't know this part, and neither does anyone else. Only me, just me.*

"Darling, you're stressed. You've been through a ringer. The hospital, the treatments." Frank drew his wife's hands to his chest. "Love, it's Lizzie's illness eating at you. Remember what the doctors said. You have to take it easy, let it go."

"Take it *easy*?" Snatching her hands back, Meredith let out a cawing, almost crazed laugh. Her hands fluttered like broken-winged birds. "Let it *go*? Look where I am, Frank! It's one thing to visit; it's another to be *brought* by *her*, and there are these *others* who shouldn't be here at all, who don't belong outside their . . ." She choked that off. "And you don't think I have the *right* to know what the hell's going on? What that *bitch* means by the *first*?"

"Temper." The crazy lady did a tut-tut, like Mary Poppins gone over to the Dark Side of the Force. "I mean precisely what I said. Everything *you* are, what you see when you look in the mirror, my dear? You owe all that to me."

"No." But Emma could tell that this was the kind of *no* that meant *no no no, I can't hear this*. "No," Meredith repeated. "That's not right. Look where you are. It's the other way around."

"Deep in your soul, you know that is not true. You know that *I* am the template, the first and the last, your alpha and omega," the crazy lady said. "I am the original Meredith McDermott, not you."

ELIZABETH

We

1

I KNEW IT. We're the originals. These others are only impostors and pieces.

As she'd watched and listened to everything unfold through the mind's eye in Emma's down cellar prison, Elizabeth thought she would feel more smug about that, but something her mother said gnawed: *I am the template.* The first Meredith; the original Meredith; Meredith, the person. Yet if that was true, why had her father felt the need to make a copy at all?

Her eyes strayed to the other Meredith, her bandaged arms. Her own mother had done that. The scars were hidden by her long sleeves, but they were there.

And I've done the same. Her hand strayed to her scarred left forearm. *But mine was for a purpose. There was a reason. I needed to understand the symbols.* But for her and her mother and now this *other* Meredith . . . for them *all* to do so was wrong. She'd have thought her father would have corrected that in the copies. *Unless he can't. Maybe it's as fundamental as the color of our eyes.* So each and every piece of her or her mother was contaminated? Like mother, like daughter? Self-murder was inevitable? Is that why, every now and again, she actually thought she sometimes heard her mother's voice

can't you see how sick she is

that's not your father

in her head as well? She never had understood that.

But no, that can't be. Mother's not a piece. She's original. She is herself, as am I. She was hearing a . . . a memory, some argument between her parents drifting to the fore, that was all.

Her destiny might not be fixed or inevitable either. That copy's daughter—that Meredith's Elizabeth—had died from a disease she'd never heard of. Leukemia? Yes, and *that* was the event that unhinged her. She wondered when that had happened, at what age the other Meredith's daughter took ill. *Because I am sick.* There were moments she thought she really *might* be dying and that living a life cooped up in hospital was *all* the life she knew.

Ridiculous, of course; that constable had come on her fleeing some horror. *But I can't remember from whence, or what it was I saw, other than vague impressions of coming on bodies in some underground labyrinth.* Like this place, down cellar? No, ridiculous. Absurd. *My father was* doing *something to the bodies, those girls and boys, if I remember right.* They'd been roughly her age—although had there been a younger, smaller child, or two? She couldn't recall.

Here was something else that didn't tally. When Doyle found her, she'd been bleeding, badly. Yet if her father had been there with her, wouldn't he have done something to staunch the flow, bandage her? Prevent her from being injured in the first place? So why hadn't he? *Unless he really wasn't there at all—and where was that, exactly? Was it even in this* Now?—*and I only imagined it.*

But there *were* bodies. That inspector, Battle, said so, as did Kramer. That hadn't been her imagination.

My God. Her stomach tightened. Kramer said that what had bound itself to her blood would save this world and remake it. He'd said that *her* blood, rich with shadows, was responsible for healing Weber's injuries. The shadows hadn't always been there, of course; they'd come with Emma.

Yet what if her father had been after roughly the same thing? *I carry pieces. I hear voices.*

So did her father require what she carried in her body and mind: a certain piece, an animus that would infuse a spark in a way that was wholly different from the faceless, anonymous man-things of Kramer's construction?

What if her father needed her blood to make those girls and boys . . . into people?

2

SOMETHING ELSE NIGGLED.

How had she escaped her father? He was strong, a man, and she was a slip of a thing and ill, besides.

Perhaps the correct question was, *had* she escaped at all?

What if he'd let her go, returned her to this *Now*?

Or if she'd never left it . . . how had he gotten out?

And why hadn't he taken her with him?

3

"I TOLD YOU," she said, slipping her gaze from the mind's eye to her right. "You're pieces and copies, and that's all you'll ever be."

"If that makes you feel better." Emma's voice had taken on the curious burr of Eric and the others, who were all clustered round as if she were the candle and they, the moths. It had started as soon as Emma unlocked their down cellar prison and Eric unfurled like a blighted black rose. Elizabeth hadn't liked that, but Bode's life had hung in the balance and there was no other way. Unnerving, too, the way Emma could be both *here*, in this down cellar, and out *there*—talking to Kramer, her mother, her *father*, the false Meredith—at the same time. Even more troubling was how the longer Eric stayed with Emma, in the very front of her mind, the closer these other silhouettes and shadows clustered.

So like those blanks in the cells, too. And what had *they* been about? Yes, *she'd* sometimes thought of the other patients as *faceless*, nothing but open mouths and sound, but *Meme* had been the one to say it.

Emma thought it had something to do with energy—*look at the way the rocks glow; everything wavers; it's like the barn in the valley*—though it was beyond Elizabeth what the other girl was babbling about.

"Whether Bode is a real person or just a piece who thinks he is, your mother or Kramer will get rid of him. They'll kill this London's Tony and Rima, too." Of them all in this down cellar space, Emma's face was the most substantial, because she really was strongest. Elizabeth had noticed that even in this gloaming, the other's birthmark was a very bright glister. Kramer was right; the shadows were Emma's power. "Obviously Meme would have to go, too, considering that she's my double," Emma said.

"But not an exact match." It was the one Emma called Rima. She was not as well-defined as Emma or even half as fleshed out as Eric, though Elizabeth could make out obsidian stones in the deep hollows of the thing's eyes. Unlike Eric, it had taken time for Rima to put together sentences. At first, her voice had been only a toneless sough. The longer Emma was here with them, though, the more defined they all became. "Your eyes are different," Rima said.

"She's way more complete than the man-things, though." It was a shadow-boy, more a smoky pillar than anything formed, but she thought that was because the stain left in Casey ran deep. He couldn't seem to settle well, and his voice oscillated amongst several registers. To Elizabeth, the boy's tones grated like a symphony of kazoos, each buzzing a different tune. He was a strange one, too, his eyes so different even from Emma's. Of the precious few glimpses she'd gotten, she saw they were indeterminate, never quite settling but slipping from black to silver to gray and back again. "I wonder why?" Casey said.

"I'm sure I don't know about Meme," Elizabeth said. "She's Kramer's creature." *Never realized the literal truth of that.* "Until now, I didn't know my mother was in league with Kramer at all. I haven't seen her in ages."

And how do I feel about that? Really? To know that my mother has been rounding up these people? She frowned over that last word. It wouldn't do to think of them as complete, whole individuals. And yet . . . her eyes fixed on the Tonys, dying in their cages. On Rima, so willing to give of herself to save another. That little girl, Emma: how she cared for them. *They bleed. They feel.*

What did she know of that kind of connection? What had *she* ever felt but anger and pain and confusion?

Have I been nothing but a pawn, a . . . a vessel? My God, if Kramer really could empty her of all the pieces, bleed her dry, what would be left? She could almost imagine that she might be like those faceless man-things: the approximation of a person, but soulless. Perhaps she was even closer to Meme than she realized? Even if they were nothing but copies and pieces based on her, Emma and the shadows, Bode and his friends . . . they all had *lives*. They could love. *Did* love and care for one another, and fiercely.

But have I ever? What am I? Who am I, really? Where is Elizabeth *in all this?*

"What about little Emma?" Rima's words oscillated like the rapidly plucked strings of a violin. "Is that really you out there? Do you remember this at all?"

"No." Emma touched her chin. "But I remember clocking myself. Took that header off my bike the week after down cellar. My *blinks* started up around the same time. But I sure don't remember *blinking* here."

"Could be a different Emma." Eric's voice was a hollow hum. "Maybe your accident is a branch-point. A pivot: you went one way, and that little girl went another."

"Maybe." Emma sounded troubled. "You know what I don't understand? For the sake of argument, let's say what we heard in the valley is the truth: we're all characters from McDermott books."

"And you're the only escapee," Eric said. "The one who got free of the page and then gave that ability to me and Casey."

"That's kind of too much to process, but okay. Think about it. So far, Elizabeth's mom has gone only into *books* I recognize: Rima's, Tony's. Chad is from *Echo Rats*. I'm not saying that we all don't feel or aren't, weren't real . . . but why hasn't Elizabeth's mother gone outside book-worlds to other *Nows*? Where's the Rima from a spaceship or something? Where's Chad as a girl, or the guy who didn't go to 'Nam?"

"Oh, isn't it obvious?" Elizabeth couldn't contain herself. "The point is to rid me of *you*, not go around murdering innocent, *true*, whole people."

"Or perhaps your mom can locate only those versions who were actually there, in the valley," Emma said.

"Doesn't explain the McDermotts," Rima said.

"No. Actually, I think it might." When Emma shook her head, her hair and face eddied and smoked into swirls of shadow that drifted and undulated before settling back into place like the coils of an elaborate coiffure. "Meredith said she dreamt about being afraid of Frank and blowing him up, remember? Well, *I* saw a lot of that in those Lizzie-*blinks*. House showed me the moment of the crash. I *know* Meredith was dying. *She* thinks it's a nightmare or a hallucination or something, but it really happened."

"Yeah, but if Elizabeth's mother is right," Eric said, "how do you know that what you saw didn't happen in a book?"

A burst of impatience. "What *is* that?" Elizabeth demanded. "This *nightmare* you all keep yammering on about. I've no idea what you mean."

"Nightmares? They happen when you sleep," Eric said.

"What? Sleep is *sleep*. Sleep is nothing. It's *blank*."

Emma and Eric looked at one another, and then Emma said, "Elizabeth, what happens when *you* go to sleep?"

"Happens?" When *was* the last time she'd slept? She couldn't recall. *Have I ever slept?* She really wasn't certain. "Nothing. I close my eyes. I open them. That's all."

"So no images, no pictures? It's just . . . black?"

"Well, yes. It's the same for everyone. Nothing is all *anyone* sees when they sleep."

"Well, clearly not everyone, right? Meredith knows what a dream is. Where I come from," Emma said, "everyone dreams. You see pictures. Stories, sort of. It's a way of sifting through your day and storing memories."

"Doesn't sound very restful. Have you considered that's something common to pieces because you're imaginary? Of course you'd insert yourself into stories, because that's all you know. Real people have no need for dreams."

"Then how do you explain your mother?" Emma said. "She knows what nightmares are. It's how she found the others."

Elizabeth felt a twinge of disquiet. "I don't know. Why is it important? Who cares?"

"You know," the shadow-Casey said, the words wobbling and reverberating, "now that we're talking about it, I'm not sure I remember *ever* having a dream. I know what they *are*, but . . ." (She noticed how close his shadowy pillar had sidled to Rima, and they *did* seem a pair, just as Eric and Emma did.) "Do *you* remember, Rima?" Casey asked. "From before?"

"No." Rima sounded troubled. "And why would *our* Tony and Chad think something that happened was only a bad dream instead of the real thing?"

"They both died there," Emma said. "Maybe that's the only way they *can* think of what happened. When you wake up, you're relieved it was only a nightmare."

"But we get right back to the same problem: why has the nightmare bled into *this* London's Tony and Rima and Bode?" Eric said. "Why them and no other?"

"For that matter, why hasn't Meme had the dream? She's your doppelgänger," Elizabeth said, surprising herself. *Why am I helping them?* Perhaps *that* was her purpose? Was *this* the pivot upon which her life might turn? "If she's so close to you in every other way, shouldn't she?"

"She's right," Eric thrummed.

It bothered her that she actually felt a flicker of accomplishment: *See, I'm not completely hopeless; I can hold my own.* "Why haven't *I* had that nightmare? Except for Eric and Casey, you're all pieces in me. Why doesn't it bleed back into me?" Elizabeth said. "Because you're right, Emma: how does my mother use a nightmare if *I* don't know what a dream is? If *no one* here does? God," she said, truly listening to herself, "what if people here don't . . . because they *can't*? What if dreaming isn't a glitch or mistake? What if no one here dreams because . . ." *Say it, make it real; look at Meme and these doubles; look at my mother and that other Meredith. It's the only logical conclusion.* "What if they don't dream because it's not in their nature . . . and it's not in mine? God"—she exhaled a quavering gasp—"what if it's because of the way we're all *made*?"

"Hey, hey, take it easy." Laying a hand at once solid and vapor, flesh and shadow, on her shoulder, Emma gave a gentle squeeze, and only then did Elizabeth feel the wet on her cheeks and the sting in her eyes. "We can't be certain of anything," Emma said.

But Elizabeth thought she was perilously close to understanding something. The words were taking shape on her tongue and then lives of their own. "If my mother is the only one in this London who dreams, doesn't that make her closer to you? And then, because I can't . . . doesn't that make me like Meme? Like Kramer?"

"They don't have us in them," Eric said. "That might explain it. Maybe we keep you from dreaming."

"Oh, how fortunate," she said, but with no venom. Her voice was watery. Through her tears, she noticed that, like Emma, Eric had moved closer. All the shadows had, and she recognized, with a start, that they *felt* something for her. Not pity so much as . . . understanding. Empathy. *We know how you feel; we are here to help you if we can.*

"What are we to do? What can we? How can we make this right? Look at this *Now*, my world. What a shambles it is. We're all wrecks of one sort or another. Kramer may have learnt something from my father. In fact, I'm certain of it. There are those man-things, after all, and what he can do with the rock here. You'd think he'd use that ability to repair this place, but I doubt he truly can. He doesn't know how, and maybe that's because he can't imagine properly. Can't"—she could feel herself groping toward something now—"can't *dream* a world in all its casts and colors, and so nothing will ever be right here, because he can't do it, and never will."

"Yesss." The sound was startling, a ghostly sough, void of inflection, that drifted from somewhere behind. "Never. *Willlll.*"

God. Shuddering, Elizabeth hugged herself. That voice stroked the tiny hairs on her neck and sent a frisson skipping the rungs of her spine. This particular shadow had spoken very little and was the least formed, quite probably because it was also the most contaminated of all, having bound itself to a whisper-man of the Dark Passages.

Odd, though, given how insubstantial and ghostly it seems now, that its voice was so strong, enough to get me to cut myself. Cupping her arm, she kneaded her aching skin. She could swear the scars actually clenched. *Perhaps that is all of itself it recognizes, this urge to form these symbols?* Or its sole purpose?

The shadows' indeterminate bodies flowed and eddied as they turned, and Emma dropped to a crouch. "Why not, Lizzie?"

Emma's tone was very gentle, as if she feared frightening this piece back into incoherence and oblivion. Or perhaps she was only being cautious. After all, this small shadow had nearly killed Emma and her friends. "Is he doing something wrong?"

"Not. Make. *Riiight*." The words were hollow and reverberative. If ever one wished to hear a proper ghoul, Elizabeth thought they need look no further.

"Make?" Eric repeated. "Don't you mean *made*?"

"No, I think she means something else. Lizzie," Emma said, "you made *Nows*. You *make* them. Can you . . ."

"Build." Pause. "A." Pause. "New."

"A new," Emma repeated after a moment. "A new . . . what, Lizzie?"

"Maybe she means *anew*," Elizabeth said. "As in *over again*."

"I don't think that's it. Lizzie, honey, tell me." Emma reached a hand to where the shadow's head ought to be, and when Emma's fingers played through black mist, Elizabeth could swear she saw the slightest shimmer of corn-tassel curls.

The more Emma names it, the clearer it—Lizzie—becomes, she thought. *Very canny, Emma. To name is to control.*

"Lizzie," Emma said, "what did you mean?"

The curls roiled like golden pythons before evaporating in black steam. *"Nooow."*

"A new *Now*? Or a start-over *Now*? A redo?" Eric and Emma traded looks, and then Eric went on. "Which do you mean? How would you do that, Lizzie?"

The answer, when it finally came, sent a chill sweeping through Elizabeth's body. Perhaps it was because the words also seemed so final.

"Not. Me." The Lizzie-shadow trembled. *"Weee."*

DOYLE

Pot and the Kettle

YOU THINK YOU'RE *the first, the original, the* only *Black Widow?* (No matter who she claimed to be, the name so suited.) Doyle's eyes wandered back to the examination tables. *Pot and the kettle, that.*

"What? I . . ." Meredith warded off Black Widow's words with an upraised hand. "That's not true." She repeated it, as if mortaring the words in place, then looked to her husband. "Is it?" As if hearing the question in her voice, she said, "No, of course not." When McDermott didn't respond, she turned to Black Widow. "I understand why you believe that. He creates you to think that way."

"Creates us?" It was the little girl, Emma. She'd bunched a shawl under Tony's head and now stood alongside Rima. "*All* of us? How?"

"Wait a minute," Doyle said, breaking silence at the same instant Chad said, "Whoa, hold on a sec." In his cell, the other Tony said, "What, *what*?"

"Yes. I know, it's a lot to digest." Meredith's face softened a little. "All writers take bits and pieces of real life for their stories.

Some of you have more than others, that's all. But that's why this all feels so *real*. Why people who read his books fall into the page, get lost in the story." A small laugh bubbled past her lips. "A little like us, I guess, although we only visit for short times, never . . ." Her eyes ticked over the iron bars of that cage, and then she slicked her lips. "We only visit," she repeated.

"Visit?" Emma echoed, and Doyle saw that Elizabeth, too, had come to attention. "How do you get in and out?" the little girl asked.

Meredith went on as if she hadn't heard. "The really good stories always *cling* to you afterward, too. It's this little *click* in your head. You can't shake the narrative, but walk around in a haze; the world doesn't feel real. It's as if, well . . ." Her shrug was almost apologetic. "You and your world jump off the page."

"Jump off the bloody page?" Doyle went hot with anger. "What the *shite* you talking about?"

Careful, Doyle. Black Dog's tone held no mockery now. **Think hard before you go any further. Think of *me* and how I came to be.**

Doyle paid it no mind. "This is real because it *is*. What, you think we don't feel nothing, suffer. . ." *Nothing.* He flicked his tongue over the no-taste blood on his lips. He thought back to the humbug, the nothing that was the hag, the ginger-haired sergeant and constables with no faces and brass smears where there ought to be numbers. Battle's tasteless whiskey or brandy or whatever it had been. How nothing *smelled* like nothing, not even his sweat anymore. Kramer had said the serum would bring clarity and strip away artifice. *He said he'd wash my mind.* Doyle could feel himself going cold all over. *Turn my mind into a clean slate.*

And hadn't he felt that happening? The layers peeling off?

My God, it could be, couldn't it? Wasn't *artifice* what a writer did? Gave a character or house or place a cursory description, a few choice bits of history to make it believable? *But then that's all there is. Take that away and there's nothing.* Give *him* a serum and then layer upon layer of life as he knew it sloughed to reveal the one moment—that little nugget—that was the nexus about which everything else that was Doyle had been crafted. *That damned hovel. My father. The moment I . . .*

And then Black Dog had taken on true *substance*, as if it were his core. *No, that's got to be wrong. Shite.* He was sweating rivers. *I'm letting them confuse me, that's all. Hang on, hang on, Doyle. This is shite; it's all bloody shite.*

Ohhhh, poppet. Black Dog leaned into him, and maybe they were propping each other up after all, one feeding off the other. **Think of it this way: you'll always have me.**

"What I don't understand is, why, Frank?" Meredith looked up at her husband. "And don't tell me I'm imagining things. I'm not insane or delusional."

"Oh no," Black Widow drawled. "You only slit your wrists as an amusement."

"Shut up," McDermott said, though without much force.

"That," Meredith said to Black Widow, "has nothing to do with you. What you are and what this place is has no bearing on me or my life."

"You can look me in the eye and say that? How do you know that he hasn't *made* you to believe that you're real and sane and a person, just as he has these others?" Black Widow said.

"Ohhh, no." Meredith let out a weak laugh. "I'm not going to get into what-ifs with you. We can argue this all day, but facts are facts. I'm real. No one made *me* out of words."

"But I *am* real!" Little Emma shouted. "I'm bleeding. It *hurts*. Tony's *dying*. Of course we're real."

"No, not quite." Kramer put a hand on his chest. "Only some of us here are the genuine article: fully fleshed-out, real people. Ingenious, too, how Franklin's managed to meld fact with fiction, reality with fantasy. As for the rest of you and all your many copies . . ." From a pocket, he pulled that glass bauble on a beaded chain. "All we need now is the Mirror. Once Franklin shows us how to reintegrate your energies, we'll use the cynosure to guide us, track down any doppelgängers that remain. Rid of its fictions, this world will stabilize."

"Cynosure? *That?*" Meredith's laugh had more heart this time. "It's a *fake*; it's got no power. *I've* got the cynosure. Not on me, but back where . . . ," Meredith began, but then McDermott cut her off: "Kramer, you and I both know you've always had that."

"What?" Meredith threw him a startled glance. "Why would you write them a copy?"

Write? Doyle could feel the scream taking shape in his throat. *Bloody fucking* write?

Her husband ignored her. "What's changed, Kramer?"

"Come now, Franklin. Don't be willfully stupid. You know it's her." Tipping his head at Elizabeth, Kramer let the glass bead and chain dribble onto a nearby instrument stand. "Emma brought the power through the shadows. She's always been strongest."

"*Me?*" Emma said.

"What you'll become, child, not who you are at this moment," Kramer said.

"You mean, like me but *older*?" Emma stared at Elizabeth. "Like *time* travel?"

"No." When her mouth moved, Elizabeth's entire visage trembled. "Tony's right, Emma. I think this is an alternate reality."

"Oh." The little girl was all eyes. "A parallel universe? A different timeline?"

I can't even pretend to understand that. Doyle armed sweat from his forehead. *Reality is reality. Time is time.*

Think, though, poppet, how changeless everything is here, Black Dog said. **The only reason you're convinced of time's passing is when there is a slight change. It grows lighter or darker. But that's all perception, how your brain works, not *because* of time. Every moment under and in the heavens is now, poppet.**

"Emma?" Meredith laughed again. "There *is* no Emma. Frank gave her up."

"But *I'm* here," Emma said.

"Yes, I *see* that, but Emma was only an experiment . . ." Meredith's voice suddenly died.

"You were saying?" Kramer prompted. "About an experiment?"

"Yes." Meredith's mouth worked as if the lips were unwilling to let what was on her tongue escape. "Frank's always been fascinated with the idea of setting one of you characters in motion, by yourself. If he left you unfinished but not sealed in a Peculiar . . . if he allowed you to actually leap from the page, you might . . . Frank." Her hand whitened on his arm. "Goddamn it, you didn't. You *promised*."

"It's not what you think," McDermott said, his voice rough.

He's not angry. More anguished, Doyle thought. *As if his world is falling apart.* Doyle nearly laughed out loud. *Well, join the bloody club, boy-o.*

"Yes." Black Widow's mouth moved in a bitter half-moon. "Our Franklin is so very good at keeping his promises. Open your eyes, Meredith. Aren't these others, these children, proof of just how often he pops in for a visit?"

"Pops in?" Meredith blinked. "Frank, you *come* here? *Why?*"

"It doesn't matter." McDermott's gaze held on Kramer. "We aren't going to talk about that, all right? That's not up for discussion. Let me get my wife out of here, and I'll come back, I promise."

"You want me to let your wife go?" With that mask, Kramer had all the innocence of a python. "Which one?"

"Oh, for God's . . . which *wife*?" Meredith bridled. "Look, forget appearances; forget that she and I are doubles, all right? You obviously know how this works; that Frank's used bits and pieces of our lives over the years, and popular culture, history— every writer does that. I mean, for God's sake, look at Doyle."

"What?" The word exploded from his mouth in a hard, percussive rap. "What you talking about, history? Popular culture?"

"I mean just what I said. Arthur Conan Doyle was a real person; he was a writer, too, actually, and very famous."

"Me? A . . ." He practically choked on the word. *"Wr-writer?"* In his mind's eye, he could see his fictitious Brother James's spidery script: *Our Doyle is quite inventive; perhaps he would consider a career in letters.*

"Yes," Meredith said. "But your life before was miserable. Your father was a drunk and died in an asylum. You were poor, lived in a slum . . . Sciennes Hill Place, I think? You ran with a gang. Probably would've ended up dead or in jail if your mother hadn't begged the Jesuits to take you, except you hated them."

My God, she knows about me. It was all Doyle could do not to shred his clothes and run stark-screaming from this place.

"And there was all that fascination you had with cocaine, drugs. You experimented on yourself at least once that Frank was able to find. Wrote a paper about it when you became a doctor."

"A doc . . ." Doyle couldn't make his throat work. "Wh-what?"

"The only reason you became a physician was to please your mother. You actually weren't all that good at it either. Couldn't make a living, and you started to write in your free time." Meredith said it all in an offhand way, as if ticking the items on a grocery list. "So Frank did a what-if. What if he took all that real history and made you into the Doyle you might have become, one that fit in with this world?"

"But . . . but"—Doyle was choking—"*wh-why*? Why would you *do* that? I'm a *person*. I had a good *life*! I was famous! You just said so!" Thinking, *Doyle, Doyle, what are you buying into? You believe this flummery? You, a doctor? A natty writer?*

Oooh, poppet. Black Dog gave him a confidential nudge. **Am I there, too, I wonder? In this other Doyle's worst imaginings? A black dog, a hellhound?**

"Because a story needs an everyman, a kind of stand-in for the reader and yet a person thoroughly in the world who doesn't know what's going on but comments along the way. That's what Frank intended, although . . ." Meredith's brow suddenly furrowed, and she looked at her husband. "I thought you decided to give up Doyle, too. Your editor never saw the point; said people wouldn't accept a Doyle who wasn't brilliant, like Sherlock. Didn't see why Doyle was needed at all."

"Yet another broken promise, I wager," Kramer said. "Look at little Emma, after all."

"*Stop* that!" Emma shouted, though the words were barely understandable through her tears. "No one made me! I'm not a *thing*!"

Neither am I. Doyle's hands curled to fists. *I'm a person. I'm a man! I'm singular. I* have *no double here.* Although . . . what if he wasn't anything but a fiction? Did that mean that only Kramer was real? Black Widow?

"What goes on with my husband isn't any of your business," Meredith said to Kramer. "I've been there for every single one of your creations *and* his failures, the fragments he never finishes. So you can save your breath. Go play your little mind games with someone else."

"Perhaps," Kramer said, "but answer this. You say you've been by our dear Franklin's side. For how many years?"

"Kramer," McDermott said.

"Years?" A fleeting look of confusion clouded Meredith's face. Her lids fluttered, and she put a hand to a temple. "I . . . it's hard for me to remember. The *treatments*, the shock therapy . . . my memory's not . . ."

Memory a little spotty? Doyle wanted to blurt. *Stick around; it gets better.* Instead, he bit his lip to corral the bark of a hysterical laugh. Thought, again, *I'm going mad, I am mad, we're all mad here.* Then: *In the right place for that, aren't we?*

"Kramer, please." McDermott interposed himself between his wife and the bars. "That's enough."

"*I* don't think so," Black Widow said.

"Meredith?" Kramer prompted.

"I'm sorry." Meredith pulled herself straighter. "I don't

remember. All right? Happy? It's the treatments, the ECT. The shots and pills."

"Yes. Of course. Well, how about your age? How old are you?" When she hesitated, Kramer *tutted*. "Come now, surely you know that."

"Thirty?" It came out small, and then Meredith tried another laugh that, this time, was no more than a timorous flutter. "No, that's probably not right, is it? Not if I've got a teenage daughter. Unless we were married very young, but Frank was in school and we couldn't afford to get married and . . ." Her fingers quivered before her mouth. "I'm rambling. I do that when I get nervous."

"Of course. The mind is such a fragile thing. I'm sure there are days you can't tell what's real and what's not."

"For *God's* sake, Kramer!" McDermott shouted. "What do you *want*?"

"What I've always wanted, Franklin. I want the Dickens Mirror."

"There is no mirror here," McDermott said.

"Don't lie to me." Kramer aimed a finger at Elizabeth. "*She's* bound to shadow, and yet she remains whole, intact. The cynosure knows her; it has *power* where it did not before. Her blood *heals* and she's seen the Mirror, which means that once you tell us where it is, she can either bring more of that healing power here or show us how to leave this accursed place. Now, again, *where* is the Dickens Mirror?"

"There is no *mirror* here," McDermott repeated.

"Liar," Black Widow said.

"Do let's not pretend," Kramer said. "You come here, regularly, to steal from this *Now*'s energy for your creations. Don't deny it. That's why this London is falling apart."

"No, that's wrong. You're mistaken. He can't come back here. There's no way in," Meredith said before McDermott could answer. "I made sure . . ."

"All right, Kramer. Yes, I do come here," McDermott said. "I . . . visit. But not through the Mirror, and it's not because of my stealing anything that this London's disintegrating."

"*Frank?*" Meredith's eyes were wide. "You come here? Frank, you *promised* not to."

"As I said about our Frank and his promises," Black Widow said.

"Shut the hell up." Meredith turned a fierce gaze on McDermott. "You *shit*. You left in a back door, didn't you? But why? Why *here*?"

"For his work, of course." Kramer gestured toward the examination tables. "Shall we take a look? See what a busy boy he's been?"

Oh. Doyle felt his insides curdle. *No, let's not.*

"Frank, answer me, goddamn it," Meredith said, "or I will find a way to smash every Peculiar, ruin *every* book, send *all* of it back where it came."

"You will." Elizabeth's features shivered, then reformed. "Or you already did; I'm not sure. It might be that everything happens all at once and then things spin out from there. Whatever. Destroying the Peculiars doesn't work. All you end up with is more of *this*." Elizabeth's gaze roved over the cavern before settling on Meredith again. "Free energy. You know the physics of it. Remember your dream."

"What the hell are you—" Then Meredith seemed to hear herself. "I'm sorry, sweetheart. I didn't mean to snap, but please,

Elizabeth, stay out of this for now. Let the adults handle this, all right?"

Black Widow grunted a laugh. "Oh, that's very rich. Listen to my daughter. She knows what she's about . . . well, that *piece* does, anyway."

"Shut up." Meredith's fists clenched. "Just shut the fuck up."

"Meredith, stop. You're only making things worse. I know what I said, but . . ." McDermott wouldn't meet her eyes. "But Kramer's right, and so is Em . . ." He stumbled. "Elizabeth. I mean . . ." He made a helpless gesture to encompass the entire cave. "Look at it all, this *potential* just waiting to be tapped."

"But Frank, a back door? This isn't a goddamned computer program! I don't even pretend to understand why you felt the need to use *me* as a template for that *woman*, but don't you realize that's how my double got out?" Meredith waved a hand at the rest of the cells. "She found it, and used that to get into *their* book-worlds."

"Would you stop saying that shit?" Chad said.

"No, that's not how she's doing it." McDermott sighed. "She's . . . she's using a different way."

"Oh, really? Which is?" Meredith asked.

"Haven't you been listening?" Emma said. "I told you. She's coming through *dreams*, the same one we've all had! You must've had it, too. How else did you get here?"

"No." Meredith shook her head. "A valley? Monsters? Snow? Not me. I had a very different dream."

"Your house has geraniums. The barn is red," Emma said. "You have a studio where you make glass, and you used tanks of . . . I don't know . . . fuel, whatever, to blow it all up, and then you made Lizzie get in the car. You made her leave her cat . . .

Marmalade? Only the fog started chasing you."

"The fog?" Black Widow said. "You mean, another Peculiar?"

"No." Meredith's voice was no more than a whisper. Her face was paler than porcelain and her eyes huge, her gaze riveted on the little girl. "A Peculiar's an energy sink. It's . . . sealed."

At her place along the wall, Elizabeth stirred. "Meredith, she's not talking about a Bose-Einstein condensate."

"What's that?" Emma said.

"Too much to explain," Elizabeth said. "Think of it as a state of matter as close to zero energy—absolute zero—as possible."

"I haven't gotten that far in school," Emma said.

"I have." Future Tony armed sweat from his forehead. He was even paler than before. "Nothing would move except on the quantum level."

"What the devil?" Kramer tossed a confused look at McDermott. "What are they all talking about?"

McDermott didn't reply, but Doyle saw the swift chase of emotions on the man's face: surprise, then satisfaction, and then that slight curve to his lips. *He's* proud *of them, as if they're all his children parsing out a thorny problem.*

"A Bose . . ." Meredith's face went slack. Her eyes roved from Emma and Tony to Elizabeth, then back. "How"—she sounded as if someone had delivered a solid gut-punch—"how do you know so much?"

"I told you," Emma and Elizabeth said at the same moment. "I studied it in school," Tony said, as Emma went on, "I saw your dream."

"You saw my dream? You?" Meredith echoed. "That's not possible."

"Why do you keep saying that?" Doyle asked. He wasn't

aware he was going to speak, but damme, this was ridiculous. "It's how *she* found them, isn't it? She came in *through* this nightmare, this . . . this *dreaming*, somehow. It's the only logical conclusion because it's the only thing they've in common."

Excellent, my pet. Battle would be proud.

Doyle pushed past Black Dog's snigger. "So why you keep saying they can't dream when they have?"

"Because," Meredith said, "it's not possible for any of them—any of *you*—to dream. Frank makes sure you can't."

"Meredith," McDermott said, "I don't think this is the time."

"Oh, shut ya bunghole," Doyle said. To Meredith: "What do you mean, McDermott makes sure we *can't*. Why?"

"Because he figured out that if he lets you dream," Meredith said, "you go insane."

DOYLE

What Remains

"INSANE?" DOYLE BRAYED harsh laughter. He nearly doubled over. "You mean . . . you mean, stark raving mad?" he gasped. He was holding his gut, he was laughing so hard. "Madam, we're in a bloody *asylum*."

"Yes, do watch that tongue of yours," Black Widow said to Meredith. "You're not precisely the picture of sanity, you know."

Reddening, Meredith tugged her blouse until the sleeves covered her bandages. "That's different. I've had a few . . . problems, that's all."

Black Widow gave her a narrow look. "Yes, I daresay. Well, if what you say is true, then how do you explain *my* ability to find any of them? To find *you*?"

"I can't, other than it's a mistake, an oversight."

"It's a little more complicated than that, honey," McDermott said.

"Oh *yes*!" Doyle was off again. "Honey, *do* tell!"

Doyle. Black Dog's tone, brittle as hoar ice, sobered him instantly. **Stop your nonsense.**

"Dreaming sort of . . . wakes you up? You *imagine*, and your imagination wrecks the story." Meredith shrugged. "You all start going off your own ways. A writer has to keep control of the narrative."

"Maybe in a book," Doyle said, smearing tears from his cheeks. But he didn't miss how Elizabeth's eyes narrowed as if in sudden comprehension. McDermott only looked like a dipper with his hands deep in a pocket only to find that the jig was up. "But this is *London*."

"Well, *yes* . . . but in a book-world, that's all. Actually," Meredith said, "not even that."

"What do you mean, not even *that*?" Doyle looked to McDermott. "What does she bloody mean?"

"I'll ask the questions here," Kramer said.

"Oh, shut it." Doyle scowled, all his hysteria gone now. "I got other words for you."

Feeling peevish, are we, darling?

"You too," he said, not caring if the others thought him a lunatic.

"Is something the matter, Doyle? Has something untoward happened?" Kramer tipped his head to one side. "Something unusual?"

"Untoward? Unusual?" Doyle waved a wild hand. "Ya gob, everything *out* there is a blank to me now. Nothing tastes like anything! People got no faces!"

"You too?" It was the little girl, Emma. "I thought it was just me. Not the people, but the food here is terrible. Like so *Wrinkle in Time*."

Wait, it's happening to the little girl; it ain't just me. He felt a sudden burst of hopefulness. *Oh, thank you, God, I am real, I am, and*

Kramer's simply mad! "Did he give you a shot?"

"No. It's been like that since I got here," Emma said.

"Started for Tony and me after the nightmare," Rima said.

"And for me." It was Bode, finally conscious and still very pale, his long hair hanging in wet ropes. But he was sitting up now as Meme stood, face pinched, at his elbow. He pressed a hand to a temple. "God, feel like I've come back from the brink of the grave."

"You have," Black Widow said.

"Are you all right?" Rima called as Chad said, "Christ, everything's the same except the accent. You okay, man?"

"Yes, I . . ." And then Bode's face drained of what little color it had. "My God. You can't be—"

"He's not. Chad's like the other Tony." Rima said it almost apologetically.

"I don't know if that makes me feel better." Bode cracked a thin smile. "But I'm glad you're alive, Chad."

"Yeah, I'm kind of happy about that myself, man," Chad said.

"But food had taste for you before, Bode?" Kramer asked.

Confusion creased Bode's face. "I . . . I *think* so?"

"Fascinating. Perhaps that's because you're a piece of Elizabeth and not cut from the same cloth as our Doyle here."

"Oh, shut up," Doyle said.

"For God's sake, stop thinking only of yourself, Doyle. Look at our world, how broken it is, how scrubbed of its features, its uniqueness. Look at *us*." With a curse, Kramer tore off his mask. "Look at *me*, my *face*," Kramer hissed. The purple bellies of exposed muscle quivered, and his naked left eye, without its lid, gleamed as milky-white as the Peculiar itself. "The monstrosity I've become. For whatever reason, *that . . . man*"—he shook the half-mask at McDermott—"that *monster* steals from us, and I would have it *back*. I would restore order, make us *whole*."

"Steals?" Doyle saw how Emma's mouth quivered. Her face was the color of the fog. "What does he take? How does that relate to *us*, to Elizabeth? Is it . . . *ohhh*," Emma breathed. *"Pieces."*

"Oh my God." Elizabeth gasped. "He's talking about energy transfer. It's probably why Kramer thinks releasing the doubles' energy bottled up in here"—Elizabeth put a fist to her chest—"will help."

"Because it will," Kramer said.

"Yeah," Emma said to Elizabeth. "Exactly. I mean, *look* at all of it."

"What are you two talking about?" Rima looked from the little girl to Elizabeth and back. "What do you mean, transferring . . ."

"The ripples. Why things waver down here. It's like that energy sink I told you about, Rima. The reason Elizabeth is important is because she's a container. Inside, there are all these different energy . . ." The girl looked to Elizabeth. "What's the word?"

"Signatures," Elizabeth said. "Energy signatures."

"Remarkable," Kramer mumbled, his blued nub of a tongue writhing over naked bone. With no nose, he had to hold his pan-ops like a pair of opera glasses. He looked at Black Widow. "You see this?"

"Yes." The woman had slipped on her pair. "It's . . . it's her and *all* of them together."

"It?" Meredith said. "Them?"

"What does she mean, Emma?" Rima said.

"The pieces," both girls said, and then the little girl went on:

"That's why Kramer and this other Meredith snatched us. I don't understand it, but Elizabeth's like . . . like a bottle, only she's got a bunch of different-colored beads all mixed up inside, which is why she's *here* in the hospital. Everyone's all rattling around inside, and it makes her kind of . . . you know." The little girl gestured toward her head.

"I think the word's *mad*." Doyle didn't recognize his own voice, or that dead tone. "Don't you know we all are here?"

Easy there, poppet.

"Kramer wants to take out all the energy signatures, all the beads that don't belong until she's only one color, *just* Elizabeth. Then, if he can do *that*, he figures he can build better, you know . . . *people* than those blank man-things." Emma looked at the older girl. "Right?"

I do believe she's got it, Black Dog said.

"Right." Elizabeth looked over at Doyle. "He wanted to see how much of you he could take away and what could be put back."

"He took it all," Doyle said, hoarsely. His hands bunched. He felt like weeping.

Oh now, darling. Not all. Black Dog gave him a long and sloppy doggy kiss. **I'm your true color, the blackness of your heart, with no artifice, no mask to obscure the monstrosity, and I will never leave you.**

"God, and how I wish you would," Doyle said, not caring who heard or what they thought. *An illusion; it's all been nothing but smoke and mirrors.*

"But I *can* put back, Doyle," Kramer said. "With the Mirror, anything is possible."

"You don't have that kind of power, Kramer," McDermott

said. "You never will." He looked at Black Widow. "It's the same for you. You came for me and Meredith? You only *thought* you crossed to a *Now*."

"What?" Meredith asked.

"Jesus," Elizabeth said.

"What?" Emma said to the older girl. "What's he . . ."

"But you didn't," McDermott said to Black Widow. "You can't. You won't ever have that ability."

"Indeed?" Black Widow's face was strained. "You forget who I *have*. I have you. I have your *wife*."

"No." McDermott gave a smile that was so sad, Doyle thought the man might weep, too. "Never. You've never had her. No one has, not even me."

"Frank?" Meredith looked frightened again. "*Frank?* What do you mean? What are you saying?"

"Please, Meredith, please remember this." McDermott smoothed hair from his wife's face. "I have loved you with all my heart. I have always loved you. I would give my soul to save you. I've tried so hard."

"Save me?" Meredith's eyes grew huge. "What are you *saying*?"

Oh shite. Doyle couldn't help but look to the bundles. *That's why she's—*

"Please, McDermott." To his surprise, Doyle saw the shine of tears on Kramer's face, dewing both flesh and raw muscle. "In God's name, *tell* me where the Mirror is and how to use it," the doctor said, holding out his hands like a supplicant. "Help us, please. Don't *leave* us to die in this blighted world."

"There's nothing I can do. I've already *told* you, Kramer." McDermott's shoulders slumped. "How many more times do

I have to say it? There *is* no Dickens Mirror here. There's only *the*—"

"Dickens Mirror. I *know*," Kramer said. "That's what you say—"

"And you're not hearing him," Elizabeth interrupted, though from her tone, Doyle thought the girl he *saw* might not be the one speaking, as if she had her own Black Dog that had taken control of her tongue. "He really means what he says, Kramer. Think about it a second, and then you'll get it. It's that little word, *the*. Makes all the difference." She looked at McDermott. "Victorian pastiche. That's what it's been called, because you were imitating a style, an era. That's it, isn't it? That's why things are the way they are here. This is like *Satan's Skin*."

"Yes," McDermott said. "That's exactly it."

"What?" Doyle looked from one to the other. "What's Satan's skin? A grimoire? A demonic parchment?"

"No. It's pieces," the girl said. "Pieces of a book."

DOYLE

Pastiche

"PIECES?" KRAMER'S LIDLESS eye bulged. "A book? A Victorian *pastiche*?"

"Yes. An imitation. That's what my Kramer called it," Elizabeth said.

Imitation. Doyle's head was hollow. *Like me. Just a bit character in a drama.*

"*Your* Kramer?" Kramer scowled. "I'm sure you're mistaken."

Elizabeth grunted a breathy laugh. "I wish. In my *Now*, you're just as obsessed with McDermott. You're still an asshole, too."

"You know about *Satan's Skin*?" Meredith said. "That's impossible."

"Well, I guess *not*. Considering that I *rewrote* part of *Satan's Skin* without knowing it, and that started this whole nightmare to begin with," Elizabeth said.

"But how do you *know* about it?" Meredith said. "It's only in manuscript form."

"Because I've read McDermott's books in my *Now*," Elizabeth said. "I saw a copy of a portion of that manuscript. We had this assignment to do a story in the style of Frank McDermott, and I ended up writing part of *Satan's Skin* without realizing it. Changed up a couple things, but my story was virtually identical. It also didn't end."

"That's right." Meredith gave a slow nod. "He never finished it. But it still doesn't explain how you know it."

"It's a really long story. I saw a . . . a *hint* in . . . well, the doctors said fugue states, but I call them *blinks*." Elizabeth waved that away. "Little side-trips to different *Nows*. Anyway, this one happened in the valley, the one they're all dreaming about? Yeah, yeah, I know." She put up a hand as Meredith opened her mouth. "They can't dream. He doesn't make them that way. But guess what, they obviously *can*, because *I* know about dreaming and *they've* all had the same nightmare. Now, maybe this London's Tony and Rima *wouldn't* have had the dream if the others hadn't lived through the valley, although if they're all connected and entangled on a quantum level or something . . ." She seemed to shake that off, too. "Doesn't matter what you call it. The point is, I *saw* a copy of a book in a series I'd never heard of called *The Dark Passages*."

"Yes, it was a projected series, but he got sidetracked and then decided he couldn't write it well enough. So it's all in . . ." Trailing off, Meredith searched her husband's face. He gave her back nothing, but he also didn't deny anything. "That book's in pieces, too," Meredith said to Elizabeth. "Notes, chapter fragments. Character sketches. Of course, it's disintegrating over time because of the ink and parchment he uses. But that book . . ." Meredith exhaled a laugh that was mostly air. "It's set in Bedlam."

"And you put all that away in a Peculiar?"

"No. Frank sent the pieces to . . ." Pressing the heel of a hand to her forehead, Meredith closed her eyes. "A vault in London. That's what he said. I believed him."

"Because I did," McDermott said. "I didn't lie about that."

"But you left yourself a back door, didn't you? So you could visit, play around, maybe swap out a character, or edit? Or maybe . . . Jesus." Elizabeth leveled a sudden, sharp look at McDermott. "It just hit me: what if you wanted a place to squirrel away stuff that had nothing to do with *anything* in that manuscript? Bits and scraps and pieces . . . Is *that* what we're talking about? That's why there are all these *pieces* inside Elizabeth? Jesus, you *made* Elizabeth this way on *purpose*. She's your own special Peculiar: a container for excess energy or whatever you grab from the Dark Passages, so you can still get at it." Wrenching her arms free of the blank, which didn't demonstrate an inclination to grab her again, Elizabeth glared at McDermott. "All this is exactly like *Satan's Skin*, isn't it? The key is . . . it's not *finished*. *That's* why this place is falling apart: because you never completed it, and now it's just rotting away."

"Oh God." Meredith hid her face in her hands. "Jesus, Frank."

"What?" Kramer rapped. "This is a *world*! It's a *Now*."

"No, it's not." Elizabeth never looked away from McDermott. "I'm right."

"Essentially." McDermott measured her with a glance. "Who am I talking to?"

"Take a wild guess," Elizabeth said.

"Emma?"

"Me?" The word came out as a high squeak. Doyle saw Rima put an arm around the little girl. "You mean, I'm *not* different?" Emma said. "I'm just like everyone else?"

"Oh no, you're very different," McDermott said. "Trust me on that, honey."

"Don't *honey* me." Turning, the girl buried her face in Rima's shoulder. "I don't know you. You're not my guardian."

"Emma," said Elizabeth . . . or was it another, older Emma residing in Elizabeth's body? An amalgam of both? *My God,* Doyle thought, *I'm actually getting used to this, and how much lunacy is that?* "It'll be okay," Elizabeth/Emma said. "I . . . we have an idea."

"We?" McDermott's eyes slitted. "Who are you talking about?"

"All of them. The shadows." Kramer sounded as broken as Weber's skull. "She can do it at will now. No struggle at all. Just that *glimmer.*"

"What about *my* Elizabeth?" Black Widow asked. She'd said so little, but then again, Doyle thought this was like screaming: eventually, even horror spun out to a certain numb resignation. "What's she to say in all this?"

"She's here." Elizabeth . . . Emma . . . seemed to turn inward a moment. "Right beside me. Elizabeth let us. We didn't force her, but it was the only way to save Bode. Actually, she's the one who figured out what Frank's doing, why he's left her this way."

"Frank." Meredith cupped a hand to her mouth as if afraid to let the rest out. "You bastard, you couldn't let Emma go, could you? You *had* to try, to see what would happen, even after I told you not to."

"What were you afraid of?" Elizabeth/Emma asked.

"You were too much, Emma," Meredith said. "Too much of the Dark Passages, too close to real. What I've never understood is *why*. *Why* try so hard? Why *keep* trying to make you work?"

"There might be a reason." Elizabeth/Emma looked at Black Widow, then back to Meredith. "I bet not *everything* this London's

Meredith says is wrong. You might be like Kramer, not letting yourself hear what she means."

"That's the second time you've said that." Kramer glowered. "Why?"

"No, Emma," McDermott said. "Elizabeth. Please. You don't have to do this."

"I don't have to . . . what?" Elizabeth/Emma said. "Lie? You mean, like you?"

"What in God's name is going on? McDermott, if the Dickens Mirror is here, where is it?" Kramer actually turned a circle. "And Satan's skin? What is that, a kind of parchment? What are you three going on about?"

"You've all got very selective hearing. I've told you." Elizabeth/Emma kept her eyes on McDermott. "We're going on about books. Books in pieces. Books *going* to pieces because of the ink he used to make sure they *would* die eventually. Books that exist in fragments and were never finished, like *Satan's Skin*. Like"— Elizabeth/Emma ran her gaze over the glowing rock before settling on Kramer—"like this place and the people here. Like you. That's why you're falling apart. That's why there's energy everywhere. You're a pot of water that's boiling itself dry, a fire burning itself out, going up in smoke. That's why the *fog* keeps getting worse."

"She's right." Black Widow looked to Kramer, who'd gone as chalky as the paint on his mask of tin. "I don't like it. But it fits."

"*What* fits?" Doyle thundered. He couldn't help himself, but they were all talking, talking, *talking* above him somehow, in their own private language, as if he didn't matter. "Can't you just *say* it?"

"Yes." Across the room, Meme—so quiet, so dutiful—was

the picture of dread. "What is she saying? What does she *mean?*"

"Yeah, go on, *Dad,*" Elizabeth/Emma said. "Cat's out of the bag now."

"You think you've got it all figured out, young lady." Anger made McDermott's voice shake. Color flooded his cheeks. "But believe me, you *don't.* This will cause more pain and heartache than you can imagine."

"I've lost everything"—and Doyle thought this was mainly Emma speaking now. "Eric's a shadow. Me, my essence . . . I'm stained by the whisper-man. I can't go back to my *Now,* can I? No, of course not. What I've built for myself would probably fall apart. It might be ruined already, like Rima's book-world. Funny, too, because I always figured this face was only a mask; that the monster underneath would show itself in the end. And now?" Her mouth moved in a crooked grimace. "It has. I'm *stuck* here, you asshole. So don't talk to me about pain. Tell them the truth. You already did. They just didn't hear what you really meant. Go on." Her face shuddered, and Doyle saw no glimmer this time, but tears spilling over her cheeks. "Don't be such a damned coward, Frank," she said.

Through the haze of his rage, Doyle had a clear thought: a coward *this* Emma was not. "Yes." He squared his shoulders. "Tell us, damn you, and devil take the rest."

Ah. Black Dog sounded as if it had found a meaty bone. **Of that, have no fear.**

For a second, Doyle thought that McDermott might still refuse, but then the other man let out a defeated sigh. "Fine." McDermott pulled himself straighter. "She's right. I said it, and I keep saying it. There is no Dickens Mirror, not the way you think of it."

"Of *course* there is." Red blotches stained the portion of Kramer's jaw that was flesh and blood. "You *use* it. How could I *know* about it otherwise?"

"Because of who and where you are. *The Dickens Mirror* is the title of a book I never finished," McDermott said. "And the reason you'll never find it, Kramer, is because you're living it."

EMMAS

Doll

1

THE POLICEMAN, THAT Doyle guy, went ballistic.

"You're saying ya come here, take what ya need, leave the rest to rot?" Doyle's accent was thick, full of rolled *r*'s and round vowels, like Indiana Jones's dad. Only he was screaming, waving his hands around and choking on his words, which seemed like they couldn't spill from his mouth fast enough. His face was redder than a beet and streaky with sweat. Emma thought he might even be crying. "Only some of us is more important, some worth the saving or caring about? Because I look around and I don't see another Doyle!" he shouted at McDermott. "*Why* is that? Because I'm a piece of scenery to move around like a tree or rock! I'm a blank, a nothing, someone you snatch 'cuz it's convenient? Who are you, who are *you*, to tell me my life is nothing?"

"*Doyle.*" It was that creepy, half-faced doctor guy, who hadn't bothered to put his mask back on. That little wormy nub of a tongue freaked her out. "Control yourself!"

"*Control?*" Doyle bellowed. "Oh, that's *rich* coming from you!

You been pulling my strings from the beginning, playing on my troubles, making *me* your sop! All very well for you, because you've your *mission*. Going to make everything *all* whole again, yeah? Fix your flipping face? Wave your arms, and the Peculiar vanishes? Well, I got a bulletin for you. You want to know just how *important* you are, who really matters?" Doyle was by those tables in two giant strides. Drawing a knife, he began ripping and hacking at burlap, which gave with a sound that reminded Emma of Sal tearing up Jasper's old underwear into rags. "I'll show you. He don't care about you. Take a good long look, and then you'll know just how much you *don't* matter to him!"

"Doyle, no, wait!" McDermott shouted. Balled fists to her mouth, Meredith was crying but with no sound and only big tears rolling down her cheeks. When McDermott tried to hug her, she pushed him away. "Kramer, please," McDermott said. "*Stop* him!"

"No." The crazy lady—the other Meredith—was white as cottage cheese. "I want to see. I need to know."

Kramer said nothing. Everyone else was only watching. Her face tight, Rima was holding Tony. When she saw Emma looking, she held out an arm. "It'll be all right," the older girl murmured as Emma slid close.

"What if they're rotters?" When someone hugged you like this, it was hard to believe bad things could happen, but Emma thought this wasn't over yet, not by a long shot. In the cell next to theirs, Chad had dragged the other Tony away from the bars. Across the room, Emma saw that Bode was standing now, a hand on Meme's arm. A finger of uneasiness tickled her neck at that, but then she felt eyes on her and shifted her gaze. Elizabeth— and the other Emma, along with whoever else was in there, and how freaky was *that?*—was watching *her*. As soon as she caught Emma's eye, the other girl moved her head in a tiny nod. Just a quick up-and-down.

Like . . . *be ready.*

Ready? Ready for what? Or maybe she was only imagining things, her eyes playing tricks because of the energy wobble.

Rima looked down at her with eyes that were clear now and not bleeding. "If they're rotters, then I guess we're done for."

"N-not yet." Tony's voice was barely a whisper. He raised a trembling hand to Rima's cheek, which had ceased eeling. "We . . . still have to f-find our farm . . ."

"On a high cliff, near the sea." Rima pressed her lips to his forehead. "In the sun."

I don't want to die. Eyes burning, Emma looked away. *I don't want anything to happen to Rima and Tony either.* For some reason, she again looked over at Elizabeth, trying to look behind that girl's face for the other Emma. She thought as hard as she could to that girl, *Tell me what to do, and I'll do it.*

"There! You look at *that!*" A rope of white spit hung from the policeman's mustache, and there was more lathered on his chin. Stepping back, Doyle aimed his knife, and Emma saw that he'd laid open two of the sacks and only started on the third. There was a big gaping hole over the chest, but either Doyle had thought better of it or decided the first two were enough. "You look at *them* and then you tell me just who in the hell matters here and what in God's name it *means!* Because *where* they going? Where do *they* belong?"

There was a moment's silence as everyone stared. Then McDermott let out a long moan and let his head fall forward until his chin touched his chest. His knees kept crimping like he was trying to fall, and he probably would've if he hadn't been hanging on to the bars.

"Dear God," Kramer said, very quietly. "They're breathing."

2

BOTH WERE GIRLS, without any clothes on at *all*, which would've bothered Emma any other time except this. The littlest one looked like she was in kindergarten or maybe first grade. Her hair was bright yellow like a sunflower, and her face was a heart, the chin delicate and fine but with baby fat still. She had very pink cheeks, and her lips were the color of spun cotton candy. Her eyes were closed.

The woman's face was a little square, but with high cheekbones and an angular jaw. Her hair, a rich, reddish chestnut brown, tumbled around her bare shoulders to curl over her breasts. What Emma noticed, right away, was how smooth her skin was: not milky white but tawny, as if she liked to spend time in the sun. No scars at all.

The bodies were Elizabeth, as a little girl . . . and Meredith.

There was a muttered *holy shit* from Chad. Both he and the other Tony had pulled themselves upright, the better to see, and Chad had threaded an arm around the other Tony's waist. They listed, leaning into one another. Across the way, Bode had an arm around Meme now, who'd covered her mouth with both hands. She looked like she wanted to puke. Kramer's face was half stony, half twitchy, those exposed muscles jumping. From his expression, Emma thought even Kramer was thrown for a loop.

Doyle's face was gray. His eyes were as buggy as a cartoon's, like Wile E. Coyote's after he'd just run off a cliff with a stick of dynamite in one hand: *Wuh?* He kept looking at the knife, like he couldn't understand how it had gotten there.

"Oh." Rima's hand tightened on Emma's shoulder, and it was only then that she realized she'd moved out of the other girl's protective embrace and closer to the bars. "McDermott made them *again*? Why?"

Actually, with Meredith, Emma thought she might know. *This book-fragment is all about an asylum. Kramer's a psychiatrist or something.* She bet the crazy lady, this London's Meredith, had been his patient. And, look, this other Meredith, the one who thought she was real, had been in a hospital and there were fresh cuts on her arms. *How many other Merediths are there?* Did they *all* do that eventually? Because you'd have to be brain-dead not to see it: McDermott was starting his family over again, from scratch, for . . . for a new book? Or another *Now*?

Gosh, what if for him, it's the same thing? What if he writes a new him, too? What if life in a book with his wife and kid is better than nothing at all?

Next to the new Meredith, the new little Elizabeth swallowed. Her lids twitched, then briefly flickered open. Someone in the room gasped; Emma didn't know who, because her gaze was riveted. The little girl's eyes were intensely, deeply blue, but there was nothing behind them. It was like she was a doll, or an android waiting for someone to download a program. Her lids slid down again, but not before Emma caught a glint of gold, and she knew that it was a birthmark . . . just like hers and the older, other Elizabeth's. The little sleeping girl let go of a long sigh, and her mouth made little sucking movements. If you didn't know better and with her eyes closed like that, you'd swear she was a baby having a dream about a nice warm bottle.

But why make Elizabeth a little kid again? She couldn't tell what the older version was thinking, but somehow Emma thought Elizabeth—the other Emma inside—had a hunch. *Maybe he thinks that if he starts from when she's younger, he'll get more time. That he can change other things, too, and then nothing bad will happen to either his kid or her mom.*

"What is this, Frank?" For a lady who had only just met an earlier version of herself (because that was who this London's Meredith had to be) and now gotten a peek of the copy that was supposed to take her place—*God, when she finally cuts in just the right way and deep enough?*—Emma thought Meredith sounded pretty calm. A little deadly even. "What have you done, Frank?" Meredith said. "What are you planning?"

"Isn't it *obvious*?" But the London Meredith's voice was a little breathless now, like someone had gotten her good, right in the stomach. "He's preparing to discard you as he did me. You've become obsolete, a drudge."

"No." McDermott reminded Emma of those pictures they showed of disaster victims when a monster twister's made matchsticks of their houses, or a guy who went out for a jug of milk and came back to find fire trucks and his family still inside, burned to a crisp. "Never. That's not . . . not what this is about. It's never been that."

"Then what *has* it been?" Meredith asked, still in that deadly, even voice that was starting to sound an awful lot like the crazy lady in black's. Emma kinda wished Meredith would go ballistic and get it over with. But maybe there was a limit to how much screaming a person could do, the same way you could be afraid for only so long before you had to deal. "Why have you done this? Why have you made them?"

McDermott gave her a long look with his disaster-victim eyes. When he did speak, he kept it short and sweet.

"Because she always gets sick. Elizabeth always dies," he said. "And then, my love . . . so do you."

EMMA

Escaping Destiny

HOLY SHIT. FROM her place behind Elizabeth's eyes, Emma watched McDermott, how calm he was now. Meredith too. He'd said it to Meredith in a Lizzie-*blink* when Meredith couldn't quite remember how much in love she and her husband once had been: *There's some spark, an essence I can't quite wrap my hands around and put where it belongs.* That essence was like Bode and tunnels, or Tony and his tentacled nightmares out of Lovecraft. *Just like me and my skull plates, the scars, this is the fundamental that holds constant in every version and cuts across* Nows: *Meredith always kills herself because Lizzie always dies. No matter what he tries, McDermott can't write any of that out.*

I've always been ill. In her head, at the mind's eye, Elizabeth sounded as worn out and defeated as McDermott looked. **Ever since I can remember.** The other girl paused, and Emma could almost hear the rustle of a hem on poured concrete as Elizabeth shifted. **Mother was always so melancholy, too.** Elizabeth gave a laugh with no humor in it at all. **That's why I've heard Mother, with you other pieces. He placed part of her here**

for safekeeping, too. Why else craft a new Meredith here?

That would make sense. But Emma bet McDermott wasn't the type of guy to put all his eggs in one basket either. Guy wrote a lot of books; there must be tons of notes, and she knew there were other unfinished manuscripts. Her Kramer had said so. She bet he visited other places. She'd just happened to land here.

"Well, now we know what he's been doing here," she said. It was internal, a thought directed at them all, but it felt better to imagine it as speech. "It's the free energy, here for the taking, and he doesn't have to worry about binding anything from the Dark Passages. He must know that if he reaches into the Dark Passages and binds those things too many times . . ."

She let that go, but she could supply the rest: do that too many times—or do it even once with something very powerful and hold on a second too long because every ounce of your being screams not to let go—and you ended up like her: stained. Nowhere to go.

I'm sorry. She felt Eric as a sigh along Elizabeth's neck. *I didn't mean to stain you. I thought I'd let go in time.*

"Don't, Eric. I don't feel sorry for myself. I'd do it again." *I would try to save you, no matter what.* Maybe she could understand McDermott after all. Eric felt so real, as if the longer they all spent time together, the more solid they became. Not that Eric would spring back to life or anything; that would never happen here. Maybe, in some other *Now,* an Eric would find an Emma, but it wouldn't be her.

Rima: *Wonder who's in the third sack.*

A new McDermott? Casey, a flicker.

A good guess, but she didn't think so. Size was all wrong.

Emma. Eric, again. *If we're going to do this, now's the time. While they're all focused on the bodies.*

He was right. She might never get a second chance. But God, she was scared. She didn't want to do this, not really, but she didn't see another way out. She couldn't go back to her old life. So it was either do nothing or this one last thing and hope for the best. *But I don't want to be* nothing*; I'm not ready to die.*

We don't know if that will happen. Eric felt so close. *But at least it'll be our choice. Better than waiting around for something else to make that decision for us.*

So you are really going through with this? She couldn't tell if Elizabeth was scared or skeptical. **And you'd do it voluntarily?** Elizabeth said.

"We can't stay here, inside you, forever," Emma said. Just the image of Kramer looming over her with a syringe made her flesh creep. "It's your best chance, too."

Perhaps. Elizabeth sounded thoughtful. But **I was made for** *this* **place. Perhaps there's no escaping destiny.**

"I don't believe that. I got out." So she might again, just in a different way. Sweeping her eyes around the room, Emma mapped out positions, mentally choreographing her moves. Bode and Meme were behind and off her left shoulder. Weber was slumped even further back, and the blanks had retreated to slots along the far wall. Frank and his Meredith of the moment were to her left; Rima, the Tonys, Chad, and Emma were the furthest away, in the last cell to her right. Between her and them were Kramer, London's Meredith, the examination tables, and Doyle.

And the cynosure's where Kramer left it. She snuck her eyes to the instrument on her right, within arm's reach. *Quick snatch and grab, nothing fancy.* After that—she slid a hand into her right skirt pocket and felt the keen steel scalpel, the one that Weber had stolen and which she'd swept up from her cell's mattress what seemed ages ago now—she had to hope the others were fast enough. If she was really lucky, she'd pass on a suggestion, too. She hoped it would stick. But she'd settle for getting little Emma out of here and letting the chips fall where they would. She couldn't control everything.

Do the best we can, Eric said. *Besides, you heard McDermott: you're in it. It should work.*

"Yeah." But *should* wasn't the same as *would*. There was little Emma, another wild card in all this. *Have to trust the cynosure knows what to do.*

There's no guarantee you'll be able to stay where you're going, if you even manage it. You might only make things worse, although—Elizabeth's tone took on a wry note—**difficult to imagine how that could be.**

"But maybe not. This place is in pieces. McDermott never finished. There's no coherent organizing principle, nothing that pulls it together or directs all this potential energy. But our Lizzie knows how to build *Nows*. So if *we* pull together . . ."

To write a nice story, make this world over?

"What other alternative is there? If we're right . . . Hey, look." Their interior exchange had lasted only a few seconds, and now Emma saw the constable, hands up as if warding something off, blunder back from the examination tables. "You see Doyle?"

Yeah. I don't think you're going to get a better shot. She felt Eric and the others gather themselves. *Get ready,* Eric said. *And Emma: I will hold you to my heart, across times . . .*

It was not and never had been her thought, but his, from that moment before they'd charged the whisper-man to try and rescue Casey and Rima. But Eric was in her, and she in him, and she knew the rest.

"To my heart, across times, Eric," she said. "To the death."

DOYLE

Creature

DEAR *GOD*, WHAT had he done? *I'm not a monster. I've never been cruel when it wasn't called for in kind.* Gasping, Doyle threw up his arms but couldn't blot out what lay on those tables. Core his eyes from their sockets with his black blade, and he'd still see them: fresh, unmarred flesh and yet that awful emptiness. *Like dolls.* His gaze flitted to the third bag, which he'd not torn open. Best to leave that.

No, *better*: get Meme out of here. He jerked his head around. With that bandage round his head, the boy, Bode, looked like a battlefield survivor, but it was Meme who tottered and Bode who slid an arm round the girl's waist. The sight was acid and ate at his eyes. No, *he* would save her, back slang it from here. They would start fresh, just him and Meme, and to hell with . . .

"So they're for you," Meredith was saying. Her voice was queer, a little dead already. "For when you start over. How many times, Frank? How many other copies of me are out there? Or do you only bop over to a nicer, less crazy Meredith in some other *Now*?"

"No," McDermott said. "It's not like that."

"Then what's it like?" Meredith asked in her dead-voice. "Tell me. I really—"

"Constable, what is in the third bag?" Everyone turned, though Doyle couldn't, not right away. "Constable?" Meme called again. "What's in it?"

Face her. Don't be the coward we all know you are, darling.

He did what Black Dog asked. Meme had taken a step away from Bode and now stood, uncertain, one hand outstretched toward Doyle but the other still lingering after as if tethered to the other boy by an invisible thread. "What . . . who is it? You must know, because you brought these here," Meme said. "Show us."

"Yes, Doyle." Kramer was still as a sphinx. "Do."

Black Widow stood, regal yet ashen, by the doctor's side, and for the first time, Doyle thought how much a pair they were. How they looked so like the McDermotts, come to think of it. Why, sculpt Kramer a new jaw and he might be a double at that. And why not? McDermott had peopled this fiction with other bits of his life. Why not a bizarre, broken, half-lunatic version of himself with the same obsessions and mad desires? It hit Doyle that if a man lost his wife, that *might* just feel as if a good half of him had been carved away, his innards gutted . . . and now here was Kramer, face eaten and in ruins, the loss plain as day: half man, half monster. Considering his own Black Dog, that did seem to be quite the theme, didn't it?

"Hasn't Doyle done enough?" A blank had more life in its voice than McDermott. "What's the point?"

"Because I want to know," Meredith, his wife of the moment

in whatever *Now* they inhabited, said. "I need to see this."

No, trust me. None of you needs this. But he'd no choice, did he? He felt Black Dog shuffle softly alongside as Doyle worked his blade into the slit he'd already started. This time, he worked the blade with care. He felt the supple glide of skin under his fingertips, the shudder of a heartbeat, the throb of a pulse along the neck. The head was swathed in light cotton, but loosely: a trick he'd learned when watching the undertaker do his pap. Then, too soon, he was done. Sack cut, wrappings laid aside.

It was at that last second, too, that it came together for Doyle. McDermott had returned, oh, who knew how many times to fashion these, over and over again. So Kramer must've seized a chance and stolen one, but without understanding exactly what came next. It also made so much more sense now why Kramer always said it in that most peculiar way of his: *my creature*.

It was also clear that Meredith was right. McDermott was obsessed.

But not only with his wife and daughter.

2

FIVE SECONDS AFTER Doyle flayed that sack, Meme began to scream.

But it was another ten before she snatched the knife.

EMMA

The Third Body

1

THEIR VIEW WAS blocked, so she couldn't see what—*who*—was in that third bag right away. But boy, she had a hunch, and before that policeman stepped back, Emma shot a glance at Elizabeth. Their eyes locked and Emma just *knew* the other girl was thinking the same thing. Emma turned to Rima. "You were right," she said.

"What?" Rima's brows folded. Her arms tightened around Tony, who was more awake now, so maybe Rima had drawn enough from him after all. "What do you mean?"

"When you looked through the glasses at Meme," Emma said, "and saw noth—"

That was when Meme started screaming, the sound like a spike. It was *that* loud. Beyond the cell, everyone was focused on that third body, and Meme. Bode kept trying to pull her back, but she fought, biting and kicking until he backed off.

"It is not right, it is not *fair!*" she shrieked. "This cannot be *right*! I am *not* a monster, I am *not!*"

The others jostled, like seagulls squabbling over a dead fish, and then Emma could see why Meme was freaking out.

The third body was *her*.
The third body was Emma.
The third body was Meme.

2

"MEME, I'M S-SORRY, so sorry!" Doyle, the policeman, was blubbering like a kid who knew he'd done something he couldn't take back, while, beyond, in the far cell, Meredith was shouting at McDermott: "You couldn't let her go, you couldn't let this die, could you? What were you *thinking*? A world built just for *her*? Your grand experiment? They're *things*, they're *creations*; you can't set them *loose*."

"And what are you?" McDermott roared. Snatching Meredith by the arms, he shook her hard. "I have been trying to set you free for *years*, across *times*, and still it's never enough! I can't save our daughter, and I can't save you from yourself!"

"Meme!" Doyle held out his arms as if he expected a hug and a kiss would make everything all better. "You're the last person I wish to harm!"

"But I am *not* a person! Can you not *see*?" Raging, mouth hanging open, she rounded on the creepy doctor. "What did you do, Kramer? Steal me from McDermott to see if you could breathe life into the clay of my body? Do better with me than you have accomplished with those . . . those *things*?"

Kramer said something, but Emma couldn't hear what. It was chaos; except for those android-like things and the guy with the lumpy head, everything was a swirl, the perfect gambit for an escape except for the stupid iron bars, and Emma was thinking, *If there was ever a time for Lara Croft*. Then there was a flicker, way off to her left, and she turned.

Elizabeth was moving, darting for a table. No one except her saw; they were all clustered around the tables and Meme, with their backs turned, and the blanks and messed-up Weber . . . well, they didn't count, probably couldn't think. Elizabeth made a running grab for the glass pendant. As soon as she touched it, the glass began to glister and glow, and Emma's heart gave a leap. *It works for her, it works for* her*!*

She scrambled to her feet. By her side, Rima started, called her name, but Emma was already flying across the cell. She dropped to her knees as the older girl dashed up. "What, *what*?" she asked.

"Here," the other girl said, though her voice had a weird hum that reminded Emma of when Superior really got going right before a big storm and the wind grabbed the windows and made them *brrrr*. Elizabeth thrust the necklace through the bars. "Put this on, and don't take it off!"

"Okay?" It came out as a question. This was not what she expected. Keys to unlock the cell—that would be good. Or a gun, a knife, *something*. But a necklace? Still, she slipped it on. To her, the chain looked like something soldiers used for dog tags, and those scraps of metal . . . was there writing on them? "But I don't know . . . ," she began, and then realized that the glass hadn't stopped glowing. There was something else happening, too, right between her eyes, under her lacy skull plate: the thump and throb of a new, fresh headache. *Like I had right before crazy London Meredith showed up in my window at home.* The same she'd felt when the secret door opened down cellar.

"Listen to me. There's only time to say this once." Elizabeth was talking low and fast. "When I say go, you *go,* understand?"

"G-go?" Emma felt Rima come up and drop alongside. "Go where?" she asked.

"It'll be obvious." Elizabeth flicked a quick glance over her shoulder. Following her gaze, Emma saw that none of the adults were paying any attention. Meme was shrieking; the McDermotts were shouting at each other; Doyle was screaming again. Lots of noise and plenty to distract them. By now, Chad had scurried over, half-dragging the other Tony. "But if this works," Elizabeth said, "you have to go right away. Don't look back, don't hesitate."

"If what works? What are you going to do?" Chad asked.

"Get you out." The older girl drilled Emma with a look. "When the time comes, you grab *only* the other Tony and Chad, you hear me?"

"What?" She heard the high squeak in her voice. "I can't leave Rima and—"

"No," Rima said. "She's right, Emma. We have to stay, Tony and I. This is where we belong, but not you." To Elizabeth: "You're Emma now?"

"Mostly, but we're all here," the other girl said. "Elizabeth, too, and she'll still be here when this is done."

"Done." Emma stared. "What do you mean, done? Why aren't *you* coming? Where am I *going*?"

"Don't let her scream, Rima." Elizabeth grabbed Emma's wrist. "Honey," Elizabeth said as, a second too late, Emma saw a flash of steel, "you're going home."

3

IF RIMA HADN'T slapped a hand over her mouth, Emma would've yelled plenty good and loud. The scalpel sliced a bright red ribbon on her palm, the pain like the thin line of a hot laser. Cheeks ballooning, she was still blowing the trapped ball of a scream when that steel flashed again as Elizabeth—the other Emma—cut herself, then slammed their bleeding palms together.

The sensation was an explosion, a black, icy rocket blasting through her body, racing from her toes to shatter through the top of her skull. Emma's vision reddened. Orange spangles bloomed, and there was a rushing, almost metallic clatter in her ears, like hundreds of birds snapping their beaks at once. Her body went limp. She might even have passed out a split second.

"Hurry." It was Rima, bracing her up. "Hurry, Elizabeth, now!"

"Blood of My Blood," Elizabeth said. A dark red rivulet was threading from one nostril. "I bind you. Breath of My Breath, I invite you, I take you . . ."

Emma was having trouble breathing. There was a cold hand in her chest, working its fingers up her throat and down into her lungs, reaching around to cup and squeeze her heart. Another, very thin, slipped into her head; she could feel it walking her brain, picking its way across crevices and crooks before finding one very dark, very deep slit and worming its way in.

"Together, we are one and there are the Dark Passages and . . . and . . . that's enough, Emma!" Grimacing, Elizabeth threw her head back as her face glimmered, the features rippling and shifting, now a boy, now a half-girl, now a scaled creature with a silver swirl for an eye. "That's enough, Emma," Elizabeth growled, her voice a good octave lower. "Don't hang on too long. She only needs a suggestion. Now, let her go, let her *go*, let her . . ."

"Stop!" Rima wrenched their hands apart. "That's *enough*!"

The icy fist gripping her heart melted away in an instant.

That weird sense of a finger stirring and poking the meat of her brain eased, though it wasn't quite . . . *gone.* It stuck there, the way a shred of pot roast got between her teeth, and she could feel a mental tongue sneak to worry it. In Elizabeth's eyes, Emma saw the gold birthmark flare with rage and hunger, and Emma had the sick feeling she was the bunny and that was the wild animal out there ready to eat her alive.

"Sorry. Right." Elizabeth glanced askance and Emma wasn't sure the other girl was even talking to them. When she looked back, her eyes had cleared. She reached through the bars. "Rima, let me . . ." As the other girl hesitated, she said, "You saw Weber. My blood heals. It will *help.*"

"All right. Do it . . . *ah!*" Rima stiffened as Elizabeth pressed her bleeding hand against an open wound on Rima's forearm. The contact was brief, no more than a second, but Emma saw Rima's head rock back and then her eyes widen. "God, what . . ."

"Save Tony." Elizabeth surged to her feet. "And make sure Emma goes, Rima."

4

FIFTEEN SECONDS GONE.

Fifteen before Meme.

ELIZABETH

The Moment Electric

YES, YES, YES! She didn't know if that was her or Emma's voice, but it didn't matter because this was what she wanted, perhaps was even why she'd been created. Blood singing, Elizabeth lunged for the blank rock wall immediately to her left. Her palm was still bleeding, but already the muscles were wriggling, the edges of her skin worming and sewing themselves together. Her arms writhed, and as waves of energy swirled, she felt the hard ridges and lumpy pillows of her many scars begin to soften and disappear. They were all there now, the many pieces perched at the front of her mind, clamoring for release, and none stronger than Emma and her shadows. The pull was immense, this imperative to let go a tidal surge.

Go! Slamming the rock with her hands, she cried out, the moment electric, her back arching. At once, she felt them streaming from her fingertips, all the pieces gushing like high water loosed from a dam. Her pulse was thundering, her heart smashing her ribs, and she thought the rest, gathered round the bodies, were still screaming, and Meme loudest of all: "No, no, *no*, I will not *let* you!" The inside of her skull ached with a lancing pain that shot from her forehead to the top of her spine, and yet her consciousness ballooned, that mind's eye widening like a pupil until all that remained was a huge expanse: like a night sky with no stars. Her mind was clearing, the cobwebs tearing apart, as if someone had finally decided to sweep back a pair of heavy curtains, open the windows, and let in light and fresh air.

And she thought, *Go, Emma, go! Hurry!*

No reply. Although she didn't think the girl was completely gone. She might never be, if it was true that every essence—a *whisper*, as Rima would've called it—left its mark.

But she got her answer when, around her, the cavern groaned. Stone bucked and heaved under her feet, but unlike the quakes, there was no loud crack or bang of stressed rock giving way. This was like riding heavy swells in a sleek kayak.

Kayak. That must be an Emma-thought. *Because I don't know how that feels, or what a kayak is. I've never seen the sea.* Under her hands, the rock was shimmering, the ripples spreading wider and wider in a mirror image of that mind's eye, and it was happening fast, within seconds: the stone smoothing, growing glassy and black.

Almost there. It was Emma, a remnant anyway, still with her. *Elizabeth, when the Mirror opens, you have to get out of the way fast. If you're pulled in . . .*

"Don't worry about me," she said. "Only say when."

Just a few more . . . The black-mirror rock suddenly seethed, and then she felt the give under her hands. *Way's opening,* Emma said. *The cynosure ought to . . .*

A roar: "What are you *doing*?"

EMMA

Following the Light

1

"**WHAT ARE YOU** *doing?*"

It was a guy's voice, that doctor. Emma tore her eyes from
Elizabeth, still hunched over that churning rock that was going
mirror-smooth, and looked across to the others, still gathered
around the bodies. Meme was screeching like someone was ripping out her heart. Crap, *she'd* feel the same way if she saw herself
all laid out like an empty-eyed Barbie.

Kicking free from Bode, Meme lunged at Doyle. Crying out,
the constable stumbled away from the examination tables and
threw up his hands (maybe he thought she was going to scratch
his eyes out or something), and that was when Meme got her
hands on that knife. Snatching it free, Meme let out another of
those crazy, ripping shrieks and dashed for the bodies.

That's when everyone over there went nuts.

"Meme!" Bode shouted. "Meme, don't!" And Kramer was
bawling, "No! Stop her! Don't let her . . ." The London Meredith
only stared, stunned, with disaster-victim eyes, but in her cage,

the other Meredith was screaming, maybe for both of them: "No, no, not my little girl, *please!*"

"Meme, *no!*" It was McDermott, pressed up to the bars. "I can help you, but please, *please* don't ruin them! Not when I'm so close, not when I think I've found how to make things right!"

"No, no, nothing makes this *right!*" Meme snarled. "It is their fate, their destiny to *die*, and who are you to play *God?*" Rearing, she plunged Doyle's dagger down in a hard, fast stab—and straight into the smallest body: little Lizzie.

"AAAHHH!" Meredith wailed as the knife sank all the way up to the hilt. Lizzie's eyes jammed wide open, and her cherry-red mouth widened in a soundless scream, like that weird painting of the guy on the bridge against an angry, churning sky.

"Noooo!" Meredith was practically clawing her eyes out. "Stop, stop! Don't hurt my baby!"

Too late for that, Emma thought. Blood boiled, spreading in a slick red lake over the little girl's belly before leaking down the sides. Little Lizzie—although she really wasn't yet, was she?—flopped and jerked and looked so much like a hooked salmon flip-flapping on the deck of Jasper's boat, Emma wished she had a club or something to put the poor thing out of its misery.

"Don't!" McDermott shouted again. "Meme, stop! Not my baby, not my *child!*"

"She is *nobody's* child, as I am not," Meme shouted. On its table, little Lizzie's mouth still hung in that silent shriek, but what feeble light there'd been in those doll's eyes fled as fast as blowing out a birthday candle. "She is no more *real* than I!"

"Meme!" Bode grabbed at her arm, but Meme wrenched

free, then brought the blade around in a whickering, backhanded arc. Bode jumped out of the way just in time as the knife flashed down again.

"You are not *me*!" Meme slashed at the third body—the empty doll of a person that had Meme's face. The skin over its cheeks and forehead, across its eyes, opened in wide, gaping, spurting red slashes. "You are *not*!"

"Kid!" Emma jerked back around to see Chad's eyes bugging from their sockets. He'd draped the other Tony over his shoulders in a fireman's carry, like soldiers did when they got a wounded buddy out. "Holy shit, kid, look at the bars, look at the *bars*!"

She did, and her heart gave a huge kick in her chest. Their iron cells were dissolving, just like a special effect. She could see straight through, and in another second or so, there wouldn't be any bars there at all. The whole room was like that, going molten as lava and shifting, and it was so *fast*. With every ripple, she felt the ground surge up and then sink as if she were on the deck of Jasper's boat or a floating dock. The stone was like that, too, going as glassy as the surface of the big lake, and she thought, *That's Emma and the others.*

Her cut hand still tingled, and she could taste the quicksilver sparkle of an icy essence on her tongue. Her brain had turned into one giant Van de Graaff, arcing with electricity. At every pulse, she felt the cynosure's heat, like something radioactive. It was so bright she had to squint.

"Be ready!" Craning over her near shoulder, Elizabeth shouted, "As soon as the bars are gone, grab Chad's hand and think of *home*, Emma, think of *down* . . ."

2

ELIZABETH NEVER SAW what came for her next. Neither did Emma, so focused on the evanescing bars and *home*. As soon as Emma thought that, the cynosure seemed to *crackle* with new life. All at once, a searing beam of light shot from it, unspooling in a ribbon, and Emma just had time to think that Einstein *was* right: light could be solid. She was staring, dumbfounded, and then Chad was shouting and pointing as the bars vanished—and *that's* when she finally caught, from the corner of her eye, a ferocious flurry that was *not* this room reshaping itself.

And Emma heard Bode: *"NO!"*

"Elizabeth!" From her place beside her, Rima started to her feet and shouted, "Elizabeth, behind—"

Whatever Rima said next was lost when Elizabeth let out a sudden, agonized shriek.

Because that was when Meme stabbed her.

3

THE DAGGER SLICED into Elizabeth's back, close to her spine. Arching, Elizabeth screamed again as, across the room, the London Meredith finally came out of her stupor and shouted, "No, no, no, *please!*"

Meme paid no attention. She was snarling and grinning like something feral and pretty crazy. Teeth bared, she drove deeper, harder, *twisting* the hilt, and this time, when Elizabeth opened her mouth, a gout of blood boiled onto her lips and chin like water from a bubbler.

At that, the room *bellowed*. The sound was enormous, deafening, a howl that reverberated and swelled and overlapped on itself in a shuddering chorus, as if some prehistoric giants had suddenly awakened. Along the wall, Emma saw that the blanks' faces had split; they were nothing but mouths and teeth all lowing the same note. Even Weber was moaning.

It's them. Emma cast a wondering look straight up at the seething whirl that had once been rock. She wasn't *quite* sure, but she could've sworn that, for just a second, there were faces up there and all of them were shrieking. The room shuddered. *It's Emma and the shadows and everyone else.*

Not ten feet away, Elizabeth tottered, her now-deadening weight dragging her and Meme toward the Mirror's edge. Before them, the glassy rock dilated and trembled. Emma thought that one step in the wrong direction, they'd both fall in and be gone, like getting sucked past the event horizon of a black hole.

Please. Emma aimed a look up again at the faces that might be only her imagination. *Help her!* Could they, or Rima? She didn't know, and there was no more time. Dangling from its chain around her neck, the cynosure's bolt of light arrowed straight through and into the Mirror, scorching a path.

"What are you doing, Meme?" Bode was there now, screaming. "What have you *done*?" Hooking his hands around her elbows, he yanked the other girl away. As soon as Meme let go, Elizabeth rocked back, blundering on her heels. Her knees gave. She sagged, knife still in her back and so deep that Emma could see the hilt ticking with her pulse. She sank onto her side in a widening crimson pool. There was blood everywhere, and the room was still howling.

"Stop them! Don't let them through!" Jerking her head to the left, she saw Kramer and the London Meredith now, maybe twenty feet away. They would be here in three seconds flat. "The girl's got the cynosure!" Kramer cried.

"*Go*, Emma!" Rima was on her feet, Tony's arm draped over her neck. "Run now, *run now!*"

"Come on, kid!" Still bowed under the other Tony's weight, Chad was lunging in an awkward bounding leap for the Mirror. "*Move!*"

"Wait! *Jack!*" Sweeping up her cat, she turned and dashed for the rock—a second too late.

"No!" It was Kramer, and she and Chad both faltered, turning a last glance. His ruined face loomed, the one lidless eye bright as a headlamp. His hands clawed and shot out for a grab. "Give me the *cynosure*," he foamed. "I *want* . . ."

Gasping, she whirled. Kramer's hands whisked through her long hair, and she cried out, but then Bode hurled himself into the doctor, and the two of them crashed to the bucking, heaving rock in a tangle of legs and thrashing arms. Behind, she heard the London Meredith keening, and then she stopped worrying about what was behind and focused only on what lay ahead and what she had to do.

"Grab my hand!" she shouted, leaping for Chad, who waited at the Mirror's lip. As soon as they touched, her vision seemed to erupt in a fan of colors, but it was gold and cobalt that were the brightest of them all: two threads racing down her arm to lace round their joined hands and cinch them tight.

"GO, EMMA!" It was McDermott, somewhere behind all that. "*Don't look back, honey! GO-GO-GO-GO-GO!*"

Put us all where we belong. Take me home. And then, something she didn't understand and that might not have been entirely her thought: *Take me back BEFORE . . .*

Hurtling for the Mirror, Emma plunged into the dark, following the light.

RIMA

Into the Abyss

AND LIKE THAT, they were gone. Standing with Tony, supporting his weight, Rima watched as the cynosure's light lanced through black-mirror rock. The surface, dark as tar, went molten and then swallowed them up like a thick pool of lime: the little girl and her cat, Chad, and the other Tony.

"No!" Thrashing free of Bode, Kramer staggered toward the Mirror. He nearly tripped over this London's Meredith, on her knees by Elizabeth. A short distance away, hair wild and all eyes, Meme stood, hands slack by her side, her fury spent. "Get up!" Kramer wrestled this London's Meredith to her feet. "Take us, *take* us!"

"I don't have the cynosure." This Meredith's tone was dead. Elizabeth's blood had soaked into her skirt, turning it a queer shade of purple very like her glasses. "I can't follow, not through the Mirror. I'll never find her again."

"Haven't you been paying attention to all that's transpired?" Spittle foamed through the ravaged flesh of Kramer's jaw. "You found McDermott and *that* Meredith because he let that copy of you dream! That little girl, *that* Emma, dreams as well! All you need do is use the Peculiar as you have before. Find her through her dreams, and we get her back!"

"But the Emma that bound them all together is *here* now." This London's Meredith raised her eyes to the rock. "The tie's broken. *You've* not been listening. They're not the same girl anymore. They were only the same girl at the pivot point where I found her. The cynosure *works* for her now, which means that whether she knows it or not, she carries the power to launch her life down a different path."

"Stop this!" Kramer pointed at the still-glimmering Mirror. "We need to go, and we need to go now while the way's open!"

"Doctor, take me with you, *please*." Hair dragging round her face, Meme caught at Kramer's arm. The girl's hands were slick with gore. "I belong to you! Have you not always said?"

"*You?*" Kramer jerked his arm free. "You're filth, a creature, fit for nothing."

"No, *please*," and then she cried out and clasped a hand to a suddenly flaming cheek.

"Stop!" Bode was struggling to his feet. He looked as if he'd plunged into a tub of bright red paint. "Don't hit her, *don't*!"

"But Doctor," Meme began.

"Did you not hear?" Grabbing Meme by the throat, Kramer drew back his hand for another blow. "Are you not *listening*?"

"She may not be," said this London's Meredith, "but I am." With a sudden wild shout, she spread her arms and barreled into them both.

"What are you *doing*?" Staggering, Kramer reeled, Meme still in his grasp, and both wrapped up in the woman's iron grasp. "Are you *mad*, woman?" he screamed. His free hand shot for a handhold—

And he made it. He did. Rima saw the instant his fingers found purchase on rock and hooked. He had a grip; the tendons on the back of his hand strained and went taut. He had saved himself, and Meme.

But then . . . the rock pulled back.

2

SHE WATCHED IT happen: how the stone knob shrank, withdrawing into itself, retreating like a tortoise, to leave Kramer with thin air, and nothing to stop his fall.

"Rima?" She heard the note of wonder in Tony's voice. "Did you . . . ?"

"Yes. It's them." She raised her eyes to the churning rock above. "It's Emma."

"No!" Bode started for Kramer and the others. He was big and strong and they were still within reach, so he ought to have made it to them in time. But all of a sudden, he stumbled, and Rima saw a stony knuckle on the floor that had not been there a fraction of a second before—and knew that Emma had saved him.

Sweeping forward, this London's Meredith propelled Kramer and Meme with the force of an inexorable tide. She drove them all past the edge, and into the abyss.

In an instant, the mirrored surface stilled. Although she was a good fifteen feet away, Rima saw how it coalesced and hardened to a surface as obdurate as cast iron.

The way was closed.

The Mirror was gone.

RIMA

The Way

1

"RIMA." TONY'S VOICE was husky, cracked with pain. To her relief, however, his face had smoothed and his bleeding had diminished. The shadow-Emma had been right: her blood healed. "Can you help Elizabeth?" Tony asked.

"I could try," she began, but the room gave a convulsive shudder, a bump that made her stumble. There was a sharp crack and then a sound like a rush of water over a falls as a shower of rock came cascading down the walls—and she thought, *Maybe not.* This was different; was the cave breaking up now? Another hard bang, a pop, and now a spray of debris shot out in a stony geyser from the far wall. From above, there was an odd groan that was different from the bellow that had sounded when Elizabeth was stabbed. A moment later, she felt stone patter her hair and arms and heard it rattle along the floor.

"What's going . . ." Shielding her eyes against another rain of scree, she looked up and then gasped. "Oh my God. Tony, look up, look at the ceiling!"

"It's coming down," he said. "It's not just breaking apart. It's actually . . ."

"Lowering. I know." *We'll be buried alive, entombed here like insects in amber.* "Come on, lean on me," she said, draping one of Tony's arms around her neck to take some of his weight. "There's nothing more we can do." *Or that the shadows will allow. Perhaps Elizabeth truly belongs to and with them now.* "We need to go."

"How? Where? Kramer came from over there, but . . ." With his free arm, Tony pointed toward the far wall, past the examination tables and on the other side near where the McDermotts' cell had been. "Look."

"I see it," she said grimly. The cave was still heaving and falling, the walls ebbing and flowing, but the ceiling was starting to come down as the space contracted. *Sealing itself off.* As she watched, a span of rock immediately behind the man-blanks elongated. Two molten lips opened and then closed around the blanks and Weber.

"God!" Tony said. "Did it just *absorb* them?"

"I think so." She saw the McDermotts, arms clasped round one another, huddling near the one intact body, that new Meredith, but they were making no moves to get out. *Maybe he knows a way and is waiting for the right time? Elizabeth . . . the other Emma . . . said he used a back door.* But that was probably only useful for the McDermotts, not them. From what she understood, and that was precious little, she, Tony, and Bode either couldn't pass through or might only end up like Kramer and this London's Meredith and Meme: adrift in a dark limbo. Or perhaps this was where the McDermotts would stay, in this rocky tomb. Somehow she didn't believe McDermott would, or that the shadows would stop them if they tried to leave. This was a man who made and remade those he loved. If he'd wanted to die with them, he could have, many times over. Perhaps, a version of himself already had—and would again. When you couldn't save the woman you loved or your child, maybe a piece of the heart died, too.

Emma, come on, help us. Show us the way. Blinking against another hail of stone, she eyed the lowering ceiling, the crinkling walls that were beginning to collapse in on themselves in fanlike folds. *You can't have done all this only to let us die here.*

"Rima!" Tony was staring behind them. "Look!"

She turned in time to see the rock part just wide enough for them to pass through. The way was dark, like a long throat. If there was an end, she couldn't see it.

"Where do you think it goes?" Tony asked, then gasped as the floor turned a slow roll, as if nudging them forward. "What the blazes?"

Right, Emma, I hear you. This is the way to whatever future awaits. Her gaze fell to Bode, who was still where he'd fallen, on his knees by Elizabeth's body. "Bode, get up. Let's go."

"What for?" Bode's face held a stunned look, and the hopelessness in his eyes scared her a little. Using the side of a hand, he brushed a fall of Elizabeth's hair from a cheek. She'd lost so much blood that her skin had gone glassy and nearly transparent. Her half-open eyes were already glazing. Bode looked up at them. "First Meme and now . . . I was supposed to protect Elizabeth. That's what I was to do and . . ."

"And so now what? You're to die as penance?" The brutal edge surprised her. "*We* still have a chance. Elizabeth gave it to us then, just as Emma and her shadows are now." She jerked her head toward the mouth of the tunnel, still patiently waiting. *But not for much longer.* Another splintery smash as rock shattered, and she thought, *Only a few more minutes and there'll be nothing left here, no space at all.* What was above them now? *Doesn't matter.* "Stop feeling sorry for yourself and get up!"

For a split second, she thought he would argue; do something incredibly stupid, like wave them on and then lie down and wait for the rock to smother him. *No, Emma, you wouldn't let that happen, would you?* No answering bump of reassurance this time.

"Right," she said as Bode pushed to his feet. "Let's . . ."

"Wait!" It was Doyle. She'd completely forgotten about him, but now she saw the constable pulling himself up from where he cowered in a corner not far from the examination tables. His uniform was undone, the coat hanging open, and most of the buttons missing. His hair was a fifteen puzzle of corkscrews, as if he'd been trying to tear it out by the roots. Like Bode, he was awash in gore, much of it on his face, so his eyes started from a mask of red. "Take me with you!" He began clawing his way around rubble. The floor was strewn now with boulders. "Don't leave me here!"

"Then come on!" Tony shouted. "Hurry!"

"Yes. Coming! Don't—" Doyle yelped as the floor suddenly shifted. A huge crack sketched itself over the rock, and then widened in a crooked black smile. Crying out, Doyle flung himself forward as the stony slab tilted, and then all of a sudden, the man was looking at them across a gap too wide to jump. *"No!"* Bawling, he looked to the lowering ceiling. "It's not fair! What did I do? I only done what I was asked! I was only . . ."

"You kids!" McDermott was standing now, an arm about his wife, as more debris showered down. "Rima, *go!* Don't you see? She's giving you a way, but you have to be brave enough to take it! Go on, all of you, and live your lives!"

Live our lives? As rats? And a way to where? To what?

"No!" Doyle cried again. Beyond, two of the examination

tables had toppled. The bloodied bodies of the new Meme and the little girl were limp as cast-off rag dolls. "What about me, what about *me*?"

"Come on." Bode had taken Tony from her, but now he stretched out a hand and gave her wrist a gentle tug. "It's a chance, chuckaboo. Let's take it."

At the tunnel's mouth, she paused for a last look, sweeping her eyes right to left, and frowned. Elizabeth's body had vanished, and her blood, too. Absorbed like the blanks? Across that chasm, Doyle was still shouting and shaking his fist. *Emma, why not let Doyle come with us?* There was no reply, no surge in the rock, but she wondered if, like Meme, Doyle was a creature of this place, with no part to play in whatever future awaited—and so here he must remain.

And what about the McDermotts? *Emma, don't try to stop them going. Whatever his reasons, McDermott's our creator, our father. You can't blame him for trying to cheat death.*

It was then that, beyond and at the limits of this dwindling space, she thought she saw something . . . dimple. Was it the air? The rock? For some reason, she was reminded of the moment the Peculiar spat first that cat and then little Emma out onto the snow and into the tangle of their lives, where perhaps she'd been a thread all along. She thought about the rock and how it had absorbed the blanks, Weber. Elizabeth, too, folding the girl into its embrace.

That was when she realized: the McDermotts were gone.

Back door. A huge wave of relief coursed through her. *They took it.* Or Emma and the shadows let them. Either way, it amounted to the same thing. But to where?

And what of *them* now?

"Rima!" It was Bode, his voice echoing down the tunnel's throat. "Come on!"

Now the floor *did* bump, just the once, its meaning clear: *Go.*

Right. Turning away from what was left of Bedlam, she followed, as Doyle's screams chased after.

2

SOMETIME LATER, AFTER they'd walked and jogged five hours or five seconds—there was no telling—Rima thought she saw a fiery glister of milky light far in the distance.

"Oi." Pulling up short, Bode cocked his head. "You hear that? That . . . sound?"

She did, and it was really two sounds: a barely discernible *thump* . . . a pause . . . and then a *boom*.

"You know what it reminds me of?" Strong enough now to stand on his own, Tony took a few steps forward. "When the Thames runs high. The way it slaps the abutments. Got the same rhythm."

"Oh, *wonderful*," Bode said. "We're probably running in an old sewage tunnel, along with the rest of the offal. Either that or we're about to hit an underground river."

Somehow she doubted Emma would do that to them. "But there's *light*," Rima said, and then she sniffed. "Is that . . . do you smell *salt*?"

DOYLE

Back to the Future

1

"GODDAMN IT, GOD*DAMN* it!" Frothing, Doyle watched as those accursed rats disappeared only for the tunnel to pucker in on itself and vanish. McDermott was gone, too, and his wife. There one second, then *poof!* He noticed McDermott had left the body of his new Meredith behind, too, like so much rubbish destined for a dustheap.

Oh, but you'll just make yourself another, won't you? If not here, then you'll dip your nice sharp nib somewhere new. Doyle knew: once a sneak, always a sneak. Breaking the rules the first time was the hard part. After that, you could justify anything.

"What about *me*? I'm not so bad." All right, all right, maybe it was one thing to try and cheat fate; when your daughter withered no matter how hard you worked, and your wife always went mad on a road to self-destruction. Maybe what McDermott had done wasn't so monstrous. Oh, but what about Meme? What had *that* been about? He'd been fashioning Emma at various ages, in different ways? What was it about Emma that McDermott couldn't give up?

"I don't bloody *care!*" he shouted. "I am *not* a monster. Everything I did, I *had* to. What did I ever do to you?" Another shower of debris raised a cloud of dust, and he began to cough. Rocks nipped his cheeks. One particularly large stone, big as his fist, bulleted onto the back of his neck and nearly knocked him flat. He felt the shock of it all the way through to his chest. The ceiling was now so low that in another few moments, he'd be able to clamber up on a table and touch it. God, if he'd only hung on to his black blade, he could slit his throat. Better that than to be ground to paste.

Wait. He snuck a hand into his coat. His fingers slid over metal, and then he was drawing out his Webley. *One bullet. That'd be all it would take.* His hand was shaking. He was afraid to thread his finger through the trigger guard for fear the gun would go off. But this was a way out. The mouth would be best. Blow out the back of his skull. Over in an instant. At the last second, he could be master of himself. *But maybe not yet.*

"Come on. You helped the kids, that McDermott. You helped everyone but me. Why? What, you going to squash me flat?" he croaked. "I *saved* you." Though he had no earthly idea who he was really talking to, or if that balanced out the fact that he'd killed Battle and, well, done so much more. For all he knew, whatever had invaded this place had turned it over to new management, maybe even the devil.

That was when he realized. "Black Dog?" He turned a complete circle. "Where are you?" He went so far as to push up his sleeve. The death hound's maddened gaze stared back, but it was only strange ink and didn't answer. "God*damn* you, where did you . . ."

Here. It was a growl at his back. He spun round, and then a cry of joy rocketed from his mouth. There, across the way, not ten feet distant, he saw two fiery eyes peering out from the ebony maw of a tunnel. **Come, poppet. This is the way.**

He started forward, a single step, then stopped. There was something here he didn't quite like, but it was like having to choose between a needle or going without, wasn't it?

Crouching, he bounded for the tunnel, only just ducking inside as the ceiling behind slammed down. It was like watching a giant eye close. Now he was completely in the dark. Standing there, nerves vibrating, he listened to rock settling around this space. *I've no guarantee this is a way out. Maybe it's not a tunnel at all.* Maybe it was only a room, or a short open seam that would eventually close down to a narrow slit the deeper and farther he went. How thin, through what width, could a man wriggle? Worms did it. So did squirmers. God, the image of him as an infection threading beneath the skin of the earth sent shivers racing up and down his spine.

"Black Dog," he whispered. Silly not to use his full voice, but his heart was knocking so hard he felt the pulse in his teeth. His eyes strained for those telltale glowing slits. This wasn't like the death hound. It never led . . . well, except with the hag. It always slunk behind, nipping at his heels, the monkey on his back—like the needles, the pints, the pipes. "Black Dog?"

This way. To his left. He looked but saw nothing. Then he felt a tiny nip at his bum. **Go. You want to stay here until you become wizened as a mummy?**

"But I can't see. What am I supposed to do, feel around in the dark?" But then he remembered: *match safe.* He always carried one for his bull's-eye. Patting around in his trouser pocket, he drew out the rattling metal case, tweezed out a match, then ran it over the ridged striker. The match caught with a spit of phosphorus and a stink of sulfur, and he thought, *God, I smelled that.*

"Oh, thank you," he breathed into the dark. Perhaps this *was* the way for him, and now things would go back to normal, or better than. First his sense of smell coming back, and then perhaps taste . . . *God, what I wouldn't give for a biscuit, a good strong cuppa. A humbug. Anything. Just give it all back.*

The match's reach wasn't much, but enough to show a narrow straw of a tunnel just high and wide enough for him to pass without knocking his shoulders or head. He sniffed. Above the fading aroma of sulfur, the air wasn't stale, although it was a bit . . . fishy? His nose crinkled. *Mildew and something rotted.* An animal, perhaps. He shook out the match before it could scorch his fingers.

Onward, my darling. Black Dog gave his rump a nuzzle. **Back to the future.**

"Is that a joke?" He waited for the hound's reply, but none came.

So Doyle began to walk. It wasn't as hard as he thought it would be. The tunnel was so snug there was no way to turn around or bumble into a wall. The floor was a little odd, a touch concave straight down the center in the way of a sewage conduit, something that allowed for very little deviation. He could swear he felt the smooth indentations of boots worn into rock, as if many souls had walked this way before. *You watch; I'll end up in the Thames with the rest of the city's leavings.*

Not at all, poppet. What is it they say? Black Dog paused as if in thought. **In a man's end, one may find his beginnings?**

"I think it's the other way round," he said, and then stopped again. That fishy smell was stronger. How long had they been walking anyway? His stomach rumbled. He was suddenly famished. *Have to be close to the end*. Surely he wasn't fated to wander the bowels of the earth for all time? He heard something then, a faint . . . trickling? *Shite, water?* "Damn," he said, pulling another match from his silver-plated safe, "I *have* wandered into a sewer . . ."

And then, from somewhere ahead—perhaps only a few inches—there came . . .

a soft . . .

moist . . .

slithery . . .

rustle.

2

OH. HE FROZE, match poised above the striker. All his hair was on end. He could feel his lids peeling back and the whites of his eyes drying as they bulged. He was quivering.

Black Dog? He didn't dare let a breath escape the fence of his teeth, much less a sound. *Is that you?*

No answer, although ahead and again . . . a slight, papery, slithery rustle. *Like something shifting position*. Snake, shedding its skin? Snakes liked sewers. So did rats.

That made him think of the Webley. Yet that meant a choice. Revolver or match: he couldn't have both. *Gun don't do me no good if I can't see what I'm shooting*.

"Goddamn it, Black Dog, stop yer games," he hissed. "Where are you?"

No answer. The air was nasty, the taste coating his mouth foul, as if he'd licked a privy clean with his tongue. *Just my luck,* he thought, running his match over the striker. *Get my taste back now, and what do I get?* The match spluttered a shower of tiny yellow sparks, then resolved to a finger of flame that he lifted to light the way ahead. *I get . . .*

"Shite." The word fell from his mouth, and then nothing more came for a time.

For a time.

3

IT WAS NAKED and in tatters, decayed skin peeling away in greenish strips as he'd always imagined. Its head was bulbous, the long hair dragging in dank tangles like wet seaweed. Its jowls sagged, sloughing from bone. Its man's breasts already had, exposing a bird's cage of ribs and the soft and blackened rot of dead muscle and putrid, liquefied fat. When it flexed its gnarled, clawed hands, a scatter of moist, scaled skin flaked off to drop with sodden splats on stone.

Only the eyes were different, and they were black mirrors, smooth as stones, and captured the light so well Doyle saw himself—his pale, horrified face—twice over.

"*Arrrtieee.*" When this monstrosity gave his ruined head a rakish cock, there was a wet ripping sound as the skin over his neck and decayed tendon unraveled. There was a series of crackles as vertebrae crumbled, so that when his father smiled, he did so on end, with his left ear flat on that shoulder. "Been waiting on you, oh . . . a long time, son."

Yes. Black Dog chuffed from somewhere behind. **And do you know, poppet, that quote? I believe you're right. In your beginnings, you *do* find your end.**

4

THE SCREAM FINALLY came then.

It didn't last long.

THIS IS . . .

NOW

"WHAT?" BLINKING, TONY snaps to. For a moment, his mind is a little muzzy, as if he's just swum to consciousness from a drugged sleep. But then the world firms, and there's slick, cool tile under his bare feet and light dew on his cheeks from a steamy shower. Mist veils the bathroom mirror. Behind the fog, a vague silhouette of a boy waits. Water drips from the ceiling because he's forgotten the exhaust again, and his father's going to bust his chops about that because the parsonage is so goddamned old and the last thing he needs is to go hat in hand to the deacons and blah, blah, blah. Next to the shower stall, a tongue of wallpaper has come unglued, and that sucks. He'll have to fix that before school. Superglue, this time: Christ, that stuff never comes off.

Must've zoned out. Michael Jackson's tinny soprano sputters from his piece-of-crap Sony transistor, and for what must be the ten trillionth time, old Michael's warning that they're going to *geeeet* you. Tony clutches his tired Snoopy electric toothbrush in one hand, a half-strangled Crest tube in the other. If Matt were home, he'd have a cow, bitching about Tony not rolling the tube up from the bottom. Tony guesses the Marines make tight-asses out of everyone. Sometimes he thinks he squeezes the Crest around the middle just to give his brother something to complain about and settle them into their old ways again: Matt busting his balls, then wrestling him into a headlock for a knuckle rub while Tony squirms and yells, *Quit it, you asshole, quit it!*

Mainly, though, it's because every time Matt walks through that door, a huge surge of relief washes through Tony because, thank Christ, his brother's still alive. Like, *I didn't imagine you.* Which is so damned crazy.

No way he'll tell anyone about that either. The doe-eyed social worker'll probably say he's not dealing with his mom and all, but she can screw herself. Let cancer eat up your mom from the inside out, lady, and then see how great you feel. (The social worker is his dad's idea. Says they all need to come to a state of grace, which is weird coming from a pastor. But his dad's a total basket case. So Tony goes.)

He can't recall what he's just been thinking. Probably nothing, but he does that a lot these days. His eyes drop first to the Dickens novel he's got to write that damned paper for: a ten-pager comparing and contrasting Dickens's use of doubles in this monster with either *Great Expectations* or that story . . . *The Haunted Man and the Ghost's Bargain*? Gag him with a spoon. At least *Haunted Man* is short, the last Christmas book Dickens published, and anyone with half a brain can see that Evil Genius is really Redlaw. Thank God, they're going on to Sherlock Holmes next. *Hound of the Baskervilles*—now *that's* a story. That black dog gives him the shivers. He wonders if he can talk the teacher into trying Lovecraft after that. Talk about . . .

"Spooky," he whispers, and for no reason he can figure,

a shiver races through his body. His arms go sandpapery with goose bumps. His eyes slide from *Our Mutual Friend* to the *Twisted Tales* he snagged in April. Moist air's curled the comic's pages, but whaddaya expect from cheap paper? Hacker's wondering if maybe they've been in this foxhole forever. Like Hacker's entire life is that one day, lived over and over again. Of course, the kicker's that Hacker and his men are toys who only think they're real.

And now, Tony can kind of relate.

Have I been here before? His eyes roam his bathroom, the fogged mirror. "Of course you have," he says. "You live here. It's time for school."

You're stressed, that's all.

His mom's cancer, for one. His eyes find Hacker, frozen on the page. He's obsessed with this story; reads it over and over again. The social worker would say he's not "metabolizing" his brother's deployment, like the fact that Matt might wind up with his brains splattered all over the insides of a helo off the coast of Grenada has given him terminal heartburn.

On the other hand, she might have a point. Like his friend Trey's already seen *The Dead Zone* ten trillion times, but him? Walked out, chest tight and sweat lathered on his neck. Thing that got him? The whole bullshit about dead zone visions, like you could or *should* change the future. If you did, where did it end? Like, okay, save his brother from getting on the one helo that'll take a nosedive into the ocean, right? But what about the guy who takes his brother's place? He has a family, too.

See, you can go nuts thinking about stuff like that, which is probably why his science teacher, Steele, says he outta go into theoretical physics, because it's so loopy. Like there are all these other Tonys in all these other universes and timelines. In at least one, yeah, his brother dies. Or there's a Tony with a mom who doesn't have lung cancer, or who does but gets better, and blah, blah. Thing is, he's having a hard enough time dealing with the life he already has, thanks. Steele's a nutjob. Get away from him with that crap.

So he couldn't watch *The Dead Zone*. Walked out of *Blue Thunder*, too. That Roy Scheider loop-de-loop scared the shit out of him. Pull that crap in a real helo, you'll drop like a fucking stone, same as Malcolm McDowell. (And you're supposed to cheer about that? *Yay, the bad guy cracked up. He's paste. Real Marines crash during training missions all the time. Yay.*)

Trey says they ought to stick to Disney movies, ha-ha. On the other hand, *Something Wicked This Way Comes* was pretty boss, what with old Mr. Dark and his freaky Mirror Maze, which showed you yourself at different times and ages, like those multiverses Steele talks about? And where your image might get trapped in a mirror and then you never get out? Scared the pants off him. He's already seen the movie five times. Doesn't know why. But it feels . . . familiar.

On the radio, Michael Jackson winds down. There's a pause, a burp of static. A span of dead space in which he hears his mother, muffled but distinct, dying down the hall: *kak-hakak-kak-kak.*

For that split second, Tony thinks—and maybe for the first time ever: *I'm like Hacker. This is the only morning of my life and the only day I'll ever know, and that stupid song will start over again, you just watch.*

So he snaps off the radio. He can't remember if he's ever done that. But what the hell's he going to do if Michael starts up again? Never leave the goddamned bathroom? Hang out like Schrödinger's cat and wait for someone outside this box to decide?

"Screw that," he says. Hiding behind mist, his fuzzy reflection has no opinion. But in the center of his chest, his heart gives a sudden, hard kick. (Has it ever beat before?) He senses that what he does next is important; it just is.

He puts the toothbrush down, but carefully, and squares his mangled tube of Crest alongside. Then, he uses the side of a hand on the mirror. Has he ever done this? He can't remember. Why is he breathing so fast?

His face, from his light blue eyes to his mop of curly brown hair, appears first. Everything looks . . . right. Normal. He squeegees the rest of his face into being: squared cheekbones, an aquiline nose, thin lips. Naked from the waist up because of the towel around his middle. It's him all right. Shower stall in the background, the edge of the toilet. Shit, he better put that seat down, though.

He huffs a relieved sigh. The knot in his stomach unclenches. Fear-sweat has pearled his upper lip, which he now wipes dry. "Well, what the hell did you expect, you nut?" he says. Other than parroting his every move, his reflection has nothing to say for itself.

From beyond the bathroom door, his mother calls, "Honey?"

She'll give him a kiss that tastes of death. He will brush his teeth again. Cut him a break. He's not a monster. He loves her. But he's only a kid.

And look on the bright side: he's not a toy; he's not Redlaw, haunted by himself, or a character in a comic book, like Hacker, that poor schmo.

"Coming, Mom." Picking up his toothbrush, he throttles the tube into letting go of a green worm of Crest. The ooze of it sickens him a little, and for a fleeting moment, he eyes the glistening, sluglike glop and thinks, *Squirmer*. Something that makes no sense but which also gives him a queasy, frightened feeling in the pit of his stomach.

"Stop it, you moron." The boy in the mirror doesn't disagree. So he sets to work on his teeth.

Yeah, yeah, his life isn't perfect. A lot of the time, it's not even all that great. But it's better than nothing.

Tomorrow, though . . . different toothpaste.

If he remembers.

NOW

"OH, THAT'S A fabulous question. There's actually a reason for that change from the first book to the second, and it's right out of Ray Bradbury," the writer says. She's standing at a lectern in the store's café. Behind her is a table piled high with stacks of books, and the bookstore's manager is off to the side, a clutch of Sharpies in one hand. "He wrote this great story all about this guy who goes back in time to hunt dinosaurs, only when he gets back, everything's changed because he stepped off the path and crushed a butterfly. This was before the whole chaos theory thing got going, the butterfly effect? You know, a butterfly flaps its wings in Kansas, and there's a tsunami in Japan? Bradbury's point was that one small change can produce ripples that have profound effects for the whole system. So I did the same thing. I've been playing with multiverses and different timelines throughout both books, right? And the nature of reality? Like how do you know you're really in one, or awake at all?"

"Oh." It's a guy in the second row. "I get it. So that's why the book is by McDermott in the first novel, but you know, the *real* book"—the guy holds up his copy—"has your name on it. It's kind of this metatextual clue that something *major* has changed in that particular timeline."

"Or I'm just messing with your head, and you're going to freak when you get to that part and read what you just said and realize you're all characters in my novel, and I'm the only real person in the room," the writer says.

"Or crawled in through a back door for a visit with all your book-people," a girl chimes in.

"There's always that," the writer says.

The first guy frowns. "Yeah, but so you're saying they were all book-people, or they *were* real, only some of them weren't, or maybe even some were book-people who kind of wrote themselves into our reality, only they can't tell the difference and only *think* they're real?"

"Yes," the writer says, and everyone laughs.

"See?" An elbow to her right ribs, and then Lily's leaning closer. "She *totally* speaks your language," Lily whispers. "Please?"

"No, Lily, I already told you," Emma mutters. They're standing way at the back, out of earshot of the crowd. All the chairs were filled, but that was fine. From the number of people, Emma figures the signing line's going to stretch halfway to the front door. "Great, she knows physics, but so what? It's really not my kind of book."

"But I don't want to talk to her by myself." Lily heaves a tragic, long-suffering, *if-you-were-half-the-friend-you-say-you-are* sigh. "She probably gets a trillion requests for this kind of crap."

"Come on, she's not Stephen King. Have they made any movies of her stuff?"

"No."

"Well then, see? You're only a big deal writer if they make a movie."

"But I'm afraid of sounding *duuumb*." Lily scrunches up her entire face. "Her stuff is *weird* and there are a lot of characters and it's *hard*. Like there's this science and stuff? You have to really *think*. Although you'd love this. One of the main characters, Emma? *Sooo* totally you."

Which she so *totally* couldn't take. That report on Jane Austen her freshman year just about killed her. Every time she sees her name in a book, her mind trips. She has to remind herself, *No, you nut, that didn't happen to you.*

"Wow, *thinking* as you read, keeping track of characters—that's rough." Zero sympathy on this one; Lily stepped in this cow patty on her own. Emma flicks an appraising glance at the writer. Fifties, probably; short red hair that has to be a dye job. Tank top, cargo pants, one of those paracord survival bracelets. Steampunky glasses. At least she doesn't look like anyone's crazed Aunt Bertha, let out of the attic for a little air.

She glances at the book Lily hugs to her chest like a shield. Nice cover, if a touch freaky: all smoky purples and swirling bright blues, with ill-defined but clearly Victorian-era chimneys, like something straight out of Dickens via *The Twilight Zone*. Set it alongside the first book in the series, and she could see that the designer had echoed those crazy-ass crows in that explosive white glister at the center. A little Jack-the-Ripperish, actually, and not her kind of read; her life's been enough of a horror show, thanks.

"Sorry," she says, "I'm not the one who decided to take Kramer's course." Though that had been a near miss. When time rolled around to select her junior year classes, her schedule allowed for only one of two electives: animal husbandry, where she'd learn really useful things like neutering piglets (Holten Prep might be in Madison, but shit, this is Wisconsin), or Kramer's überserious course on creativity and madness.

Anyway, when Emma saw the choices? These little internal bells went *ding-ding-ding.* Like those red-alert *whoop-whoops* in the old *Star Trek.*

Alarms like that happened rarely, but she always paid attention. The first time, she was twelve and had taken a header over her bike before awakening, splayed like roadkill, to the pop of gravel under a truck's tires and gulls pinwheeling high above and laughing, *A-hah-hah-hah, look at the stupid huuumannn.* Completely freaked her out—*my face, my face!*—and Jasper, too, who'd just gotten this *feeling* and lit out from his boat for home faster than greased lightning. The craniofacial doc went apeshit, of course: *You have to be careful of your face.* Like, *duh,* yeah, tell me another.

It was later that night, when Jasper checked up on her, that *ding-ding-ding* had gone off, and then this little voice—kind of soft and big-sisterly—suggested that she really did have to suck it up and tell him about down cellar: that inky square that had opened when she touched it. It was something she'd been worrying about all week: *Do I or don't I?* Like this was a really important moment and her life could go one way or the other, depending— and then that big-sister voice came out of the blue.

So she told him. Jasper listened, then kissed her forehead and told her not to think about it anymore. Oh yeah, right, like *that* would happen. The secret door was an itch in her brain. So, of *course,* she'd gone down cellar two weeks later, just to see.

But the door was gone. Not just painted over. *Gone.* Like someone had . . . taken it out. She must've mashed that cinderblock ten trillion times before giving up. She didn't ask, and Jasper never said, although sometimes in dim light and when he tilted his head a certain way, she would think, *Pair of glasses and dark hair . . .* She could swear she'd seen him somewhere before, and wondered if, maybe, Jasper had been sent special just to watch out for her. Like some kind of guardian angel, or secret protector.

Most recently, there'd been the whole deal with the head-aches. Didn't take her meds. Didn't like them. Made her all zombified. Whenever a headache came on, though, there'd also be this burn beneath the skull plate between her eyes and a *tug* in her brain, as if she were a baited hook a salmon had decided to test: *Hey, you there?* Like there was something out there, wait-ing to grab her, take her places. Set her on a different path. It was during those times that she'd think back to down cellar and wonder just who Jasper kept from creeping in or dropping by for a visit.

Anyway, the big-sister voice spoke up again: *Tell your doctor about the headaches.* To her surprise, her doc was cool and all about her not being zombied out. Put her on a different med. The head-aches vanished, and so did the burn, those tugs.

So when the alarms went off and that big-sister voice *suggested* she get a little creative about the whole Kramer thing (and no way was she lopping off Wilbur's balls), she talked her adviser into an independent study centered on the physics of glass, which, considering she gets to spend a ton of time in the hot shop, is sweet. Mainly, it got her out of Kramer's class, and that was all that mattered.

"You dug your own grave here, girlfriend," she says now, pat-ting Lily's shoulder. Everyone in Kramer's class has to interview someone from the reading list. (Lily had added that they had to

be *living* writers, which Emma's let slide. Lily's so clueless sometimes.) "She's not going to bite you. Just talk to her. Anyway, I
got my own crap to do. Come get me in the science section when
you're done."

The store shelves science, philosophy, and poetry in the
very back, where virtually no one visits—which is exactly why
she loves it. Nice cushy leather chairs. Plenty of legroom, with
enough space between standing shelves to sprawl on the carpet
if she wants. Finger-walking spines, a title catches her eye: *Glass
of the Alchemists*. Book's huge, one of those coffee table things,
but it's put out by the Corning Museum people, who know their
stuff. Hefting the book under an arm, she heads down the aisle
for what she thinks of as *her* spot: right corner, round table, faux
Tiffany lamp, deeply cushioned red-leather wingback with an
ottoman. But as she rounds a standing shelf, she pulls up short.
Thinks, disgusted: *Shit*.

And then gets another, better look and thinks, kind of breathless: *Holy shit*.

He's heard her coming, because he looks up from what he's been
reading, a question in his dark blue eyes. "Hey." Not an invitation
but not a *get lost* either. Nice voice, baritone, smooth. Like good
chocolate you've let melt in your mouth.

"Hi." *Moron*. She teeters, uncertain if she should turn back or
take that empty wingback.

"Oh, hey, sorry." He's stacked books on the table between the
two chairs and now he moves his closer. "Sometimes I spread out.
There's plenty of room, you want."

Okay, so he's not a creep. Her gaze sweeps his stack, though
she only recognizes one book because she's just seen it. *Probably*

waiting for that writer to finish up with the questions. Or maybe he doesn't like crowds either and will wander back when the signing line's winding down. She watches him through her lashes as she lays the glass book on an ottoman. In the soft light of the faux Tiffany, his hair is military-short but still shimmers an iridescent purplish-black, like the velvety wing of a red-spotted purple butterfly. His shoulders are very broad and muscular. Yet when he turns a page, he does it with long, delicate fingers. Maybe . . . a senior? She's never seen him at Holten. Could be he's in college or something. ROTC, maybe. That makes sense.

"It's Plath"—and, startled, she looks up to find his eyes on hers. "Not her poetry, though I really like that, too."

"Oh." A blush creeps up her neck. Shit, this is so meet-cute, it ought to be in a book. This is her cue to ask him more, discover how sensitive he is, blah, blah. In ten minutes, he'll offer to buy her coffee, and by that evening, they're having a food fight with a tub of popcorn before they collapse, giggling, on a deep shag carpet and her shirt's rucked up and then he slips his hand under . . .

She veers away. "I don't know much poetry." *Okaaay, conversation killer right there; you go, girl.*

He shrugs. "I do, but I'm not sure I would've looked at this either, except the writer back there? Mentioned Plath a couple times, said she'd read a bunch of Plath's poetry and her diaries, and one of the characters gets all hung up on *The Bell Jar*, so . . ." Handing over the book he's been reading—*The Unabridged Journals of Sylvia Plath*—he opens to a page and points. "I got curious."

She reads. It's a passage about remembering every moment— every *now* is how Plath puts it. Recalling what the writer said about timelines and multiverses, she thinks: *Hunh.* "All that talk about *nows*? Bet your writer knows Barbour, too."

"Who?"

"Julian Barbour. He's this theoretical physicist?" Flipping open her backpack, she tugs out a book.

Eyebrows arched, he scans the title. "*The End of Time?*"

She nods. "Basically, what he's saying is what Plath does, and I think it's what this writer's getting at. For Barbour, every moment is its own *Now* and exists forever. The only reason we even dreamt up something like time is because we notice there's a difference between one *Now*—one moment—and the next. It's like, uh, you know . . . when you were a kid and got those books where that drawing of a horse is just a little bit different than the one before?"

"Yeah." He nods. "Flip 'em really fast and it looks like the horse is galloping."

"Exactly. But it's an illusion. We only think there's motion because our brain processes it that way." She taps Barbour's book. "Same concept. There's no time. There's only this *Now* and the next *Now* and the next, except they all kind of happen at once."

"Well . . ." He opens to the page he's been reading. "To me, Plath is more about living in the moment. She was writing about how *aware* she was of every second and how that completely freaked her out, especially since each was precious, singular. Like you always have to be aware of the fact that the end might be just around the corner. You know, walk out of this shop, get hit by a bus . . . it's over. Life turns on a dime. So you can't waste a single second or let one go by without realizing just how remarkable this—all of life—is." His eyes play over the shop, the books, and then drift back to her face. "When the *Now* is gone, it's gone, and no getting it back, no do-overs or second chances. And what if you let pass the one *Now* that was so special, you'll never see its like again? Where your life could go one way or another, only your chance slipped past because you weren't paying attention?"

For some reason, tears sting the backs of her eyes. *Don't cry, you nut. What is there to cry about?* She has to swallow around a sudden knot. "That's so sad. It sounds . . . final."

"Yeah." His face is still, and his eyes shine. A moment passes, and then he says, "My unit's shipping out in ten days. Afghanistan? They say advisory role and training and support, but we'll be armed and on patrol with the ANA—Afghan National Army. We'll get shot for sure. So I think a lot about *what if.* You know, not making it back. Thing about this *Dickens Mirror* thing that lady wrote? Friend of mine read it and says I'm in it, and so is my brother and his girlfriend. You know, our names? Except, in the book, we're all dead. We're ghosts."

She thinks back to the writer: *Or I'm just messing with your head.* At that, she feels an eerie, almost surreal sensation that is not a tug but breathless and expectant all the same. As if this moment is . . . a pivot, a branch-point in time: one Emma goes this way, another goes that, still a third does something different, and on into infinity.

"Kind of freaked me out," he says. "Made me think where I'm headed and how I might not make it back." After another, longer pause, an edge of scarlet bleeds over his jaw. "That wasn't a pickup line."

"I know that." She slicks her lips. "My friend said I'm in the book, too. I mean, not . . . not"—she stumbles a little—"you know, a character based on me or anything, or even, you know, *me.*" *God, babble much?* "That would be impossible, right?"

"Not if you believe the book."

"Well . . . but it's a *book*. It's made up."

"But I think that's her point. We could be book-people hanging out in the real world, or this could all be something one or both of us wrote ourselves. Or we're real people visiting a book-world, or we live in a *Now,* an alternate timeline that's a near double for another. In the end, how would you know?"

"You would just *have* to. I mean, all we've got are our perceptions to tell us what's real."

"Dreams feel real when you're in them."

She could've sworn that was her thought. Or was it from a movie? She can't recall.

"So, since you're in this lady's book, too . . . I mean, your name . . ." When his mouth quirks, she sees a dimple in the left corner. "Does that ever bother you?" he asks. "When writers do that?"

"Oh yeah." She tells him about Jane Austen, but now she knows: she is *so* never reading this *Dickens Mirror* crap, even if they make a movie out of it. "So what happens to them?"

"Dunno." His muscular shoulders rise and fall. "I haven't read it. I might not, actually. I don't know if I want to find out what happens to that guy with my name."

"So why are you here? Why bother getting the book, or having her sign it?"

"Just felt . . ." He shakes his head. "Like this was where I was supposed to be, right now." He lets out a little laugh. "In this *Now,* I guess. I can't explain it any better than that."

"Oh." She knows she could end this right here. Settle back. Some desultory chitchat. For God's sake, he's a soldier and he's leaving the *country*. She's got a test to study for.

But at that moment, there is that tiny mental *ding*. Not an alarm, but it does get her attention, and then the big-sister voice whispers a suggestion.

"Look," she says, "you want to get a coffee? We can hang at the café and you can get your book signed. I have a friend up there anyway." She adds, quickly, "This isn't a meet-cute, okay? I'd rather take out my tonsils with a fork."

"Me too," he says, and does her the favor of not smiling.

They'll have coffee. He'll get his book signed. The author is actually an interesting lady. Even spent time in the military, so the writer and he hit it off. The writer tells him to be safe, keep in touch if he wants. She's also a little goofy, but Emma knows a couple glass artists with some screws that need tightening. (When Lily spots him, she will do the whole eyebrow *he-is-so-HOT* thing, which Emma will pray he doesn't see, and he doesn't seem to—or, if he does, won't let on.)

Most of all, it will definitely not be meet-cute.

But there will be a moment, and it will be a perfect *Now*, because it might also be the last.

As they walk out—Lily's already fluttered off with some bogus excuse, which is completely stupid, like Emma and this guy are going to lip-lock right there—he says, "I like your necklace. Where'd you get it?"

"I'm not sure. I've always had it." She toys with the glass pendant on its beaded chain. "Since I was twelve, anyway. It's why I'm so interested in glass. I want to figure out how the artist did it. You know, put a whole galaxy in there."

"It's beautiful." He cups it in a hand, but his eyes fix on hers. "Like a message in a bottle."

"Or a *Now*." Why has she said that? Why is her heart pounding like Superior thrashing Devil's Cauldron, *ba-boom, ba-boom?* "I mean, if you could bottle a single, perfect moment."

"Yes, and if you could"—and *now* . . . he touches her, very gently, running the side of a thumb over that slight thread of a scar under her chin—"I'll settle for this."

NOW

IT IS HIGH summer. The sky is so bright the blue's paled nearly to white. Brassy sunlight splashes the cliffs and spills hot and molten over Rima's shoulders. Threading around black basalt boulders and through tall cliff grass and stands of hot pink thrift is hard work, especially with the basket. She'd be sweating more if not for the wind, clean and cold with a salt tang, coming off the water. Rounding a corner, she heads for a large thumb of sparkling gray-black rock at the far end of a bluff densely carpeted with yellow bird's-foot trefoil, where she stops to rest.

This promontory is the island's tallest, and juts out in a massive overhang, well clear of a jumble of sharp boulders. Below, waves thrash the shoreline in rhythmic thumps and booms that send up huge founts of white spray. To her left, though, is a crescent-shaped tidal loch with a dark-sand beach where the boys will bring in the boat. A perfect spot for a picnic. The water's calm enough for the scuttling plovers and snipes to poke at the sand. At the loch's edge, she spots the sleek, oily roll of an otter.

Puffing a little, she sets down her basket. "Hot," she says, then sighs as a cool tongue of sea wind licks sweat from her neck. "Thank you, Emma, but that wasn't a hint."

Of course, Emma doesn't answer. Rima keeps hoping that, someday, the other girl might. On the other hand, maybe Emma's out of practice. She's in so many other things now. In a way, she and the shadows are everything. *And what is that like, to be so . . . expansive?* Perhaps a body is too limiting now, like trying to cram yourself into a whalebone corset.

Resting, she watches deep orange and black Slender Scotch Burnets float over yellow trefoil, the moths flitting from flower to flower. Bright gold spangles dance on the sea and cut tears. Shading her eyes, she looks to the southwest, her gaze skimming over the lower, slightly humped hills of Little Colonsay to the deep green hummock that is Staffa. From here, she can just make out the island's massive hexagonal pillars, rising from the surface like stilts upon which the rest of the island is balanced. If she looks a little off-center, she can even make out the occasional black flit of puffins darting in and out of the island's cliffs. It is the very picture of everything she has read and can remember.

"You know the one bird I've not seen yet?" she murmurs as her eyes skim the far horizon. *Only want to check, see if it's still there.* "I've yet to see a single golden eagle. Isn't that . . ." The word *odd* curls like a snail on her tongue.

Beyond Staffa, there is nothing but mist on the ruler-straight blue line of their horizon.

Her stomach shrinks in a queer little clench. *The sea's always misty; don't be ridiculous. It's not the Peculiar.* Of course, there's no way to be certain. They've never sailed that far, however far it really is. No call. Everything they need is here.

"I know you wouldn't let anything happen to us, not now."

She hears the slight quaver. "It's only a little . . . unsettling."

Shouldn't there also be other islands? "Look north and there ought to be Ulva," she says, trying to dredge the pages up from memory. "Perhaps Coll or even Skye. At least . . ." How many islands in the Treshnish had that book mentioned? Eighteen from this shoreline alone? She couldn't recall.

But I've never been here. This is all what I've built up in my mind, from descriptions. From a few paragraphs in a long-ago book. She licks beaded sweat from her upper lip, and saliva pools under her tongue at the salt tang. Perhaps that's why she's not seen a single eagle: because there's no firm picture of one in her mind.

Or perhaps this is all we need. The most she could dream up, and this *is* a reasonable facsimile. Now that they're here in this . . . dream? Illusion? She's unsure what to call it, but she knows that the old story about the boom and roar of the island's monster in his cathedral of black basalt, the one she and Tony heard once upon a time, isn't a fairy tale. Or maybe it is, but not in this place. Staffa's, what, six miles away? The sound shouldn't carry, but it does, and at night, she will frequently wrap herself in a good blanket and sit out for a long time to listen to the distant *ba-boom, ba-boom.* Sometimes, she will think, for no reason at all, *Matchi-Manitou, in his deep dark cave,* or about a place called Devil's Cauldron.

"That's you, isn't it, Emma? Something from your *Now*?" She smiles a second later as the waves below intensify and grow very loud: *BA-BOOM, BA-BOOM.*

She remembers London and the Peculiar. Of them all, she remembers everything of their past that is, to Tony and Bode, only a blur. As soon as they exited that tunnel, stepping from the dark into bright sun and a cool breeze, both boys behaved as if this was the way things had always been. There was their wood and stone cottage to the right, with rooms of belongings she didn't recognize but which the boys treated as theirs. A short distance beyond stood a good strong croft and white shaggy sheep. There was a stone barn with two horses, plows; a vegetable garden, in full bloom; and even apple trees, which Rima was fairly certain shouldn't grow here, but she wasn't quibbling. They had food, a good well, and there was always plenty of wood to be had in copses of scruffy trees and wild rhododendron. There is rain when they need it, and bright sun when they don't. The seasons change, and there's always snow for Christmas.

Yet even I've no idea how long we've been here. She holds out her hands, no longer as work-roughened but tanned and strong. Whatever happens, they'll never be creamy and silken. No kid gloves for her. "A fine *laaadeee*," she drawls, in an exaggerated singsong. One thing she'll have on all those priggish ladies, presuming they ever existed: she hasn't aged. Her hair never needs a trim. She is sixteen, probably for as long as she wishes, or even if she doesn't.

As soon as she saw the sea, she knew this all had to be the work of Emma and the shadows, plucking this fantasy from her mind and then building a world for them to live in. Emma and Eric and the others are in every leaf, every rock, every breath of wind, every flower, each and every bird. They are the sun by day, and the millions of stars at night. But they're not gods, and she understands that this world has limits. For example, there's a village not far away: a jumble of houses along an inlet with cobble streets. There are people, but their faces are rudimentary, so many blurs, like the blanks in that cave beneath Bedlam. The boys don't seem to notice, and sometimes she has to bite her cheek to keep from screaming when Bode makes a joke and a blank throws back its head in a roar of laughter.

But they don't go often. This is enough world for them. Neither Tony nor Bode are curious about what lies beyond what they can see. She guesses it's a small price to pay, and no different than the generations of real people who live their lives in such places, with no curiosity about the wider world.

Although . . . at times . . . she thinks Bode has an inkling. She worries about him. She and Tony have each other, but Bode's alone, and there are moments when she spies him staring out to sea, a wistful melancholy in the turn of his mouth, a sparrow of something dark spiriting through his eyes.

Someday, Emma, if you can—if you remember how—maybe . . . let her suddenly walk up from the beach? Or across the high meadow?

"It's a lot to ask," she says. "I think he was *driven* to protect Elizabeth. Perhaps, even . . . created that way? But Meme . . . she could have been different. So, your face, your body, but Meme's . . . personality? Though I guess she didn't have much." She still remembered the jolt when she looked through those panops and saw the clay blank that was Meme. Not a monster under the skin, but close. "But maybe you could start her off, give her a push in the right direction, and then whatever she becomes will be because of us. Because of Bode."

A lot to ask. She isn't ungrateful, truly, but it's a little like pushing the limits of this world. No one has bothered them, and since she believes that McDermott or his many other selves is/are still out there, that must mean Emma and the others have closed *them* off somehow. No back doors, no tinkering, no stealing.

She wonders about McDermott, though. He got away; he's out there. If she had the power, would *she* stop trying to remake a Meredith who would not die? A daughter she would never lose? For that matter, how many times had McDermott remade himself?

She's thought a lot about this. The London Meredith found them all through dreams, including McDermott and his . . . well, Meredith of the Moment. But Meme didn't know what it was to dream, and neither did Kramer or Doyle.

Which means the ability to dream is the essential ingredient. Take away Meredith's ability to dream and imagine—to go her own way—and there is no Meredith. You'd have only a shell, a blank. Someone like Meme, nothing more than a pale imitation. *But it's a self-fulfilling prophecy, too. If you re-create Meredith in all her complexity, she* must *dream. Which means she will kill herself, eventually, because Lizzie's fate is a constant, too.*

There are times when, if she closes her eyes, she swears she sees McDermott. He stands at a large window overlooking green pasture. In the distance, there is a little girl with corn-tassel curls and her cat, big and orange, beside her, and she is once more the child he remembers. Then he turns . . .

And there she is: asleep. Perfect. No scars, not yet, and maybe never—and he is both afraid and so full of love his heart should burst. *Please, God,* he thinks as he bends to brush her lips in a kiss. *Please, maybe this time . . .*

It hits her then that this might explain McDermott's obsession with Emma: a creation that could dream and be set free to write her own life and escape destiny. Emma had mentioned a back door, so maybe he even visited her on occasion to see how she fared. Just . . . to observe from a distance.

Perhaps this is why he'd never given up trying. McDermott must've wondered what might happen if he created a Meredith he would then make certain never to meet? If they never crossed paths, they would never have a daughter and then Meredith would live. Oh, he might be able to visit, drop in from time to time and look in on her, but her life would not include him—and of course, *his* Lizzie wouldn't have a life at all. Robbing Peter to pay Paul, that.

Say he accomplished it, though. How then could McDermott live without Meredith? Would he even *be* McDermott then? Were Meredith and Lizzie necessary ingredients to make *him*, too?

For that matter, would *she* have the strength to do the same . . . say, for Tony? Leave him be, set him free—and never, ever know that kind of love? She wants to think so, but the sudden hollowness in her chest gives the lie. Love was quite a selfish emotion, wasn't it?

And where is little Emma? Is her life rewriting itself even now? Or is she destined to always find herself back here, with us, in some fashion? Or perhaps, in some *Now* she will never know, Emma is a creation of the mind, only so many words on a page, each leading to their scripted, preconceived, and inevitable end . . .

There's a shout, distant but clear. Blinking, she looks away from that misty horizon and down to a spot closer in. The boat's there, white sails full and cupping wind. Bode, muscular and bare-chested, is at the jib sheets . . . or is it the boom? God, she can never remember and doesn't really care. Tony's monkeying over the deck, and she sees the flash of his face as he tilts a look. Standing, she waves, then bends for her basket.

Trudging back over the promontory, she watches moths rise in a spray of orange and black. But as she nears the edge where she'll turn right and make her way down a corkscrew path to shore, a large shadow ripples over a near hill. A cloud? A little surprised, she looks up . . . and gasps.

Gliding past, no more than fifty feet away but very low to the ground, the eagle is a dark bronze, almost as if it's been dipped in sunlight, and massive, with wings that span an easy twelve feet from tip to tip. The eagle is close enough that she sees the yellow curve and black hook of its beak and wicked talons. Riding the air, the bird is absolutely silent. A cloud would make more noise. The eagle is also swift, and in three seconds, the bird's swept behind a hill to the left.

"Oh," she says, and that's when she realizes she's been holding her breath. "That was . . ." Her voice dies away as the eagle suddenly reappears, banking in a wide arcing turn. This time, it doesn't head to the right, back the way it came. Instead—and still very low, maybe no more than seven feet off the ground—it rockets straight for her. By the time she understands it could take her eyes out with those talons, the eagle's dipped level with her head and then abruptly veers off in a steep, high climb. Its face flashes across her vision, and it is so close, she feels the suck of air, a flutter of her hair on her neck and cheeks, as the eagle soars away, pulling with its massive wings.

That bird was so near she saw one thing more: the impossible color of its eyes and, in one, a burning gold glister.

"Hello, Emma," she whispers, and then has to swallow a lump. "I'm so glad to see you."

And, perhaps, this is the start of something new: a first step in another direction. For Emma? For them all? "I don't care," she says as she follows the bird that is spiraling up and up and up. It's so high that if she stuck out her thumb, she'd blot it out completely. An absurd thought: *Wonder what it all looks like from there.*

At that she feels a slight prod, like the poke of a finger, right above her nose in the center of her forehead. It feels like a suggestion: *Close your eyes.*

Their bloods have mingled; if she reaches deep inside, her mind closes around a faint, dark, icy stain. It is, she thinks, why she remembers and the boys don't. But this is a first.

Heart thumping, she does what the voice asks. "Do I relax, do I think of some . . ." Her breath jumps in a sudden quick inhale as a white clear space unfurls in her mind—as if her brain's fresh, clean parchment upon which nothing has yet been written.

In the next instant, Rima is airborne, wind in her face and over sleek feathers and a powerful body that cleaves and soars through thin air and blue sky. Far below, there are emerald hills and their home and that indigo sea and all that binds her to this life and those she loves, for however long it lasts.

But for a time, Rima lets go of all that and flies: higher and ever higher, heading for the bright coin of the sun above to test the limits of this boundless sky.

ACKNOWLEDGMENTS

EVERY NOVEL IS an education, but the fun of doing a quasi-historical is you get to travel to fun places and meet interesting people and see terrific sites because, hey, it's all research. The challenge is knowing what to leave out because there's the urge to put in every single scrap. After all, I did all this *work*, and for God's sake, you should appreciate that. (And who knew the Victorians were such potty-mouths? I suppose they got away with it because it all sounds better with an accent.)

In the end, though, novels are stories, not histories, so consider yourselves spared. Therefore, for every bit of history I got right, I take full credit. I also take the blame for anything I got wrong.

Remember, though: this is why it's called *fiction*, folks.

For making this novel a reality, my deepest thanks go:

To Greg Ferguson and Elizabeth Law: for understanding what this series was all about from the get-go.

To Jennifer Laughran: for making a call that afternoon in April and saying, point-blank, *Nu, kid. It's time.*

To Jordan Hamessley: for picking up the ball and running with it and challenging me to make this even better.

To Ryan Sullivan: for ruthlessly killing every word that didn't belong—but, oh, the blood—as well as being the most superb fact-checker I've ever known.

To Bonnie Cutler: for catching what everyone else missed.

To Margaret Coffee, Michelle Bayuk, and Alison Weiss: for your unfailing support and good humor and always finding ways to get my work out there where and when it counts.

To the entire Random House sales force: for your continued advocacy and hard work at putting my books in the hands of kids, our readers. They are, in the end, what we're all about.

To the very kind people of London's Royal College of Surgeons: for tracking down all the source materials I requested and providing great photographs to boot.

To Dean Wesley Smith: for reminding me to get over myself already because no one book is all that.

To my daughters, Carolyn and Sarah: for listening to me blubber while never once making me feel like <cue eye-roll> *Mom* . . .

And, again—always—to David: Without you, I couldn't. I just couldn't.